THE PICASSO PROVENANCE

*THREE PICASSOS ... BUT HOW CAN MURDER,
VENGEANCE AND DECEIT PAINT A PRETTY
PICTURE?*

DANN FARRELL

NEW YORK, NOVEMBER 9, 1999

S arah Hastings shivered and turned her coat collar up against the stiff night wind that blew in off the Hudson and funneled between the tall, forsaken buildings. She walked deeper into the crowding darkness that could harbor anything, making her way toward her father's loft studio.

She had been home now for over three hours after a tiresome transatlantic flight, and she still hadn't seen anyone. So much for surprise visits, she thought. Her mother wasn't in her apartment when she arrived, and when Sarah dialed her cellphone, it rang out in the bedroom. What was the damn point of having a phone if you always left it behind? She jotted a note on a yellow Post-It pad and stuck it onto the cellphone's face. Anyway, she would see her mother later, and visiting her father was the primary reason for her visit. Today was Jack Hastings's fiftieth birthday.

The streets around her, a patchwork of old cobblestones, asphalt and concrete, were wet and shiny-black. The only sounds were the blustering of the wind and the occasional whoosh of distant traffic. There were no streetlights here. Why would there be? There was nothing here but decrepit nineteenth-century warehouse buildings that had outlived their original purpose. Even during the day this section of the neighborhood looked grim.

Tonight, the only illumination was the ambient glow of the city reflecting off the cloud cover. On either side of her, tall gateways and overhangs soaked up the night's luminosity, niches of gloom in countless gradations of black. She reached her father's building with relief, pressing the buzzer with growing assurance, chiding herself for her childish imaginings.

But there was no answer; she buzzed again. Still no answer. Sarah could feel the inherited testiness of her mother rising and she hated it. Where the hell was he anyway? She pressed again, then scrabbled in her shoulder bag for her mother's bunch of keys, gratified that she'd had the foresight to take them from the apartment earlier. She turned the lock and pushed open the big steel-faced door. Inside, high above her head, a single faded fluorescent bar lit the dingy, peeling paintwork of the entrance hall.

Slamming the door against the bitter wind, Sarah approached the vintage elevator's metalwork cage and hesitated. Her nostrils flared at the rancid stink of years of neglect and decay. The utter silence above her boomed in her ears. The musty oak-paneled cubicle was dark, though she guessed the interior light would come on once she pulled the metal gate open.

As far as she knew, the building was vacant apart from her father's studio on the sixth floor, so she decided to take no chances. The last thing she needed was to become trapped in an antique elevator, in an empty building, on her first night home. She pressed the grimy Bakelite timer button on the wall, and the skeletal stairway fluorescents flickered into light as, keys in hand, she began to climb the stairs.

This warehouse building was one of several in the locality owned by Sarah's maternal grandmother. Despite their dankness and their aura of abandonment on a night like this, Sarah viewed them with affection. They were part of the legacy of her great-grandfather's once disreputable, but successful, mercantile history during the Prohibition era. Now, of course, their time was approaching. They were all in line for improvement, conversion and inevitable gentrification.

Her father had been painting here for as long as Sarah could remember. His studio was a high-ceilinged, bright and airy space which afforded expansive views over the Hudson to the New Jersey shore. Recently, since Jack and her mother, Liz, had parted, it was no longer simply his studio but also doubled as his home.

The staircase was lined all the way up by the original cast iron balustrade, the once crisp details blunted by a century of over-painting and topped by a mahogany handrail. Sarah climbed quickly, her rubber-soled shoes making little noise on the stone steps. She was halfway between the second and third floors when a thump echoed from down below. She froze; her hand clenched the rail as she strained to hear. It felt damp and sticky to her touch. There it was again—a thump, followed quickly by another, and then another. The door—someone was beating on the front door.

She peered over the railing into the stairwell. Had someone watched her enter? Waited to make sure she was alone? Sarah turned and started upward again, taking the steps two at a time, fleeing from the hammering that was now becoming sharper and more insistent. Then, as she approached the next landing level, she tripped and lost her footing—just as the lights went out. She thrust her hands out in front of her to break her fall, and in the darkness she heard the metallic tinkle of the cluster of keys as they hit the stairway. With approaching panic, she ran her hands along the width of the step. Nothing there—they must have fallen down further. Still on her hands and knees, she inched back down, one step at a time, scrabbling along each one in the dark. Below her, the hammering at the door was incessant now—whoever it was knew that she was there. Then her groping hands found the keys. This time she thrust them deep into her coat pocket as she leaned back against the wall and eased herself upright.

Sarah edged up the stairwell, her right arm extended into the blackness ahead, sliding along the cold, damp paintwork. Reaching the turn on the landing, she almost fell again when she anticipated a step where there wasn't one. She felt relief as her fingers brushed over the Bakelite button. Pressing it, the light strips stuttered into life once more.

Fueled by adrenaline, she bounded upward, slamming each timer button she passed to avoid a repeat. By the top floor she was panting, and upon reaching the door of her father's studio, she collapsed against it. The hammering below had stopped. With her forehead pressed against the cold paneling of the door, she tried to compose herself. She could see a light through the wrong end of the peephole; maybe he was there after all. He could have simply been in the shower. She retrieved the bunch of keys from her pocket with shaking hands, and using the heavy brass key ring, she rapped on the door and waited.

Her parents had only separated in the past few years, while she had been away studying in Europe. It had happened so cleanly that it seemed to Sarah that they had just been waiting for her to leave home. But, despite their living apart and leading separate lives, she had heard no mention of divorce from either of them.

Hearing nothing, she knocked again, louder this time, but there was still no response. With trembling fingers, Sarah sorted through the bunch until she found the key labeled "JACK". She managed to insert it in the lock, turned it, and pushed. As the door opened, a loud, rasping noise made her jump—it was the entrance buzzer being pressed from the street. Then Jack's phone started to ring. Sarah dashed inside, slammed the door closed and leaned back against it.

The scene before her made her choke. She could do nothing, not even draw a breath. Bile rose in her throat, making her cough and jump-starting her breathing. Mesmerized, she could only gasp and stare.

Spot lit, the girl hung motionless, suspended from the high metal sprinkler pipes by a thick blue polypropylene rope around her neck. Garish as a tableau in an Amsterdam whorehouse window, her blonde shoulder-length hair fell forward, half concealing her heavily made-up face. Erect brown nipples protruded through circular cut-outs on the black neoprene basque.

Her long, black-stockinged legs dangled, one still wearing a shiny, black patent, high-heeled shoe. The other shoe lay two feet below, on its side on the floor, alongside an overturned molded plastic chair.

Paralyzed by the horror, Sarah remained slumped against the door. The phone stopped ringing as the machine cut in. Simultaneously, the door buzzer ceased its rasping. "Sarah!" a voice shouted from the machine. "It's me—if you're there, release the catch and let me in!" It was Liz, Sarah's mother.

❧ 2 ❧

Adam Kennedy and a female companion sat at the end of the last row of seats in the Christie's Rockefeller Center saleroom. Tonight was the first important Twentieth Century Art evening sale of the season. The room was packed with bidders, collectors and dealers, while the banks of telephones manned by the Christie's team were either buzzing with activity or poised in a state of readiness. Adam, despite having no stake in any of this evening's paintings, was present to witness what the major Picasso on sale would fetch, for he had a personal interest there.

The painting hung on display, a powerful image of a reclining nude in a black armchair, the luminous flesh tones striking against the contrasting background colors. Over five feet tall and four feet wide, it had been painted by Picasso in 1932 and, as the seventh lot in the sale, it was about to be auctioned.

From the start, at thirty million, the bidding was lively, coming from within the room and on the phones in million dollar increments until, with a final "Fair warning" by the bespectacled, silver-haired auctioneer, the hammer fell at forty-one million dollars. There was no applause, no excited gabbling, only the power of the painting resonating throughout the room as it was taken down by the porters and replaced by the next lot.

"A magnificent painting and an excellent price," Adam said in discreet tones to his companion, London-based dealer, Catherine Bentley. She merely nodded her head in agreement and turned the page of her catalog to the description of the next lot.

What a bitch, Adam thought. Nearly two days of escorting this woman around New York had been demanding—like trying to charm a cobra and not being sure you are playing the right notes, always waiting for the venomous strike. Now, it seemed, she was even making a pretense of ignoring him, making him pay. Sure, for some reason Belloc was being tardy on this deal, but hell, when it came down to it she was being way too presumptuous. She might not even end up being the winner in this contest, which would damn well serve her right.

He peeked at her out of the corner of his eye. She seemed engrossed in the sale catalog, making occasional marginal notations in red ink, glancing up only to inspect each new lot as it was displayed. From this position, the angular lines of her profile gave her a predatory look. She had made no secret of her annoyance upon hearing that the bishop had flown back down to Florida just before she arrived and that no substantive discussions could begin until his return. Downright disrespectful, she had complained, despite Adam's apologies; just not how she was used to doing business. Granted, she had a reputation as a major dealer and negotiator in Europe, but now she was behaving like a spoiled child, making no effort to disguise the impression that she was being forced to hobnob with the monkey rather than the organ grinder.

Adam checked his wristwatch; the bishop's flight had been delayed earlier, but he was due here at any moment. The organ grinder would know exactly how to deal with Ms. Bentley, irrespective of her conceits. He turned his attention back to his catalog, making notes as the succeeding items either sold or were bought in.

The sale was coming to a close and already a substantial portion of those assembled was moving out. Adam turned to her again. "Catherine," he whispered, "shall we wait in the lobby? The bishop shouldn't be much longer." She nodded as the hammer dropped on the item being sold.

Adam stood alongside her at the rear wall of the lobby, in a position where he could maintain a good view of the entrance while the departing crowd flowed past them now that the sale had ended.

"There he is . . ." Adam said, then, raising his voice sufficiently to be heard above the hubbub, he called, "Phil!" A man in a dark overcoat stopped and turned toward the sound of Adam's voice. A glimpse of a clerical collar flashed at his neck as he smiled and lifted his arm in a wave of acknowledgement before weaving in their direction across the current of exiting bodies.

Bishop Phil Connor's physical appearance belied his sixty years: cropped grey hair, taut, even features, and a physique and complexion of a younger man. He was a well-known and popular figure around the fine art salerooms of the East Coast. As an auxiliary bishop attached to the New York Archdiocese, his brief was to appraise, allocate, or dispose of the various fine art legacies that were bequeathed to the Church from benefactors on the Eastern seaboard of the United States. But this evening he was not on Church business.

In a few steps he was by their side.

"Adam, sorry I missed the sale—events beyond my control. I hoped you might still be here . . . and I assume this must be Ms. Bentley?" He spoke with an Irish brogue, only a little inflected by his lifetime in the United States.

"Catherine Bentley, Bishop," she said, holding out her right hand. "I'm glad to meet you at last."

"Call me Phil, please," the bishop said as they shook hands. "I must apologize for not being here to greet you, but Paul Belloc had some last-minute thoughts on the sale of the paintings, and I had no option but to fly down."

"Well, I trust your meeting was fruitful and that we can come to a mutually satisfactory agreement soon."

"I hope so, too," he replied, then without directing the question at either one of them in particular, he added, "How did the sale go?"

"I reckon they must've grossed close to one hundred million in total. Not bad when you consider not all of the fifty-three lots sold," Adam said.

"And the Picasso?"

"Forty-one million—a little above expectation, if you can call six million *a little.*"

The bishop paused. "Hmm . . . If you include the auction premium and taxes, that'll bring it over forty-five, back up to the level of ten years ago." He checked the time. "Still, it's all over now," he said, smiling. "But we have time for a bite to eat, or some refreshments, if that suits?" Adam turned to Catherine, his eyebrows raised, mirroring the bishop's question.

"Thank you, Bishop," she replied, nodding.

The bishop fished his cellphone from his pocket and said, "My car's nearby; I'll call André."

§

Installed in a comfortable and intimate corner of a nearby restaurant, the bishop ordered drinks and they settled back to browse through the menus. After a cursory scan, Catherine excused herself to visit the bathroom.

Once she was out of earshot, Adam asked in a low, urgent voice, "So, what did Belloc want? Why did he need to see you in person? What's the problem?"

"It was nothing, Adam . . . it's just his health. He hasn't fully recovered from surgery. He's been told to take things easy and to avoid stress. He's inclined to proceed with this deal at less than breakneck speed, so I agreed. Let's face it: we wouldn't want anything to happen to him."

Adam sat back and turned his head to look straight into the bishop's eyes. "Phil, I'm not a kid any longer. I don't believe in the Tooth Fairy, or Santa Claus, and I sure as hell don't believe Belloc dragged you all the way down to Florida to discuss his health—he could've done that on the phone. We both know that the sale of these Picassos is a big deal by anyone's standards, and even if Belloc was on his deathbed he'd be putting the Grim Reaper on hold till the deal was done!"

The bishop smiled, but Adam interrupted him with a pointed index finger. "I'm not calling you a liar, Phil. I know you've always had my best interests at heart, but if there's a problem, I'd rather you shared it with me instead of trying to feed me half-truths."

"Okay . . ." He shrugged, looked back into Adam's eyes and, after a moment, nodded. "Yes, Belloc wanted me down for a face-to-face with Paul Junior."

"Why?" Adam insisted. "Old Belloc makes his own decisions. He always has, and particularly where his art collection is concerned, he's always been hands-on. What would his pain-in-the-ass son have to do with it?"

The bishop shook his head. "Who knows? Hospitalization and major surgery bring mortality home to you—you realize that you're not bulletproof. And you know that young Paul is becoming more hands-on throughout their businesses."

"No, I don't know. He's not exactly high on my best-buddy list."

"Well, anyway, he thinks we're unnecessary, and obviously, if we were cut out of the deal it would save them a fortune."

Adam grunted.

"But don't worry," the bishop said. "Belloc wanted me there for a three-way meeting to resolve things. He made no bones about how I had helped him over the years—but he also emphasized that he had given his word that when the time came to market the Picassos, the business would be ours and he would not renege on his word."

"And you believe him?"

"One hundred percent."

"How did Paul Junior react to that?"

"In a nutshell, he was seething. But what could he do? He'd

been overruled. The upshot is that there will be no change: we have the sale of the paintings, and we can proceed to open negotiations with any interested parties—like your friend, Catherine." He smiled. "Has she mentioned the paintings yet?"

Adam rolled his eyes. "All the time. But I explained that until you returned from Florida I wasn't in a position to discuss it—and she wasn't happy about that. In fact, it's gotten so bad that I think she's stopped speaking to me."

The bishop laughed. "Don't worry about it; we'll deal with that when she returns. And what about Jack? Have you spoken to him since I left?"

"Yes, we had a meal with him yesterday after she arrived, and she's been to the studio and likes his work, which is doing well at the moment. Did you know that two of his paintings changed hands last week for fifty thousand each . . . ones I sold only five years ago for twenty for the pair?"

"I'm sure he was pleased with that."

"Well, you know how negative he is. He just complained that it didn't make much difference to him since he didn't profit on the deal," Adam replied.

"Yes, he's becoming more irritating the older he gets. I hope he didn't upset her."

"No. He may be irritating, but he's not stupid. He's happy to have her handle him in Europe."

"Through you, I trust?"

"Yes, of course."

"Here she comes now," the bishop said.

Adam glanced over his shoulder to see the Englishwoman returning in the distance. "Tell me, has old Belloc decided on a price for the Picassos?"

The bishop nodded, and, with one eye on their approaching guest, leaned over toward Adam and whispered into his ear.

As Catherine Bentley returned to her seat, the waiter arrived to take their food order and their drinks were served.

As they sipped their drinks the bishop said, "We were just talking about your promoting Jack Hastings's work in Europe."

Catherine replied directly to the bishop, "Yes, we have discussed it. However, as you know, developing the market for Hastings, or indeed any living artist, isn't my primary purpose here in New York."

The bishop nodded. "So I understand."

"My client is very keen to register an interest in the three Picassos before they are offered on the open market."

"Yes," the bishop replied, "Adam has already explained that, and I have informed our principal of this interest."

"In which case, I can accompany you to Florida tomorrow, if you wish."

"Not necessary, Catherine," he replied. "Arrangements are being made as we speak to have the paintings packed and dispatched to a high-security depository here in New York. My client doesn't wish to participate directly in any of the negotiations; he's leaving that entirely up to Adam and me."

Catherine raised her eyebrows in an expression of mild surprise.

"In which case, what time scale are we talking in terms of?"

"The paintings will be available for your inspection in one or two days at the most, God willing," the bishop answered with a wave of his hand. "Your client can wait that long, I'm sure?"

She pursed her lips. "I suppose so."

Adam's cellphone began to ring. Excusing himself, he checked the caller ID and answered. He sat immobile; it was apparent something was wrong. He had to clear his throat to reply to the caller.

"Jesus, Joe . . ." he croaked. "When did that happen?" He was struggling not to choke up.

"Yes, yes, I'll do that . . . Phil's here with me at the moment," he said. "I'll tell him . . . I can't believe it!"

The others looked at him with concern. Neither of them spoke. They could see the watering in his eyes, the swallowing action in his throat, the exaggerated displacement activity as he put his phone back into his jacket pocket and tried to compose himself enough to speak.

Turning to the bishop, Adam placed a hand on one of his and gripped it tightly before speaking. "That was Joe Rooney. Jack's dead! They've just found him hanged in the studio!"

Detective Joe Rooney patted his jacket pockets. He removed a pack of cigarettes and a lighter from one before pushing the mess of photographs and crime scene reports across to the other side of the desk. Although he'd finished his last cigarette only minutes earlier, he already craved another—but this was strictly a non-smoking building. Stress pricked the nicotine monkey, and he was finding today very stressful, for although he had come to view his own end with equanimity, friends' deaths were still disturbing.

He rose from his chair, then paused. He stuck a cigarette in his mouth, lifted the flame to the tip and inhaled, and sat down again. He pointed a finger at his young partner, Carl Lummus, and said, "I want you to pretend I'm not here. Just spend a little more time examining this stuff. Triple-check that there's nothing we're missing."

As Lummus sorted the paperwork into piles before him, Joe eased back into the worn office chair and picked at its foam-padded forearm rest with a fingernail. The image of Jack hanging refused to fade. Eyes open or closed, he could still see him. And it had been the same all through the night, allowing him little rest.

He could feel the sour acid of the sleepless night rising in his stomach.

Sure, he'd had his share of disagreements with Jack Hastings in the past. Let's face it, who hadn't? Jack had never gone out of his way to endear himself to anyone, so they no longer kept in regular touch, but a long time ago he had been very friendly with Jack and Liz, and he was finding it difficult to look at him like this.

Carl skimmed one of the Crime Scene Unit photographs across the desk toward him. Another shot of the same subject, only taken from a different angle: an upper torso shot with the wig pulled back to allow a better view of the rope securely knotted around the main sprinkler system pipe that led down to and through a chromed metal eye to form a tight noose around the neck.

"He must've been a good looking girl when he was alive!" Lummus observed with a smile. "Great tits!" he added after studying the next one and tossing it on top of the other in front of his partner.

Rooney liked Carl Lummus. Still only in his late twenties with short blondish hair and even-featured, Nordic good looks, he and Rooney generally meshed together well. He was intelligent, conscientious, and hardworking. An ambitious young cop, Rooney believed, who, with luck, was destined for the top. Always eager, he had only recently returned from a well-reviewed, six-month placement in England with the London Metropolitan Police. But he had one very annoying habit, and one that would only prejudice his opportunities promotion-wise. He just tried to be too fucking funny.

Rooney leaned forward, jabbing his right index finger at his partner. "Listen to me, Carl—it's nothing personal, I enjoy a joke as much as the next guy, but there's a time and place for everything, and this morning and this department are definitely not either."

Carl looked at him with surprise, then realization. "I'm sorry, Joe, I didn't mean to upset you."

"Look," Rooney said, "let me give you one piece of advice. In this department you can get so far on your qualifications and hard work, but there'll be plenty of others who'd just love to see you fuck up. To them, and to your superiors, being funny about the job is just not appropriate. It may have been acceptable in London, but believe me—here it'll do you no favors. Here, it just indicates that you're not worthy of being taken seriously—that you're just a flake. Okay, you're a college graduate, a high-flyer with lots of talent, but just remember that this is the NYPD, not the set of Seinfeld, so enough with the comic one-liners!"

Carl nodded and leaned over to retrieve the photographs.

As Rooney closed his eyes, tilted back in his office chair and drew deeply on his cigarette, Carl began re-reading the reports.

Rooney was simply putting in his time. His father went at fifty-three, which had seemed old to Joe at the time, and none of his three uncles had made it to sixty. All the same; all cardiac victims. And he had no reason to expect to last any longer himself. His wife, Anna, wasn't dead a year yet. It'd been hard to come to terms with. She'd had the operation, endured the grueling post-operative treatment, and all the tests had shown she was clear. Then at the six-month check-up, the bad news. Three months, they told him, but they were wrong again. She was gone in three weeks.

They were childless—not by design, and not for any want of trying. Joe told himself that it didn't matter to him, but he would've liked a family for Anna's sake. Maybe it's not such a bad thing after all. With Anna gone and his chances of longevity very slim to zero, they would've soon been orphans anyway. But then, he thought, most of us end up orphans.

At fifty-two and with over twenty-five years on the force, he could've opted for retirement, but what would he have done with himself then? This was all he had left; this was what made him get out of bed in the morning, and more often than not, kept him out of bed. It had become his template for living, a Treasure Island map superimposed upon a garbage dump. Now he was heading for the black spot.

Since her death, he'd taken up smoking again after a break of fifteen years. He was surprised at just how easy and comforting it was, like meeting an old friend. No guilt at backsliding. It just didn't seem that important anymore. It was a bit like riding a bicycle; he hadn't had one for years, and already he was back up to three packs a day.

"Well?" Rooney asked as Carl neared the end of the paperwork. He straightened up in his chair and fanned the smoke from in front of his face. "What do you think?"

"Still looks the same to me. Classic autoerotic asphyxiation, with all the usual fantasy props. He's even arranged the dressing mirror so he could see himself during the action."

He laid out the photographs on the table, displaying segmented views of the room; there was the one with the long mirror and another with the chair lying on its side just behind the ankles.

"See," Carl said. "There's nothing out of the ordinary for this type of scenario, except, of course, that for a hanged white male, the photos show a painstaking attention to detail."

"Doesn't surprise me. Jack was an artist," Rooney said. "He put a lot into his work, and this just turned out to be his last creation."

"According to the notes, he put a lot into the condom he was wearing, as well," Carl said, scooping up the photographs and turning them facedown.

Rooney glared at him before taking another draw as his cigarette neared its end.

"There were no signs of any forced entry. All the doors had been secure when the girl opened them with her mother's keys." Carl paused, pursed his lips and shook his head. "Jesus, how must she feel after finding her dad like that? And then her mom turning up. What a homecoming!"

"She's heavily sedated, so I don't think she's feeling a hell of a lot at the moment. And in a way it's as well that Liz returned home when she did and found her cellphone with the note stuck to it. She was able to give the kid the support she needed and to make all the calls."

Carl sat staring at the backs of the photographs spread face down on the desk in front of him. "You knew him, Joe; was he gay?"

"Gay isn't a term, in any sense of the word, that I'd have ever used to describe Jack Hastings—and I've known him since he was a kid. He's always been intense. Even when he was young, he was more interested in his work than partying. He was one of those driven people; he even had a sideline going restoring pictures for the Catholic Church. It was through him that I became friendly with Bishop Connor."

"How did you come to know him?"

"His dad, Harry, was a friend of my dad's—they were on the force together."

Carl straightened up. "Hastings's dad was a cop?"

"Yeah, but he was shot when Jack was about fourteen . . ."

"Shot?"

"Yeah . . . terrible; he wasn't even on duty," Rooney said. "One evening he'd gone down to the local 7-Eleven. According to the cashier, the store was empty apart from Harry, who was at the back checking out the beers though the cooler doors, when two guys walked in. They had a quick look around but didn't spot Harry, then produced two pistols and told the clerk to empty the register. Harry must've heard them, and he'd have been able to see what was going down through the high mirrors. Anyway, he always carried a small Walther when off-duty, and when he racked the slide, the noise alerted them. Harry shouted to them to drop their weapons. They didn't and started firing. He took a couple of hits and they escaped; he died on the way to the hospital."

"Jesus! He didn't even get one of them?"

"No, it jammed—he didn't even get a round off."

Carl shook his head. "That's the trouble with an automatic; it can let you down when you need it most."

Rooney nodded. "Yeah, Harry only carried it when he wasn't in uniform. My old man reckoned he never maintained it properly; he said it just gave him a false sense of security."

Rooney stubbed the cigarette end against the side of a metal waste bin. "As you can imagine, Jack took it hard. From then on, he did nothing but study and paint, getting top grades in everything. But it was the painting that he'd become obsessed with, and that was the direction he took, even though he could've had scholarships for law, medicine, or anything. He had a lot of talent.

"Then, in about seventy-five he got married to Liz, who was the only child of a wealthy family."

"This the same lady, the mother?" Carl asked.

"Yeah, they've only ever been married once. She was a real stunner back then, though maybe a bit of an art groupie—hanging with the Warhol crowd, that sorta thing. Still looks good though."

Carl flipped over a few of the photographs. Rooney stared at them but said nothing.

"Jack and his wife, they weren't together anymore?" Carl asked.

"No, not for a while, but they've never divorced. However, he's since taken up with another, younger girl. She's an artist as well."

"She's not living with him?"

"No. Jack wouldn't have been an easy person to live with. Too intense and moody. Too driven. He knew the Truth, and if you disagreed you were wrong, period. He would've been hard for anyone to put up with, especially a young girl in her late twenties."

Carl consulted the pile of notes in front of him. "According to this, the daughter, Sarah, is twenty-two. No other kids?"

"No, just Sarah. I hadn't seen her in a long time; must be ten or twelve years. She's been away studying for the last few years in Europe, something connected with the Fine Arts—London, I think. Hell of a way for her to find him."

"So he had a wife, a child, a girlfriend and no history or hints of homosexual activity?"

"You've got it," Rooney said.

"Apart from what he was wearing," Carl added.

"Give it up, Carl. You know he's basically hanged himself by accident while beating off. Probably did it regularly, but in the gasper game there's no room for mistakes, and I reckon he's paid the price, that's all. As you said — it's classic autoerotic asphyxia, and, as in most cases, the AA perp creates this sort of erotic scenario just to intensify his climax."

"Yep, AA; except in this case it's been the One-Step Program—just take one step off a plastic chair into fresh air."

Rooney shook his head. "I've told you—enough already!"

Carl made no immediate response, just continued perusing the material on the desk. Eventually he spoke, "So, the girlfriend? You know her?"

"Yeah, met her once or twice through Adam Kennedy. He handles her work as well as Jack's. Her name's Zannah Koller, a real knockout; couldn't contact her last night but spoke to her on the phone earlier this morning. Said she was elsewhere at the time with friends, which checked out."

"She was out with friends on her boyfriend's birthday?" Carl said.

"Hmm . . . apparently she didn't even know it was his birthday," Rooney replied. "Doesn't surprise me though—typical Jack. Anyway, she was probably only with him on a coat-tail basis. His work's making big bucks now. Maybe she was hoping to hitch a ride."

"Did you ask her if he normally dressed so formally?"

"In a sense. Obviously, I didn't explain too much. I merely asked about Jack's sexual inclinations."

"Which were?"

"In a word: catholic, with a small 'c'."

"So it's possible he decided to indulge in a little extra-curricular activity without her? In the art world, he must've had a lot of gay friends and acquaintances?"

"Why are you keeping on at this?" Rooney growled.

"I'm just thinking that now that he's been rooting around in this Pandora's Box, he may have expanded his horizons. You just said it: he's into all sorts of exotic and erotic with his new girl-friend and is maybe tempted by something entirely different."

"No, I can't see it. I knew him. He was one hundred percent hetero, I'm sure of it. Maybe you're right in a way though. Maybe he was experimenting with all this super-feminine stuff: the makeup, the wig, the latex breasts, the stockings, and the heels. The self-strangulation ended up being the extra element that was literally his downfall."

"Well, I agree it's probably not a suicide, but something bothers me about it. Something just doesn't feel right."

Rooney made no comment as Carl continued.

"He invested a lot of care in his cosmetics, clothing and accessories. He had become the exemplification of a whorish sort of female sexuality—except for his dick, of course, and it doesn't count as it was doing the thinking. Even I, Joe Normal, could see the erotic after-image of his creation in the photographs. He'd spent a lot of time and care creating this image . . . not surprising, really, since he was experienced in the plastic arts. Even to his fingernails: they'd been augmented, though some of them were torn off, probably in his attempt to save himself. And this is where I see a problem. If he had been gently and gradually inducing this oxygen deprived euphoria and accidentally slipped into unconsciousness, it's unlikely that there would have been any scrabbling at the rope. He would've just drifted off into that sleep you don't wake up from."

"That's quite an assumption," Rooney objected. "Look how a chicken can still run around even after its head's been chopped off." Rooney rubbed his eyes with his thumb and forefinger. "If that's all you've got, I'm going for another smoke."

4

The weak November sun irradiated the limestone façade of the eighteenth-century chateau with a honeyed glow. The property, on the southern outskirts of Paris, served as the corporate headquarters of TC-SPEED, the major document and parcel express delivery company in Europe and Australasia— and one that was rising fast in the Americas. Out of view, some distance from the chateau and its ancient outbuildings, clustered a small modern hamlet of company dwellings, and beyond that, warehousing facilities and the headquarters' security infrastructure.

From the south-facing French windows of his first floor apartment suite, Ray Mitchell gazed down over the tightly patterned parterre garden to the long lake that shone in the middle distance. Though it was a pleasing vista, no thoughts of strolling out of doors passed through his mind. It was just too damn cold after the tropical warmth of northeastern Australia, and though agreeable, Ray just couldn't shift the notion that it was a poor second to the view from his rainforest veranda that looked out over the Coral Sea and toward the Barrier Reef.

His desk phone pealed. He checked his wristwatch: two thirty. "Yep," he said.

"Mr. Tanaka has arrived, sir," a female voice replied.

"Terrific," Mitchell said, "would you show him straight up, Marie-Anne?"

He pulled open one of the ormolu mounted drawers, removed two document folders, and placed them on the desktop. Glancing at his watch again, he passed through an adjoining reception room and opened one of the tall paneled entrance doors which led onto the corridor.

Standing in the open doorway, Mitchell could see Marie-Anne approaching, accompanied by a young, formally dressed Asian man in his thirties, carrying a briefcase.

Mitchell took a step into the hallway and held out his right hand in greeting.

"Welcome to France, Taiki. I'm Ray Mitchell."

Tanaka shook hands and said, "Pleased to meet you, Mr. Mitchell."

Mitchell, dressed in a crewneck sweater and blue jeans, guided Tanaka through to the brocade-lined salon which served as his office. He indicated one of a pair of tapestry-covered gilt fauteuils. "Take the weight off your feet," he said, adding, "Will you join me in a beer?"

Tanaka concurred and Mitchell left the room, returning with two chilled cans of Australian Four-X beer.

"Taiki, the job I've brought you here to discuss is just a wee bit delicate. It concerns acting on my behalf as an intermediary, and it deals with some very personal matters, which mean a hell of a lot to me. If you go for it, it'll just be between us two. No one else will know I'm involved—at least until I decide otherwise."

Taiki Tanaka had spent the past three years working in London since being recruited into the middle management stratum of TC-SPEED. However, this was his first involvement with management at this most senior level.

"If you don't mind me asking, sir—why me? You have no personal acquaintance with my work, do you?"

Mitchell smiled. "Not firsthand, Taiki. Though you come well recommended. *All wool and a yard wide*, is what your Aussie boss in London tells me. When I said I needed a discreet negotiator I could trust, he immediately recommended you. This job involves a little bit of—shall we say—playacting. You might say I'm type-casting you as the inscrutable Oriental."

He paused, assessing the young man for any signs of reserva-tions he might have, then added, "But don't worry; nothing I need you to do is either dangerous or illegal. You've just got to be a front for me, and rest assured, I won't forget it."

Tanaka remained silent for a moment and took a sip of beer. Then, nodding, he said, "Thank you, sir. I'm honored to be working with you."

Mitchell's bronzed face beamed. He leaned over and shook Tanaka by the hand.

"Good decision, Taiki. Now, my position as the major share-holder in TC-SPEED is a close secret and not easily identifiable as it's routed through several other holding companies. With you as company spokesperson, I'm rendered as remote from you as the man in the moon."

"I assure you, sir, no one will learn of your involvement from me without your explicit permission."

"Good," Mitchell said. "Now, I'll give you a bit of background to the problem."

He leaned forward and picked up the top folder from his desk and removed an unframed colored photograph of two middle aged men leaning against the rail of a boat, just clear blue sky and the sea as background.

"The one on the right is my dad; the other is an American named Paul Belloc. They were both keen sport fishermen and great mates—or so my dad thought. Back then, Belloc was a regular visitor with us in Queensland and there was quite a bit of friendly rivalry between them, whether in fishing, business, or their shared passion, art collecting. Both of them loved the early twentieth-century stuff: impressionism, cubism, surrealism. They both bought widely, and, as it turned out, wisely. However, there were three paintings—early buys of my dad's—that Belloc really envied. As a nipper, I remember Belloc often nagging at him to do a deal for them, but they were his favorites as well, and he always refused to part with them."

Mitchell produced another photo from the folder, this time in black and white, and handed it to Tanaka. It was an earlier shot of Mitchell's father against what looked like an art gallery or museum backdrop.

"They're a bit hard to make out, but you can see them hanging on the wall behind my dad. This was taken when they were on temporary loan to the Art Gallery of New South Wales as part of a twentieth-century art exhibition they held."

Tanaka peered into the photo. "Are they Picassos?"

"On the nose." Mitchell nodded. "Each is a painting of one of Picasso's mistresses—though it'd be hard to tell that by looking at them. Right up to the line he refused to sell them. "They're Picasso's Sheilas," he'd say. "They're not eating any grass." But then came the mid-eighties and he had a lot of money tied up in oil, and it just went through the floor. Something had to be done, and, whaddya know, his good old friend, Belloc, came to the rescue.

"At the time my dad had some mining interests which were still profitable. So when Belloc offered to do a deal involving a small gold mine in Indonesia that he owned eighty percent of, in exchange for the three Picassos, he didn't immediately knock it back, as he'd have done before."

Mitchell opened his can and took a slug.

"A gold mine for three paintings?" Tanaka asked.

"Well, my dad knew the background to the mine, or at least Belloc's version of it. New core samples promised big underground deposits, but Belloc had got a bit shirty with the local powers-that-be. He effectively shit in the nest. This was a big problem. He knew, of course, that as my dad had been doing business there for years, he was well-connected. Dad knew exactly who to bung to get things moving. And, as you know, in certain parts of the world, if you're not dealing with the right people, you're not dealing at all. End of story."

Tanaka nodded. "So your father agreed to the deal?"

"Not at first. He tried to do some other sort of a deal with Belloc. But no luck. Belloc wanted the paintings, and that was it. In the end, and against his gut feeling, it was my mum who convinced him that it was an opportunity too good to miss. Of course, it was a big mistake."

"What went wrong?"

"Well, first—there was fuck-all gold!"

Mitchell's voice had raised; he took a swallow of beer and forced a cough before continuing.

"The core samples had obviously been buggered with; traces had been scattered in the cores before being assayed. Belloc, of course, denied it, as you'd expect. Further testing revealed surface traces of gold, but the mine was no longer viable. It wasn't worth working any further. He reckoned one of Belloc's geologists, who has since disappeared from the face of the earth, had been responsible for salting the core samples. It was a piss-poor situation that just couldn't be salvaged. And if that wasn't enough, then came the final shellacking."

Mitchell paused and took another sip from the can he was grasping. "Yeah, it knocked the stuffing out of both of us, and it came totally out of the blue. It was my mum; she left us—me and my dad. Or rather, she simply didn't come back."

Tanaka half lifted a hand. "No, Mr. Mitchell, it's okay. I don't need to know this."

"No, it's better you hear the full story. You'll see why I've gotta lie low in this deal." Mitchell's eyes focused on the beer can in his fist as he continued. "She'd been in the U.S. for a couple of weeks, visiting my young sister, Rosa, who was at school there. My dad just got a phone call from her to say it was over; that she'd been involved with Belloc for some time and wanted a divorce. That was it; she never came back—and she kept Rosa with her."

Mitchell shrugged. "I suppose it's nothing new. People screw around and marriages break up every day. Even so, it was rough, and it nearly finished my dad off. Not surprising, really. The business was in the shit and his wife had left him, taking his only daughter with her, after having conned him into making the worst business decision of his life.

"It knocked the heart out of the old man, and after that he more or less hung up his boots. I took over, cut our losses and diversified where I could. I was lucky, of course. Whole blocks of land along the coast that he'd bought for buttons in the sixties started to come good. Hotels were going up and the tourist boom really took off. It saved us."

"I take it you haven't been reconciled then?" Tanaka asked.

"No. Though when my dad died, Rosa flew over for the service. It was the first time I'd seen her in over four years, and you see big changes in a teenager in that time; she'd turned into an American, accent and all. After that, she and I sort of kept in touch from time to time, but that was about it. Then out of the blue I got a call from my mum; she was terminally ill and wanted to see me." Mitchell paused. The beer can gave a weak metallic crack from his grip. "So, we arranged a private visit, and she died shortly afterward. There were no recriminations, but you couldn't have called it a reconciliation. Just a goodbye."

"And your sister, Rosa?"

"By then the States was where she called home. I've invited her to come out to Queensland, but she's never taken me up on it. So she still lives there, in Florida, in the Belloc household, as his stepdaughter."

Tanaka said, "I'm sorry."

Mitchell waved his hand. "That's okay—you couldn't have known," he said, and lifted the photograph of the two friends on the boat, tapping it with his forefinger. "To get back to the point. This bastard, Belloc, is no longer a well man. He's had major heart surgery, which wasn't entirely successful. The prognosis looks good—at least from my point of view. He's going to drop off the perch soon, and he knows it. On top of this, I'm happy to say, he's had a few business setbacks recently. Not that he's on his uppers, but I suspect he could do with a healthy injection of funds. Consequently, the word is he's going to sell my dad's paintings. And this is where you come in. I want you to buy them."

"It's not exactly my area of competence, Mr. Mitchell . . ."

"That's not a problem. What's important is that Belloc doesn't discover that I'm in any way involved. He hasn't forgotten about me; he blames me for a lot of their misfortunes over the past years, and not without reason. I've tried to undermine the bastard every chance I got, and it was a bonus if he suspected that I had a hand in it. So I reckon he would sell the bloody things to anyone else for less than market value if he found out I was after them."

"So you want me to approach them on behalf of TC-SPEED?"

"No, the company has already enlisted the services of a London art dealer to do the actual face-to-face negotiations. You will liaise with her. She, of course, knows nothing about me. As far as she's concerned, you will be the person who has the ultimate mandate to negotiate—the top banana. You do the deal."

"What's the name of this lady?" Tanaka asked.

"Catherine Bentley." Mitchell stood up and lifted the bottom folder from his desk and handed it to Tanaka. "All the relevant background and contact information is in there. She's in New York at the moment, has been briefed, and is expecting your call.

"I've had one of the company houses here allocated for your accommodation until this thing is over. Tomorrow, I want you to contact her. Remember, my name mustn't come up, but if an alarm bell rings—even if you hear a suspicious sounding fart—I want to know. All my numbers are in the folder. Anyway, I won't be too far away, so don't hesitate to contact me. Any time, day or night, it makes no difference. No matter what it takes, I want these paintings back. Any questions?"

Tanaka tapped the back of the plastic folder. "I'll study this first, and then consult you with any questions I may have." He paused. "But there is one thing you could satisfy my curiosity about now."

"Shoot," Mitchell said.

"How much are these paintings actually worth?"

Mitchell drained the last of the beer from the can, wiped his mouth with his hand, sat back in his chair, and with a faint smile addressed the wall somewhere over Tanaka's head. "Hard to be precise, but in today's market, in U.S. dollars, they are probably worth in the region of thirty to forty million . . ."

Tanaka's eyes opened wide before he heard the next word.

". . . each! But, strictly between you, me, and the black stump, the price is irrelevant. You just get them. Nothing else is an option."

5

Shortly before eleven, the sleek, black hearse glided through the entrance gates followed by two limousines and the funeral procession. Having left early in case of hold-ups on the New Jersey Turnpike, Adam was already there, waiting. As the parking lot began to fill, Adam checked his black tie and appearance in the rearview mirror. This was it: he got out and joined the tail end of those lining to shuffle inside.

The small chapel brimmed as subdued organ music thrummed in the background. Adam squeezed onto the end of the last pew.

Hard to think that this was the end of Jack. He bowed his head and lifted his hands up to his face in imitation of prayer. Hard to imagine that he would never have to listen to him complain about prices, the bishop, or anything else, ever again. He had known him since his teens, and though Jack had projected an aggressive, inflexible persona to the world, Adam had known his kinder aspects. Jack, he knew, in his inimitable way, had cared for him. He pressed the corners of his closed eyelids with his fingertips as he felt a wave of sorrow wash over him. The music quieted as Bishop Connor's familiar tones began to resonate from the concealed speakers. Adam felt himself relaxing, and regulating his breathing, he sat back on the bench, letting his friend's words comfort him.

As the casket hummed downward out of view, Adam steeled himself. He knew it wasn't over yet—it might be the end for Jack, but the difficult bit, dealing with the survivors, was yet to come.

He watched his fellow mourners file out of the chapel and form a long, untidy line outside to pay their respects to the bereaved. The family group was small: Liz, Jack's widow, held a supporting arm around her daughter, Sarah, who stood with a vacant expression on her face—doubtless still stunned from the horror of her homecoming. On Sarah's other side stood her grandmother, Maria Halliday, Liz's mother, who had flown up from her winter quarters in Florida "to make sure the pain-in-the-ass is really dead", as the bishop had confided that he'd overheard her saying.

Adam decided to wait until the line shortened a little before approaching them, and he scanned around the other mourners. Yes, there she was.

Zannah Koller, Jack's girlfriend, was normally easier than this to pick out in a crowd. She was standing with a gaggle of fellow artists who had no doubt attended to give her moral support in what she probably considered enemy territory. Her usually startlingly blonde hair was sheathed in a black beret, and drawing closer to her, he could see that her face was largely unmade-up, except for around the eyes, where she had been trying to disguise the ravages of her tears. As Adam joined the group and exchanged nods with several others, Zannah edged him to one side.

"Adam, I'm so glad to see you," she whispered.

Adam took one of her black gloved hands and asked, "How have you been holding up?"

She shook her head with small side to side movements. "I'm really worried. I need you to help me."

Adam put his other arm around her waist, becoming aware of the swooping line of her hipbone beneath her clothing. "Zannah, anything I can do for you, don't hesitate to ask."

"I told him it was dangerous, but I never thought it could get him killed."

Adam tensed; was this an inappropriate comment? He had to

say something. "Well, there's no denying that," was the best he could do.

She was gripping his hand tightly now. "Christ, I could be next. What am I going to do? Can we come to some sort of arrangement?"

What was she raving about? Was she implying that she does something similar to reach orgasm? Was this some sort of a come-on or confession?

As he hugged her closer in silent reply, his fantasizing was interrupted by Bishop Connor's voice.

"Good morning, Adam," he said, then, "Zannah, my dear, I've been looking for you everywhere."

Adam removed his arm from around Zannah's waist as she and the bishop exchanged greetings.

"Zannah," he said, "I've been thinking about what you were saying yesterday. Let's step over here for a moment and have a quiet word. Will you excuse us for a moment please, Adam?"

With a conspiratorial wink toward Adam, he put an arm around her and wheeled her a little distance away, just out of earshot.

Adam stood waiting. Their heads almost touching, Zannah appeared riveted by whatever the bishop was saying. Unlike her conversation with Adam, this one was being dominated by the bishop. Zannah barely spoke, just nodded while the bishop cradled her with one arm as she clutched the back of his overcoat. Whatever he said reassured her, for as they rejoined his company, Adam could see the desperation on her face had faded.

"Now, I have to have a private word with Adam, if you don't mind," he said to her, "but you don't need to worry, I'll be in touch with you the moment I return."

Looking relieved, she bade swift goodbyes to both of them and moved off to greet other mourners, who, having done their duty with the officially bereaved, were now approaching her.

"What was going on there? Adam asked.

"The seal of the confessional." The bishop smiled, forefinger vertical in front of his lips. "She was just a bit upset, but she'll be grand. Anyway, never mind about Zannah, there are more important things in the offing. I have to go back down to Florida . . ."

"Again?"

"Yes, but don't worry. The paintings are packed and ready to go, but Belloc just wants to go over the minutiae one more time."

His gaze moved over Adam's shoulder to a group just walking away from the chapel. "There's Catherine Bentley talking to Liz. I know she can be a bit intense, but you need to keep her on the boil. Who knows, she may not turn out to be the major player, but whatever the case, competition can only be good for us. I'll have to go now. I've got one or two things to do before I leave, but I'll contact you and let you know when I'm returning. I shouldn't be away more than a day, two at the most. With luck, I'll be back by Monday."

"Fine," Adam said. "Let me know and I'll pick you up."

As the bishop walked away, Adam smiled to himself. There he goes, the professional propitiator, more puff than product as usual, but he was familiar with the bishop's modus operandi: reveal as little information as necessary. Generally, though, this maxim did not extend to him, as the bishop had guided and mentored him ever since the traffic wreck that killed his parents, orphaning him at seventeen. The bishop had been his dad's closest friend, and since then, he had encouraged him educationally and vocationally, teaching him everything he could about the fine art business and looking after him like a son. Recently, though, things had been seeming just a little more opaque than normal; nevertheless, Adam's trust in the bishop was implicit.

Adam turned and walked over to pay his respects to the Hastings family and to speak with Catherine Bentley.

With collar length dark hair, dark toned complexion and fine facial features, there was no denying that Liz Hastings was a very attractive woman. Under her open black topcoat, she was wearing a tailored black suit with dark shaded stockings and black suede formal shoes. Looks like a fashion plate, Adam reflected, but then she always had.

During the summer before his first college semester, the bishop had introduced Adam into the Bohemian art world of New York, where he first met Jack and Liz Hastings, an unconventional couple. Adam's head had been turned by the attention of this beautiful older woman, and it wasn't long before they became involved. However, the affair left Adam feeling confused and guilty —despite Liz's assurances that Jack didn't give a damn. "Sauce for the goose," she used to say. But, for Adam, the emotional turmoil had been too much, and after every assignation Adam was crushed by remorse. There had been no alternative but to put an end to all contact. For him it was the only way.

Even much later, after becoming Jack's agent, he managed to minimize any personal contact with her. Not difficult, as Jack's artistic life had long been separate from his personal life. Now, as he approached the group, he wondered if he had simply been too young to appreciate his good fortune.

With Jack's death things were bound to change. Now, Liz would be the beneficiary of Jack's body of work. He would have no option but to deal with her.

Already he had made a difficult visit to the family before the funeral rites, making all the right noises, trying to submerge their own personal history. Fortunately, Liz's mother had been present at the time, which had cushioned the awkwardness. He was probably being ridiculous, he told himself. For Liz, it was probably just a faded memory from her past, whereas for him it was different. It felt like a fixation, a hangover from his youth. "Grow up!" he scolded himself as he approached the four women walking together.

Liz's mother spoke first. "Adam, will you be joining us for the lunch?"

"No, I'm sorry, Mrs. Halliday, I have a few commitments later this afternoon," he said. Was that a relieved look he caught in Liz's eyes?

"Well then, perhaps you might see Sarah home? She's not feeling up to it either."

Adam saw Liz looking at her mother with surprise bordering on alarm. Sarah gave a weak smile, as if indifferent to her fate.

"My pleasure," he answered, avoiding looking at Liz.

As they walked toward the funeral cars, Adam turned to the Englishwoman. "Oh, Catherine, perhaps we could have lunch sometime soon? There are a few things I'd like to discuss with you."

"Me too," she replied, "give me a call later today if you can."

As the others slid into the front limousine, Sarah stood beside Adam, docile as a well-trained dog, while Liz insisted to her that she go straight home to bed.

"Okay, Mom, don't worry, I'll be fine." These were the first words Adam had heard her utter; she was evidently beginning to revive.

As the funeral car pulled off, Adam guided Sarah in the direction of his own vehicle. Hearing his name being called, he turned —it was Joe Rooney. Adam had noticed him earlier, standing, almost hiding, he thought at the time, at the back of the chapel. Glimpsing him later, Adam noticed that he was avoiding having any extended conversation with Liz and family—obviously still bad blood there, for whatever reason.

"Joe, I saw you inside, but then you disappeared."

"Yeah, well, I didn't want to intrude too much on the family."

Turning to Sarah, Adam made the introductions. "Sarah, you remember Joe Rooney—the detective that's handling the case?" She nodded and extended her hand. Adam continued, "Joe's an old friend of your dad's from years ago."

"Oh, I didn't know that," Sarah replied.

Joe clasped her hand. "Apart from the other day, it must be about twelve years since we met, so you wouldn't remember me from then. Anyway, I've changed a bit in the meantime." He stroked a temple with one hand and rolled his eyes upward to indicate his thinning pate.

She smiled. "Probably not as much as I have."

Adam and Joe chuckled in agreement.

Yes, it was good to see Joe becoming a little more animated, chatting as they strolled. Since his wife's death, Joe's enthusiasm for life, and the interests he and Anna had pursued together, had disappeared; from a convivial and caring friend he had become a chain smoking misanthrope. But this morning his mood seemed brighter. What's this, Adam wondered, "the child Anna and he never had" syndrome? Anyway, whatever the reason, it was good to see Joe this way. They had reached Adam's car.

"Do you need a ride, Joe?" Adam asked.

"No, I'm okay, thanks." Joe turned to Sarah. "It's been really good seeing you again. I'm just sorry it's been under these circumstances." He shook her hand. "Hope it's not another twelve years till we meet again. Take care."

Sarah smiled at him while Joe nodded to Adam and headed off in the direction of his vehicle.

"What a nice man," she said, as Adam opened the car door for her.

Firing up the engine, Adam asked, "Where to now, Madame? Paris, Rome, London . . .?"

She pulled a wry face. "Sorry, it's going to have to be New York. And please don't forget . . . it's Mademoiselle, not Madame."

"Well, Ma'm'selle," Adam said, "I'm sure it doesn't have to be New York right away?"

She looked at him.

"Not when we have the entire gamut of New Jersey's culinary delights spread before us."

"You're right," she said, laughing. "I could murder a pizza!"

Adam sat opposite her in the booth and watched her cut into her thin-crust, spicy pepperoni with anchovies while absently tapping along with Bob Seger singing "Against the Wind" on the piped Muzak playlist. His tuna salad lay barely disturbed in front of him. The booth was tomato red in every dimension, with a false ceiling suspended only a few feet above their heads. He took a mouthful of tuna, lifted his glass of Diet Coke and took a long drink.

"It's like having lunch inside a post-Caesarean sectioned mother . . ." she said with a grin before biting into another forkful.

Adam almost choked. He couldn't breathe; carbonated liquid and bubbles foamed-up in his airways until Coke began to erupt in uncontrolled sprayings from his nose and mouth. Tears streamed down his face as he tried to control his spluttering laughter.

In seconds, Sarah was beside him with fistfuls of paper napkins from the chromed dispenser, mopping his face, suit, and table top.

"Jesus, you're a messy eater," she scolded, smiling.

Adam began excusing himself, embarrassed by the glances of other diners. He grabbed some more napkins, dabbing at the bits she'd missed. She moved back to resume her meal, dismissing his apologies with a wave of her fork.

"It's okay. Once you get used to eating in company, you'll soon get the hang of it." Her teasing was relaxed and calm. Quite a difference from an hour ago, Adam thought as he aped normality and took another careful mouthful.

"So, what are your plans next?" he asked.

Sarah shrugged. "Not sure. Maybe stick around a while, let the dust settle. What about you? You were Dad's agent. Where does that leave you?"

"Well, he was quite prolific; there should be quite a body of work in the studio." Adam felt uneasy. Talking this way almost devalued Jack as a person—just transforming him into an asset to dispose of as profitably as possible. "Anyway, I handle several other artists, and I'm still involved in the gallery downtown."

"And working with Bishop Connor as well?"

"Still moving whatever he puts my way," he agreed. "You know, minor surplus stuff the church wants to dispose of." As he heard himself speak, he knew he sounded blasé and felt guilty since this represented the bulk of his income. "And long may it continue," he added, by way of private contrition.

"So much for business." Sarah made an invisible tick in the air. "What about your personal life?"

Adam smiled. He was being cross-examined by a girl almost half his age; a girl who had seemed an inconsolable wreck just a few hours earlier, but who was now trying to take control. "Just the usual, a bit of theater, movies . . ."

"Alone?"

"Simply because I hang around with clergy doesn't mean I'm a monk."

"No, no, I'm sorry," Sarah said, "I wasn't casting aspersions. I was just wondering if you were involved with anyone at the moment."

"No, still making my own breakfasts."

Smiling, she indicated the unfinished platter in front of him. "Must be a big one if what you eat for lunch is anything to go by."

He tapped his waistline. "When you hit forty, you've got to keep your eye on the pounds. You'll see for yourself—in another thirty years or so."

She wiped the corners of her mouth with her napkin before scrunching it into a ball and bouncing it off his head, laughing.

"Well, I'm ready if you are. Just need to make myself look human again first," she said, lifting her purse and sliding out of the booth.

Adam smiled, and as she went off to the bathroom he paid the check.

DRIVING WITH THE BRIGHT BLUE SKY OVERHEAD AND THE climate control set at a comfortable seventy-two degrees, it almost felt like early summer. Adam indicated a service station ahead. "Need to get some gas before we hit the highway."

He pulled up alongside the self-serve island and jumped out. Swiping his credit card, he flipped the lever and started refueling. Standing and pumping the gas on the passenger side, his eyes were drawn to Sarah in the front seat. There was little of her visible, just her shining dark hair and the sight of the side of her face through the glass.

Crazy, he thought, how in the space of an afternoon she had been transformed from this morning's pitiful soul into this vivacious creature before him. He couldn't deny it; he was experiencing a thrill just being with her, even looking at her like this, through the window, at a distance.

The pump clicked off, shocking him out of his reverie. As he removed the nozzle and turned to holster it back in the pump, his eyes caught the exterior mirror. Sarah's face smiled at him and winked. He felt himself reddening; she'd been watching all the time.

Flustered, Adam went through the routine of replacing the filler cap and closing the flap with deliberation as he tried to compose himself before getting back into the driver's seat.

"I was beginning to think there was something on my hair or my face by the way you were inspecting me there," she said with a laugh.

"No, no. Sorry . . . I was just in a bit of a daydream." He was all thumbs as he tried to get the ignition key into the lock.

He felt her hand on his arm. "It's not a complaint," she said, placing her other hand on his chin and turning his face to her. "I've enjoyed peeking at you as well."

Adam looked into her soft brown eyes that were no longer smiling but were widening, getting closer. He placed his right hand over her hair, cradling the nape of her neck. "I was just admiring the sheen of your hair," he said, the sentiment no longer sounding inane.

"Be my guest."

Her words barely registered at a conscious level as he felt her body moving toward his. As if he was being reeled in, his face moved across to hers. Their lips touched, just as the blaring of a horn jerked Adam back to reality.

"Jesus! We're blocking the pumps!" Adam pulled his seat belt

back on and gave an apologetic wave to an angry-looking driver in
a battered Chevrolet pick-up behind him, before driving off.

During the ride back, Adam didn't say much. He just drove and
listened to Sarah chatter. Is she as embarrassed as I am? he
wondered. Christ, she's not much more than a child. Once she's
alone, is she going to think that I tried to take advantage of her
when she's been at her most vulnerable? The disquiet churned the
tuna in his stomach.

As he pulled in to drop her off, she thanked him, then leaned
toward him, grabbed his tie and kissed him full and moist on the
mouth.

"Thank you, Adam. That's the most human I've felt since I've
come home," she said. "Brush up on your dining etiquette, and I'll
see you soon." With a wave of her hand and a generous smile, she
jumped out. Adam, not really sure what had just happened, waved
in reply before driving off.

❧ 6 ❧

Despite appearances, Bishop Phil Connor was worried. Jack's death had really put the pressure on. Now, as a result, the Bellocs needed him back down in Florida again, and quickly. There was no doubt what they wanted—information and results—and he was no longer confident of being able to provide either. At least not at such short notice.

As the Mercedes drove away from the funeral with André at the wheel, he turned his attention to the sheaf of documents on the seat beside him. It contained a backlog of African charity-related paperwork that he couldn't continue to ignore. He had dedicated over twenty years to establishing his charity as a small flexible outfit that wasn't hobbled by the constraints of the larger, higher profile organizations. In general, this method had proved successful, injecting funds and developing projects on a specifically targeted basis.

But success in African relief terms was as frustrating as trying to empty the ocean with a bucket—even the success could be depressing. Most depressing of all were the inter-charity professional jealousies, which threw up problems that were as time-consuming and awkward to deal with as the real life-or-death issues on the ground. Often you found yourself in a world of professional

41

fundraisers, especially here at the source of the funding, rather than in the field. People whose entire lifestyles were financed not only by generous salaries but also by percentages of the amount they raised. "Incentives", as they unblushingly called them. These people regarded you as a competitor, a rival who was poaching funds that they were therefore unable to access and benefit from.

This was one of the problems of becoming more successful; these sorts became more difficult to avoid—they wanted to "help" you. What they really wanted, of course, was to absorb you and enhance their own organizations and their own personal wealth. Often, these were people who should know better; people who have actually been in the field; people who have seen human beings dying in front of their very eyes for the want of a dollar. It was a mystery how such sights did not automatically confer humility upon them. Did they not know that they too were going to die? And most of them very soon; after all, what were twenty or thirty years in the scheme of things?

From the document he was reading, he saw that one of these rivals was now trying to muscle in on a little fund-raising venture that Father O'Hara, an old clergyman friend, had been operating annually on his behalf in Boston for over fifteen years. Unfortunately, this evening's Florida trip meant he wasn't in a position to deal with it personally. André would have to go as his envoy. However, it would make little difference. André took no nonsense from anyone.

André was not a priest, despite the dark-colored garb which gave him a clerical air. He and the bishop had met many years earlier in Djibouti, northeast Africa, where the bishop's charity was involved in refugee relief work and André was an NCO with the French Foreign Legion. From the beginning, he had been impressed with Bishop Connor's pragmatism. For a priest, André thought, the bishop was remarkably worldly, and he was happy to help from time to time, sorting out various local problems. In fact, André had proved so invaluable that the bishop created a position for him when he retired from the Legion. He had now been employed by the bishop for over five years as his personal assistant.

Fifteen years' service had been enough for André. Belgian by birth, he had joined the Legion in his late twenties, and in common with a lot of recruits who wished to vanish, he had adopted an assumed name. He had served in Africa, with occasional stints in Madagascar and Tahiti. But fifteen years was enough, and it entitled him to both a retirement pension that was payable anywhere in the world and French nationality in the identity he had assumed upon enlisting.

In a way, by joining the bishop, he had merely swapped one family for another and was now as dedicated to his new employer as he had been to his old. Though he may have settled into this less physically demanding role, he had not allowed himself to become soft. He still had a job to do. He was a firm's man, and now the firm was Bishop Connor. The only visible vestige of his old martial life was the small stylized "Flaming Grenade" gold signet ring he wore on the pinkie finger of his left hand—the emblem of the French Foreign Legion.

§

By the time they arrived back at the episcopal residence, a spacious suite of rooms assigned to him from the portfolio of Archdiocese property, the bishop had made his decision. Just two charity-related problems needed personal intervention: the one in Boston and a minor matter back in Africa. He knew André was competent to deal with both, so he directed him to fly to Boston and address that problem first, then travel onward to Africa.

The Picassos were now on top of the agenda. With his bag packed for the Florida trip, he went to his study. There was one more thing to do—one call to make, the one he had been delaying.

He sat down at his desk and relaxed back into the chair, closing his eyes. Slowly, while easing his head from side to side and from front to back, he began to massage each side of his neck muscles with his right hand. But it was no good; this was simply procrastinating, delaying the inevitable and solving no problems. Jack's demise was taking its toll: sorrow, worry, and the restless nights. That was enough; he checked his wristwatch—he could postpone the call no longer. She wouldn't like it, but she needed to know the truth. He lifted the handset and began to dial.

§

Liz sat opposite her mother in the back of the limo as they left her apartment for the airport. What a hell of a day, first the cremation and then the massive blow-up with her mother over her meddlesome interference between Sarah and Adam Kennedy. Now piqued, her mother had changed her plans and insisted on heading back home immediately. They traveled in silence; there had been enough angry words over lunch. In any case, by tomorrow her mother would have forgotten about their tiff, especially after having escaped down to the more congenial climate of southern Florida.

The past few days hadn't been easy. Liz wasn't used to having to accommodate another emotional whirlwind so like herself within such close confines, and that was without taking account of her daughter. Sarah, however, because of the trauma, had spent a lot of the time becalmed by medication, and she hadn't really entered into the equation at all. Until this afternoon, that is.

Her mother didn't look her age. She never had, thought Liz, as she stole a glance while avoiding eye contact. They hadn't seen each other in a few months, and since her arrival Liz had begun to notice certain fleeting aspects of her: a familiar profile here, or an evocative smile there. But what she recognized wasn't purely her mother; the open smile and fine profile line reminded her of a previous bereavement, that of her grandfather, Romano, the last man she had truly mourned.

Mario Romano had doted on Liz and devoted a lot of his time to her as she was growing up. He was a keen huntsman, and in her teenage years, she accompanied him on regular trips upstate where they fished, hunted and bonded. Under his tutelage, she learned the practical skills of woodcraft; they taught her patience, stealth and self-reliance, and they honed her natural resourcefulness. Liz never forgot those trips.

However, in the sixties, he could no longer sustain the power base he had established during the Prohibition years. His son-in-law, Stephen Halliday, though not incompetent, was more inclined toward the Arts, and he struggled to keep the business profitable. Now, with her father dead ten years and the business interests sold off, the backbone of her mother's fortune and income lay in trust funds and the remaining property her grandfather had amassed in the course of his lifetime.

Yes, Liz thought, as she stole a glimpse at the ghost of her grandfather in her mother's face, he had overshadowed all the other men in her life. Firm but supportive, he had never castigated either Liz or her mother for their marriage choices. However, this, she felt, was his cardinal error, and she resolved not to repeat it. Liz would ensure that Sarah would not continue this serial misjudgment on the distaff side.

§

It was late afternoon before Adam made it back home. The episode at the gas station still played on his mind, and each time he reran it he felt more embarrassed. Had he taken advantage of an emotionally fragile girl, someone so many years younger and less experienced, someone who may even now be alarmed by his audacity? Damn it, he had to admit that not only had he felt a rapport developing between them, but he also found her extremely attractive. Despite their physical resemblances, Sarah just seemed so different from her mother. More kindly and humorous, her sarcasm without rancor—even Liz's humor tended to be barbed. Yes, he would have to see her again. However, as she was staying in her mother's apartment, there was another problem: to call her or not? He had no doubts that Liz would less than welcome such a contact.

Then there was the problem of Zannah. She had been niggling at the back of his mind since the funeral. Yes, Jack had died in an appalling tragedy, but the self-obsessed urgency of her behavior today was still incomprehensible. It wasn't the passive devastation of being face to face with the undeniable—and furthermore, Adam realized with more embarrassment, it wasn't a sexual proposition.

She had obviously been worried about something, and before Phil had intervened, he had hoped that he might be able to help her. There was something going on that didn't quite make sense, and he really needed to try to find out what it was. He looked up her number and dialed.

Her phone rang so long that he was expecting the machine to pick up, so he was surprised when he heard her subdued voice saying hello.

"Zannah, it's me, Adam. I just wanted to check on you—how are you feeling now?"

"Oh, I've been lying down, Adam. Sorry if I came over a little excitable this morning, but after Jack, I've been so worried."

"You'll be fine in a week or two," he reassured her, cringing at the cliché as he heard himself say, "It's been a big shock, but life goes on . . ."

"Yeah, well I want to make sure that mine keeps going on."

"Sorry?" he said, wondering if he'd misheard her. "How d'you mean?"

"Come on, Adam! You know what I mean. I don't want to end up like Jack. I'm not greedy. Sure, we all know he was his own worst enemy and getting weirder by the day. Said he just wanted to concentrate on his own work. Didn't want to do anything more for Phil. But it was shameful to turn his back on him like that, after all the bishop had done for him. But now all he would say was, "Fuck Phil!" That's when he involved me at the sharp end. Used me as the messenger, the go-between, 'to sweeten the pill,' as he put it."

Adam made non-committal noises whenever she paused, letting her think she was telling him something he already knew.

She continued, "What made it worse was that Jack was refusing to talk to him face to face, refusing to negotiate at all. It put me in an impossible position and Phil was furious—I'd never seen him angry before."

"What did Jack want?"

"You don't know? Phil didn't tell you?"

"No . . . not in detail . . . just that he wasn't happy about it," he stammered.

"I'll tell you, then. Jack wanted ten million before handing them over, and if he didn't get it he threatened to not only burn them but to spill the beans on the last twenty years!"

Ten million dollars? The last twenty years? Blackmail from Jack? Adam needed to know more, but he knew she would just dry up if he asked her directly.

"But," she continued, "as I said to Phil this morning, I had nothing to do with it. I was just the messenger. Now that Jack's gone I'd be happy with a share of the original deal they'd agreed on."

Everything she said required some sort of reciprocal comment, but he was flying blind. He had to say something. "How did he react to that?"

"He understood. Phil's a very sympathetic, understanding man, as you know. I explained that as Jack has shared his confidences with me and has involved me so much, it just wasn't fair for me to be side-lined now. On top of that, the way things have turned out, nothing can go ahead without my cooperation. But as I've already told him, I'm not greedy, I'll settle for five hundred thousand—but I want it up front."

Adam felt as though he was doing a crossword—another clue. "And he agreed to this?"

"He said he'd do his best, but he was sure they wouldn't be enthusiastic about it. He said they might regard it as a bit late to be doing that kind of a deal. That I should just give them up and merely walk away. But I reckon Phil was just giving it a try; you can't blame him after all Jack put him through. So, I stuck to my guns. I deserve something. After all, the bottom line is that I control the access to them, and you guys need them."

"So Phil's reassurances this morning took the pressure off you?"

"Yes."

"And things will be settled when he returns from Florida?"

"Yeah, I hope so, and everyone will be happy." He could hear a smile in her voice.

Adam paused, then said, "Except Jack."

Hanging up, Adam reflected. Instead of having any questions answered, the call had raised even more—one hell of a lot was being kept from him.

His cogitations were interrupted by the phone in front of him ringing into life again; he answered it.

"Adam, Catherine Bentley here." Her no-nonsense tones chimed in his ear. "Now that Hastings's funeral is over, I thought we should lose no further time. When can we proceed on the paintings?"

"Catherine," Adam said, "let me first apologize for this terrible delay. I know what a busy lady you are, and I have to thank you for being so patient under these tragic circumstances. Jack's death has been a blow to us all—to the family, the Bellocs, and especially to the bishop. So much so that I'm afraid we've been rather guilty of neglecting you."

"Look, I don't want to appear insensitive," she said, "but let's get back to the paintings. My client is becoming a touch impatient."

"Catherine, I understand, and I assure you we are on the verge of being able to finalize something. However, the vendor has just requested that the bishop should go back down to Florida to see him. He's flying there this evening."

"Again?" Her tone was irritated. "I understood the decision was made. What's the problem?"

"Between ourselves, Catherine, old Belloc is a very volatile character; but the bishop and he have done business together for a long time, and I believe he can handle him. Don't worry, there won't be a problem."

"I hope you're right," she said, "I must tell you frankly that I find it very frustrating to be negotiating a deal at so many removes. Especially one that is lurching around like this one is. It would be so much more efficient to be negotiating with the vendor in person."

"Catherine, believe me, I understand your situation," Adam said. "And, to tell you the truth, I feel compromised myself by our client's vacillating—but, without reflecting on your professionalism or reputation, I can assure you that a direct approach by you to Belloc might result in your client being excluded as a potential purchaser."

"Very well," she replied, sharp as a knife. "In which case, I don't think there's much point in us meeting again until such a time as you have substantive news for me. You know where to find me. I'll be waiting for your call." She hung up.

"And fuck you, too." he growled into the dead handset.

A frustrating conversation, but at least he had stalled her for the time being. He could understand why she wasn't happy—he wasn't happy either. He hoped that he hadn't upset her too much; she was too valuable, but he couldn't allow her to even contemplate that there was any possibility of subverting his and the bishop's role in this sale.

Her arrogance had not only annoyed him, it had seeded an alternative scenario: the possibility that these paintings could indeed be marketed without his or the bishop's involvement, something that the bishop had assured him was out of the question. But what made Phil so confident? Paintings of this stature needed no real selling. They would sell themselves. Even placed quietly on today's market, buyers would be lining up for them. Maybe Phil was fooling himself, placing too much faith in his long relationship with Belloc. There was so much money involved here that it was difficult to conceive why anyone, even someone with a fortune such as Belloc's, would willingly forgo millions of dollars in commission. For old time's sake? Unlikely.

Furthermore, it was now evident from the conversation with Zannah that something very important was being kept from him. He felt powerless, a spectator at the edge of the action. Merely the message boy. At least, he consoled himself, he had stood up to Catherine Bentley—she had sounded quite disgruntled by the end. By Monday the bishop should be returning from Florida, and this time Adam was determined to hear the full, unabridged story.

❧ 7 ❧

Phil Connor cruised north of Miami along the I-95 high above the regular free-flowing Sunday morning sedan traffic in his Ford Explorer rental. Usually, the Florida weather heartened him, particularly at this time of the year. This morning, however, the brightness bothered him, even through his dark-tinted glasses. He'd passed another restless night, sleeping fitfully.

He wasn't by nature a worrier. All his adult life, in times of anxiety, he had found reassurance in the truth of the dictum that "ninety-eight percent of the things you worry about never happen." Consequently, he tended to regard worrying as an emotionally wasteful and pointless exercise. However, over these past few days he found himself being consumed by the remaining two percent.

He knew he was in a difficult situation. There was a lot of money involved—not that he was any stranger to that. His usual brief was to deal with the fine art and antiques that the Catholic rich donated to the church, either as tax write-offs or as legacies— either way, they were attempts to curry celestial kudos. But this deal had nothing to do with the church and involved more money than usual. One hell of a lot more than usual—probably comfortably in excess of one hundred million dollars, and the one thing he was sure of was that old Paul Belloc wasn't even distantly related to a fool, whether he was dealing with a long-time friend or not.

Aware that eyes would be studying him through the entrance security cameras, he tried to appear relaxed as he waited for the tall ornamental front gates of the Belloc Palm Beach mansion to open. As they glided apart he lifted his foot from the brake pedal, eased on the gas, and, displaying an air of nonchalance, rolled up the shrub-lined driveway to coast to a stop in front of the white pillared portico of the replica antebellum colonial home.

To his dismay, he saw Paul Belloc Junior appear from the front entrance of the building even before he opened his driver's door.

Paul Junior had a trim and athletic appearance. In his late twenties, current fashion had done him a favor in allowing him to wear his hair tightly cropped, which helped disguise his impending male pattern baldness. His features had a not unattractive angular Germanic line to them, but to the bishop's eyes, they were compromised by a strange translucence to his skin that reminded him of a frog's underbelly. Routinely described as "handsome" by the social columnists, the bishop had to assume either that they had never met him up close, or they were out and out sycophants.

"Paul! Good to see you!" the bishop boomed, proffering a handshake, which was returned impassively. "How's your dad?"

"Just the same as he was the last time you saw him," young Belloc said. "Before you go inside, I think you and I need to have a talk about this new situation. I don't want my dad unnecessarily upset."

The bishop joined him, and they walked away from the house along a garden path flanked by fruit trees and shaded by young palms. It was already in the eighties and promising to be another baking hot day.

Belloc continued, "As you know, he's aware of Hastings's death. But I haven't told him the full story—that you're still empty-handed—and I'm not inclined to. I don't want the stress causing a relapse."

"Relax, Paul. Jack had them squirreled away safely, and I'm on the verge of acquiring them. Just leave it to me; there's nothing to worry about."

"Listen, Phil, I find myself worrying about a lot of things, and they all seem to be linked. This was supposed to be straightforward. You said there would be no problems if we let you handle things, and my dad went along with you. I know the two of you go back a long way, and I was happy to remain loyal to this quaint little tradition. But honestly, now I'm not so sure it was such a good idea. It's taking too damn long."

Belloc paused and turned, wordlessly indicating that now that he'd had his say, it was time to head back toward the house.

"Be patient for just another couple of days, Paul. That should do it—you'll see."

Phil Connor knew that Belloc's little speech was all fatuous bullshit. Not for the first time, he felt like slapping the arrogant brat around the ears, but he strained hard to conceal the contempt he felt. If Paul Senior were to die, in a matter of weeks this same brat could be in control of the Belloc fortune, business, and extensive art collection—another excellent reason to pursue the completion of this deal as quickly as possible. In the meantime, Phil knew that he was the only game in town, no matter what this kid said. He had all the necessary connections. He even had a serious buyer waiting lined up in New York, and most importantly, he knew the full story from the very beginning. This knowledge alone ensured that he couldn't be side-stepped.

He couldn't resist. It was time to show this upstart who held the wild cards—time to let Junior know that he wasn't a mere stooge in this game. He paused on the path and touched young Belloc's sleeve, more for emphasis than to interrupt his stride, and spoke to him.

"Look, Paul. I know you're frustrated and upset. We all are. I'm on the brink of doing a deal right now, and believe me, the deal will be done in a matter of days. But to be truthful, I'm annoyed by the implication that you and your dad are only cutting me in on this for old time's sake. I know you were a lot younger then, but it's not that long ago—only nine years—and you knew the situation at the time. So just don't forget that when your family was faced with an intractable problem, it was me who provided the solution. Remember that the whole scenario surrounding the Picassos was totally my idea, and up until now it has been an unequivocal success."

He could see by the surface tension of his skin and the tightening of his lips that Paul Belloc Junior was furious, but he made no reply to the bishop's outburst. They resumed walking back up toward the mansion.

Having made his point, the bishop continued in a more conciliatory tone. "But none of us know the future, and life tends to spring surprises and complications on us. Jack's death has merely created another little complication . . ."

Young Belloc swung around in front of him, blocking the pathway, his eyes popping wide, his skin stretched by his facial grimace, his voice strident and rising. "Hastings alive was creating the complications! He was out of control! Don't forget his crazy demands . . . or his threats!"

The bishop raised an open hand in a calming gesture. "Look, I'm not making any accusations. I'm just saying that at the moment we have another problem to solve. But let me assure you, it is only a small problem, and I can solve it."

"So you've been saying for months," Belloc Junior said, regaining some composure. "And maybe you can. But let's cut out all the stalling and inject a little urgency into this. From where I'm standing, it's obvious that you aren't able to handle this yourself. I think it's time I arranged for a bit of assistance."

The bishop held his hand, palm-out, in a halting gesture. "That won't be necessary, Paul."

"I'll be the judge of that," Belloc Junior said and strode ahead.

The bishop followed him into the air-conditioned entrance hall where they almost collided with Paul Belloc's stepdaughter, Rosa. Dressed in a matching white top and short tennis skirt, she was on her way out, a racquet tucked under her left arm. She, too, was in her late twenties and tall, blonde and tanned with the toned physique of an athlete. Her open, friendly manner contrasted with the surliness of her stepbrother, and though not of his bloodline, she appeared fully integrated into the Belloc family and was the pride of Paul Senior.

"Bishop," she said, "back again so soon?" adding with a mock shiver, "Don't blame you really. That New York climate wouldn't suit me either at this time of the year."

"Nor me, Rosa," he replied. "I'm glad to hear you appreciate your good fortune."

"Oh, I sure do." She beamed in the direction of her step-brother, whose petulance dissolved before her smile. "See y'all later!"

The bishop gave her a parting wave. Yes, he thought, she's grown into quite an asset to the Belloc household – personality and a born manipulator, just like her stepfather.

She disappeared outside in a flash of shapely brown limbs and sun-bleached hair.

Before the tall, white painted and paneled door, with one hand on the handle, Belloc Junior turned to the bishop and said, "Remember, it would be better to say nothing to my dad about what you call 'this little complication'." He opened the door and ushered him inside.

Paul Belloc Senior did not look ill. His neatly trimmed silver hair complemented his tanned complexion. He was casually dressed in a polo shirt, cream colored chinos, and tan loafers. His only adornment was a gold watch. Sitting in a deep-buttoned leather wing chair to one side of his large mahogany desk, he folded the newspaper he was reading and set it down as the bishop entered.

"I see the New York salerooms have had a pretty good week, Phil. Christie's and Sotheby's must have grossed about four hundred million between them in four days, from what I can tell."

He spoke while indicating to the bishop to take a seat by the front of the desk.

"Yes, and two Picassos alone accounted for nearly a quarter of that, as I'm sure you noticed," the bishop answered with a smile as he sat down.

Young Belloc sat on the periphery of the bishop's vision, behind the desk. His father asked if anyone required any refreshments. No one did; Belloc himself sipped a goblet of iced water, the bowl misted by the chill.

Then he asked the question, "Well, Phil, now that Jack has come to a sorry end, where do we stand?"

The bishop didn't hesitate. "I was just telling Paul before we came in that everything is in hand and should be operational within the next few days. Already, as you know, I have one of the major European dealers just sitting in her hotel room and champing at the bit."

"Are you telling me that despite all Hastings's saber-rattling, you have actually managed to get your hands on the paintings?" Belloc Senior shot back.

The bishop's eyes met the son's. They both registered surprise.

Belloc answered both their looks. "It's my heart that's giving me problems, gentlemen, not my head. I know all about Jack's death, when he died, and how he died. What I don't know is where the paintings are. Do you, Phil?"

There's that two percent again, he thought as he felt the goose-flesh rise on his skin. "Bear with me, Paul. I know where they most likely are, and rest assured, I'll be able to get my hands on them."

Belloc set his glass down on top of the newspaper on the desk, and, fingertips steepled together, leaned forward in his chair. He enunciated each syllable clearly and deliberately. "At this moment, hand on your heart, can you assure me that you one hundred percent know where the paintings physically are, Phil?"

The bishop grimaced, tight-lipped, but said nothing and indicated nothing.

"That's a 'No,' then." He held his hand up to halt any stalling objection the bishop might make. "Phil, we've worked together well over the years, and, fool that I may be, I trust both you and your judgement—but only up to a point. There's one hell of a lot of money at stake here, and I want it realized sooner rather than later. Do you follow me?"

"Paul," the bishop began in a reasonable voice, "we both know Jack Hastings tended to be a bit capricious from time to time. And he certainly did present us with a problem or two. Furthermore, his death didn't exactly make it easier . . ."

"But did it make it less expensive, Phil?" old Belloc said with a sigh, "Did it save us money, or, as I'm beginning to fear now, is it going to cost us more?"

❧ 8 ❧

Adam had slept little. Thoughts of Sarah and Zannah had disturbed him throughout the night, and now, as he lay awake staring at the ceiling in the pre-dawn dark, he felt as though he had barely closed his eyes.

Most troubling was that last phone call with Zannah. He had mulled over everything she said on the line—every strange thing she had said after the cremation, every nuance and intimation— and in the darkness it had become clear. She believed Jack had been murdered and that her own life was in danger. She and Jack must have been involved in some secret deal with the bishop that he was unaware of, an arrangement that had been kept from him, and by her own admission it involved paintings.

Beyond that, deductions were difficult. Certainly, a large painting by Hastings was starting to make reasonable money, but even a large cache of them wouldn't justify anyone being murdered, and his entire body of work, all that he had produced to date, wouldn't fetch anywhere near the ten million dollars Zannah had mentioned. The fact that he, Adam, had an exclusive contract with Jack to market all his work, made it even more puzzling. Adam's entire career in the art world was due to the bishop, and to a great extent he still depended upon his patronage. After all these years, it was inconceivable that Phil would cheat him, especially over paintings of Jack's. No—it could only be about the Picassos.

But what did the threat about the last twenty years mean? Adam had been involved in the art scene for most of them, and despite torturing himself all night for an answer, he was still at a loss. He decided he was just going to have to pursue these questions, both with Zannah later today, and with the bishop when he returned. This time he would resist his evasions and insist on knowing the answer. This time he was determined to find out.

Now, at seven thirty, with no chance of salvaging anything from the unsettled night's sleep, he rolled out of bed. Fifteen minutes later, he was just stepping out of the shower when he heard the entrance buzzer. Before eight was early for any kind of visitor, especially on a Sunday morning. Toweling himself dry as he went to the intercom, he lifted the handset and said, "Hello?"

"Adam, it's me, Sarah. I didn't wake you, did I?"

"No," he said, hiding his surprise, "I'm just out of the shower." He pressed the release button. "Come on up." He snatched on a tee shirt and jeans and slipped his feet into a pair of loafers while the very last person he had been expecting made her way up.

Well bundled up against the morning cold, she apologized, "Adam, I'm really sorry to be annoying you at this time of the morning, but I had to get out of the apartment, and I didn't know where else to go. Living under the same roof as that woman is driving me crazy!"

Adam poured two mugs of coffee at the breakfast bar, helped her out of her winter coat, and sat down opposite her.

"I take it you're referring to your dear mother?"

Her mouth full of hot black coffee, she nodded.

"Yeah, she's not the easiest person to get along with."

"Between being raised with her, my grandmother, and my father—all self-opinionated know-it-alls—it's a miracle how I turned out to be so well-balanced," she said, smiling.

Despite the early hour, she appeared recovered from her ordeal of the last few days. Apart from occasionally bumping into her at her father's studio over term breaks when she was home from her studies, Adam hadn't seen much of her since she was a schoolgirl. Yesterday afternoon was the longest time they had ever spent in each other's company, and the only time they had ever been alone together. Adam was relieved to see that his impulsive behavior hadn't generated the negative reaction that he'd feared. In fact, watching her sipping coffee opposite him helped him submerge all his concerns of Zannah and the paintings. He was just happy to see her sitting there. To hell with the age difference, he thought as he savored her dark Mediterranean looks and shining black hair. She was beautiful, no question, and though young, her maturity belied her years. Even dour old Joe Rooney, Adam remembered, had been entranced upon meeting her after the funeral yesterday.

"So what's the problem?" Adam asked, now that her evident agitation had calmed.

She rolled her eyes. "By the time you dropped me off yesterday, she and my grandmother were already back at the apartment after having had an argument. My grandmother's bags were sitting in the hallway already packed, and she was about to go back to Florida. Of course, that wasn't an earth-shattering surprise. They do tend to spark off each other, but I'd expected her to be staying with us for another few days. They were both pretty tight-lipped as her bags were taken down and Grandma said her goodbyes to me. So when my mom got back home from dropping her off at the airport, I just tried to stay out of her way and keep a low profile, thinking that their disagreement had nothing to do with me. But I was wrong."

Adam just raised his eyebrows, encouraging her to continue.

"Turns out she'd blamed my grandma for my disappearance with you. She insisted I should've been at the funeral lunch, or at least that was what she made out. I reckon it was more to do with the fact that I was with you!"

Adam frowned. "Why? I was just doing what your grandmother asked," he quickly added with a smile, raising his coffee mug. "Thanks, Grandma!"

Sarah smiled in return and clinked her mug of coffee against his in a toast. "My mom doesn't see it quite that way. It mightn't have been such a big deal if I'd gone straight back to her apartment after the cremation, but arriving back after she did seemed to be a problem. Plus, the fact that I had obviously spent the time with you definitely made things worse."

"Yes, it's been a long time since I was flavor of the month with your mother and, personalities aside, I'm sure there's no way she would approve of you having anything to do with someone nearly twenty years your senior."

Her brow furrowed. "Listen, I've been away from her apron-strings a long time now, and I'm twenty-two years old. I'm an adult, have been living overseas on my own, and I'm well used to choosing my own friends."

"Yeah, I know, but I'm only trying to explain your mother's attitude, and it's because of your age that the few years you've been independent seem like a long time. By the time you're my age, two or three years will seem like nothing."

"Yeah, there's no denying that," she said, smiling again. "By the second quarter of the twenty-first century, I'm sure my outlook on a lot of things will have changed."

Adam held an index finger up and shook it at her. "Careful, now—don't push your luck." He topped off both mugs with coffee as she relaxed and looked around her.

"Nice apartment," she said, and added with a sweep of her hand around the room. "Though any Hastings are noticeable by their absence."

"Not at all," Adam replied, gesturing with both hands in her direction, "his best work is right in front of me."

Sarah spun her head around to look on the wall behind her, then, catching his meaning, began to redden. "Sort of walked into that . . . didn't I?"

Adam smiled and reached over to squeeze her hand. "Who could disagree with me?" He took another mouthful of coffee before asking, "What about your dad's paintings . . . the canvases still in the studio? Has there been any mention of them?" He felt a niggle of guilt as he asked the question. Now that Jack was dead, all his remaining paintings would belong to his estate, even the ones that Adam had in storage or on display. His contract had been with Jack, and he was curious what Liz's plans would be. She would probably even be within her rights to demand their return and control all future disposals herself.

"Not really, though I think I did hear my mom discuss something about paintings with that Englishwoman, Bentley, the other day. It seems like a dream though. I wasn't quite with it then."

Yeah, that would be just like Liz, he thought, to screw him on anything she could. He needed to have another word with Catherine Bentley.

Sarah interrupted his thoughts. "Anyway, I reckon I need to find somewhere else to live if I'm going to stay in New York for a while, and I suppose I'd better get myself something to do in the meantime."

She moved over from the breakfast bar to the big tan leather couch, kicked off her shoes, and curled her feet up under her as she snuggled into the corner of it and sipped her coffee. She looked very comfortable, very at home. For a moment, Adam felt his euphoria at having Sarah here, in his apartment, alone with him, checked by a shiver of unease.

Yes, he liked her. He was very attracted to her and was not dismissing the possibilities of pursuing some sort of a relationship with her, but a raft of reservations began to flood over him. There were obvious objections apart from the age difference. Was he entirely comfortable with her being the only child of his old friend, Jack? Then there was Liz's attitude; she seemed to be in over-reactive high gear. There was no doubt she would be incandescent if she discovered that her daughter and he had become involved—and there were material implications there.

But most of all, she came with a lot of baggage. They had too many friends in common. Sure, things might be fine as long as their relationship was fine, but if things changed—and, let's face it, things do change, and particularly with the age difference—it might just prove too difficult.

The phone rang, and excusing himself to Sarah, he lifted the handset and answered it. Zannah's soft, husky voice whispered in his ear, "Adam, I'm sorry for being such a nuisance yesterday. As you can appreciate, I was upset, and I'm just phoning to thank you for your concern."

"Zannah! I'm glad you called. Feeling any better this morning?" Handset to his ear, Adam was facing Sarah as he spoke, and as he uttered the words he could see her posture stiffen.

"Yes, thanks. You know what they say, 'another day, another half a million dollars'," she joked.

"Bear in mind what else they say," he replied, " 'don't count your chickens.' "

She laughed. "We'll see—I'm a positive thinker! Can I buy you lunch today, to make up for being such a pain in the neck?"

"Sure," he said, and as they finalized arrangements, Sarah picked up a glossy copy of the arts magazine, *Apollo*, from the coffee table and was flipping through it much too fast to be actually reading. She was clearly annoyed. Understandable, really. Zannah probably symbolizes a disturbing side of her father. Furthermore, even though she wasn't a catalyst in Jack and Liz's separation, it was possible that she represented 'the other woman' in Sarah's perception of events.

"She's certainly a piece of work," Sarah said as Adam finished his call, "not that I'm surprised after yesterday; she must've had her Rolodex with her, lining up a list of any suitable new victims—and I reckon you'll chart pretty high on it."

Adam stared at her, speechless, for a moment. "Actually, Sarah, I think you're being a bit unkind," he said. "I'm Zannah's agent, just as I was Jack's, and I've known her for a while now. Believe me, she was pretty cut up about your dad, and she still is. She approached me yesterday about some ongoing business and some complications that have arisen, and so I need to discuss things with her. That's all there is to it. I understand you may resent her and why, but it's in the past. You need to get over all that."

Adam could see the tension rising in her as she replied, "Maybe you think I'm a bit out of line here, but I'm not very good at misrepresenting my feelings. I believe in plain speaking—it's the way I was brought up. This *Zannah*," she sneered the name, "I saw her yesterday playing up to Bishop Connor, you, and God knows how many others, looking for sympathy—what a joke! From what I hear, she was just a parasite using my dad for her own ends!"

Adam tried to calm the situation, to reason with her. "I think you're overstating it a bit there, Sarah. Whoever told you that probably had their own agenda. Sure, her name being linked to Jack's maybe brought her a bit more attention than otherwise, but believe me, from where I stood it looked like a pretty symmetrical arrangement. He got as much out of it as she did."

Sarah's gaze didn't flicker, but her head shook slowly from side to side in mock disbelief. "Sometimes I wonder how you men manage to survive at all. She's a transparently manipulative bitch who's in need of a new meal ticket, and although I don't *know* what she's up to, I could make a damn good guess!"

"What can I say apart from 'you're wrong'? You're condemning the girl based on hearsay and prejudice. I've told you, my business with Zannah is just business—and that's all."

Sarah screwed her feet back into her shoes and, standing up, she struggled into her heavy coat before Adam could reach to help. Slinging her satchel over her shoulder, she opened the door and blurted, "Well, I don't know about you, but I have my suspicions about the sort of business she's doing with the famous Bishop Connor," adding, "Enjoy your lunch." before slamming it behind her.

Adam stood open-mouthed and unmoving at her furious exit before turning back toward the breakfast bar, lifting the coffee mugs and starting to rinse them in the sink. What an over-reaction, he thought. Maybe she's got quite a bit of her mother in her, after all. There is one consolation though – she certainly won't be expecting to be moving in here tonight.

§

Adam and Zannah sat in a quiet corner alcove in a dim, secluded section, well away from the usual Sunday lunchtime bustle at the back of the restaurant. Air kisses and pleasantries had been exchanged and the meal was under way. Adam poured another glass of wine for Zannah and topped off his own glass. He hated drinking red wine at lunchtime. It made him feel heavy and lethargic; too often it ruined the rest of the day for him. But Zannah needed to be cotton-wooled. She must feel safe in the knowledge that he was there as her confidante and her support.

Her collar-length, bright blonde hair was startling against her black blouse as she leaned back against the banquette. The alcohol was doing its job; she looked relaxed and secure. Her black-lined, cornflower blue eyes sparkled. Despite faint traces on her wineglass, the dark red wax glowed evenly on her lips; her perfect white teeth gleamed when she smiled. She was smiling a lot. He was aware that their knees were touching, more like lovers than friends. He judged that she must be feeling relaxed enough by now, after two full glasses of wine, to be ready to reveal the whole story.

Adam began, "Zannah, I've got a confession to make to you." Leaning closer to her, he could smell the perfume of her hair. "Our conversations after the funeral yesterday have left me a little confused. I need you to flesh out the bare bones of what you told me."

"What's there to be confused about?" she asked, taking another swallow of wine. Suddenly, her tone changed. "Is there a problem? Has Phil contacted you from Florida?" Behind the glow of the wine, fear sparked in her eyes. She grasped his left hand; his right still held his glass of wine. Her grip was tight—drowning, not flirting.

"No, I haven't spoken to him yet," Adam assured her.

She moved even closer to him, still gripping his hand. He felt the length of her thigh against his and the swelling pressure of her breast against his bicep as she lowered her voice and bent over to him. Like an urgent kiss, she whispered in his ear, "Adam, I know I'm way out of my depth. I couldn't believe it when Jack told me the amount of money involved in these paintings . . ."

Adam knew he had guessed right.

"It all seemed so simple, and the way Jack put it, so appropriate, so just . . ." "Just?" Adam said. He knew she was talking about the Belloc Picassos—it could be nothing else. Some months ago, the bishop had talked about quietly bringing them to New York for Jack to clean before their sale. Adam had argued that it seemed like a big security risk, and anyway, a clean wasn't going to add anything to the value of paintings of that stature. But "just"—where does justice enter into it?

"Yes," she said, "Jack felt that as these paintings were going to be sold for maybe as much as eighty or ninety million dollars, and as the sale couldn't proceed without him, he believed he was entitled to a substantial share of any commission that would be paid out. That's why he wanted ten million."

Confused, Adam delved into the dustiest corners of his imagination for any likely explanation. Had the bishop gone ahead with his cleaning plan, enabling Jack to get his hands on the paintings? Seems completely out of character for Jack—he'd been doing restoration, cleaning and repairs to canvases, including many quite valuable ones, for the bishop for years without any previous problems. More than that, it was a totally crazy scenario—suddenly, because he had three Picassos in his possession, he holds them for a lunatic ransom? Then he demands ten million from the bishop, who, in turn, neglects to share this new development with him, his business partner?

"Sorry, Zannah, you've lost me." Adam whispered back. "Ten million for doing what? Cleaning some paintings? That only makes sense if you are talking in terms of Italian lire. In fact, yesterday you mentioned a figure of five hundred thousand. From where I'm sitting, that's just as ludicrous, and furthermore, what was that you said yesterday about spilling the beans on the last twenty years?"

Zannah loosened her grip on Adam's hand and groped beside her in the dim light for her purse. "Excuse me, I need to go to the bathroom," she said as she stood up.

Adam watched her shapely silhouette disappear around a corner into the main body of the restaurant. He savored another mouthful of wine and, closing his eyes, he leaned back against the heavily padded leather upholstery. From the seclusion of the booth, he didn't see Zannah walk out the front door of the restaurant. She didn't return.

Back at his own apartment, his machine was flashing. It was a message from the bishop. He had spoken to the Bellocs and would be returning to New York in the morning. Leaving his flight details, he asked Adam to collect him from the airport. Adam felt drained and exhausted. He blamed it on the red wine and the lack of sleep, but in his heart he knew that wasn't the reason.

Obviously Zannah was terrified and was carrying a secret that she had thought he shared. But he'd been clumsy and displayed his ignorance, which must have scared her even more. That could be the only reason for her running off. She believed that Jack had been murdered, and somehow this involved the Picassos. If it involved the Picassos, it necessarily involved him, and this made him uncomfortable. Adam preferred all his personal links with violent death never to exceed the gastronomic.

❧ 9 ❧

I t was well after one in the morning when Joe Rooney killed
the Technicolor glow in the corner. The sound had been off
for hours, but the flickering movement was company, like a
dog you didn't have to walk. The big glass ashtray overflowed onto
the pine coffee table in front of him. Marlboro country. He sat
with a photograph album open on his knee, with others piled on
the table beside the ashtray. He tipped his head back and drained
the last of the soda from the can. Apart from the occasional light
beer, he had been off the booze for over six months.

After the death of Anna, his wife, Rooney had found himself
being consoled by colleagues in the traditional male fashion: at the
bar, over a drink. So began a routine that ensured oblivion—often
before he was ready for it, since he frequently woke in the cold
dark mid-night, bursting to piss, finding himself still clothed and
sprawled in the La-Z-Boy. It was also affecting his mourning, his
recovery. Sure, it numbed the anguish, but he needed the anguish.
To avoid it felt like cheating on Anna, so he stopped drinking.

He stopped a lot of things. He became chaste. It wasn't a
conscious decision and it represented a significant change from his
previous life. Anna and he, though married for fifteen years, had
still enjoyed an active sex life until nearly the end. And of course,

before they met and got married, his libido was regularly exercised. But since she died, things had changed. He hadn't noticed it at first, probably due to the booze blindness. Since it would have been considered unseemly in his circumstances, his fellow cops didn't inflict the usual sexual banter upon him that other, normal single cops were subjected to.

In the beginning, he noticed the change in himself as one might notice a small lump—almost imperceptible. One wonders if it wasn't always there, always like that. Then, as it grew, denial became impossible. But it didn't disturb him. He was simply a neutral observer of it, an anthropologist in the world of the pathologically bereaved.

He did find it interesting though. Young women that he encountered in the everyday scheme of things had started to look subtly different. Difficult to pin-point at first, he realized that they all would remind him, maybe by just a small feature here or there —around the chin or a crinkle at the eyes—of someone else. This someone else was always female and always much older.

The more he looked, the more he saw. It seemed as if he was seeing every girl's mother in her, or how he imagined her mother would appear, no matter how firm and taut her visage was. Their entire genetic program fast-forwarded through his eyes. Though not quite crumbling into crones, he saw their terrible potential realized, their inexorable future before him. Cute jawlines revealed their budding jowls to him; wide-eyed hope bagged and drooped. Laughter scoured the faces with deep, wrinkled lines.

Desire was gone and he didn't miss it. The early morning erections still arose, but the connection was gone. Just as a gourmet doesn't relate the feast of the night before to the morning's bowel evacuation, the link was gone. He had come to terms with it. He just got on with his job. Smoked his cigarettes. And waited for the inevitable.

Sure, there were moments of despair. Who hasn't felt the pointlessness of routine? The getting up and going to work and going to bed and getting up again. For nothing, for no reason, to do what? Sit and watch the mental chewing gum on the television? Just suck on another cigarette. Once or twice, in darker moments, he'd almost sucked on something more metallic. Life is a death sentence anyway, and in these moments he was glad that he and Anna hadn't condemned an innocent child.

But unaccountably, things were changing. The album on his knee was full of snapshots of the better days of his youth, photographs taken in an era when everyone smiled and everyone posed for the camera. There he was as a rookie cop, his arm around his mother who was beaming at the lens with maternal pride. Her glistening black Mediterranean curls and swarthy complexion were echoed in his own. Now dead as well, she had been a beautiful young woman, the daughter of Italian immigrants from the poverty stricken south. Birth problems resulted in Joe remaining an only child, allowing him to bask in undiluted love and attention as he grew up. His mother became the lynchpin of both Joe's and his father's lives, and he still missed her. Joe turned to an eight by ten portrait taken of her when she was in her late teens, just after her marriage, and looked into her deep brown eyes—even though it was in black and white. She was probably pregnant with me then, he thought.

He rested the open album on his knees and lit another cigarette. This will be the last one before I hit the sack, he promised himself. Amazing how things change. It seemed like only yesterday when these tight white tubes were the essential fashion accessory, signaling glamor and sophistication. Now you had to huddle in doorways with like-minded lepers, relegated to a status somewhere below drunk drivers, or suck them like this, lonely at home. Marlboro man.

The funeral yesterday had been disturbing. Not that he and Jack Hastings were still friends, but in the years before meeting Anna, he had spent a lot of time socializing with him and that whole artsy crowd. These days it was only the bishop and Adam whom he kept any regular contact with, but through them he still came across some of the others from time to time. Mostly at funerals—they didn't live long either, these artists.

It had been interesting to see Liz, Jack's widow, again. The passing years had matured her into a classic beauty, but he no longer felt any stirrings for her. And judging from her reaction to him, she appeared to have forgotten that they'd ever had a liaison in the first place. For his part, he had been cured a long time ago. Meeting, falling in love with, and marrying Anna had fixed that. Liz belonged to a cleanly amputated aspect of his past, leaving no phantom limb.

Seeing Sarah had been a bombshell, however. He hadn't encountered her since her childhood, and she evidently had no recollection of him. Outrageously, he cringed, it was love at first sight, and as he admitted this he felt the guilt swell inside him. Anna not even a year dead yet, and he finds himself fizzing like a firework after a brief introduction to the daughter of a ghost from his past.

In turmoil, he gazed down at his mother's photograph again for consolation and comfort before closing the album and placing it on top of the stack of others. Time for bed and, with luck, sleep. He levered himself out of the couch, feeling the aches from every old injury he'd ever had. Growing old surely is a bitch, he thought. Just as he was on his feet, the phone rang. One thirty in the morning held no significance here—probably the office. Crime never sleeps.

He was right; it was Carl Lummus, his partner.

"Joe, I'm sorry to phone you so late. Did I wake you?"

"No. I'm still up. What's going on?"

"I'm afraid I have some bad news. Your old buddy Jack Hastings . . ."

"Yeah? What . . ." For a moment his mind raced ahead of the news. He could feel the hairs on his arms rise on top of the goose-flesh. It's Jack's daughter, Sarah. He's going to tell me she's dead. His throat tightened. He could ask no questions.

"His girlfriend, Zannah Koller," Carl said. "She's been found dead in her apartment."

He felt the relief flow over him. He coughed to clear his throat and compose himself before asking, "When? What happened?"

"Don't know exactly yet, Joe. The news just came in minutes ago. It seems other residents in her building returned home and saw her door ajar. They discovered the body and made the call. The uniforms say the room's like a slaughterhouse. Her body was lacerated, but it was having her throat cut that killed her."

"Okay, you go ahead. I'll see you there," Rooney said before hanging up. Christ, the last thing he felt like confronting was another cadaver he knew. Routine kicked in as he emptied the ashtrays, tidied away the photograph albums, empty soda cans and the other debris from the evening's self-entertainment.

Definitely no chance of getting much sleep tonight, he thought as he moved back over to the telephone. He checked his watch and dialed Adam's number.

✤ 10 ✤

Joe Rooney arrived home from the crime scene mess shortly before five, physically and emotionally exhausted. He had to get some sleep. Carl was picking him up in five hours' time. He shed his clothes quickly, throwing them onto a chair. He set his radio alarm for eight fifty, and despite the turmoil in his head, he immediately fell unconscious.

Feeling miraculously refreshed, he woke to Elvis Presley singing *Return to Sender* on the oldies station. Despite the horror of Zannah's apartment, his sleep had been like death—just oblivion, nothingness. He felt reborn.

In the bathroom, he spent more care than usual on his morning rituals, going to the extreme of foaming up and wet shaving twice until he was content that a caress along his jaw line would be enough to excite even the passion of a pedophile. No more heavy, greasy diner breakfasts for him, he decided. It was time to take control and shape up again; time for a new regime. He found an almost stale English muffin in the refrigerator, sliced it in half, popped it in the toaster and poured himself a steaming mug of coffee. The hard part was not having a smoke with it.

As he ate, he reflected on Zannah's murder. It had been a horrible death. She had been sliced up, probably by someone who enjoyed it. Most of the cuts looked horrific but were not life threatening. Rather, it looked more as if she had endured an extended, deliberate torture. She had been alive throughout, then her throat was cut, deeply and with enough force to slice right through the windpipe. It was a bloody mess. On the face of it there appeared to have been no sexual assault. None of the neighbors had seen or heard anything, and there was no sign of the murder weapon. By the end of the night, all he had was a far out lead that would have to be followed up. Unlikely, but he had no alternative; he would have to interview Sarah.

By the time Carl Lummus arrived, Rooney's earlier elation had faded a little. Maybe it was the lack of sleep or the light breakfast, but he had a hollow ache in his stomach and was certainly not looking forward to making this next visit.

"Where are we going?" Carl asked as Rooney climbed into the passenger seat.

"Liz Hastings's apartment. I want to have a word with her daughter, Sarah."

Carl looked at his partner without surprise. He had been present when Rooney had checked Zannah's machine and had overheard the message. They had been at the Hastings's once before, very briefly, just long enough to hand deliver a sympathy card after her husband's death. Carl guessed Rooney was uncomfortable at the prospect of having to make a return visit in his professional capacity.

"Look, it's only a routine follow-up. You don't need to do it. I'll go in your place. I'll just drop you off at the office first."

Rooney dismissed Carl's concern with a wave of the hand. "It's OK. I know it's routine, but these people are old friends and I owe it to them to try and make the process as easy as possible."

"Oh! So they're expecting us?" he said in a tone that made it obvious that he knew they weren't.

"Shut up and drive." Rooney growled.

Liz Hastings sounded so surprised to hear him on the entry intercom that she buzzed him up without the third degree he had been expecting. She opened the door and invited them in. To Rooney, the apartment smelled like a spring day. He glanced around. Sure enough, vases of cut flowers were everywhere, decorating nearly all the flat surfaces. Where the hell does she get those in the middle of winter, he thought? As they walked further in, the aroma of coffee coming from the open plan kitchen and dining area beyond told him breakfast wasn't long past.

For the first time since Anna's death he became aware of the stink of his own clothes. His jacket, he realized with embarrassment, couldn't have smelled any worse if it had been used to wrap tobacco bales. He decided to try not to stand too close to anyone in the hope no one else would notice.

Rooney briefly introduced Carl to her before asking, "Is Sarah at home?"

"Yes, she is," Liz answered with a puzzled expression, motioning them to take a seat. "You want to speak to her? What's it about?"

Carl sat down on the couch, but Rooney remained standing. "I'm afraid there's been another death." Liz just stood, waiting for more. "Zannah Koller . . . Jack's . . . well, you know . . . she was killed last night."

For a moment, Liz said nothing before looking down at the floor, shaking her head. "That's terrible." She shrugged. "I only knew her to see and by reputation. I had no particular affection for her, but I'm sorry. What happened? And what does it have to do with Sarah?"

"She was murdered in her apartment last night. Messily. And as Sarah was trying to contact her yesterday, I thought I'd better speak to her."

Liz looked appalled. Instead of her usual self-possession, she suddenly looked tired and vulnerable. Maybe the shock of these deaths was knocking the hard edges off her after all, he thought. In an obvious attempt to recover her composure, Liz insisted that Rooney take a seat and offered them coffee, which they accepted.

After so little sleep, Rooney was beginning to suffer the effects, and he looked forward to another injection of caffeine.

As she poured she said, "I'll call Sarah. We'd just finished breakfast before you arrived. She should've showered and dressed by now."

Rooney said, "If you'd prefer, we can discuss this privately, just the three of us."

Liz looked at him for a long moment. Rooney inferred that she was trying to decide whether or not to allow this floating derelict from the past to become involved in their current lives.

"All right, I'll go and speak to her," she said and left the room.

Rooney straightaway turned to Carl, his right hand held up, palm facing outward in the universal halt sign. "Don't say anything. Just sit there and keep quiet. Imagine that this doesn't really have anything to do with you."

"Easy to say, Joe, but I think maybe you're going a bit too far. I know you're an old friend of the family, but if it ever came out, it would look very much like unprofessional conduct," Carl said.

"Look, this is all happening in private. Who's going to mention it? You?"

"No, but . . ." Carl stopped speaking as he heard footsteps returning.

It was Liz. She beckoned to Rooney.

"We can talk in the office. It's through here," she said, indicating the direction she had just arrived from. She turned to Carl. "That is, if you don't mind excusing us, detective. Can I get you some more coffee?"

Carl thanked her but refused, assuring her that he was just fine as he was.

Liz's office was a small room without much of a view. A computer monitor and keyboard sat on the main desk to one side of the window, while a long oak table with filing trays and correspondence ran at a right angle to it along another wall. There were two swivel desk chairs. Sarah was already seated in one. Her mood looked somber, her greeting reserved.

Liz indicated to Rooney to take the other seat. She half sat, half stood against the long table. She spoke first, "I realize the police have got to do their job, and I'm sure you're aware that the past week has been a very trying and emotionally stressful time for us, especially Sarah."

Rooney nodded. "I know."

"Then let's get right to the point. What are you doing here? What's Sarah got to do with this?"

Rooney could see the familiar Liz resurfacing.

"We're dealing with a particularly brutal homicide," he explained, trying to keep himself in check. "I've been up most of the night, and I have a duty to follow up any and all leads. Don't forget, Liz. I did at least wait until daylight. I didn't come here and wake you up in the middle of the night."

Leaning against the table, holding her chin in one hand and her elbow resting in the palm of the other, she neither moved nor responded.

His eyes moved to Sarah. "Sarah, I need you to answer a few questions." He didn't pause for a response. "When did you last see Zannah Koller?"

"On Saturday, after the cremation, just before I met you."

"And when did you last speak to her?"

"I've never spoken to her," she answered.

"But you did leave a message on her machine?"

She made no response while Liz looked at her with narrowing eyes.

"Did she get back to you?"

"No, I've just told you I've never spoken to her. I've never met her . . ."

"Listen, Sarah, I'm trying to help you here. I could've taken you downtown to the interview room—done this formally. I'm trying to do you a favor. Just tell me why you left that message on her machine."

Liz interrupted. "Is no one going to tell me what this damn

message was? Sarah, what were you phoning her, of all people, about?"

Sarah ran her hands through her hair, then, turning and looking out the window, she said, "I was annoyed. She phoned Adam Kennedy yesterday morning when I was in his apartment, and she arranged to have lunch with him."

Liz slammed the edge of the table with her fist and stood upright. "You were in his apartment yesterday morning! What the hell were you doing there?"

Sarah ignored her. "She annoyed the hell out of me by flirting with her extensive retinue of admirers after the service, and suddenly there she was, on the phone to Adam before my dad's ashes had cooled down. I was pissed at her, so I called to tell her what I thought of her. The machine picked up, so I left a message."

Liz rolled her eyes. "Are you crazy? What does anything Adam Kennedy does have to do with you?"

Sarah turned back toward Liz, her voice strong now. "Look, Mom, he's not an ogre. He's amusing, friendly, good-looking, and he's a nice guy. I don't know what you've got against him."

"He's twice your damn age!"

"You're exaggerating. He's not. Okay, he's older, but what the hell? He's not exactly decrepit!"

Rooney interrupted. "Calm down, both of you. Adam's suitability is neither here nor there. But it answers my question: whether it's resentment at Jack's girlfriend dishonoring his memory by playing the field so soon after his passing, or a simple case of jealousy—they both fit the bill." Neither of them spoke, so Rooney continued, "Unfortunately, both categories are serious contenders as motives. Even simple jealousy accounts for a big percentage of homicides."

Sarah looked at him in silent horror.

"Have you gone totally mad? Are you suggesting Sarah had something to do with her death?" Liz was shouting now.

Rooney gestured for her to quiet down. "Take it easy—this is why I'm in here alone with you. I'm just stating the facts, but believe me, I want to eliminate Sarah from the inquiry as much as you do." Liz's face assumed an expression of distaste as he said the words which insinuated that her daughter could have had anything to do with this.

Sarah spoke first. "How do you do that?" she asked.

Rooney lowered his voice to not much more than a conspiratorial whisper,

"This is totally privileged information I'm about to share with you," he said. "It mustn't leave this room or be revealed to any other party. If it does, I'll deny ever having had this conversation. Do you agree?"

Sarah looked up at her mother and, taking her lead from her, nodded assent.

Rooney looked serious. "This was a savage killing, and it has all the ingredients that will assure it a lot of press attention. This in turn puts the investigating team under a lot of extra pressure to get results and to be seen to be turning over every stone in order to get these results. So, in order to do this, we have to pursue every obscure possibility, every long shot, and eliminate everyone that enters the frame at all. You understand?"

They both nodded again.

"Unfortunately, Sarah, you're in the frame, and I want to help eliminate you."

"How?" both of them asked simultaneously.

Rooney looked around the small room as if checking for eavesdroppers and continued, "There would appear to have been one piece of hard physical evidence left by the killer at the scene!"

"What was it?" Sarah asked.

"I'm not at liberty to divulge that. Doing so could cost me my job. I can only tell you that it can be biologically matched to the killer."

"So, it's hair or something like that," Liz interjected.

"Something like that," he said, before turning to Sarah "Usually, in these cases, if there's any resistance by the suspect, we seek a court order for a DNA sampling. Once that's done, of course, such things can become a matter of public record and you run the risk of the media discovering it, and then, well, I don't have to tell you what that could mean in nuisance or publicity terms."

"Absolutely," Sarah said, "We'd have The National Enquirer and all their buddies camped outside on the street!"

"So what do you suggest, Joe?" Liz said.

Rooney noted the question as the first time in many years that she had actually called him by his first name.

He answered, addressing Sarah, "Let me take a tissue sample from you, totally off the record. I'll have my friends at the lab expedite the processing, and then, when it's not a match, you'll be eliminated."

"The testing, what does it involve?" Sarah asked.

"It's simple, just a cotton bud swab of the inside of your cheek. That's all. Only a matter of seconds, and I can do it here or wherever you wish. We'll just keep you away from the station, though."

"Can we do it now?" she asked him.

"No, I don't have the sterile kit with me," he said, allowing a smile for the first time. "But if it suits you, I'll pick it up and come back later. I can take the sample then."

Sarah looked at her mother again before agreeing. Rooney, aware of the brooding figure of Liz standing to his side, pushed himself to his feet.

"I'll see you later then," he said, nodding to Sarah with a slight bow.

"Thanks, Mr. Rooney, for all your help," she replied.

"Entirely my pleasure," he said, "and the name is Joe."

She smiled back at him. "Thanks, Joe."

11

Rooney's early morning call left Adam numb. Zannah was dead. No—she wasn't just dead—she had been murdered. Murdered just hours after walking out of the restaurant on him. Adam's reflex reaction was to contact the bishop.

The bishop had been his dad's friend since Adam's childhood and, since his parents' death he had tacitly assumed the paternal role without complaint. He had guided and advised him; he had helped him become established in the fine art world. Adam suffered no illusions about himself; to succeed in this business you needed both luck and contacts. The bishop had provided the latter in abundance and personified the former. Without him, Adam knew, he would not be in the position he was in today, especially with the prospect of his share of the commission on the sale of the Belloc Picassos just around the corner.

Yes, the bishop's administrative role produced the greater bulk of his business since it provided access to an ever-regenerating reservoir of paintings and artifacts from bequests to the Catholic Church, with no financial outlay. The arrangement between them had long been that Adam would take a thirty percent commission of the gross of any sale, fifty percent of this commission then being credited to the bishop's offshore account. The remaining seventy percent balance was passed over to a Church account maintained by the bishop which, in turn, allocated a further percentage to his Third World Aid charity, which operated mainly in deprived, arid African regions, with the rest going into the Church's coffers. The amounts Adam received varied, but they usually added up to a substantial monthly income that allowed him a comfortable life-style and a healthy bank balance.

However, without this regular business, Adam's enterprise would barely be viable—and Adam knew it. Not only was the bishop an indispensable mentor and benefactor, but he was also his longstanding friend.

Nevertheless, the events of the past few days confused him. Something was happening that involved the bishop but excluded him. Yesterday it became obvious that even Zannah had been in on it, and disturbingly, it was most likely related in some way to the upcoming disposal of the three Picassos. This was a sale that any art dealer or auction house in the world would ache to have an interest in. Their market value was so huge that being involved in it in any capacity was worth a considerable figure. But time and again Phil had assured him that the handling of this sale was exclu-sively theirs—the result of an arrangement between the bishop and old Belloc himself, satisfying Belloc's desire for a minimum of fuss and publicity and avoiding the paintings having to be displayed on the world auction stage. Dealing with the bishop, as everyone who had ever done business with him knew, ensured discretion and security. Until now, it seemed. Where so many millions of dollars were concerned, no one was predictable.

Curbing his impulse to phone Florida at this early hour and wake Phil with this latest devastating news, he decided to wait and tell him face to face. He would be seeing him soon enough. He was due to pick him up at the airport in the morning.

§

As usual, the airport terminal concourse was hiving on a Monday morning, and Adam scanned the bobbing crowd for any sign of Bishop Connor. At last, he spotted him and attracted his attention with a wave. He was uneasy at the prospect of revealing the news about Zannah to him and the inevitability of a confrontation over what he had learned from her. However, doing his best to hide his feelings, he greeted him as warmly as usual, grabbed his case from him and struggled to behave normally.

As they strolled to the airport parking lot, Adam asked, "Well, how did things go down in Florida?"

The bishop's mouth tightened. He shook his head. "I'm getting too old for these damn early morning flights—too much hanging about in airports . . ." Then, noticing the strain in Adam's face, he added, "You look rough! Are you feeling all right?"

"Yeah, I'm okay. Just couldn't sleep much last night. A lot of things on my mind."

The bishop nodded. "You must take after your mother. She was a bit of a worrier as well."

"Hmm . . . maybe," Adam responded. "Anyway, what about the paintings? Is everything okay?"

They had arrived at the parking space. As Adam unlocked his Mercedes Benz wagon, he slipped his hand into his pocket and turned off his cellphone. The bishop only nodded in reply before opening his door. Once they were both seated inside, Adam turned to him, looked him straight in the face and insisted, "Phil, is the sale ours, or have they changed their minds?"

The bishop reached up over his shoulder with his left hand and pulled his seat belt down and over his torso to secure it by his hip. He brushed imaginary specks from his dark clerical suit and settled himself in the beige leather seat before replying, "Adam, don't worry. The deal is ours."

"So, can we proceed immediately?" He still hadn't started the engine. There were questions to be answered, and the confined quarters of the Mercedes were ideal. Here the bishop was a prisoner; he couldn't escape by ducking off somewhere else.

"The short answer is 'Yes.' Obviously no deal can be finalized without the agreement of the Bellocs, but I can assure you—unequivocally—we have the sale."

The bishop looked more comfortable now, more relaxed. However, Adam knew him long enough to know that this might merely be a part of his pastoral repertoire, and it often couldn't be taken at any more than face value.

"So what's Zannah's problem, then?" Adam asked.

"Zannah? What's she got to do with it?" For the first time there was an edge of annoyance to his voice.

"That's exactly what I want to know, Phil. I had lunch with her yesterday and, judging from her conversation, she felt that she had a pivotal role in it—to the tune of somewhere between half a million and ten million dollars!"

The bishop smiled—a from the heart, relaxed, everything in the garden is rosy sort of smile. Blarney, Adam thought as Phil addressed him with his soft, hypnotic brogue.

"Adam, you might say Zannah is suffering from a delusion or two. She thinks she has some embarrassing information about Jack and regards it as a sort of legacy—something she can capitalize on. Leave it to me. I'll speak to her later today. I'm sure I can deal with her problems, but believe me, they don't concern you, and furthermore, she's mistaken."

"That's bullshit, Phil!" Adam replied. "When I spoke to her she was convinced Jack was murdered and was worried about ending up the same way. She told me that she wasn't as hard-nosed as Jack and was happy to do a deal for less than he wanted. But the thing that really pissed me off was that she thought I knew what she was talking about, and, as you know, I don't!"

The bishop paused. A sad, reflective look had taken the place of the smile. "Adam, we've known each other for a long time. I know I could trust you with anything: money, information, or my reputation. I've always tried to help you in any way I could. You're like a son to me—you know that. Yes, I admit that occasionally I may be over-protective toward you—and this may be one of these occasions. Let me assure you again that Zannah is not a problem that you need concern yourself with. Forget about her ravings; her silliness doesn't affect you. I swear to you before God!"

"Phil, you're an atheist," Adam replied.

The bishop dropped his eyes and shrugged. "Well, certainly agnostic anyway, but then I'm a victim of circumstances, too."

"What circumstances?"

"The circumstances of my youth. Unlike you, when I was growing up I didn't enjoy the luxury of self-determination. I could never be myself. Life for me turned into one long pretense."

"Don't try to change the subject, Phil. I'm talking about the Picassos and Zannah."

"In a way it's all related, Adam. I don't mind admitting that to you. Once the paintings are sold, you'll be set up for life. You'll be able to do most anything you want, go anywhere you want, with anyone you want. Relatively speaking, you don't realize how fortunate your life has been."

Adam's tone became firmer. "Listen, Phil. I know what you've done for me over the years, if that's what you mean. I'd be the first to acknowledge it, so don't try to make me feel guilty."

"No, that's not the point, Adam. I was, and am, happy to help you in any way I can, but at the moment I'm talking about my misfortune, not your good fortune."

Adam shook his head slowly. "I'm not following you."

"For me, when I was growing up there weren't a lot of choices . . ."

Adam interrupted him, "Yes, I know, you've told me the story of leaving the farm, life in the seminary and being transferred to the US before."

The bishop's voice became insistent, "No, Adam, you've no idea. I had no real choices. Everything happened to me more by accident than design. Even being appointed as an emergency replacement for the deceased secretary of the old bishop, who was my predecessor in dealing with church bequests. He was expected to follow his secretary at any minute, but he didn't. I was just lucky he lived long enough to allow me to develop the expertise and contacts. But, life just clicks by. Suddenly you're nearly sixty, and the regrets you've been agonizing over for years are still there—they've just become more urgent. My home is here now, but escaping from this religious prison was never far from my mind—and it still isn't."

"Still isn't? You can't be serious!"

"Adam, you know me better than anyone; you know my doubts and you've probably had suspicions about my proclivities, but you've been just too well-mannered to ask."

Adam half-smiled, and though aware that the conversation wasn't going the way he had intended, he said, "You mean sex?"

The bishop nodded as Adam added, "You can just tell me it's none of my business."

"No, it's okay. You know as well as I do that there are plenty who have abandoned the cloth for marriage or a relationship. For myself, I've never felt the need of marriage or constant companionship—I suppose a bit like you."

"So what are you saying . . . that you've had affairs?"

The bishop nodded. "Even in Church terms, celibacy is merely a prescription—an ancient one, granted—but it's just a discipline, not a matter of theology, not a tenet of faith. So over the years, just as I've accommodated my beliefs with my official role, I have similarly accommodated my sexuality."

Adam exhaled in a mock whistle.

"Both by training and temperament, I'm a discreet type of person," the bishop said, "but once this Picasso deal goes through, it will be the end of all pretense. I am more than ready to retire, no matter how belatedly it may seem after all I've just told you."

"Which brings us back to the problem with Zannah . . ."

"Trust me, Adam, as I have trusted you. We have the sale of the paintings, and Zannah is no more of a problem than a tiresome insect buzzing around our heads."

"A squashed insect, Phil."

The bishop looked at him, brows drawn.

"She's dead. She was found in her apartment late last night, murdered."

The bishop sat mute and motionless, deflating like a poorly sealed balloon. His normally taut, tanned face slackened.

Realizing the bishop was on the verge of tears, Adam's own tight-reined vexation began to melt. He wanted to put his arms around him, reassure him, tell him that it wasn't true, and that everything would be all right. He had to remain strong and resist that urge. He needed to know more.

Since his parents' deaths, this man had provided Adam with almost every substantial opportunity he'd had in his life. He began to feel guilty for even entertaining the notion that Phil might be trying to outflank him. How ungrateful to corner him like this in an airport parking complex, accusing him, setting him up, then felling him with the news of Zannah's murder.

The bishop leaned back against the headrest, eyes closed, clasping his hands together in the reflexive attitude of prayer. Neither man spoke, the Mercedes a cocoon of quiet amidst the reverberating traffic noise of the parking lot.

After some minutes, the bishop asked, "Are you sure she was murdered?"

"I'm afraid so. Joe Rooney phoned about one thirty this morning to tell me, and apparently she was cut up quite badly. Most of the wounds were disfiguring but not life-threatening, he said. She would have survived except for finally having her throat cut back to the bone."

As Adam spoke, he could see the bishop struggling with his emotions. He straightened up, cleared his throat with a cough, licked his lips and dabbed the corners of his eyes with a Kleenex.

His evident distress made Adam uncomfortable, and he was hesitant to add to it by pursuing his own agenda, which seemed crass and materialistic now. But, he reminded himself, the bishop was a professional mediator, trained to reconcile the wayward with their god. A performance like this would be all in a day's work to Phil. This could all be just a ploy, an attempt to derail him.

He was determined to continue. "Why was she killed, Phil?" His voice was low, sympathetic. "What was she talking about?"

The bishop shook his head slowly. "I don't know why she was killed. I find it impossible to believe that it had anything to do with the paintings. Good God, we're talking about a human life here!"

"Yes, but she was talking about a lot of money, and just take a look around you. People are mugged and murdered in alleyways all over the world for small change compared to that."

Adam paused, but there was no response from the bishop, who sat staring at the windshield. He placed his hand on the bishop's shoulder. "Phil, you've got to share this with me. From what Zannah said, it obviously involves me somehow, and in that case, I have a right to know. Preferably before I too have my throat cut!"

The bishop moistened his lips with a quick flick of the tip of his tongue. Adam could see his turmoil, could see him weighing his alternatives and trying to gauge their effects. Half turning in his seat, he gripped one of Adam's hands.

"Okay," he said, "but first I want you to suspend judgement until you have all the facts. The early answers aren't always the right ones. What I'm going to tell you hasn't been withheld for any selfish reason, but rather that you simply didn't need to know or be implicated. In fact, in the beginning, it was an advantage if you didn't know. Now, I'm just asking you not to overreact or rush too quickly to condemnation. Try to understand, and please try to forgive me for keeping you in the dark about so much for so long."

Adam listened, a blank look on his face.

"Another thing I must beg of you, is to keep what I'm about to tell you from Joe Rooney. He may be a friend, but he is also a police officer, and it would be unfair to place him in a situation where his loyalties may be stretched."

Adam just nodded his assent and sat behind the steering wheel, listening.

"It began over twenty years ago, while you were still at college. As you know, Jack was an unparalleled draughtsman and a skilled and meticulous restorer. Apart from his own painting, and almost as a form of therapy, he adored cleaning and repairing the various canvases that were part of my portfolio for the Church. I paid him, of course, and at that stage he was grateful for the freedom an independent, regular income of his own allowed him.

Then, among a sizeable bequest with a lot of valuable paintings in it, I found one, a seventeenth-century Italian scene, which would've been a glorious picture except for the damage. It had a hole in the center of it that was as big as a turnip. He was keen to see what he could do with it, and since it wouldn't have been worth a lot of money even in perfect condition in those days, I agreed. He handed it to me a week later, and I couldn't believe it. It was perfect, and it looked its age. I was delighted, he got paid and the painting sold. And so it continued."

None of this was a spectacular disclosure. It was commonplace in the trade to have paintings cleaned, holes and tears repaired, deteriorating canvases relined, even areas with major damage repainted. It was all discoverable to the expert eye, particularly nowadays with so many scientific tests available to uncover all such over-restoration and trickery.

"So far you're not telling me anything new, Phil," Adam said as the bishop paused. "I always knew he did a lot of restoration work for you."

"Jack's skill, the fulfilment he got from the work, and the financial rewards encouraged both of us to experiment a little further. Many old genre paintings that ended up in my possession were virtually worthless, but they were on old canvases and in their original frames. Jack took them and created something original, but of the period; he aged them a bit, added a minor signature and "Presto!" we had something from virtually nothing."

"You and Jack were faking?" Adam butted in, his voice strident. "Is that what Zannah knew?"

The bishop ignored the interruption. "Nothing but good came from it. All the paintings were sold to willing buyers with ease. You know as well as I do that it's nothing new. Painters have been copying and misrepresenting other painters' work since time immemorial. Very often it's the only thing that's kept them from starvation. And we had the biggest of advantages that ensured us total security from discovery."

Adam interrupted again. "Yeah, the surplus art disposals of the Catholic Church would certainly be above suspicion. Plus, of course, any that were discovered to be fakes would only reflect on the poor luck or judgement of whoever had bequeathed them to the Church."

"That's right. Provenance is the cornerstone of authenticity, and the fact that any particular work coming on the market from collections bequeathed to the Church renders it virtually beyond reproach," the bishop agreed.

"Since the arrangement with my superiors allocates me a large percentage, after expenses, to help fund hospitals, irrigation schemes, education and famine relief work in the Third World, I took advantage of it. This, I realized, was a heaven sent opportunity to do good. Globally, collectors were paying obscene amounts of money for paintings, often by painters who never managed to sell a canvas when they were alive. Many of them were paintings that I personally couldn't even relate to. How much better if such enormous sums could be put to better use?" The bishop shrugged his shoulders and made a wry grimace. "So, we just produced a slew of minor works. Not copies, just paintings in the style of, say, minor impressionists or even minor sketches by prolific major figures—and signed them appropriately, of course."

"So, you've been slipping fakes into the system for years? Representing them as *sleepers* you discovered in collections that were passed into your charge? And I suppose I've been involved in some of this?"

"I'm afraid so," the bishop said. "In the beginning, you didn't need to know. Then, as time passed and Jack produced more and more, I couldn't tell you without having you feel hurt or resentful that I'd kept it from you in the first place."

Adam sat, both hands gripping the steering wheel, staring. This was not merely a case of passing off a few decorative period paintings as something they weren't and pocketing a few hundred or maybe a thousand dollars. From what the bishop was intimating, this was a deliberate, well planned and executed cottage industry designed to feed the demand for whatever was the current fashion. And they'd been doing it for years.

"How many?" Adam asked. "Are we talking tens here? Hundreds? Thousands?"

"It's irrelevant, Adam. In the first place, I don't know. Only a fool keeps records of that sort of thing. Further, they are all in galleries and private collections, and no one is unhappy about any of them, so there's no good reason for you to be. Just rest assured that you were never cut out, and you always received your percentage."

"Do you think I'm worried that I've been short-changed? That I haven't received my share of the spoils? After all these years, do you know me at all?"

Adam's voice was rising; the windows were beginning to steam up. He turned the ignition key a notch, lowered the two side windows a fraction, and continued in a quieter tone. "I'm not a naïve innocent, and I don't mind cutting the occasional corner, but what I do object to is being treated like a fool."

The bishop put his hand on Adam's. "I can only ask your forgiveness, and your forgiveness is all that I want. Personally, I have no regrets for any of it. I'd do it all again. Just think about it, Adam. Fifty-three million dollars for Van Gogh's "Sunflowers" in eighty-seven, over fifty-one million for a Picasso in eighty-nine. Crazy amounts. I hate to make moral judgements, but I felt it was reprehensible when millions of people were dying in Africa from lack of a handful of maize or a drop of drinking water."

Adam found himself nodding in agreement.

"But with Jack's death, it's all over. Fortunately, by now the pump has been primed. The success of the charity is attracting other funding, and I'm tired. I need a rest from it all. And, as I said, I've a lost lifetime to make up for.

"There's just one more thing to do, however. Unfinished business. And what I'm about to tell you involves the pinnacle of Jack's entire body of spurious work. This is what he was proving awkward about. And it's what's going to make you rich and allow me enough to retire on."

"The Picassos? Where do they fit into all of this? They can't be fakes!"

The bishop indicated the window ventilation gaps and lifted a finger to his lips. "Keep your voice down, Adam. There is too much at risk here."

They both scanned around the parking lot before the bishop continued. "You remember when the prices for twentieth-century art started to rocket in the eighties?"

Adam nodded in reply.

"And the Bellocs were advised by their insurance company that if they were going to have their collection on publicly accessible display in their headquarters, they were either going to have to replace several of the core paintings with copies or all insurance coverage would be withdrawn?"

"Yeah, of course I remember. They wouldn't cover the Picassos unless they were kept either in a bank vault or in a high security area of their own home, not accessible to public view. That's when you commissioned Jack to paint those super copies—but I remember him under-painting them with his own signature and dating them. In any case, they were destroyed years ago in the fire."

The bishop said in a low voice, "Certainly that's how it appeared, and anyway, it would be virtually impossible to introduce a high-profile fake of that caliber into the marketplace—without a convincing provenance, that is."

Adam sat back in the driver's seat and stared out of the clearing windshield, reflecting on what he had just been told. Astounding and so simple. A lot of those paintings would have changed hands time and again by then, generally for more and more money. They'd just become a convenient currency; the present owners all had their money's worth, and that's how it would remain unless he blew the whistle. Sure, they'd all profited from it, but the lion's share had gone to charity. It had doubtlessly saved countless lives. What did it matter if a portion of it had gone to Phil's pension fund or Jack's?

"Jack!" Adam jolted from his reverie. "What happened to Jack? And where does Zannah fit in?"

"That gets us back to the Belloc paintings."

"The ones Jack painted—the copies?"

"Yes, he painted and aged them, and on the wall, they were indistinguishable from the originals. However, once Paul Belloc had them, and the insurance company was satisfied that the replacements were on display, he simply took them home and put them into storage."

"You mean the originals," Adam corrected him. "He put the originals into storage?"

The bishop shook his head. "No, the copies. He didn't put the copies on display at all. He told the insurance company he had, but the originals never moved. They were still hanging on the walls."

"What? He kept the real Picassos hanging on display after having copies painted to replace them? What was the point of that?"

"You know how stubborn he is. He's used to doing things his own way, and he resented being told what to do by a faceless insurance company. As with the rest of his life, he made his own decisions and wanted the collection displayed in what he considered its authentic entirety."

"So when they had the fire . . ." Adam interrupted.

"Yes, the originals were burned to cinders—along with one or two others—though otherwise, most of the collection was only lightly smoke damaged. The insurance company paid out on the minor ones and compensated Belloc for the copies."

Adam shook his head, then he spoke slowly and deliberately. "Let me get this straight. Are you telling me that it's been Jack's copies that have been posing as the originals for the past nine years?"

"Yes," the bishop said.

"But, if they're under-painted with Jack's signature . . ." Adam stopped mid-sentence. "Jesus! Jack's been doing replacements— that's what Zannah was talking about! He'd upped his price to ten million—and she said that's what killed him!"

"Hold on there, Adam. Don't race to too many conclusions. That was a combination of paranoia, hysteria and bereavement talking. I'm far from convinced there was anything suspicious about poor Jack's death."

"Well, there certainly was about Zannah's!" Adam retorted.

"A tragedy," the bishop said, his eyes misting again. "Jack involved her too much and told her too much, and she certainly had become something of a problem. But I still can't believe her death could have had anything to do with the paintings."

"Where are they? Who has them?"

The bishop sighed. "That's the problem we're now faced with. Jack faked discreetly; he never did it in his regular studio. To be on the safe side, he's been renting a section in a high security self-storage facility for years, and I'm pretty sure that's where they'll be. When Jack died, Zannah had the access card and the keys in her possession. She was nervous about holding them, aware of the responsibility, but I was confident I could've done some sort of a deal with her when I got back."

"So not only have the originals not existed for years, but Jack's replacements are locked away. Do you know the location?"

"Yes, it's over in New Jersey. But the storage depot is tight on security. Access is straightforward enough if you have the magnetic card, the pass code, and the keys, but without them you'd need a court order."

Adam thumped the steering wheel, shaking his head. "This is crazy! All this time you've been telling both me and Catherine Bentley that the Picassos are just about to be shipped up from Florida, and you don't even know where they are for sure!"

"No, don't worry. I'm ninety-nine percent sure they're in the New Jersey studio. Otherwise, Zannah wouldn't have been trying to do a deal. So, what about Catherine Bentley, the Englishwoman? Have you spoken to her since the funeral?"

"Yes, I've spoken to her, but I don't know what the point is. She was annoyed then, and she's going to be flaming mad now."

"OKAY, CONTACT HER LATER, APOLOGIZE FOR THE DELAY, AND AT least initiate proceedings. Demonstrate to her that we are acting in good faith."

"Acting in good faith! Have you totally taken leave of your senses, or am I missing something here? You want me to continue this charade without having the paintings in our possession?"

"It's the best we can do, Adam," the bishop explained. "She's already been in New York over a week, and the main purpose of her visit has barely been discussed. We've procrastinated long enough; we mustn't allow the line to go slack."

"Phil, we're talking at cross-purposes here. Even if we continue with this transaction, you're ignoring the fact that we don't have the damn paintings—and you've already said it would take a court order to gain access to Jack's studio."

"Calm down, Adam. I know our options seem limited at the moment, but I'm doing my best to deal with this awful news of Zannah and bring you up to speed at the same time. I have no choice but to assume we'll be able to locate the paintings, one way or the other. We only need the keys and the magnetic card. I've been to the studio countless times. I know the pass code, which was the one thing Zannah didn't have, and without it, the keys and card are useless. So, contact Bentley today."

"Jesus, Phil! What can I say to her about a timescale?"

"Stick to the story that we're in the process of having them packed and shipped up from Florida at the moment. That'll give us a couple of days' grace to find them."

"Must be wonderful to have such faith," Adam said, half to himself.

"More logic than faith, Adam," the bishop said. "Those paintings are valueless to anyone else but us. No one else can sell them, except through us. Sure, it's conceivable that somehow, some anonymous third party has them and wants to hold them for some sort of ransom. But if they've killed Zannah to get them, then they must proceed very carefully. One way or another, the Picassos are bound to surface, and surface in our direction. Consequently, I'm confident that we'll end up with them."

It was evident the bishop regarded the matter settled. Adam powered up the Mercedes and reactivated his cellphone. He was uncomfortable with his own evolving reaction to the bishop's explanation. Before meeting Phil from the flight, the overriding preoccupation was Zannah, her behavior yesterday and her murder last night. Now, his priorities had altered. Now, the primary concern was revolving around the paintings, and not merely the fact that they were fakes. Phil was right; copper-bottomed provenance was the critical element in the fine art market. They had the provenance—they just didn't have the paintings. With the prospect of a guaranteed multimillion-dollar payday dissolving in the course of a conversation, he assured himself, such a reassessment was certainly justified.

The tires squealed on the dry concrete of the parking structure as he swung onto the exit ramp. "What do you think, Phil? Should I contact Joe Rooney and perhaps try some excuse to get into her apartment?"

"Absolutely not! Don't do anything that'll draw attention to you. I know Joe is a good friend, but there will be other people involved, and expressing an interest in the murder scene may well be part of the profile of the actual murderer. Even as it is, since you were perhaps one of the last people to have seen her alive, you'll routinely come to their attention. Don't make things worse for yourself."

Adam nodded in agreement as he drove down the ramp. The

last thing he needed was to become a suspect in a murder inquiry. Poor Zannah. Hard to imagine that she was no longer the dazzling living creature that he had lunch with yesterday. Despite Phil's reservations, it's most likely that her death was painting related. And that only meant one thing. "Phil, I hate to say this, but the likelihood is that whoever killed her has the keys."

"Yes, if the paintings were indeed a factor, then you're probably right," he agreed.

As they drove out into the winter sunlight, Adam slowed the Mercedes, indicated to pull over, and stopped at the side of the service road. He turned to the bishop. "Phil, I've just had a thought, something I don't think you've considered." The bishop's grey eyes stared back at him. "There is one scenario in which the paintings don't need to filter down to us, one way that we can be completely cut out of the loop."

"What's that?" he asked.

"If Zannah's, and perhaps Jack's, killer is under instruction from the Bellocs. That way, they'll have possession and market them through one of the big salerooms on a no-commission deal, thereby cutting us out and saving themselves millions."

It was clear from the bishop's initial expression that he hadn't considered that possibility, but then relief began to spread across his face. "They couldn't do that. They'd be running too much of a risk. They know we know the truth, and we could undermine their authenticity."

Adam pulled a wry face. "I hoped you could've read between the lines, Phil. I'm not too happy about saying it out loud, but you're right. It certainly would be too much of a risk for them— unless they dealt with us the way Zannah has been dealt with!"

The bishop looked solemn as he digested Adam's words.

Adam's cellphone began to ring. Joe Rooney's voice sounded urgent in his ear. "I've been trying to contact you for the past hour! Where are you?"

Adam, concerned, glanced over at the bishop as he answered,

"I've been picking Phil up from the airport. Must've just been in a poor signal area for a while. What's going on?"

"I don't want to say too much on this line, just that there is a possibility of you being implicated—"

"What?" Adam interrupted. "You mean—"

"Yes! But say nothing else. Just drop the bishop off and come straight over to my place. I'll meet you there."

☙ 1 2 ❧

J oe Rooney was not smiling as he invited Adam in. Declining the offer of coffee, Adam took a seat on the sofa facing Joe's regular La-Z-Boy seat. The stale smell of cigarette residue hung in the air like a fumigation bomb, but at least the drapes were open. Too many times in the past, Adam had visited only to find Joe sitting alone in semi-darkness.

"Adam," Rooney said as Adam took his seat, "I need you to tell me something truthfully, and I'm asking as an old friend, not as a cop. If I'm going to be able to help you, I need you to answer me on the same basis—with no bullshit."

Adam broke in. "Before you insult me by asking—No! I had nothing to do with Zannah's death! Jesus, I didn't even know she was dead until you called and woke me!"

Rooney ignored his words. "Were you screwing her?"

Adam stared straight into Rooney's eyes. Despite all his assurances, they were the eyes of a police officer. "No, I wasn't," he answered with emphasis, "and what's more, I never have." He paused. "That's not to say I wouldn't have minded, of course."

Rooney stared back, as if trying to probe into Adam's mind with his eyes.

"Why do you ask that? Had she been raped? Were there signs of recent sexual intercourse?" Adam asked.

Rooney shook his head. "No, there wouldn't appear to be any sexual aspect to the killing—except maybe sadism."

"Then why ask me that?"

Rooney didn't reply immediately. He fidgeted, as if searching for a cigarette, before speaking. "Because she was in the early stages of pregnancy. And she knew it."

Adam's eyes widened with surprise. He found it hard to imagine Zannah as a mother.

"The Crime Scene guys found a pregnancy testing kit in the trash. The lab confirmed she was pregnant later this morning."

"But why me, Joe? She's been with Jack for the last couple of years, and even then I imagine they had a pretty open relationship."

Rooney straightened up in his chair. "Why do you say that? Do you know that she's been seeing other guys, and if so, who?"

"Not exactly, but from certain comments that I've overheard in their company, it's conceivable that Jack got a bit of a buzz from the possibility. In fact, knowing him and his history, nothing would surprise me."

"Yeah, well even if that turns out to be the case, it still keeps you in the frame. You were the agent for both of them and you also mixed with them socially. That's common knowledge, and now we hear that you enjoyed an intimate lunch with her yesterday that, the waiter says, came to an abrupt end when she stormed out, leaving you alone."

Adam admitted, "Yes, we had lunch. She was upset and left suddenly—that's all. I've never had sex with her, and I certainly didn't kill her! I can't imagine why anyone would even dream of that."

"What upset her? You?"

"Jesus, Joe! Her boyfriend was just cremated the day before— she's been upset for days!"

Rooney absently patted his jacket pockets. "Adam, this wasn't just some break-in that went wrong. This poor girl was sliced up before she was killed; you might even say she was tortured."

"How could it happen without attracting attention? What about the neighbors, did nobody hear anything?"

"No, her radio was playing music loudly, and the top floor occupants were out until late. They were the ones who called it in. The apartment below is vacant; Carl checked it out. He says the ceiling is stained from her blood seeping through. From the final cut."

Adam sat back in the sofa. His arms felt heavy, and he wanted to get away from this interrogation.

Rooney continued, "Our problem is that you were the last person seen with her. To all appearances, you left on bad terms, which just might provide some hint of a motive. Furthermore, according to the waiter, the way you and she were behaving before she made her exit was a little too cozy for just good friends, which might suggest a possibility of paternity."

"Okay, so there's a little circumstantial indication that we were physically involved. As I've told you, we were not, but this can all be cleared up quite easily. A comparison of DNA profiles between Zannah, the embryo, and me will establish beyond doubt that I'm not the father. Am I right?"

Rooney sat back and looked at him with undisguised surprise. "You're happy enough to do that?"

"Joe, believe me, please!" Adam said. "Stop being a cop for a second. I'm not happy about anything to do with this. I'm just agreeing to a comparison with tissue from poor Zannah's dead body. The thought of it turns my stomach, but I'm not involved, so I'll do whatever is necessary to establish that. You just tell me where and when."

Rooney smiled for the first time since Adam had entered his home. "Jesus, that's a relief. I didn't know how I was going to ask you to give a sample. I thought it would make you think I didn't believe you."

"So when can we do it?" Adam asked.

"I have testing materials right here. We can set it up now, if you have no objections."

"Go get them; it's fine by me," he said.

Rooney went into the bathroom and returned with a screw top glass phial and a pack of sterile, cotton-topped sticks. Adam surrendered, open mouthed, as Rooney took three buccal swabs for the profiling.

"Until this DNA test clears you, it's almost the only thing they've got. I'll get this done immediately and phone you the moment I get the results."

"You said 'almost the only thing'?" Adam asked as Rooney sealed the top on the phial.

"It's privileged information, so no further than this room, okay?" Rooney said, continuing as Adam nodded in agreement, "It's probably nothing, but there was a message on the victim's answering machine timed at yesterday afternoon. The tone and content were hostile, could even be construed as threatening."

"Who left the message, do you know?"

"Oh yeah, she considerately left her name, though I'd have recognized the voice." Rooney took a deep breath and paused before leaning forward toward Adam. "It was Sarah Hastings's voice, and I'm afraid she mentioned you!"

"Me? What would Sarah have to say to Zannah about me?" As Adam spoke the words, he knew the answer.

"Well, she didn't exactly spell it out, but from her tone, one of the inferences you could draw was that she too had a little something going on with you and was just warning the competition off."

Adam felt himself reddening.

"Yes, she came to see me, totally out of the blue, at the apartment early yesterday morning, and Zannah phoned shortly afterward. Sarah overheard me arranging to have lunch with her, and after I hung up, she made it clear that she didn't approve of her father's mistress or her conduct. I thought she was being a bit presumptuous, as it was no business of hers. I can have lunch with anyone I want, and I told her so. I assumed it was because Zannah was 'the other woman', so to speak—you know, coming between Liz and Jack. I certainly thought that she overreacted, but to call Zannah later!" Adam stood up, and without asking, he went into the kitchen and helped himself to a soda from the fridge. Walking back in, he said, "It seems she has her mother's temper, but—"

Rooney interrupted him. "You and I know the people involved. This makes it very difficult to be objective, but when you look at it objectively, links like these are all we have to go on, so they've gotta be examined. Shake them about a bit, see what falls out. Technically, there is no room for favoritism or prejudice. I like Sarah; there's something about her. But from an investigative point of view, you and she are the best bets at the moment."

❧ 1 ₃ ❧

A s the bishop opened the door to his New York quarters, he could hear the phone ringing inside. Dropping his case in the foyer, he closed the door behind him and dashed to answer it. It was André.

"Allô, Bishop, I was hoping you would be back. I'm leaving Boston this evening for Paris, and will be connecting to Africa from there—"

"André, I've just had terrible news," he said, breaking in on him. He walked down the hallway into the big living room, handset at his ear.

"What's happened?"

The bishop lowered himself onto a couch. "You're not going to believe this, but Zannah Koller has been found dead in her apartment."

"Zannah? Jack Hastings's girl, Zannah?"

"Yes."

"She is dead? How?"

"She was murdered, brutally, sometime last night. Adam told me when he picked me up from the airport this morning."

"The poor girl. That's terrible, Bishop. I'm so sorry. Shall I cancel my flight? Do you want me to come back—you know—for the funeral?"

"No, that won't be necessary, André. I don't even know what the arrangements are. But it has come as a terrible shock. It's all I can think about. What about your trip? How have things gone up there with you?"

"No major problem," André replied, "just one of those little misunderstandings that arise when one person thinks they can intimidate another with empty threats."

"So, you were able to resolve it?"

"Yes," André answered. "Yesterday I visited the person who was causing the problem and, after I made our position clear, he apologized and became very amenable."

"Good man," the bishop said. This was one case where he had no difficulty reading between the lines. André was invaluable. "I'd just arrived home when I heard your call, so I'll go and unpack now. Take care in Africa, and contact me if you have any problems."

"Certainly, Bishop. I'll see you sometime later in the week, au revoir."

The bishop fetched his case and went into his bedroom to unpack. He was almost finished when the phone beside his bed started to ring. Lifting the handset, he heard an unfamiliar male voice inquiring if he was Bishop Phil Connor. He answered yes, and asked to whom he was speaking.

The speaker, ignoring the question, said, "We have a mutual acquaintance in Florida. You were visiting with him yesterday. He asked me to come to see you."

That interfering brat, the bishop thought wearily, the last thing I need is some Neanderthal breathing down my neck. But he replied, "Sure, I'm available anytime."

"Good. I'm close at hand. I'll be with you very shortly."

The bishop was put at ease by the stranger's appearance as he opened the door, greeted him, and showed him in to the office. He was of medium height and medium build. With well-groomed blond hair and formally attired in a dark grey business suit and dark overcoat, he looked more like a bank official than any sort of enforcer. The bishop sat down at his desk and indicated a chair for his visitor.

"Thank you, but no. I prefer to stand."

As the stranger spoke, his tone was neutral and to the point. His English was unaccented with the stilted phrasing that reminded the bishop of a poorly translated instruction manual. He introduced himself.

"My name is Mr. Snow. Mr. Belloc has asked me to attend you, to assist as necessary in the retrieval of the missing items, and to report all progress back to him personally as it occurs."

"I assume this is Belloc Junior?"

Snow only nodded in reply.

"I told him it was unnecessary. Everything is under control."

"Mr. Belloc does not see it like that. He feels that perhaps you are struggling, out of your depth. Consequently, he wants you to acquaint me comprehensively with the details of all the problems, to see if I can aid in the resolution of any of them."

"Mr. Snow, if that really is your name," the bishop said, raising his voice, "I've already told you I don't need any assistance. You can report back to Belloc that I will not have any impositions like this thrust upon me."

"Bishop," Snow said, his voice stoic, "I have my instructions, and I intend to follow them." He walked over to the bishop's open roll-top desk and scribbled a number on a yellow Post-It pad before tearing the top sheet off and handing it to him. "My involvement is total, and continues until I have physical possession of the merchandise." He paused and pointed to the Post-It. "I am the only person at the end of that cellphone. I expect you to contact me with breakthrough news by this evening at the latest. Otherwise, you and the extortionists will have to face the consequences. My mandate here is open-ended and free from any restraints. I have freedom to follow my own procedures, to whatever degree I should deem necessary.

"Be aware, I have been monitoring your problem here for some days now, and I have my suspicions as to probable suspects. Do not underestimate me!"

The bishop sat motionless in his chair as Snow turned to the door and, without a word of goodbye, made his own way out. He remained sitting, becoming aware of the dryness in his mouth. He licked his lips and looked down at the quivering yellow note between his fingers. He had just been threatened by a robot and, judging by the hammering he could feel in his chest, effectively. Paul Belloc Junior had just turned the corner from mere verbal intimidation to blatant thuggery.

Adam had been right. Yes, maybe they were dispensable as well. What should have been just another, admittedly uniquely profitable, deal had now turned into an extremely dangerous situation. He went to the buffet and poured a whiskey for himself, downing it in one gulp. He poured another. Sitting on his desk chair, he closed his eyes and began to breathe deeply through his nose, calming his racing heart. That's all I need to round off a memorable day, he thought, a cardiac incident. Suddenly, there seemed to be nothing but dead ends. In twenty-four hours the situation had been transformed. There were no choices left. In this desperate position, a dilemma would be a luxury. He didn't know what to do, or where to turn, but he couldn't admit it or let it be known. Such a revelation would eliminate any iota of influence the Bellocs believed he had left, and God knows what such a discovery might entail for him. On top of which, he would be letting Adam down.

He sipped his whiskey without enjoyment or savor. What was needed was sound, sympathetic, and practical advice. He lifted the phone handset, and after a brief moment's hesitation, he dialed.

❧ 14 ❧

A dam arrived back at his apartment to see his answering machine flashing its warning: five messages. Since his meeting with Joe Rooney, he had kept his cellphone off, needing the solitude to reflect. But first he needed to have a shower and try to energize himself.

Showered and changed, he dealt with the machine. The first one was an earlier call from Rooney, leaving no details, just asking him to contact him. Then a call from the bishop; a call from Robin Brew, who shared gallery space with him, no doubt dying to gossip about Zannah; a call from Sarah saying she'd been trying to reach him all day on the cellphone, and would he call her; and, most surprisingly, a call from her mother, Liz—terse and to the point: she would call him back. Playback finished, the machine was resetting as the phone started to ring again.

He answered it on its second ring and recognized her voice immediately.

"Hello, this is Liz Hastings here. We need to talk." Her tone had an aggressive edge; it was almost an order.

"Hi, go ahead. What's the problem?" Adam tried to sound casual, as if there was nothing unusual in speaking to her alone, intimately, handset to handset, for the first time in over twenty years.

"I'm in the neighborhood. I'll come up . . ." the pause in her speech indicated reluctance as she said, "if that's all right with you?"

"Fine, come ahead. I'll buzz you up."

Adam felt his arteries surge with adrenaline. It wasn't entirely a surprise; they really did need to talk. Guiltily, he realized that he should have made the first move. After all, he was the one who had most of Jack's finished work in his possession, in storage or in the gallery, the work that she would now own as his widow. This had become an exceedingly stressful day.

Minutes later, the entrance intercom buzzed: it was Liz. She refused all the civilities Adam proposed. Coffee, tea, soda—they were all rejected as if they were inappropriate, frivolous suggestions. She took a seat, not on the couch or adjacent easy chairs, but perched on the edge of his flat-topped desk over by the window. Even dressed casually in a navy blue jacket and jeans, she still looked glamorous. The advantages of good genes, he thought. Pity about her personality.

She interrupted his thoughts. "Look, I'm not just here to pass the time of day."

"Yes. No doubt, you're here about the paintings."

"What paintings?" she said, surprise in her voice.

"Jack's paintings. All the Hastings I have in stock, of course!" Adam replied.

She waved her hand. "We can deal with that later. You represented him, which is fine. I'm not inclined at the moment to get into all that. I can live with the status quo for now."

"What is it then?"

She gazed out the window as she spoke, "We had a visit from homicide this morning. From Rooney—I suppose you've heard?"

Adam nodded. "About Zannah? Yes . . . terrible."

"Well, do you also know that he wanted to question Sarah

about a message they said she left on her machine?" She turned to face him, her tone cold and controlled. "Do you know what the message concerned?" She continued without allowing Adam any opportunity to reply. "You! Sarah wanted to talk to her about you!"

Adam shrugged; there was nothing he could say without revealing that Rooney had shared a confidence with him. He could see the anger building in Liz's eyes. "You're asking me to respond to an accusation I know nothing about," he said, keeping his tone as even as possible. "Plus, you may be overstating the case a little. Sure, I'm aware that Sarah may have had a slew of problems with Zannah, but I suspect that any involvement I had with her wouldn't have rated that highly."

"Well, though I may not have heard the actual tape, Rooney was pretty unequivocal that the tone of Sarah's message was abusive and that you were implicated in it."

"I must admit, it seems strange," Adam said, half to himself.

"Strange! Hardly strange!" Liz replied, almost shouting. "From what I hear, you've been flirting with her ever since the funeral, and she's only a child."

"Child? Now, you're being ridiculous. She's in her twenties!"

Liz stood upright, glaring at him. "She's much too young for you to have any interest in. I want you to assure me that there has been nothing going on between you."

Even though Adam was on home ground, the force of Liz's presence was intimidating. She had controlled the meeting so far; she was steamrollering him.

"Hold on, Liz!" He noted her look of distaste as her name left his lips. "I think you're over-reaching here. Sarah may be your daughter, but she's an adult now and can make her own decisions. And as the same can be said for me, I owe neither excuses nor explanations to you." Adam saw her face tighten and prudently stood up as well—she might throw something. He heard his voice grow louder as he spoke, "What Sarah cares to tell you is up to her, but don't think you can come over here and start cross-examining me about my private life. You lost your right to know anything personal about me a long time ago!"

He knew he'd screwed up. This could have been smoothed over in minutes—just admit there had been nothing sexual between him and Sarah—but he just couldn't allow Liz to manipulate his life like this. He would see whomever he wished.

Her voice was icy. "I can be a formidable adversary. I'm warning you now: stay away from her, or I'll make sure you regret it."

She turned, went straight to the door, and without another word, left.

How pathetic to allow this specter from the past cause such emotional disruption, he thought. Who the hell does she think she's talking to like that? The annoyance had filled the air in the room like static. But she's gone now; get over it, he told himself. Sure, her presence, even after all these years, had made him feel uncomfortable and intimidated, but she had little practical power over him. Jack's paintings would be the only sphere in which she could have any influence, and if it came down to it, she could just have them. After all, compared to his share of the commission for the upcoming Belloc transaction—if it ever happened—Jack's work represented only pennies.

With this in mind, Adam steeled himself and called Catherine Bentley at her hotel.

"Catherine, sorry I haven't managed to speak to you earlier, but this morning has been hell. I presume you've heard about Zannah?"

"Yes," she said, "Hastings's girlfriend murdered—that was terrible."

Her voice sounded sympathetic and friendly. He didn't relish having another confrontation so soon.

"Do they know who did it? Or what happened?" she asked.

"Not yet, but they're working on it. Her body was found by neighbors late last night, but nobody else was seen around at the time, and as far as I know there are no suspects." This was not a topic Adam wanted to dwell on overlong. "But that's not why I was calling. The bishop came back up from Florida this morning. I picked him up from the airport."

"In that case, are we in a position to proceed?"

"Yes. The situation is just as I explained before. We're marketing them quietly since the vendors would prefer discretion. However, should the offers fall short of their not unreasonable expectations, they are prepared to offer them with a higher profile and global publicity."

"When can we meet to discuss it, in that case?" she asked.

"Whenever it suits you."

"Good. Let's not waste any more time. Why don't you come over here? I'll meet you in my hotel bar, about six. Does that suit you?"

Against every instinct, Adam agreed, his voice concealing the anxiety fallout from the day's events. She hung up.

Here I am about to try to do the biggest deal of my life and the damn paintings are fakes. On top of that, we don't even know for sure where they are, or if we can get them. Assuming, of course, that I'm not charged with Zannah's murder. What a hell of a situation! The phone rang again

"Hello," Adam said.

After a moment of pause, Sarah's voice asked quietly, "Are you alone?"

"Yes, I am now, but I did have a visitor who was asking after you about thirty minutes ago."

"Liz?" she suggested.

"I'm afraid so."

"I'm terribly sorry, Adam. She's just so lunatic, so unreasonable, so controlling, so . . . so . . ." she stuttered, lost for words.

"So accusatory?" Adam suggested.

"What did she accuse you of?" Adam heard her voice harden, her apologetic tone fading.

"It started out as sexual abuse of a minor, sort of . . ."

"A minor?" Her voice registered disbelief.

"Yeah, you, of course. I did point out that you were several stages removed from diapers, but since she hadn't actually swung by for a rational discussion, I was at a bit of a disadvantage."

"What did you tell her?" she asked.

"I told her that what I did in my private life was none of her business and that you were old enough to make your own life choices and friends without any intervention from her."

"And you're not in the Emergency Room!" Sarah laughed, sounding relaxed for the first time. "I wish I'd been there to see that."

"No, I don't think that would've been such a good idea at all," Adam said, adding, "She told me about your visit from Joe Rooney."

"Yes. That was earlier this morning." Adam could sense the embarrassment in her voice. "He explained that since my message was on the machine they would interview me routinely. However, it seems they have found some other forensic evidence that may be linked to the killing."

"I hadn't heard that," Adam replied. That's peculiar, he thought, why would Rooney share details of evidence with her?

"Yes, he wasn't explicit," Sarah said, "It must be hair, or saliva traces or something like that, because he told me that if I gave a DNA sample it would help eliminate me from the inquiry."

"Yeah, just as long as you didn't do it. You didn't seem too keen on her the last time we talked."

But Sarah wasn't that easily cowed. "Listen, if I was driven to kill everyone I didn't like, I'd have my own apartment block on death row by now. Uh-oh! Here she comes back. Got to go, talk to you later." She hung up.

So, Rooney was taking a sample from Sarah as well. Why? It certainly wasn't to check for a match with the embryo. Rooney is keeping secrets as well.

§

Adam arrived at the hotel some minutes early and was surprised to find Catherine Bentley already seated at a corner table with a vantage view of the bar entrance. Few other guests were around at this early hour. As usual, she was dressed in a conservative, understated fashion, a style normally associated with ladies much older than she was. She waved as if to attract his attention—unnecessarily, as he was already approaching her table.

She stood up and proffered her hand. "Adam, how have you been keeping?"

Very formal, Adam thought, as they shook hands and exchanged a handful of further mundane pleasantries. He wasn't surprised though. After their telephone conversation on the afternoon of Jack's funeral, she had left him in no doubt that she considered him to be not much more than a nuisance, an impediment in the process of acquiring the paintings.

Before he had time to arrange himself on the upholstered bench seat, there was a waiter beside him. She was drinking Scotch on the rocks, so he ordered more of the same. The interval between the drinks being ordered and arriving was spent discussing the events of the last few days, with Catherine remarking how unfortunate it was that these occurrences were no doubt proving a powerful distraction for Adam at such a critical time in his career. Her concern was expressed in such condescending tones that Adam baulked at agreeing. Instead, he pointed out that, at least, he was in the enviable position of still being alive.

The drinks arrived, and as they mock clinked their glasses, Adam had to admire her unambiguous directness. No half-hour of schmoozing here, just straight for the throat.

"Adam, what sort of a figure are we talking about here? What will it take to own these paintings?"

Normally, Adam never felt uncomfortable about discussing money, but now he was less than confident. Here he was inhibited by realities—negotiating to sell paintings he didn't have in his possession, didn't have access to, and to top it off, he knew were damn well fake.

"Well, the figures we have in mind," he began, speaking with slow, deliberate diction, "the largest Picasso, which is possibly the. . ."

"No, no, never mind a breakdown," she said. "We both know what they are. What is the total amount your clients want?" She lifted her drink and took a sip, her eyes never leaving his face.

Adam lifted his own Scotch, grateful for the cool, sour wetness in his mouth and the momentary respite it provided. She was being clever, getting in first. If he had to quote a figure, it had to be higher than anything the paintings would conceivably fetch on the open market. Once that figure was mentioned, there was only one way the negotiation could go—downward. In situations like this with only one active buyer, no one ever bids higher than the asking price.

"One hundred and seventy-five," he said, trying to sound casual.

Catherine pursed her lips, her nostrils flaring as she inhaled sharply. Her gaze remained on him as she idly swirled the whiskey and ice around in her glass, making no sound for what Adam felt was an inordinately long time.

"It's somewhat more than we were expecting; more than I am at present authorized to go," she said eventually.

Adam felt relief. Maybe he wasn't going to be put in the situation of having to produce these problematic paintings immediately after all. But he had to make a show of negotiating.

"You know that in an auction situation they'll make well over one hundred, on a good day maybe even one twenty, one thirty. Once you add fees and taxes it's in the same ballpark," Adam said.

"Plus about fifteen million dollars." Catherine snorted. "Either way, you are looking for all the advantages of a saleroom without being penalized by any of the drawbacks."

"What drawbacks? The big salerooms would eat their own children to swing the sale of these paintings and you know it; and there would certainly be no seller's premium charged. Their sale would cost the vendor nothing," Adam countered.

"Certainly, I accept that. But whereas your principal might be paid whatever the hammer price was, you are suggesting that we should stump up an extra figure, probably in excess of auction fees and local taxes. It seems to me that you want things all your own way without allowing us any consideration for being prepared to deal on your terms. After all, my principal is very flexible. He is prepared to arrange payment however and wherever your clients wish. He too prefers anonymity and is quite amenable to the amount agreed upon remaining totally confidential. Should your clients wish, for tax reasons, the amount can be represented as any credible figure and the balance paid into an offshore account."

Adam nodded and took another sip.

"One hundred," she said.

Adam slowly shook his head from side to side.

"One hundred would negate any advantage that my client might gain from your last suggestion. Come up another sixty and we have a deal." He was heartened at the gap between them. A failure to reach an agreement at this stage would give them a breathing space.

Catherine Bentley shook her head and, with an air of finality, said, "One hundred and sixty million is beyond my authority."

Adam drained his glass. "Sorry, Catherine; looks like we can't do business in that case. We just couldn't go to Belloc with an offer like that. As you may imagine, there are other interested parties in the wings, and it has simply been a matter of courtesy, as you were the first, that we have given you first refusal. Thanks anyway, and who knows? Perhaps we may be able to do business on some future occasion."

Adam moved to leave and she put a hand on his shoulder.

"One fifty, but I'll have to okay it tomorrow."

Adam relaxed back into his seat. One hundred and fifty million dollars. The bishop would be more than happy with that amount.

Just a pity about the small underlying problem, he thought, and lifted his hand to summon the waiter. "Two large Scotches, please."

On the way home in the cab, Adam reactivated his cellphone. Despite the looming shadow of their difficulties, he found himself elated at having done the deal. Yet, there was something ridiculous about it; he knew it was like selling the Brooklyn Bridge and promising to accept payment on a COD basis. Nevertheless, he was eager to share the news with Phil. He speed dialed the bishop's private number.

Immediately, he answered. Adam was aware of a tremor in the bishop's voice. "Adam, I've been trying to contact you for the last two hours."

Adam felt the last traces of elation swamped. More bad news?

"I had a meeting with Catherine Bentley. What's wrong?"

"I'm concerned that there may be something in what you said this morning about the Bellocs. I had a visitor earlier, sent by young Belloc, supposedly to assist in locating the paintings. You might say he had quite a forceful manner."

Adam understood.

"But that's not all. I received a small package by messenger late this afternoon. It contained a magnetic access card and two keys."

"The storage keys?"

"Definitely."

"Who sent them?" As Adam asked the question, he knew it was stupid.

"They didn't leave a return address—or a card."

"What are we going to do?" he asked, at the same time recognizing another foolish question. There was only one thing to do. After all, the deal he had just done necessitated taking possession of the paintings. There was only one thing to do.

"We need to talk," said the bishop. "Pick up your car and come over here as soon as you can, but don't mention a word about this to anyone in the meantime."

"I'll be there as soon as possible," he said, adding, "By the way, I've reached an agreement with our friend, Bentley."

"For how much?" asked the bishop.

"One hundred and fifty," Adam answered. His elation had passed.

The bishop's response sounded devoid of enthusiasm. "Good."

By the time Adam was firing up his Mercedes station wagon, the rain was starting to fall in big, lazy drops. Then the thunder started.

❧ 15 ☙

The keys and the magnetic card sat on the coffee table. The bishop, unease in his eyes, nursed his whiskey on the sofa while Adam sat opposite him.

"Whoever killed Zannah is the one who sent these," Adam said, "maybe even the guy who visited you earlier."

"Yes, it's tempting to think that, but, throughout this dispute with Jack, I haven't mentioned her down in Florida at all. I can't imagine how they could've known."

"Come on, Phil! Your visitor this evening is proof that young Belloc hasn't been sitting on his hands. For all you know, they've had our phones tapped from the beginning. Christ, with their resources, there's no limit to their eavesdropping capabilities— they could even be monitoring our conversation at the moment!"

The bishop said nothing, merely nodded.

"Okay, we have the card and the keys—and you definitely have the code?"

"Yes, that was the one thing Zannah didn't have, and so couldn't have revealed. But over the years, I've been there so many times, often on my own, that he shared the password with me. That's why the keys and card were useless to her on their own."

"Or anyone else—including your mysterious benefactor," Adam added.

"Phil, we have to make a decision here. We can make a call to Joe Rooney, and maybe help set this guy up, or we go get the paintings ourselves and forget about Zannah. But, let's face it, we're not the Lone Ranger and Tonto."

The bishop, uncharacteristically silent, took a moment to reply. "The reality is, if we report this we are, firstly, in danger of being implicated in Zannah's murder. Remember, I was in Florida when she was killed, and if the whole story comes out, you fill the bill quite nicely as the primary suspect—motive and opportunity. Secondly, there would be a substantial risk that the paintings would be exposed as being fake, and God alone knows what ramifications might arise from that. Thirdly, we would lose our percentage on the sale, which would be an awful lot of money to turn our backs on."

"Yeah, but this way, merely by withholding what we know, we're implicating ourselves in her murder as well. Anyway, you can't really need the money. I'm sure you could comfortably retire on what you've got stashed away offshore."

"Maybe, but it would make the difference between being simply comfortably off and never having to worry about money again. And the same could be said for you."

In response to the wordless urging of the bishop's empty raised glass, Adam stood up, went over to the buffet and fetched the whiskey bottle, then he went into the kitchen and fetched himself a soda from the fridge.

As he cracked the pull tab, he said, "Yes, but if we just lift the paintings, do the deal, and say, "Thanks very much, nice doing business with you" to the Bellocs as we walk away with our millions, we're as bad as they are. It makes us totally complicit in her murder. Don't forget, Phil, we both knew Zannah—she's not just a cipher. Christ, I had lunch with her yesterday. I even liked her." He shook his head in disbelief at the enormity of what had befallen her. "To the Bellocs, she was just an obstruction, a bump in the road to be flattened."

The bishop said, "It may look that way, but I don't think that not being personally acquainted with her counted for anything. They knew Jack intimately and for a long time. And now, I have to admit, it seems possible that he may have been their victim as well."

He appeared more relaxed thanks to the sedative effects of the alcohol, and he continued in a more assured tone, "Then, on the other hand, if the Bellocs were responsible, and they want to cut us out, why would they deliver the keys for the warehouse into our hands? Why would their hired thug not simply have reappeared here and marched me off to New Jersey?"

Adam just shook his head. "Good question, Phil. It's impossible to know."

"The one thing we do know, Adam, is that we're up to our necks in this deal. We can't stagger around in denial like headless chickens —so we've got to be proactive. One way or another, these paintings are going to be sold, and for us to stall here could send out the wrong sort of signals. We might be in danger of being classed as impediments rather than as enablers. And as you've already pointed out, as impediments, we may be in danger ourselves. Even standing back and bowing out, we could be regarded as knowing too much— as outsiders without a vested interest in maintaining the status of the paintings. We could never be sure, never feel really safe."

This was true. Simply by making the accusation, surrendering the storage keys to the police and telling them the story, they would certainly risk prison for the both of them, and undoubtedly every painting that had ever passed through their hands would come under scrutiny. Suddenly the victimless crime would start claiming victims—starting with themselves—and no matter their fate, no doubt the Belloc machine would do its damnedest to ensure they suffered for it. One hundred and fifty million dollars was a lot of money at stake. They really only had one choice.

§

Rain was falling in torrents as Adam's Mercedes exited the Holland Tunnel onto the dark New Jersey shore. The visibility was so poor he was forced to drive slowly, peering through the rhythmic momentary clearing in the wiper sweep. Fortunately, traffic was light and they didn't have too far to travel.

Concentration in these road conditions ruled out idle chat. The bishop confined himself to giving directions as they came to intersections. Throughout, Adam kept checking the rearview mirrors to ensure they weren't being followed—he could see no lights behind him.

As expected, the tall front barrier gates were closed at this time of the evening, but a pressed metal hood canopied a digital card scanner beneath a high floodlight and remote camera on the driver's side. The bishop handed Adam the magnetic card.

"Put it in, enter the pass code at the prompt, and the gate should roll back."

Adam slipped the rectangular card into the machine and it sucked it from his grasp. Almost immediately, it spat it back out. Nothing moved.

"I didn't get a chance to punch in the code," Adam said. "Maybe they've changed the system!"

"Try it the other way around," the bishop said, "is there no indication which way the magnetic strip needs to be?"

Adam peered through the deluge. There was something, a pictorial representation, but it was hard to make out. Turning the card back to front, he inserted it again. A small digital keypad glowed green.

"Remember, zero, one, zero, one, five, zero." The bishop prompted.

Adam tapped the numbers in, grabbing the card as it slid out. A yellow beacon on top of the gates started its slow blink.

"That's it," said the bishop.

In the time it had taken to process the card through the

machine, the cuff and lower arm of Adam's jacket was soaked. He pulled his hand back in and whizzed the window up. The big steel gate gave a sudden jerk, and then began to roll back on heavy six-inch diameter metal wheels. Once through, the gate began to close behind them. Following the bishop's instructions, Adam drove alongside a modern block built warehouse incorporating a row of loading docks until he came to the original nineteenth-century hulk ahead. Everywhere looked deserted, but the high floodlights glared through the downpour, rendering the headlights of the Mercedes superfluous. Lightning flashed almost overhead, quickly followed by a rumble of thunder.

"Drive up to the ramp ahead, just beside that covered walkway. It leads to the pedestrian access. One of these keys should fit the door," the bishop said.

The bishop jumped out into the downpour, beckoning Adam to follow. As anticipated, the key fit, and the big steel door opened into a glass-fronted reception area, the office closed for the night. A high camera pulsed a rhythmic red at them as the bishop made for the elevator.

"We're home and dry now," he told Adam. "It's twenty-four-hour access here as long as you have the card and the keys."

"And the cameras?" Adam asked.

"Routine security, the watchmen monitor them in between making their regular patrols. They'd have no reason to interfere with us."

Despite the age of the building, the elevator was modern. It was large, clean, and fast. The bishop pressed the "ten" button, the top floor.

"How long has Jack been renting this place?" Adam asked.

"Years. Twelve, maybe even fifteen. It was a precaution, that's all. Not a lot of people knew about it."

"Evidently," Adam replied. All those paintings, all those years, and they hadn't ever taken him into their confidence.

Stepping out onto the tenth floor, the bishop flipped the light switch and led the way down the long, wide corridor. He stopped

DANN FARRELL

in front of a pair of large doors. Sheeted in heavy gauge steel like all the others, they opened with the remaining key.

Adam stared wide-eyed with amazement as the lights flooded on and the extent of Jack's secret atelier was revealed before him.

"Jesus Christ Almighty! It's like Dr. Frankenstein's laboratory—complete with sound effects!" he said, raising his voice to compete with the storm's battering.

Half of the two outside walls were almost entirely glass, leading up to a sloping glazed roof section of about the same area. The rain lashed against it like the sea. "This is so much bigger than his regular studio," Adam exclaimed. Nine-foot-high steel shelving containing hundreds of old frames, grouped according to size, lined one wall. At the end of it stood a huge cube, taller than a man, with a sky blue ceramic finish. "What's that?" he asked, pointing. "A walk-in freezer unit?"

"No, on the contrary, it's a kiln that he had custom made," the bishop replied. "Just one of the things you sometimes need for aging a painting. Remember, some of these pictures are so large they wouldn't even fit in a commercial size oven."

"He baked them?"

"Only the important ones. Soft paint is a giveaway, and after a painting is finished it can remain soft for decades. Even with baking them in the oven, they need to dry naturally for quite a while first of all, otherwise the paint can end up bubbling with the heat. Time is a critical factor in the procedure. Jack used to say, 'You need at least a year from making to baking.'"

"And the ones we're looking for . . . the Picassos?"

"Yes, they were painted for over a year before he put the finishing touches to them."

Adam could smell the familiar cloying aroma of linseed oil tempered by the sharp, resinous pine smell of turpentine, though there were no paints, varnishes, jars of solvents, or brushes sitting about. Jack had been an obsessively tidy worker, and all the paraphernalia of his craft would have been cleaned and boxed up before being stored away. Two large, six-drawer, architect's plan chests sat side by side, butted up against a long, four-door, turn of the century, dark stained pine cupboard, leading into what looked like a kitchen area.

Indicating the chests and cupboard, the bishop said, "Both Jack and I collected all the old canvases, both used or virgin, we came across. We even built up a stock of old wooden panels from drawer bottoms and backs of armoires from all different periods. Nails, tacks, stretchers, old newspapers, even old wrapping paper and string. Everything was kept; you never knew what might come in useful to reinforce the impression of age." He walked over between two large adjustable wooden artist's easels and stared out into the storm. "Over the years, I've managed to buy the contents of several deceased artist's studios. Some of them had original unused paints, canvases and artist's supplies dating from the beginning of the century and before; materials worth their weight in gold, for as you know, the composition of nearly everything changes with time, but these would withstand any chemical analysis."

"So it wasn't just a matter of knocking out the occasional little fake then? It was full-scale forgery." Adam spoke half to himself as he looked around. There were paintings in low-level racks everywhere, but the bishop remained silent, his back to Adam. "It's a one-man production line... a fucking fake factory! I'm amazed Jack managed to get any original work of his own done at all."

The bishop turned around; there was an irritated tone to his voice, "What does it matter? Jack's dead, and all of us benefited from it. Most of all—and don't forget this for one second—thousands of human beings who were teetering on the edge of death from hunger, thirst, or disease have survived, thanks to Jack and what you call his 'fake factory'. Irrigation and agricultural schemes have been financed, hospital facilities improved, and all sorts of medical aid have been provided."

Adam could see that Phil was almost on the verge of tears.

"I have no regrets, and there has never been a whisper of suspicion concerning any of the paintings. Provenance is everything, and I provided impeccable provenance for them all. It's over now, but as I said, I'd do it all again."

Adam felt chastened. It was the shock of being confronted by the immensity of the operation. After all, this was why he was here, to locate the missing Picasso fakes and take possession of them. He grasped the bishop's upper arm and squeezed. "Sorry, Phil. I was just a tad overwhelmed for a moment there."

The bishop forced a small smile and nodded. "Never mind, we're not finished yet. Let's find what we came here for," he said, his voice barely audible above the battering of the rainstorm.

The bishop knew where to look. In the corner away from the glazed walls, he folded back a large cotton dust cover draped over a partitioned tubular metal frame, about six feet tall and just as deep. There they were, the three of them, racked, one in front of the other, looking for all the world as though they had been painted in the first half of the twentieth century.

Adam lifted the paintings out, one at a time, and examined them. He had seen his fair share of accredited fakes before, paintings that had been exposed as spurious for many different reasons. Some of them had been poorly executed, and some expertly well. But everything about these ones, from the years of grime and dust on the backs of the paintings, which had impregnated the very weave of the material, the obvious age of the cut canvas edges and the creased folds over the stretchers, to the maturity of the dried paintwork, these were self-evidently old. Unexceptionally old, just the way you would expect them to be. Amazing.

"I'm astounded, Phil. They are the real thing!"

"Yes—but let's not take too long here. Let's get them into the back of your car and get out."

The paintings were large but unframed: two of them measured just over four feet by three feet. The other, the one that was supposedly a nude, was slightly larger; it was in excess of five feet in height and just over four feet wide.

"We'll leave the biggest one to last, Phil. The smaller two

should fit between the rear wheel arches. We'll pad them up well; the big one should lie along the top."

One by one they manhandled them into the elevator, along with blankets and packing to lie between them when they were placed one on top of the other in the back of the station wagon. The bishop locked up behind them and they descended back down to the warehouse reception area. They carried the paintings to the steel front door beyond reception and the bishop instructed Adam to reverse the Mercedes up the ramp and under the cover of the awning.

In the brief moments it took him to dash to the vehicle, Adam was soaked. Even beneath the awning, the wind and rain swirled furiously. With the rear seats already folded down flat to accommodate the load, he raised the tailgate. It was still a distance of some fifteen yards from the shelter of the doorway along the partially covered walkway to the Mercedes.

"We'd better cover them with blankets before carrying them out, Phil. That storm is ferocious," Adam said once he was back inside.

The bishop agreed. "You wrap them," he said. "I'll go ahead and lay some padding down in the back to set the first one on and you can bring them out."

The bishop grabbed the thick felt rectangular pads that were already cut to approximate size and, holding them close to his body, rushed through the storm out to the vehicle. Adam watched the bishop leaning into the darkness of the open tailgate, arranging the bed of packing, and then emerging from the back and beckoning to him. He draped a blanket over each of the two paintings, lifted them pinch-grip fashion by their edges, and sprinted toward the car.

He hadn't covered more than two steps with his precious cargo when he felt the power of the wind hitting the paintings. They both lifted like kites. Adam gripped them tightly, straining to regain control. There was nothing he could do. Squinting against the rain driving into his face, he could feel his center of gravity being pulled ahead of his feet so suddenly he could not keep up. He felt a toe catch and he went sprawling along the walkway, abandoning his grip on the paintings in a reflex attempt to save himself from injury.

Glancing up from the wet concrete, he saw them bounce once on their sides, the blankets billowing off like parachutes, and then skitter and skid erratically along the walkway toward the vehicle. Like a surreal goalkeeper, the bishop intercepted the fugitive paintings, and with only a cursory glance at them, he stashed them in the back of the Mercedes before running toward Adam.

"Are you okay?" he asked, his hand under Adam's arm, helping him to rise.

Adam looked down, his trousers were both torn at the knees and his hands were scraped. He felt like a fool.

"Sorry, Phil. They just carried me away. Are they damaged?"

"Just a few scuffs as far as I can see. What about you? No bones broken?"

Adam brushed down his soaking clothes with his dirty, bleeding fingers. "No. Main damage is to my pride. Let me see the paintings"

Apprehensive at what he was going to see, he turned on the Mercedes's interior light and inspected the two paintings. Apart from being rain-soaked, the canvases were undamaged. Only the folded over canvas on the rear edges suffered some scuffing, and there were small signs of bruising on the corners where they first impacted onto the concrete.

"That was lucky," he said, relieved, "though there is some minor damage along the edges."

"Don't worry about that," replied the bishop. "It'll just help add to the illusion of age." He smiled and put his arm around Adam's shoulder. "Now let's get the final one."

This time they took no chances. The tops of the first two well protected with padding, they went back to the reception area. They wrapped the largest one with two quilted packing blankets and gripped it tightly, a hand on each corner. With their heads down against the wind and the rain, they hurried along the walkway to the ramp and slotted it on top of the others in the back of the station wagon.

"Now, let's wedge the rest of the blankets around them so they can't move, and go and dry ourselves out," the bishop suggested.

Driving away from the storage facility through the thunderstorm, Adam felt at last able to relax. His torn palms stung against the steering wheel and the rest of him ached as though he'd been kicked, but otherwise, he was on a high. For a while, Jack and Zannah had slipped his mind.

"Just drive straight to my place," the bishop said. "We'll keep the paintings there overnight—that should be secure enough for the moment. I'll contact the Bellocs and tell them that everything is back online and that a deal has been reached. Then, first thing in the morning, I'll have them moved into the high-security depository." Adam nodded, and the bishop added, "And for God's sake, just make sure you drive carefully. We certainly can't afford to be rearended tonight!"

They looked at each other and smiled. Adam headed straight for the eastbound entrance to the Holland Tunnel.

❧ 16 ❧

Snow sat alone in the darkness in a far corner of the half-deserted New Jersey supermarket parking lot while the rain pounded down. With the wipers stopped on the Dodge rental, it was almost impossible to see through the deluge flooding the windshield. It was important to stay vigilant.

Always cautious, Snow had arrived thirty minutes early for the meeting. He had driven up close to the market entrance and, while scanning for any vehicles that might be likely to signal a threat, acted out the routine of the single commuter shopper. With his overcoat collar turned up, he sprinted through the downpour for cover. Once inside, he picked up a plastic shopping basket and made the normal purchases: frozen pizza, six-pack of beer, bag of Doritos. There was nothing to alert him, no one watching, or worse, ignoring him. The storm ensured that there were few casual shoppers. No one was hanging about in the lobby watching the parking area. No panel vans or other vehicles were parked close to the rendezvous area. He paid cash for his purchases and dashed back to the Dodge.

Snow hated the cold and the wet. He always had, even while growing up. And he was far from happy now. He liked nothing at all about this entire Tri-State area: not the grim faced, hard-voiced people, the extreme weather or the close-quarters congestion. This was not the America he had come to live in, the America of the big skies and far horizons, the America that promised it all. No, that America was located elsewhere. In fact, he thought, sitting in the storm-lashed vehicle, it was almost everywhere else within the United States. This was too much like what he had left behind—a vast, high-density, European-style, tenement slum—except that here it was tacked onto the northeastern seaboard of the wide, empty vastness that was the real America.

Now based in Florida, he had thawed out the frost from his bones and begrudged having to spend any more time than necessary in this inhospitable northern clime. Sitting here in the parking lot with the hard rain pounding and the freezing cold outside, he felt chilled, but to have the heater operating, the motor would need to be running. It was too easy to draw unnecessary attention. The windows were beginning to steam up. He checked his wristwatch: 2105. They were already five minutes late. Still, with this weather he knew the traffic would be hell. He prepared to give them a little longer.

He saw the headlights first in his rearview mirror, then the dark mass of the approaching vehicle bore down from behind and drew up along the passenger side. The rain seemed to intensify as Snow's reflexes primed themselves. This was what he loved—the adrenaline surge and the money. This was what he was good at.

The door of the other vehicle opened. The driver was well geared for the weather, Snow observed, the sheen of wet oilskin striking only a small note of incongruity. In his youth, where he came from, they had been commonplace. The driver opened the Dodge's passenger door and, without even a nod of greeting, jumped in. Snow looked over and relaxed a little. As promised, the newcomer was alone. Without speaking, Snow started up the Dodge, shifted the gear lever into Drive, activating the central locking system, and circled several hundred yards over to an isolated, more brightly-lit area where he could cover all approaches. This time he left the motor running, turned the heater to defrost, and switched the fan on full blast. From here, he could view the other vehicle through the intermittent wipe, just in case.

A strong smell of rubber invaded his nostrils. Instantly alert, Snow turned toward his passenger. Smells and sensations from the past. What was it? Neural memory involuntarily stiffened his penis. Yes, of course. He recalled the odor clearly, but he recognized the connection too late.

The muzzle of the small automatic pistol kissed the soft underside of his jawline, just below and in front of his ear. The cloying, oily condom smell engulfed him. He barely heard the muffled shot that whisked around his cranial cavity, scrambling his brains, but not the second one.

✣ 17 ✥

T anaka was fast asleep in the house Ray Mitchell had allocated to him in the mini Versailles-style hamlet of nineteen others that nestled to the rear of the chateau. Discreet security lights glowed throughout the enclosed landscaped site, the cameras monitored on a twenty-four-hour basis by a crew located in the administration block some distance away.

It was two eighteen and Tanaka was in a very deep sleep. It was the third ring before he lifted the handset of the direct line beside his bed. The neon glow of the clock radio alarm blinked at him. 02:18, 8:18 p.m. in New York; there was only one possible caller on this line.

"Mr. Tanaka?"

"Speaking," Tanaka replied, suddenly wide-awake.

"Catherine Bentley here, calling from New York. I think we have a deal."

"You think?"

"I told Mr. Kennedy that the bid was provisional upon your agreement. His asking price is, in my opinion, too high. I know my instructions were to buy them, but I'm confident that if you were to cool off at this juncture, I could renegotiate at a lower price later. Even on the open market, which, granted, is very strong at the moment, I would expect to pay less—including the buyer's premium."

"What was the price you agreed upon?" Tanaka asked with a curt tone.

"One hundred and fifty million dollars." Tanaka made no comment, and Catherine Bentley continued, "Kennedy asked me one seventy-five initially, which I felt was absolutely ludicrous. My counter offer was one hundred, which was more than I would want to open with, but—"

Tanaka didn't allow her to finish. "That's fine, Ms. Bentley. You can assure Mr. Kennedy that one fifty is acceptable to me, and that we do indeed have a deal. You can proceed to make the necessary further arrangements to take possession of the paintings. Please continue to keep me informed."

Once she was off the line, he swiveled out of bed, pulled on his bathrobe and speed-dialed Ray Mitchell's cellphone.

It was answered immediately, the line loud and crystal clear.

"Mr. Mitchell, Tanaka here. I've just heard from Bentley in New York."

"Good! What did she say?"

"The deal is done at one hundred and fifty. She is confirming with Kennedy tomorrow and will be getting back to me with further details at that time."

"Good job, Taiki. Just keep me up to date with all develop-ments, no matter when you hear."

Ray Mitchell ended the call and rolled out of bed. He pulled on his heavy dressing gown and made his way to his office, where he sat down at his computer and composed an email:

Good news. The deal appears to be done for one fifty. No further arrangements have been made regarding delivery, payment, etc. yet, but I can't foresee any problems. I'll keep you apprised regarding developments. Keep in touch in the event of any difficulties or hiccups arising on your end.

Love, R.

❧ 18 ❧

Not long after eight o'clock in the morning, Adam's phone was ringing. It was Liz Hastings, her voice bearing no hint of yesterday's aggression. She sounded normal, almost friendly, in a business-like sort of way.

"Adam, sorry to call you so early at home, but I wanted to make sure of catching you."

"That's okay; what can I do for you?"

"I was thinking of what you mentioned yesterday . . . you know, Jack's paintings . . . well, I suppose we should check what there are, compose an inventory."

What's going on? Adam thought. Where has all the mother-hen belligerence of yesterday gone? He knew she was unpredictable, so he was determined not to relax his guard too much just because she addressed him by his first name. Okay, they were having a more civilized conversation, but prudence dictated caution; wait to see what her true agenda might be.

"Certainly, "he replied. "I have several on display in the gallery. On top of that, there are maybe another dozen in the storeroom at the back. They are all documented. I'll organize a copy inventory for you, and you can come view them whenever you wish."

"Good. What about any others?"

"There should be a substantial number at the studio . . . where he was found."

"How many do you think? A ballpark figure?"

"Maybe thirty . . . maybe a little more. You'd need to check it out."

"Well, the forensic people have finished with it. We can have a look whenever suits you."

Astonishing; she was being as good as her word and obviously content to allow him to continue to handle Jack's work. "Fine, how does around two tomorrow afternoon sound?"

"Perfect. I'll see you inside, so try not to be late; it might be a bit spooky for me on my own."

Her vulnerability made Adam relax, reminding him of the girl he had known all those years ago. "Don't worry," he assured her. "I'll be there on time."

She even said goodbye by politely thanking him. Maybe he had been too inconsiderate in his attitude to her lately. After all, she had just been through a hell of a stressful time and, to be realistic, no one could criticize her for her reaction to her daughter's apparent involvement with a much older man like himself. Suddenly, the only reason he wasn't looking forward to tomorrow's studio visit was because it was where Jack had died so bizarrely.

Leaving the apartment, Adam headed for the gallery which he shared with another dealer, Robin Brew. He and Robin had a symbiotic business relationship. As well as sharing the space, Robin managed the day-to-day running of the business, displaying work by his own stable of artists while at the same time handling sales for any of Adam's artists' works. This allowed Adam to devote time to his other dealings, mainly aiding the bishop in the examination, appraisal and disposal of Church bequests.

As Adam pushed open the tall glass doors to the sound of a discreet three-bar chime, Robin looked up from the pages of the morning newspaper he was reading. Immediately, Adam could see that the other's pleasure at seeing him was modified by a slight expression of annoyance on his face. Ignoring it, Adam asked, "Morning, Robin. Anything new?"

"Well, if there was anything new, I certainly wouldn't have heard it from you. I don't know why you bother to have an answering machine at home at all—or a cellphone. You never return my calls on the former, and the latter is always turned off!"

Robin was English. Taller and slightly older than Adam, his lean, angular physique gave him the unfortunate appearance of a wading bird in tweeds. Though friends, they were civilizations apart in attitude and personal style. Robin smoked a vintage Peterson briar pipe with a Sherlock Holmes-type bend to it, though, by agreement, never in the gallery. Even so, in moments of relaxation he dry-sucked on it, to Adam's annoyance, and he always reeked of aromatic pipe tobacco. However, they amused each other, as Robin possessed not only an iconoclastic sense of humor, but an obsession with gossip and an alternative sexual bent.

"Sorry, Robin," Adam apologized. "I've been having one hell of a time recently."

Robin took Adam by the shoulders and steered him to one of the blond wood desk chairs. "Spare me no details," he said, pressing him down into a seat and sitting down at the chair opposite him.

Adam gave him an edited version of his time since having lunch with Zannah to his interview with Rooney, telling him some of what he knew about the murder but excluding any reference to the Picassos.

Robin nodded. "Normally, as in Jack's case, death can be quite a good career move for any artist, but poor Zannah, while she may have had the body, she just didn't have the body of work behind her to capitalize on it."

Adam shook his head and narrowed his eyes. "What an awful thing to say!" He remained quiet for a moment, adding with a reluctant smile, "But I suppose you're right."

"Of course I'm right. We've had a lot of interest in Jack's paintings since he passed. Just this morning we had a couple in who took some digital shots of the ones on display. They were very enthusiastic. I'm sure we'll be hearing from them again."

Adam flicked through his unopened mail on the desk.

"Oh, I almost forgot," Robin said with a smile. "Jack's daughter, Sarah, called, looking for you."

"What did she say?" Adam replied as he scanned bills and circulars.

"Just wanted to know if I was expecting you today. Said she's been trying to contact you." Adam didn't look up so Robin continued, "She's turned out such a lovely girl, don't you think? Not a bit like her father though—lucky her."

Adam paused before answering in an off-hand tone, "All the same, I think she'd be a bit young for you."

"Her age would be the least of it," Robin replied. "What about the funeral arrangements for Zannah? Have you heard?"

"Yes, her brother—her folks are already gone—is arranging for the remains to be removed upstate for burial in her home town once the body is released. From what I'm told, she and her brother were estranged. He didn't approve of her lifestyle or friends. Not a bad judge, I'd say. He is insisting on a private burial with family only, and no flowers." Adam scrunched up the empty envelopes and junk mail and threw them into the wastepaper bin. "It's a relief in a way. I hate funerals, and two a week apart would be too much for me."

"Oh, I don't know," said Robin, now leaning back and sucking on his unlit pipe. "Sacramentally, it celebrates entering a stage of existence that is at least more enduring than a christening or a wedding, since generally the subject never changes his or her mind. And taking account of that aspect alone, I'm inclined to pay them a regard that I cannot allow for the other two."

Robin's comments barely registered with Adam. Their attitudes were more out of synch today than usual.

His cellphone rang. It was Catherine Bentley.

"Adam, I'm pleased to say we have a deal."

Adam stood up from the desk and moved out of Robin's

earshot. "That's excellent, thank you," he replied, trying hard to put an enthusiasm he didn't feel into his voice.

"When would suit you to meet to go over the fine details and make the arrangements to finalize the transaction?" she asked.

"As soon as you wish. The bishop is in town at the moment, and, as you know, is the primary representative of the vendor, so I'm sure he'll wish to be personally involved."

"Of course," she replied. "I can organize a conference room at my hotel. If that suits you both, we can wrap things up here."

"That's fine. The bishop is expecting my call, so this afternoon should do."

"Good," Catherine Bentley said. "We'll say around three o'clock then?"

Adam phoned the bishop and was relating the arrangement to him when Sarah Hastings walked into the gallery.

Robin greeted her effusively. "Sarah, so nice to see you! Can I fetch you a genuine, no holds barred, fully caffeinated coffee?" He guided her toward an upholstered chair to the side of the desk.

"No thanks, Robin, I've just stopped by to have a word with Adam." She turned to Adam as he ended his call. "I've been trying to contact you all morning."

"Yes, Robin told me you phoned earlier. My cellphone was turned off until a short time ago."

"And no voicemail?"

"Sorry, I find it such a nuisance that I've had it turned off. I work on the old-fashioned assumption that if anyone wants me that badly, they'll call back."

Robin interrupted, "Adam, since you're here at the moment, I'll just nip out on a little errand. I'll only be thirty minutes. That okay?"

"Sure. The bishop's meeting me here about two thirty anyway, so you're fine until then."

As Robin left the gallery, Sarah leaned toward Adam and said, "With my mom coming back so quickly yesterday, I didn't get a chance to fully explain about your friend, Joe Rooney."

"What about him?"

"I told you he suggested that I should give a DNA sample."

"Yes."

"Well, I did."

"When?" Adam asked.

"Yesterday. He said he would take it himself and have it processed confidentially, so he went off and got the testing kit and took it there in the apartment. It wasn't a big deal, just a few swabs inside my mouth, from my cheek lining."

Strange, Adam thought. Rooney hadn't mentioned to him that he had already taken a sample from her—Joe Rooney was up to something. He must have some other lead that he is simply not sharing.

"And there's still nothing new on her murder?" she asked him. Adam shook his head. "Adam, I want to apologize for being such a bitch about Zannah. I know it was totally unjustified at the time, and it seems so much worse now that she's dead." She paused, but Adam could see there was more to come. "I suppose she just represented a part of my dad's life that I'd never been a part of, and I resented her because of it. He was dead and she was still alive—I suppose, seeing her at the cremation, she became the convenient scapegoat for all my distress."

She paused for a moment before adding with a little smile, "Then, when she phoned you first thing the next morning, when I was there . . . well, maybe there was a little tinge of jealousy to add to the mix."

Adam found himself softening to her again. She was young, vulnerable, and confused, and after all, she had discovered her own father dead in the most harrowing of circumstances. He took her hand and looked deep into her brown eyes. "Don't worry, Sarah, it's been one hell of a week for us all, but especially for you."

"Yes," she said, "particularly as I've had to live with my mother. However, I've spoken to my grandmother in Florida, and so from today I'm house sitting for her until she comes back up in a couple of months."

Adam had never been in Sarah's grandmother's house, but he knew it—a large, late nineteenth-century, beaux-arts mansion on one of the east sixties, buffering Central Park. "A big place for you to rattle around in on your own," he said.

"You're more than welcome to move in to protect me if you like," she joked.

"I think Liz would be somewhat less than enthusiastic on that one," Adam replied with a smile.

Sarah lifted an eyebrow. "I don't know why you're so sensitive as far as she's concerned," she said. "At least feel free to drop by for a welcome drink . . . anytime."

"Thanks, maybe I will," he said.

As they chatted, Adam's mood lightened further. He was flirting, he realized, and enjoying it. This was better. Put the negatives behind; there was no point in worrying about events that you couldn't influence.

Robin, as promised, returned in thirty minutes, and from the smile on his face, he seemed pleased to see that Sarah was still there.

"Why don't you two go and have lunch together?" he suggested. Sarah agreed that it was an excellent idea.

Adam checked his watch. "Thanks, Robin. I'm meeting the bishop here at two thirty, so I'll be back by two fifteen at the latest."

Buttoned up well against the cold, Adam took hold of Sarah's hand and they hurried off into the street.

§

Adam and the bishop arrived promptly at Catherine Bentley's hotel, where they were ushered into a small, blandly furnished, conference room in the inoffensive fin de twentieth century style. Coffee and refreshments were provided before the three were left alone.

"Well, gentlemen," she said, "Now that we have reached an

agreement, I would like, first of all, to establish the exact where-
abouts of the paintings, as obviously, I will need to view them
personally. My principal, Mr. Tanaka, will expect it."

This was the first time either Adam or the bishop had heard
the name of the prospective purchaser. It was a name neither of
them was familiar with.

"Certainly, Catherine," the bishop said. "They should be
arriving in New York this afternoon. If you wish, I will make the
necessary arrangements and accompany you to inspect them sometime later this evening? You can arrange to take charge of them
from there on."

"Fine." Catherine nodded in agreement, taking notes as she
spoke, "I'll arrange for our people to take possession of them
tomorrow morning, in that case."

The bishop continued in a casual tone, "The name "Tanaka" is
not one I've come across before in relation to the fine arts."

"Perhaps not, bishop, but he represents TC-SPEED, the multi-
national mail and freight delivery service I'm sure you've heard of.
And though possibly a newcomer to the world of fine art collecting
at this level, they certainly have the assets to underwrite such a
bid."

"No, no," the bishop assured her, "I'm not suggesting for a
moment that this is an eccentric or frivolous offer; I'm just
surprised, that's all. Indeed, it's good to see such an injection of
new interest. After all, most of these computer billionaires are
unknowns to me as well."

Mollified, she embarked upon the other details. "Have your
clients made any decisions on how they wish the funds to be
deployed?"

The bishop removed a long yellow envelope from his inside
coat pocket. "Yes, the specific account details are all in there. Fifty
percent of the agreed amount should be lodged to my client's
account in the British Virgin Islands; thirty percent to the second
named account in Geneva, and the final twenty percent to the
numbered account, also in Geneva."

Catherine Bentley perused the document and made some further notes of her own as the bishop spoke. Then she said, "An escrow account will be established in the Virgin Islands tomorrow morning for the fifty percent. The remaining funds can be directed to their destinations confidentially once the deal is finalized and the paintings are safely in our possession. Is that agreeable to you?"

The bishop nodded assent as Adam asked, "Where are they bound for? Japan?"

"No, France. The company headquarters are situated just outside Paris. Once they arrive, we shall have them quickly authenticated and the financial aspects can be finalized."

Adam glanced at the bishop, who was displaying no concern, whereas he felt himself grow uneasy at the mention of authentication. He was being silly—of course there had to be some lip service paid to inspecting them. It was not unusual, and from what he had seen with his own eyes in Jack Hastings's New Jersey hideaway, the chances were that he had already had hundreds, if not more, fakes pass through his hands that had passed such cursory "expert" inspections. Not one of them had ever been questioned. I'm screwed up about this only because I now know the truth, he assured himself.

"In which case, we shall make arrangements to fly to Paris, say Thursday, the day after tomorrow, on the Air France Concorde, if that suits?" the bishop said.

"That should be perfect," she said and made another entry in her notebook. "I'll arrange to have you collected at Charles DeGaulle airport and brought to the company headquarters, in that case."

"Thank you," said the bishop, "and I'll pick you up here at your hotel this evening and accompany you to view the paintings."

"Perfect, gentlemen," she replied, folding her notes and standing up. They all shook hands before departing.

On the way back in the cab, Adam voiced his fears. "You don't seem to be too worried about this authentication, Phil."

"Relax, Adam," he advised. "It's just that, for the very first time, you know the whole story. Everything is fine. The canvases, the paints, the stretchers, the frames, the glue—even the very nails are of the period. They are foolproof, perfect. Jack, I assure you, was the best, a genius. Don't worry. Let's just make our reservations, pack our bags, and pick up our millions."

Adam wished he had the bishop's confidence.

§

After leaving the bishop, Adam decided to accept Sarah's earlier invitation to call at her new quarters. As well as allowing him to continue where his interrupted lunch had left off, it would also provide a break from obsessing about future problems. He didn't call ahead; he just purchased a bottle of wine and hailed a cab.

As Sarah opened the front door to him, he could see by her surprised but welcoming smile that she was delighted to see him.

"Just stopped by with a small house-warming present," he said, pressing the tissue-wrapped bottle into her hands.

She kissed him on the cheek.

"Thank you. How did your meeting go?"

She hadn't been made aware of any of the details, just that it was a very important deal.

"Excellently, I think. Phil and I go to Paris the day after tomorrow to finalize things."

"Lucky you," Sarah said as she linked his arm in hers and led him along the large ground-floor hallway toward the rear of the house and into a traditionally furnished living room, where a real fire crackled its warmth from a guarded open fireplace. She pointed to an overstuffed Victorian Chesterfield settee and said, "Make yourself at home. I'll find some glasses."

Moments later she returned, wine glasses in hand but with a look of mild consternation on her face.

"Can't seem to find a corkscrew. This house is just too damn big to know where everything is."

"Have no fear, 'The Waiter's Friend' is here," Adam rhymed, producing a small ivory-handled knife/corkscrew/bottle cap opener. He reached for the bottle.

"No, let me, you're the guest," she said with a laugh.

Opening the small serrated silver blade, Sarah sliced around the foil top, then levered out the corkscrew.

"Very handy little item, this," she said as she screwed it in.

Adam smiled. "Please treasure it forever as a gift from me."

"Thank you very much. Do all alcoholics carry these?" she said, teasing him and easing the cork out of the bottleneck with a soft pop. Lifting a small cushion from the settee, he threw it at her.

There was little hesitation and no embarrassment. By the time the bottle was empty, they were on the couch, hot, naked, and clasped in each other's arms. On a few occasions during their love-making, Adam had experienced pangs of guilt. She was a lot younger than he was. Probably most folk he knew would look askance at him. They'd see it as taking sexual advantage of someone not much more than half his age. But most of the time, passion dulled the age gap. She had something different, something he liked, and something, let's face it, he more than liked. And more importantly, it seemed that his feelings were reciprocated.

Certainly, she was a beautiful girl and he did desire her. He thought back to the pangs of lust he had felt for Zannah, both after the cremation when he had slipped his hand around her waist, and later as she had nestled against him in the restaurant on Sunday before she ran off—and those occasions did not compare to this. This seemed like something more, and he knew it contained all the elements to cause problems.

But for the moment, he simply relaxed and enjoyed these moments clasped together with her in front of the still-glowing embers. Lifting her wine glass from the floor, he handed it to her and they toasted each other.

"Will you stay tonight?" she whispered into his ear. Adam found himself wanting to say "Yes"; he found himself wanting to just move in and stay with her tonight, the next night, and the night after. However, he knew that acting upon such an impulse was invariably a bad idea, and in this case, with the extra complications of the age gap and her mother's attitude, it seemed an even worse plan. Feeling a surge of guilt, he decided that it was time to backpedal a bit. Sneaking a look at his watch, he saw it was past nine o'clock already.

"I'd love to," he told her, "but I'm sorry, I can't. I have a few things to sort out back at the apartment, and I must organize my packing as our flight leaves early on Thursday morning."

She looked disappointed, and he did his best to kiss the look away. Standing up, he began to dress while Sarah merely slipped the blouse she had been wearing over her shoulders and sat back on the couch regarding him.

"So, will I see you tomorrow?" she asked.

"Absolutely," he assured her, tucking in his shirt and tightening his belt. "I'll call you in the morning once I've organized my day, and we'll take it from there."

She nodded, smiled, and pulled her knees up onto the couch.

Leaning over, he kissed her on the forehead. "Thanks for a lovely evening."

She lifted her half-empty wine glass off the floor once again, held it up toward him and said, "Here's to many more."

Adam bent down and lifted his. "To many more," he replied.

Their glasses clinked, and they drank together, the wine smooth, warm and fragrant in his mouth.

Despite himself, he found his hand slipping up under her blouse and molding the hot weight of her breast into his palm. They kissed, allowing the wine to flood each other's mouths like a sacrament. He felt the desire building in him again, but the small remaining sensible bit of him knew what he had to do.

"Must make a move," he said, dragging himself away from her and pulling on his jacket. Standing up, she took his hand as they began to walk toward the door.

As she giggled to herself, Adam looked at her, eyebrows raised.

"I'm just thinking how pissed my mother will be." she giggled.

Adam reacted without thinking. "What d'you mean? You're not going to tell Liz I was here?"

"Of course I am," she said. "Simply because I'm back here in New York, she can't be allowed to think that she can just run my life. I'll see anyone I want, whenever I want to, irrespective of creed, color—or extreme old age." She smiled.

"Hold on, Sarah." Adam felt uneasy at this prospect. Was he simply intimidated by Liz, or was it something else? "Let's not rock too many boats in the one week. She'll be less than happy with you moving out of her apartment and moving in here. Let her settle down first and get used to the idea before you hit her with another bombshell."

"No, I think she quite liked the idea of getting her own space back. But if it makes you happier, I'll say nothing to her in the meantime," she said. "Apart from your advanced years, what's she got against you anyway?" she added with a smile.

"Beats me. I must've upset her sometime in the past. You know her, and you know that's not hard to do."

"I'll work on her over the coming weeks," Sarah said with a grin, "explain just what a wonderful lover you are and things like that."

The look of horror on Adam's face made her laugh out loud. She tousled his hair as she said, "I'm only joking, you big dope!"

Adam shivered inside as he forced a smile.

Suddenly, they both heard the locks in the front door turning, the scraping on the sill as it was pushed open, and then closing with a reverberating slam.

"Christ, it's her. She's got keys for everywhere. She'll know I'm at home as the security alarm's not on!" Sarah said, then whispered in his ear, "Stay here. I'll run up the back stairs and call her from above. You can slip out when she joins me."

Pecking him farewell on the cheek, she bundled her clothes in her arms and disappeared further into the building.

He heard Liz's voice calling from the direction of the entrance hall. "Sarah, where are you?"

Seconds later, Sarah answered, "I'm upstairs, come on up. I was just about to take a shower."

Adam waited until he could no longer hear Liz's footfalls, then he crept out into the entrance hall, and with relief, escaped into the night.

🐝 19 🐝

I t was very early, and Joe Rooney sat alone and thoughtful at
his office desk. He had just finished speaking with his old
friend and sometime fellow card-playing buddy of twenty
years, Patrick Ward, the forensic pathologist. As a favor, Ward had
pulled strings to have the DNA samples processed for him in
record time.

Amazing, Joe thought, how things progress. This type of
genetic fingerprinting was becoming so routine you just take it for
granted, the way you take driving or taking a cab for granted,
without knowing anything beyond the fundamental principles
behind the workings of the internal combustion engine.

Ward had informed him that all the results were now through,
though Joe had arranged for only one to be recorded. Adam, as he
had hoped, was not the father. The others confirmed his recent
suspicions.

The investigation into Zannah's murder was stalled. No one
had witnessed anything or anyone unusual that evening, and now
that Adam was eliminated from any more intimate link with her,
there wasn't even that long shot to go on. Maybe she had just met
the wrong guy wherever she had been earlier that night. She

wouldn't have been the first. The body was being released to her brother this afternoon, and he was taking her home.

Rooney's partner, Carl Lummus, arrived, and hanging his jacket over the back of a chair, he pulled it up and sat down opposite him.

"Joe, it's a beautiful crisp, clear, dry morning outside. You're still the right side of fifty-five. So why do you look like shit?"

"More than two days since my last nicotine hit might have something to do with it." he said.

"Oh, withdrawal symptoms. Good for you!" He paused and then asked, "Apart from that, you're okay?"

Joe assured him he was as Carl pulled a pile of paperwork toward him and started to sort through it.

But he wasn't okay. It had been stupid to try to kick this habit with all this other shit going on, and on top of that, the heartburn seems to have worsened since then. Just got to deal with it one day at a time, he thought. He picked up the telephone handset and dialed Adam as he had promised he would. It was answered on the second ring.

"Sorry, you still in bed . . . did I wake you?" He checked his wristwatch; it was just after eight thirty.

"No, I'm just about to have breakfast; I have a few things to sort out today," Adam answered. "Tomorrow I have to fly to Paris with Phil."

"Hate those long flights. And the jet lag."

"We're flying Air France supersonic on the Concorde. New York to Paris in less than four hours, so jet lag shouldn't be too much of a problem. Have you a result from the test already?"

"Yep. As you said, it's not you."

"Good, otherwise it would have been a sort of male parthenogenesis—you know, a reverse virgin birth."

"Some virgins—either of you," Joe said.

"Anything new turned up yet?"

"No, nothing. Everyone in her building's been interviewed, but still zilch." He paused. "How long d'you think you'll be away?"

"Not long, maybe only a day or two."

"Long trip for such a short time."

"Yeah, well it's a very big deal. Clients of Phil's are interested in selling some important paintings from their collection, and we are handling the negotiations."

"In that case, good luck and have a safe trip. Get in touch when you get back."

The next call Joe had to make was a shade more delicate. He decided against calling Liz Hastings's apartment at this hour. He would have to leave it for a while. He and Carl decided to go out for breakfast.

Arriving back in the office shortly before ten, he dialed the Hastings home and Liz answered.

"Hello, Joe Rooney here. Could I speak to Sarah?"

There was a longer than expected silence before she said, "She's not here at the moment, can I give her your message?"

"Yes, tell her I called and ask her to contact me, either at the office or home, it doesn't matter. She's got both numbers."

"Is this about the test? I take it she's been eliminated from your inquiries then?"

Joe paused; he had really wanted to give Sarah the news himself, one to one. Sarah was an adult, and even though Liz was her mother, she no longer had an automatic right to know. But he felt the force of her personality down the line, and this was no ordinary case.

"Well, let's put it like this: the results are back, and as far as the tissue sampling is concerned, she's in the clear."

Liz ignored his veiled implication and her tone became more assertive. "It was a ridiculous assumption in the first place."

"Maybe, but at least she's ruled out as far as forensic matters are concerned. And you've gotta admit, the whole procedure was low-key and painless. Don't forget, I've been doing my best for all concerned here."

"Hmm, yes. Well, I'll give her your message," she said, then after a pause added, "Thank you."

If that woman were ugly she would have no friends, Joe thought.

§

It was the afternoon before Sarah returned Joe's call. He was preparing to leave the office.

"Mister Rooney, Sarah Hastings here. My mother told me you phoned."

"Hi, Sarah!" He sounded upbeat. "And drop the Mister, it's Joe. I'm sure your mother told you the test result?"

"Yes, Joe, though if it had proved a match it would've been a mystery. I've never even been in her apartment. Oh, and thanks for your concern and help. I realize I've been receiving privileged treatment."

The other desk phone started to ring, Carl Lummus left the report he was working on and answered it.

Rooney continued to Sarah, "My pleasure. Tell me, if you're doing nothing this evening, what d'you say about joining me for a bite to eat?"

The hesitation was slight but he noticed it, then she replied, "No, sorry, tonight isn't good for me."

Joe immediately thought of Adam and felt a confusion of emotions.

"Though I am free tomorrow evening, if that would suit?" she added.

"Perfect; is Italian okay?" he said, his face breaking into a smile.

"But," she continued, "I do have one condition."

"What's that?"

"That it's my treat," she said, "just to say thanks for everything you've done for me."

Joe hesitated for a moment. "Deal," he said.

Carl Lummus finished his call and note-taking as Joe swung round in his desk chair to face him again.

"Strange thing there, Joe," Carl said, indicating the phone with a nod. "The call was passed through to us by one of the guys on the desk who knows you. He recognized a name and felt we might be able to help."

"Yeah, who was the call from?"

"New Jersey Homicide; a detective called Stanley Morgan."

"Don't know him. What did he want?"

"Looking for a bit of assistance. Wants to know if we could follow up something for him."

Rooney sighed. "As if we don't have enough to do."

"I think you'll be interested in this. They found a Caucasian guy with a couple of rounds in his head in a supermarket parking lot early yesterday morning. Estimated time of death was between eight and eleven the night before.

"He's proving hard to identify. His driver's license and all his other pieces of ID are fake. His credit card, in the name of Snow, is one that has been primed with a couple of thousand dollars—it's in the same name as his fake license, which enabled him to rent a car. And his cellphone is one of those pre-pay burners that you don't need to pass a credit check for. They're running his prints, but no results so far."

"What's it got to do with us?"

"Maybe nothing, but the one thing they have to go on so far is the phone. Turned out it was brand new and only one outgoing call was made on it." Carl paused. "The call was to your friend, Bishop Connor. It was made to his unlisted home number late on Monday afternoon, which was only a matter of hours before this guy was killed, and it lasted for nearly a minute."

Rooney looked puzzled. "Were there any incoming calls?"

"Only one of those as well. Made later on Monday evening from a downtown pay phone; that call lasted a bit longer. Anyway, he's sending copies of everything they've got over for us to have a look at."

"I'll check it out. I'll have a word with the bishop later," Rooney said.

Carl left the office but Rooney remained at his desk. He felt like shit. Despite what he'd told Carl, the lack of nicotine wasn't the problem. In fact, it wasn't linked to anything physical at all. Despite all his prior suspicions, the confidential information he had received this morning wasn't proving that easy for him to come to terms with. It had changed his life as well as his attitude toward a lot of the people around him. Fuck it, he decided. He had to stop behaving like a teenage girl suffering from PMS. He had to snap out of it and stop obsessing about his own personal agenda.

Poor Zannah's case still hung without a single solid lead. He had to apply himself. This guy, Snow—he was killed the next night. But people die violently each and every day—though not too many of them would have had recent personal contact with the bishop. These two had. There was no option: he was going to have to pay him a visit. To keep it informal, he decided to phone ahead. He lifted the handset and dialed the bishop's number from memory.

§

Rooney was surprised when the bishop himself answered the door.

"What! You've given André a day off?" he said with a smile as the bishop stood aside to let him enter. "Could be the thin end of the wedge. Next thing you know, he'll be joining a union."

"No, it's just that I'm in the middle of some negotiations at the moment involving a few paintings, and there are always so many other demands on my time," the bishop answered with a laugh. "As a result, I've had to delegate a few jobs to André. I sent him up to Boston to handle some charity business while I was in Florida, and from there he's headed down to Africa for a week or so to try to sort out a few problems we've been having there."

"Lucky André, escaping from this weather."

"That's one thing he never complains about. After all those years spent in arid conditions, I think he quite likes the rain and cold," the bishop said, beckoning him inside, adding, "Will you join me in a beer, Joe, or would you prefer a coffee?"

"Thanks, Phil, a beer sounds fine."

Joe took off his topcoat and made himself comfortable on the couch as the bishop returned with the beers. He sat down opposite him and indicated the thin, soft leather document case lying beside Joe on the couch.

"You here on business?" he asked, while raising his glass in a toast. "*Sláinte.*"

"*Sláinte.*" Joe responded with a smile and took a sip. The Irish toast, meaning "Good Health", was the name the bishop had aptly called his charity all those years ago, and it was a bit of a private joke.

"In a way," he continued. "I'm a bit hung up on this Zannah Koller case, so I thought I'd just call by in case you might have some insight that I'm missing. If I hadn't known her, it would be a different ball game. But I did, and well, it's really getting to me."

He unzipped the case and began fingering through the folders inside.

"Yes, it has affected us all," Phil said, "I believe she was badly disfigured?"

"An understatement," Joe replied and handed a buff-colored folder over to him. "Take a look for yourself."

Phil put on his wire-rimmed spectacles and hesitated before opening the folder. Then, with reverential deliberation, he removed the crime scene photographs, one by one. As he finished examining each one, he laid them out in a tile pattern on the low table between them. Some were overall shots of the room from a selection of different angles, and some were shots of blood spatters, but most were of Zannah, or what had once been Zannah.

For a long time, he sat and stared, saying nothing, doing nothing, just breathing deeply. At last he spoke, "They're in color? I thought they'd be black and white."

"It's nineteen ninety-nine, Phil. We even take videos—though sometimes we can still do sketches if that makes you feel any better," Joe replied, recognizing the bishop's comment as nothing more than a shock reaction at the horror of the scene.

Zannah was seated dead, wide-eyed, and naked in a cream colored, upholstered easy chair, head held tilted back. This was one piece of the three-piece lounge suite that could be seen in some of the other photographs. Except the chair was no longer cream. Now it looked more like the hide of a Friesian cow, black in parts from the soaked-in dried blood that had flowed from her wounds. It was only by looking closely at the photograph that it was possible to see what had bound her in place during the mutilation.

She had been wrapped like a chrysalis with commercial Saran Wrap, the six-inch wide version of the commonly used kitchen film for sealing opened foodstuffs. It had completely encased the chair and her naked body, from her forehead to her feet; a transparent cocoon that held her immovable, trapped and powerless. She was so overwrapped that the cuts which had been inflicted upon her through the plastic had not lessened its ability to hold her in place. Her nose and mouth were slightly vented, which had allowed her to breathe, maybe speak, but not much more.

Each sliced wound, compressed by the transparent plastic, puckered out like a pair of painted lips, decorating her corpse like a peacock's fan, except with mouths instead of eyes. From her thighs upward she had been cruelly cut, the blood running off the plastic onto the chair or dripping further down onto the floor, leaving the wounds looking clean and raw. The biggest slashed mouth of all gaped beneath her upward pointing chin. The final cut.

"My God, Joe! How could someone do something like this?"

"That's the human race for you, Phil," he answered with a shrug. "Though I'm more interested in *why* they would do something like this."

The bishop shook his head from side to side as he laid the last of the photographs down. "Sadism?" he ventured.

"That's certainly a possibility, though if it is, it's the first time he's done it like this around here. I think I'd recognize that signature if I'd ever seen it before. But it was certainly done by someone who enjoyed their work."

The bishop shifted his gaze to the floor, still shaking his head.

"We're examining all the possibilities, of course," Joe said as he started to gather up the photographs, "but to me it looks like torture."

"Oh, good God, she certainly has been tortured."

"I mean tortured for a reason, Phil, not just for fun. Tortured to reveal something—maybe information, maybe money. Who knows what? Maybe she was even tortured for having revealed something to the wrong person, or the authorities. You have any ideas on that?"

The bishop appeared to reflect on Joe's words. He swallowed the last of his beer.

He shook his head. "It's hard to imagine what poor Zannah would have had that would have driven anyone to such extremes," he said.

"Yes, that's the problem. She had no spare money to speak of, and as far as we can establish, she wasn't a known associate of any of the major drug players."

"Drugs? She wouldn't have been into drugs, not the hard stuff anyway."

"Well, it's the biggest illegal industry on the globe, and these days a lot of people are dying of it one way or the other. She wouldn't be the first," Joe replied. He downed the last of his beer. "Must take a leak."

He stood up and made his way into the bathroom.

As he stood urinating into the toilet bowl, his eyes scanned around the room. Finishing, he turned the hot water on and washed and dried his hands. He let it continue to run as he lifted the hair-brush that sat beside the sink, and taking a plastic comb from his inside pocket, he ran it through the brush. He removed a few small paper envelopes from another pocket, selected one, put the tangle from the comb inside, and sealed it. Then, opening the mirrored door bathroom cabinet directly in front of his face, he removed the bishop's wet razor. It was one of the new modern multi-bladed ones, just like his own, which gives an extremely close shave. He lifted it and the integral holder that it rested on and turned it over. Yes, there were spare blades in the back. He popped the blade that was currently in use into another of the envelopes and, turning the pack over, clicked a new replacement blade onto the shaft.

He put the envelopes into his pocket, turned off the running water, and went back out.

Joe lifted his beer and drained the glass without sitting down. "I was speaking to Adam this morning; he tells me you are both off to France soon."

"Yes, all part of this deal I'm doing at the moment on behalf of vendors down south. I'll be glad when it's over."

Joe bent over and picked up his case. "Have a good trip, and thanks for your time, Phil."

"Sorry I haven't been able to shed any new light on it, Joe," Phil said as he walked beside him out to his vehicle, "but it was good to see you anyway. Let me know if there's any breakthrough in the investigation."

"Sure, Phil," he said as he slid in behind the wheel. Then, as if an afterthought, he looked up at the bishop. "Do you know a guy named Snow?"

"Snow?" Phil pursed his lips and looked up as if checking for his details on some celestial Rolodex. "No, I don't think so. Should I?"

"Well, he's been found dead, and either he made a call, or someone used his cellphone to call your unlisted home number on Monday afternoon, the day he died."

Phil looked perplexed. "These last few days have been such a blur, with the traveling, the negotiations, and, of course, Zannah's murder. I just can't think of any such call."

"Maybe André took it," Joe suggested.

"No, André was in Boston on Monday. In fact, he phoned me from there after I got home from the airport. Maybe whoever it was got through to my machine and I missed the message somehow—or it accidentally got wiped." He paused, and murmured half to himself, "Dead . . . dreadful."

"Of course, Phil, there's a possibility "Snow" was an alias. Maybe he used another name with you?"

"Hmm, maybe, but at the moment I can't think of any stranger who phoned on Monday."

"But maybe he wasn't a stranger. Maybe you knew him as someone else. Tell you what, when I get a shot of him you can give it the once-over—see if it rings any bells, okay?"

Phil looked unenthusiastic. "I suppose so—can't say I'm looking forward to looking at another corpse though."

"Nothing you haven't seen before, Phil. I'll be in touch when you get back from Europe," he said as he fired up the engine. "Thanks for the beer."

Joe waved goodbye as he drove out of the grounds and back into the afternoon city traffic. Shouldn't have had that beer, he thought, grabbing a Rolaid in an attempt to calm his rising indigestion. Probably going to have to cut that out as well! One thing was pretty likely, though: Phil knew who Snow was . . . but was Snow's death somehow connected to Zannah?

He drove straight to see his old friend, Patrick Ward, the pathologist. It was time for another favor.

✣ 20 ✣

A dam's relief at having escaped Liz Hastings's notice at Sarah's grandmother's home had already evaporated by the time he reached his own apartment. Sarah's insistence on her own independent line with her mother had made him uncomfortable, and it bothered him as he went through the motions of preparing his overnight bag for the Paris trip.

At any other time, he thought, he would be more able to deal with her; but now, in the middle of all these recent disasters and potential problems, a confrontation with Liz Hastings was something he could live without. He poured vodka over ice and was topping off the already misting glass with tonic when the phone began to ring. He answered it with the misgivings of a guilty child who hadn't actually been found out, but feared he might.

"Adam?" It was Sarah's voice.

"Hi, Sarah," he replied, "any problems . . . has she left?"

"Yes, about five minutes ago."

"I assume she didn't see me or suspect anything?"

"No," Sarah said, "But you shouldn't pay any attention to her ravings. She can't tell me how to live my life anymore, and she sure as hell has no right to try to influence you."

Adam sat down and took a gulp of his drink. "Yes, Sarah. I

know you're right, but I just don't want to be the cause of any bad feelings at this delicate time. The strain of these deaths has been telling on everyone, and you mustn't forget that, in the short term at least, I have to continue to do business with your mother."

"How do you mean, '. . . do business with her'?" Sarah asked.

"As your father's widow, she has control of his estate, which includes his remaining body of work, and as his agent, I'm in possession of a great many of them. So I'll need to be able to interact with her on a regular basis without any bad feeling. In fact, I have to meet her tomorrow at the studio to establish exactly what there is and draw up an inventory."

"Oh!" she said, "In which case I'll come along as well."

Adam took another long drink. "No, Sarah, I don't think that would be such a good idea."

"Why not?" she said.

"No offense, but with you there, I imagine her maternal instinct might kick into overdrive and undermine any negotiations regarding the future marketing of the paintings."

"You mean you don't want to alienate her in case she takes them all away from you!" Her tone held a hint of scorn.

"I wouldn't put it quite like that. I just don't see the need to rub her nose in it—especially when she has made her views quite clear."

"Oh yeah?" she said in a petulant tone. "You would prefer to live a lie?"

"Sarah, I think you're overreacting a bit," he said, and he immediately regretted the words as he sensed her annoyance vibrating down the phone line. He tried to save it by continuing, "Listen, we've all been under a lot of stress; you, your mother, and yeah, even me! Let me just reach some accommodation with her, and conclude this other problem that I've been dealing with—"

"You mean the negotiations that you and the bishop have been having with the Englishwoman?" she snapped.

Slightly taken aback by the abruptness, Adam paused before replying, "Yes, that's right."

"So, how long do you expect that's going to take?" she asked.

"Well, it involves finalizing things in Paris, and then probably Miami. I expect that everything will be tied up by early next week, barring any unforeseen problems." Just saying the word *problems* made him feel queasy.

"And you'll be pressure and stress free by then?" He wasn't sure if he detected a hint of mockery in her voice.

"Well, I hope so," he said, not entirely happy at the corner he was being maneuvered into.

"In that case, why don't you and I organize a short vacation together for when you get back? We could go maybe mid-December, an 'ending the twentieth century together' sort of thing."

Despite the appeal such a prospect held for him, Adam baulked at the manipulation. He felt he had to make some sort of a stand. "Sarah, am I imagining it, or are you turning into your mother?" he asked in what he imagined was his most humorous tone.

For a moment there was no reply. But the hurt in her voice was unmistakable as she said, "Why? Have you been fucking her too? Well, fuck you!" The dial tone was left buzzing in his ear.

He walked over and mixed another long vodka and tonic for himself, downed a large mouthful of it, and said aloud, "And fuck you, too!"

§

The glow from Adam's radio alarm etched 08:29 into the darkness of his bedroom as the phone woke him from a deep alcohol-assisted sleep. For a microsecond he felt confused, then upon remembering where he was and what had been happening recently, the confusion quickly turned to anxiety.

Who is this going to be? he thought. Too many phone calls lately had either been unwelcome or relayed bad news. The possibility of it being Sarah calling to apologize briefly presented itself to his befuddled brain. Unlikely, he had to admit.

It was Joe Rooney, apologizing for waking him. Adam bristled a bit at what he felt was a criticism, as if Rooney was silently accusing him for sleeping late, so he denied having been asleep.

Rooney's call bore good news for a change. The results of the DNA tissue sampling had come through. It had cleared him—he was categorically *not* the father of Zannah's embryo. Even though he knew he couldn't have been, Adam felt relieved. A little more pressure off. As they made small talk about his upcoming trip to Paris, another concern began to surface. Why was Rooney asking so many questions? Does he know or suspect something about the paintings? Adam had to mentally slap himself to halt the creeping paranoia. He was going crazy; Rooney couldn't possibly know anything. He had known only a couple of days himself, though those couple of days already felt like a month.

Over a light breakfast of fruit and coffee, Adam felt himself torn. Sure, Sarah had behaved a bit presumptuously on the phone last night—or had she? He still felt a warm comfort from the memory of their lovemaking. They had devoured each other, their passion sealing them off from all thoughts of personal anguish. The outside world had not impinged on the evening—at least not until her mother's unannounced arrival. Maybe it had been his behavior that was disproportionate or unnatural in the circum- stances. Maybe her insistent eagerness was just part of being so young.

Walking over to the wall mirror, he stared at his reflection. He still looked the same as he always had. Or did he? Were those hints of greying in the hairs just above his ears? Did he normally have that worried frown tracking across his forehead? He needed to shake himself up and get things in perspective. Sarah was right; it was a mere accident of birth that Liz was her mother. If he hadn't known Liz for years, he wouldn't be giving a damn what she said, or what threats she made. He knew what he had to do.

He dialed the number Sarah had given him. "Good morning," he said when she answered.

Sarah, too, replied with a quiet, tentative, "Good morning."

"I'm sorry about last night," he said. "I'm a bit screwed up about things at the moment."

"No, you were right. I was behaving like a spoiled, demanding bitch; it was my fault."

"Whatever or whoever, it makes no difference. I really enjoyed the time I spent with you yesterday evening, and it was insensitive for me to have behaved the way I did."

"Why don't we fuck and make up, then?" she laughed.

Adam chuckled, "I look forward to it." They talked on together for another hour, as if the previous night's quarrel had never happened.

§

Arriving at Jack's studio at the appointed time, Adam found the big steel covered front door already unlocked. Liz was evidently ahead of him. As usual, he chose to trudge all the way up the wide paint-flaked staircase to the top floor rather than trust the ancient elevator. He did not regard the climb as an inconvenience. It gave him a little extra exercise, and the effort would help warm him up, as the building, like the day outside, was freezing. As he climbed, he reflected that he hadn't been here since before Jack's death. He had to admit that he wasn't looking forward to going back into the studio.

He rapped his knuckles on the paneled door before turning the handle and pushing. It was strangely anti-climactic. He felt nothing. The big room was just as he had last seen it, stacked and furnished with the scant everyday bric-a-brac of Jack Hastings's existence, though it felt not only arctic, but empty and still. He could see that Liz must be here somewhere. A dark blue wool topcoat was draped over a chair while a purse leaned over beside it on the seat. She must be feeling warm, he thought. The radio was on, tuned to an oldies station, playing Eddie Cochran singing *Three steps to Heaven*. Apt, he thought. The view of the river through the big windows, usually crystal clear, was obscured cellophane-like.

Adam walked over. It was ice; the insides of the panes were glazed with ice crystals. He shivered and called out, "Liz! It's me, Adam." He saw his breath cloud in the frigid air. Taking his gloves off, he opened his briefcase on a side table and removed the inventory details of all the Hastings paintings he had in his possession.

He looked around. Several paintings in various stages of completion leaned at awkward angles against both the wall and the easel in Jack's work area. Against the far wall, a group of canvases leaned askew. Jack would never have left them lying around like that. They must have been moved about by the police, Adam thought. Where was Liz? He called her name again.

He opened the door into the corridor that led to Jack's bedroom and the few other rooms that he had used for storage beyond it. He went into the bedroom. The Queen-sized bed had been stripped of its bedclothes, leaving the room with a bare, unfurnished look. Three large Hastings paintings that were familiar to him still hung on one wall; another two leaned, one in front of the other, against the long, book-filled shelves lining the wall on the other side of the bed. These ones were new to Adam, and he approached them and bent over to take a closer look. The voice behind made him start.

"Still making straight for the bedroom?"

He swung around. Liz was leaning against the doorframe smiling at him. Despite the cold, she was wearing only a dark blue tailored woolen dress. The dress, just above knee length, was unseasonably *décolleté* and buttoned down the length of the front, her stance displaying a long split to mid-thigh.

"Jesus, Liz, you frightened the life out of me!"

"No need to be frightened; there are no ghosts here," she said, still smiling and walking toward him, left hand extended. "Not ghosts of humans anyway. I've already checked."

"You've already taken a look around, then?" Adam replied, feeling uncomfortable as she grasped his hand.

"Come with me, I've already taken a note of all these. There are another eighteen large ones in the other rooms," she said.

Like a little boy, he allowed himself to be led by her down the hallway into the first of the storage rooms. Her hand felt hot, searing into his. His emotions effervesced in a cauldron of confusing reactions. He could feel the cathartic energy flowing from her—something powerful was happening. Was this why his life had consisted of a string of serially failed relationships? Had his natural development been stunted by the unfulfilled longing of an adolescent passion, a fixation with this woman with whom he'd had a relationship when he was too immature, too young? Was this why the teenage Adam inside him had been lying dormant, biding his time, just waiting for her to come back to him when she was free—when Jack was dead?

"See," she said, still holding his hand, "there are another eleven in here plus those few smaller ones in the corner; then there are another seven next door."

He was no longer uncomfortable or confused. Instead, a crackling current of excitement energized him. She was so close he could smell her hair and see the wet sparkle of her teeth as she spoke. She moved to the corner and squatted down before the stack of smaller paintings, pulling him down into position beside her. Her dress gaped along her inner thigh as she did so, the split revealing the taut flesh above her stocking top. In a flash of out-of-body experience, he found himself analyzing the situation. Who wears stockings during the day in the middle of winter? Is she aware of what's happening here—what is happening here?

Their knees bumped together as they steadied themselves against each other in their awkward positions. He ached to touch her. She was so close and smelled so good. Liz flicked through the few paintings with her right hand, remarking on them. Adam didn't hear a word. Then, who knows who, but one of them lost balance, and as they toppled backward to the floor, they grabbed out at each other to save themselves.

She was on top of him, her legs straddling him, her hair fragrant in his face, their mouths clamped together. Their tongues, hot, wet and sweet, entwined as they sucked each other in. It was so intense, Adam could do nothing else; he dared not even open his eyes. It was a cornucopia of delight, euphoria, frenzy, and everything rapturous, and he didn't want it to cease. There was no alternative, there was only one way to go, and he knew that she knew it as well. As he felt her fingers groping around his groin, he took over, and within seconds he was inside her. He deftly opened the top buttons of her dress and pushed her filmy bra up. Despite the cold, both her face and body grew perspiration-sheened, as he did himself. His eyes were open now, and he watched his fingers rhythmically knead her slick, dark-tipped breasts above him as his groin ground up into her in time.

As the ripple that started somewhere near the base of his brain built to tidal proportions, he erupted inside her violently while she screamed to orgasm. They jerked against each other until he was wasted.

Adam lay there, a trembling shell, feeling as though he had been amputated at the knees, and he watched the silhouette of Liz on top of him. She was recovering, pulling her bra back down into position and buttoning her dress. She produced a Kleenex from her sleeve at her wrist, and, standing upright, parted her split skirt as she slipped it inside her panties.

As she stood brushing herself down and straightening out her dress, Adam became aware of his position. He was lying, half-clothed and disheveled, on the bare board floor of his new lover's dead father's apartment, having just had sex with her mother, the widow. As he looked up into Liz's eyes, he saw her power, her control, radiate around her like an aura, and he knew it wasn't an accident.

Adam clambered to his feet and rearranged his clothing. He knew that everything was different, changed once more. She had been right—there were no human ghosts there, but their consummation had laid the other one, the specter that had disrupted his entire dysfunctional adult life. Now, he knew, he had laid his arrested development, his hang-up, to rest. He started to speak, to try to form some words, but Liz placed a raised forefinger against his lips.

"Let's finish the inventory, it's a tad cold in here," she said.

They passed the next hour in a businesslike fashion. Jack had been busy over the last six months. Most of the finished pieces Adam had never seen before, and the grand total, including the ones Adam had in storage, comprised forty-eight large paintings and some twenty smaller ones.

"I'll arrange to have these picked up and placed in storage with the others, if that suits you?" Adam asked.

"Sure, that's fine," Liz said, slipping on her topcoat.

Adam stood waiting, briefcase in hand, as she locked the studio door, then he turned and made for the stairway.

"Don't be crazy!" she said. "Let's take the elevator." She walked over to the expanded metal latticework door and hit the call button. Somewhere up above, gears whirred and clanked; naked, thick wire cable caked with years-old dried grease spun past in front of Adam's eyes. Through the open metalwork, he could see the top of the elevator emerging out of the gloom.

As the oak-lined and mirrored cubicle shuddered to a halt in front of them, Liz pulled back the outer protective gate with a noisy rattle, then the inner, and stepped in. Adam followed her. It was some years since he'd last been in this relic, and on that occasion it had jammed between floors, imprisoning him for almost two hours. Jack had heard his calls as he was leaving and somehow managed to reset it. An intermittent fault, he called it. Like everything else about the elevator, the low wattage light bulb was flickering to the end of its life as the cage doors closed over and the cubicle trembled and began its downward journey.

"Well, that was quite a pleasant interlude, wouldn't you say?" Liz asked suddenly.

There was no escape for Adam. "Yes, it was." Even to his own ears, his answer sounded stunned, trance-like.

"I hope that clarifies a few things for you, in that case?"

He said nothing in response, just stared over her shoulder at his own dim reflection and that of the back of her head in the rectangular beveled mirror panel. Where was she going with this? He became aware of a slight juddering followed by a sudden jolt. They had stopped. Two more floors to go, and they were stationary between two and three.

"Oh, Christ!" he said, exasperated, "There's no one else in the building, what are we going to do now?"

"Never mind the damned elevator, answer my question," she ordered.

Adam felt tired, felt like closing his eyes and closing the world out. Quietly, he asked, "What's the problem, Liz?" Her eyes were glaring at him now. This too had something to do with their past. But he was purged of her now. Beneath the tiredness, he knew that. Maybe she felt the same and wanted him out of her life, away from her and her daughter. Sarah, her daughter—that was it—jealousy! She didn't want him involved with her. That's why they were here alone. That's why she had been so welcoming upstairs in the studio. With Jack dead, she thought there would be no guilt reflecting on either of them. It had nothing to do with the age difference between him and Sarah at all, just the old eternal triangle.

"I thought I'd already made myself clear on that," she replied. "Just stay well away from Sarah, that's all. I've explained my position. I've been nasty and I've been nice. Are you getting the message? I'm warning you—if I find you've been encouraging her in this stupid infatuation, I'll be having a little girl to girl talk with her about you and me. She'll get a no punches pulled, totally unrestricted, blow by blow account of this afternoon, right down to the last detail," she said. "Is that clear?"

Feeling trapped and powerless, Adam nodded and said, "Yes," hating himself for being so stupid, so wrong.

The elevator started to tremble into movement again. Adam looked at her.

"Yes," she said, "I just pushed the button and stopped it."

❧ 21 ❧

Traveling alone to the gallery in the back of a cab, Adam agonized over the events in Jack's studio and Liz's role in his life. Back then he'd been a silly, unworldly, green kid who couldn't handle the fact that for her it had been nothing more than sex. His naiveté had resulted in the fabrication of a classic sacrificial myth; it was obvious now, just a case of unconscious self-delusion. A case of him transforming the emotional frustrations in his relationship with Liz into a saga of sacrifice: the sacrifice of their relationship, their love, at the shrine of her marriage to Jack. Adam found it hard to believe that he had ever concocted such a theory. The only difference between himself and those delusional folk who, imagining they have a relationship, stalk movie stars, was merely a matter of degree. Of course, she had just ended it in typical Liz fashion: unilateral decree—no discussion, no argument, no pleading. That was it, finished. How could he ever have fooled himself into thinking it was anything else?

Yes, she was still a very beautiful and sensual woman, the sort any man would feel flattered to be seen with, to keep company with. He could still see that, but the important bit—the magic that had influenced his life—was gone. He felt free of her, but was that it? Or was there now a hole in his life?

At the gallery, Robin Brew was bidding farewell to a well-dressed, middle-aged couple as Adam arrived. Adam nodded a curt greeting as he passed them and headed to the bathroom to try and straighten up his appearance as best he could. When he emerged some minutes later, Robin was seated at the desk, sucking on his unlit briar.

"Customers?" Adam asked in an attempt at normalcy.

"Be-backs," Robin answered, "another couple who are interested in acquiring a Hastings. I told them that we might have several more in the pipeline. The people I mentioned to you yesterday, the other be-backs who took the photographs, phoned this morning—they are taking two of them."

"Good," Adam said without enthusiasm.

Robin beckoned him to come and sit beside him. "Is there a problem? Were there no more paintings in the studio?"

Adam pulled a chair around and sat facing him. "On the contrary, there were more than I expected."

"And she is challenging your right to handle them?"

"No, she's happy for me to continue just as before."

"Then why the long face?"

Adam ran his fingers through his hair, shrugged, and opened his hands in a gesture of consternation. "I don't think I can continue on as before. Jack may have been a bit of an eccentric and hard to deal with for most of the time, but, at base, we understood each other and got along. We could always work things out somehow. Liz, on the other hand, is impossible to deal with all of the time. Everything has to be done the way she wants it done, no discussion and no argument. I couldn't put up with that type of interference."

"So you've told her you're not taking them on?"

"No, I didn't," Adam admitted. "I stood there like a minion toadying for approval. I feel disgusted with myself." He looked at Robin and put on a wry face.

Robin waved his pipe and laughed. "Don't feel too bad about that. I disgust myself regularly, though I must admit I always enjoy it at the time!"

Adam smiled at the reference and then joined him in his laughter.

"That's decidedly better!" Robin said. "You look a bit pale . . . have you been sleeping all right?"

Adam gave a dismissive wave of his hand. "Maybe that's the problem. I feel as though I've just woken up from a twenty-year sleep. I've just got to make some changes in my life."

Robin looked at him and raised one eyebrow. "Sounds serious, Mr. Van Winkle. Just relax on the couch there. I think you could do with a mug of strong coffee . . . but stay awake!"

By the time Robin had returned with the coffee, Adam had made up his mind.

"Robin, I've decided." Robin handed Adam his mug and regarded him over the rim of his own as he took a first sip. "When I get back from Paris, I'll tell her that I won't be handling Jack's work any longer, that I don't want to be beholden to her in any way, that I want to sever all ties."

Robin nodded. "I understand. It's a pity in a way, since Jack has become so hot. But, as the Duke always said . . ." he paused.

Adam looked at him, waiting.

"A man's gotta do what a man's gotta do."

"Oh, that Duke!" Adam laughed.

§

Liz had refused Adam's offer to share a cab, remaining standing in front of the antique elevator as he left the warehouse building. As he pulled the door behind him, she walked over and checked that it was indeed closed before turning to go back up to Jack's studio. This time she took the stairs.

Opening the studio door, she went straight to the storeroom where she and Adam had so recently had sex. A couple of stacks of boxes stood irregularly piled in one corner. Liz walked over and moved two of them apart to reveal the small camcorder on a miniature tripod, angled just as she had positioned it earlier. The little red light still pulsed intermittently on the side of the case, indicating that it was still recording. Pressing the *Off* button, she popped the assembly into her satchel and left.

She was back in her apartment inside the hour. Pleased that there was no sign of Sarah, she went to her office, removed the mini video tape from the device and stuck a label onto it. Using a black marker, she wrote "AK & ME @ JACK'S. NOV 17th 99". Then, taking a large chrome key from her purse, she opened a small metal safe that was concealed behind the wastepaper basket under the kneehole section of her desk. She removed a plastic bag containing a few cables and a charger and placed the camcorder and tape inside before replacing the bag in the safe.

§

After spending an enjoyable evening murmuring and smiling at each other over an intimate meal in a little downtown restaurant, Adam and Sarah were being driven back to Adam's apartment. The mid-week dining crowd had been sparse and, enjoying the privacy, they had lingered long over drinks and coffee in their candlelit nook. They had talked about everything; everything, that is, except the phone conversation of the previous evening and Sarah's mother, Liz. Now, however, as the cab drew up alongside his block, Adam was uncomfortable.

When picking her up from her grandmother's house earlier in the evening, Adam had been careful. He had instructed the cab driver to circle several times around the block before he was satisfied that no one was watching out for him. There had been little delay. Sarah had been ready and waiting, and he scooped her into the back seat in a lively fashion. Even the restaurant where he had reserved a table was one he had rarely eaten at before; he was taking no chances. However, as they arrived back at his own apartment, he felt vulnerable. He couldn't take the same sort of precautions here. He couldn't risk raising Sarah's suspicions.

Without making it obvious to her, he scanned the neighborhood for any signs of Liz while he was pretending to fumble for the fare. He wasn't being paranoid, he told himself. Liz's behavior in the last few days had been so controlling that incorporating a little stalking into it wasn't out of the question. She was a serious problem, and though he knew he was going to have to confront her in the near future, he wanted to placate her in the meantime. Imagining how Sarah would react if her mother carried out her threat and informed her of this afternoon's dalliance made him feel distinctly nauseous.

The freezing wet streets were deserted as they dashed into the warmth of the building and held hands as the high-speed elevator hummed its way up to Adam's floor.

There was only one call on his answering machine—from the bishop—reminding him that he had booked a limo to pick them up early next morning to take them to JFK for the Paris flight. As he reset the machine he turned to Sarah, who had taken off her coat and had already made herself comfortable on the sofa.

"I was thinking of what you said on the phone last night," he said.

"Oh please, Adam. I was hoping you weren't going to bring any of that up." Her tone was apologetic.

"No, I'm not talking about the screaming or the insults. I'm thinking of your suggestion."

Sarah thought for a moment. "You mean, about taking a vacation together?"

"Exactly," Adam said, smiling at her. "Once this deal is completed, we could take off, just the two of us. Anywhere you want, for as long as you want." She was looking at him in total surprise. He began to feel embarrassed, adding, "I haven't had a vacation in ages, and we could both do with a break."

Sarah jumped up from the couch, and running toward him, she threw her arms around his neck and kissed him deeply on the mouth. As they broke apart, she said, "Let's get to the bedroom and really finish this making-up."

Adam smiled and led her by the hand. At his bedroom door he paused, turned to her and said, "Humor me a little bit, will you?"

She raised her eyebrows and smiled. "What do you want me to wear? A nurse's uniform? Handcuffs? Just name it."

He laughed. "Let's leave that till later. No, I just want to ask you not to mention any of this to your mother. Either me seeing you, or us planning to go off somewhere together—not for the moment anyway. Okay?"

"Sure," Sarah replied, "but, as I've said already, it's absolutely none of her business."

Adam cringed, envisioning how Sarah's attitude might change should her mother explain just how it might be some of her business. But that was a problem for the future, and hopefully one of very few.

❧ 2 2 ❧

An attractive, tall, dark-haired woman in a navy blue tailored suit stood waiting, bearing a card with their last names, as the bishop and Adam emerged through French customs and immigration into the Charles DeGaulle arrivals concourse.

"Monseigneur Connor, Mister Kennedy, welcome to Paris. I hope you had a comfortable flight," she said in fluent, slightly accented English. "My name is Corrine, and I shall be accompanying you. This gentleman will attend to your luggage." She indicated a uniformed airport porter to her left. "If you would follow me, please."

They strolled alongside her, exiting out onto the damp tarmac, where a red and white Dauphin helicopter, the TC-SPEED logo emblazoned on its flanks, sat idling noisily. She opened the rear door and, with hand signals, indicated to her charges to precede her. The bishop went first, choosing one of the brown leather twin armchairs backing onto the cockpit bulkhead. Adam climbed in after him, installed himself opposite, and clicked the lap safety harness about his waist. The bishop followed suit. The clatter and roar of the rising engine dulled to a throb as Corrine followed and pulled the door of the soundproofed passenger compartment closed. A double-glazed panel separated their opulent burr-walnut and leather-trimmed section from the instrument-laden cockpit. Corrine spoke to the pilot in French via the passenger Interphone as overhead the blades began to rotate and gather speed. "Make yourselves comfortable, Messieurs. We shall be at company headquarters within thirty minutes."

Despite the Concorde flight lasting less than four hours, the six-hour difference between New York and Paris meant that it was nearly seven o'clock in the evening and already dark. From the airport they skirted southwest around the electric glare of central Paris, though Adam could see the needle of the Eiffel Tower glowing in the distance with its illuminated display counting down the number of days to the new millennium. They passed over several non-light-emitting black areas, which Corrine informed them were part of the Versailles forest, where the French sovereigns had enjoyed the hunt in the seventeenth and eighteenth centuries. Shortly afterward, they descended onto a brightly-lit helipad to the rear of a large, turreted chateau.

Once on the ground, she guided them, heads down under the buffeting turbulence of the still-turning rotors, around the side of the building, past one of a pair of illuminated fountains that graced the front lawns, to the grand stone staircase entrance of the house itself. She ushered them through a magnificent oak-paneled entrance hall into another high-ceilinged, sumptuously decorated reception room. Tanaka rose from one of a pair of brocaded giltwood canapés to greet them.

"Welcome to France, gentlemen. My name is Mr. Tanaka," he said. "I trust you had a good flight." They assured him that they had. "Your baggage is being transferred to the guest bedrooms we have prepared for you. If you would like to accompany Yves . . ." Tanaka indicated a middle-aged, tidily-dressed man, in a black waistcoat, trousers and white shirt, who stood at a discreet distance. "He will show you to your rooms, where you may freshen up before dining. I trust half past eight will suit? I can delay this should you need to take a longer break after all your traveling."

"No, thank you, Mister Tanaka. Your hospitality and timing are impeccable; eight thirty will be ideal," the bishop replied for them both.

§

Refreshed after showering and a change of clothes, Adam and the bishop relaxed in upholstered gilt elbow chairs, sipping Kir Royale aperitifs while waiting for Tanaka to join them. From the wooden parquetry floors to the delicately painted ceilings centered amid ornately carved cornices, the room exuded wealth and grandeur. Tanaka entered, followed by a tall, deeply tanned man of about fifty.

"Gentlemen, sorry for keeping you," Tanaka said. "Please allow me to introduce you to Mister Mitchell, the CEO of TC-SPEED."

Adam noticed a millisecond's jolt in the bishop's demeanor as Tanaka mentioned Mitchell's name. They shook hands, and Mitchell urged them to address him informally as Ray. Drinks were refreshed and small talk was made as Tanaka edged away from the party.

"I shall attend to the dining arrangements. If you'll excuse me, gentlemen," Tanaka said as he eased out of the room.

"Phil, Adam, thank you both for coming all this way to tie up the loose ends," Mitchell said, quickly addressing the point of the meeting.

"Have the paintings arrived yet?" Adam asked, glad to cut to business.

"Yep, they arrived this afternoon, and I've already had a look at them," Mitchell said, then looking at each man in turn, added, "However, as you know, we do have a bit of a problem."

The bishop looked surprised, and Adam felt a wave of despair wash over him.

"What sort of a problem?" The bishop was the first to speak.

"The problem is the pictures, Phil. Granted, on the face of it they look the business, but you and I know they're a bit iffy!"

"Iffy?" the bishop repeated, his voice rising.

"Yep, I'm afraid so, Phil," he said. "From a distance they're as flash as a rat with a gold tooth, but up close they don't cut the mustard. Whatever way you want to look at it, they're basically just fakes!"

To Adam's ears the word *FAKES* screamed incongruously in this sumptuous setting. It reverberated around his head and around the room. He felt shamefully exposed, like a beggar posing as a merchant banker. His throat felt tight and his mouth dry. He struggled against licking his lips, against giving any signals that would expose his insecurity. The bishop, however, wasn't so easily quenched.

"Fakes! Is this some sort of bad taste joke? Fakes?" His raised voice was aggressive, his eyes flaming.

Mitchell smiled and continued in an even tone, "Pull your head in, Phil, you're wasting your time. I *know* they're fakes." The bishop started to splutter a protest again, but was quieted by Mitchell's gesturing hands. "The fat's in the fire, boys—I know they're fakes. You know they're fakes . . . and I know you know they're fakes."

Indicating Adam, he continued, "I take it that Adam's in on it. If not, my apologies for any embarrassment."

The bishop turned to Adam and coolly stated, "Seems like we've been wasting our time here." and stood up.

Mitchell interrupted any further movement, saying, "Gents, believe me, we have no major dispute here. I know all about them. I know the history. I know the facts. I know about the fire."

Though Adam was still seated, he did not feel low enough. He wanted to sink through the floor. The bishop remained standing, though it was clear that Mitchell held his full attention.

"I know about the destruction of the originals, and I know that you, Phil, came to the rescue of the Bellocs. Since the insurance wouldn't have paid out, you proposed that the best alternative was to put it about that it was the reproductions that had been destroyed. Then, at some stage in the future, you would arrange to have totally foolproof copies made, which, with the Belloc provenance, would render them indistinguishable from the burned originals."

The bishop slumped back down onto his seat. He looked stunned. Adam was astonished. How could this stranger know so much? Could this all have been an elaborate Interpol setup designed to unveil the bishop's years of unloading fakes onto the market? Maybe Rooney had known something yesterday morning after all. He coughed to lubricate his throat and asked, "Mister Mitchell . . . Ray, where do you fit in this? Are you really involved in this company,"—Adam gestured at his grand surroundings—"or is this just the result of some misguided art fraud investigation?"

Mitchell smiled again, saying, "Let me assure you both that there's no one else involved in this. It's just between the three of us. Neither Tanaka nor the Englishwoman, Bentley, is aware of the true situation. There are no secret recordings and no hidden cameras, and I'm definitely not working with, or for, the cops. I am, as Tanaka explained, the owner of this company, and several others, and as such, I'm still prepared to buy these paintings in the full knowledge that they're fakes."

Adam and the bishop were struck silent by this new development. After a few moments the bishop spoke, "Let me get this straight. You believe these paintings are not the originals, yet you are prepared to pay well in excess of one hundred million dollars to own them. Do I understand you correctly?"

"No, Phil, on both points. Firstly, I don't want to be a pain hammering on about this, but I don't merely *believe* they are fakes, I *know* they're not the originals. Secondly, although I'm prepared to buy them, the price will have to be renegotiated—downward, of course."

The bishop glared at him and stood up again. "It seems we've had a wasted trip in that case. If you will please organize the return of the paintings to New York at once, we'll be on our way."

Following the bishop's lead, Adam rose to his feet as well. Mitchell remained seated.

"Please, guys, sit down and calm down. I know this situation may not be the one you expected, but I assure you, it's much better than the alternative."

"What alternative?" asked Adam. Knowing the truth about the paintings was causing him to have difficulty mirroring the bishop's indignation. Essentially, the paintings were fakes, and Mitchell seemed to know everything about them. He and the bishop were treading on very marshy ground, and Adam was not inclined to be swallowed up by it, especially on behalf of people who had already murdered at least one, and possibly two of his friends.

Mitchell addressed Adam's question. "As I'm sure you're aware, the French authorities take a very strong line on fraudulent works of art. Recently, a Chagall that was sent across from England, not even for sale, mind you, merely for authentication, was condemned as a fake. These people don't mess about; the painting was destroyed, and that was it. Not one cent of compensation and not a chance in hell of it being returned to its original owner. It's a sort of crusade against fakes." Mitchell paused to allow the implications of this to sink in, then he continued, "Now, I'm sure Hastings did a fantastic job on them: old canvases, old paints, the works. I've seen them and they look the business, I'm not denying that. But believe me, guys, I can ensure that they will undergo such a thorough forensic examination that they will be exposed. No matter how he's aged them, no matter how he's forced the paint to dry, the fact is that these have been painted in the last eighteen months or so, and there are going to be discoverable differences between them and ones that have been around for sixty or seventy years."

Neither the bishop nor Adam spoke.

"Now, it's up to you. If you insist on taking these back to the States with you, then I'll just lift the phone and have the tests proceed." He paused and shrugged. "Maybe you're right. Maybe Hastings can beat the testing. In which case I'll lift my hat to him posthumously and you can take them away with you. But if they fail, as I'm pretty sure they will, then they will be confiscated and destroyed, and you'll be going back to the Bellocs with your tails between your legs, without the paintings, and without a reputation. On top of that, you can be sure there will be some police interest on both sides of the pond regarding the fabricating and international trafficking of forged art works. It's a gamble, guys—your gamble, and it's entirely up to you."

Adam spoke again, "I think the bishop and I need to discuss this in private, if you don't mind."

"Be my guests. I'll leave you alone—"

The bishop interrupted him. "If it's all the same to you, I think we'll take a walk outside in the gardens."

"No worries," Mitchell said. "Take your time. I'll be here when you get back." He escorted them to the tall entrance doors, had Yves fetch their overcoats, and as they crunched down the gravel walkway into the darkness, he closed the doors behind them and disappeared back inside.

❦ 23 ❧

The bishop and Adam spoke in confidential tones as they trudged side by side along an avenue of tall skeletal trees in the winter moonlight.

"God forgive me, but I feel like strangling that smug Australian bastard. He thinks he has us in a corner, but the Bellocs won't take this lying down."

"I don't really see what they can do about it," Adam said. "This has got to be a more complex problem than just slicing some information out of a young girl in a New York apartment. We're in Europe now, inside what is obviously a secure estate, and we don't even know where the paintings are."

The bishop continued as if he hadn't heard Adam speak. "How did he know all that? It wasn't a guess. He knew everything, the entire background—the fire, Jack's involvement, everything. For all we know, maybe he was the one responsible for the deaths of Jack and Zannah."

Adam dismissed this notion. "Why? He had established himself as the primary buyer, so he was in pole position to get the paintings anyway, whether they were alive or dead. He couldn't have just stolen them, as the paintings are no use on their own. To have them he needs the provenance as well, so he must be seen to have

acquired good title to them. And there is only one way to do that
—by buying them."

He took the bishop by the arm and halted. The chateau glim-
mered in the distance behind them while the lights of Paris lightened the sky to the East. It was bitingly cold.

"Look, Phil, we can't wander aimlessly around here all night
just reflecting on the mess we're in and how the Bellocs are going
to feel. We have to deal with this, make some sort of a decision,
even though we have only very limited choices."

The bishop nodded in agreement despite the lack of conviction
in his face, and Adam continued, "As you point out, this guy,
Mitchell, seems to have a thorough insight into this whole fiasco—
much more than myself, I might add. However, he has the paintings in his possession and has presented us with only two choices.
We either allow them to be examined for authentication and run
the risk of them being exposed—in which case everyone loses: the
Bellocs, us, and Mitchell himself. Or we can admit he's right and
try to salvage the best deal we can. Don't forget, he's already gone
to a lot of expense and trouble to get this far, so he must really
want them, even though they're fakes."

The bishop stopped walking and turned to Adam. He looked
tired and older in the moonlight, but his voice was firm. "So, are
you telling me that you're happy to surrender and just say, 'Okay,
take them, you win'?"

"Take it easy, Phil," Adam said, "I'm trying to deal with the
realities of the situation and see what we can salvage. You know if
we just walk away we risk certain exposure."

The bishop shook his head in resignation. "A long way to come
just to get mugged."

Adam put his arm around the older man's shoulders as they
turned back toward the chateau. "Let's go back and see what
compromise we can reach," he said.

They walked together slowly, in silence. Despite what he had
just said, Adam was experiencing the same doubts about their
decision as the bishop had expressed aloud. Had he just railroaded

him into doing the wrong thing? It was impossible to judge. He only knew that they couldn't procrastinate indefinitely.

Inside, Mitchell was waiting for them. As the bishop and Adam stood warming themselves in front of a log fire blazing in the monumental fireplace, he asked, "Well, gents, can we do business?"

Adam spoke first, "You've gone to a lot of trouble and expense to get your hands on these so-called 'fakes'."

"Safe to say that," Mitchell agreed.

"In which case, it's safe to assume that you also have an interest in maintaining their integrity. You, too, cannot want to see these paintings undermined."

"That's true, up to a point," he replied, "but having the celebrated core of the Belloc collection publicly exposed as worthless fakes would be pretty damn gratifying as well. And believe me, I'd make sure it received plenty of publicity. They'd be jabbering about it from Manhattan to beyond the Black Stump."

Adam's eyes widened with interest and he inquired, "Are you saying that this is about the Bellocs rather than the paintings?"

"Let's just say that it would be some sort of compensation if we couldn't do business," Mitchell replied.

As Mitchell and Adam spoke, Adam noticed a change in the bishop's countenance. He saw the defeated slackness of his face begin to regain its former tone, his eyes sharpening into alertness as he listened.

Then the bishop snapped his fingers. "Mitchell! I knew there was something familiar about that name. It was an Australian called Mitchell who owned the paintings before Belloc. That's who you are! The paintings used to belong to you and you want them back!"

The ensuing silence lasted so long that Adam thought Mitchell was not going to answer.

"Not exactly. They didn't belong to me; they were my dad's," Mitchell admitted at last.

The bishop now directed himself to Adam. "It all happened just before I knew Paul Belloc, but, from the whispers I heard, he managed to virtually steal them." The bishop paused before soft-ening his voice to a sympathetic pastoral timbre, and turning to Mitchell said, "And indeed, he did steal your mother—and by extension, your sister, Rosa. I met your mother often, God rest her soul."

Gradually, things were falling into place. Adam was beginning to discern a framework, a rationale behind all of this. Mitchell wanted not only the paintings, but also vengeance, for not only had old Belloc somehow managed to acquire the paintings, but he had also enticed away this man's mother.

"That's very interesting," Adam said, disturbing the near rever-ential calm, "and you have my sympathies. But where do we go from here? Phil and I are left with a collapsed one hundred and fifty million dollar deal, and a strong likelihood of receiving a less than enthusiastic welcome if we return to the Bellocs empty-handed."

Mitchell smiled as he replied, "It would defeat the whole point of the exercise if that old bastard was happy with the package I have in mind."

Neither Adam nor the bishop returned the smile.

"So, what do you have in mind?" Adam said. "What does your alternative package consist of?"

"I'll get to that in a minute," Mitchell said. "First, tell me, what was your percentage commission of the original one fifty going to be?"

Adam remained silent. This was the bishop's sphere, and it was up to him to answer if he wished.

"Twenty percent. Thirty million," the bishop replied. Mitchell whistled in admiration. The bishop continued, "Out of that, I had agreed to pay Jack five million. Unfortunately, he got greedy and threatened to withhold the paintings until he got double that figure."

"So, being dead, he's out of the picture now, so to speak?"

"No, his widow is expecting his share to go to her."

Adam's mouth fell open. He stared at the bishop in disbelief.

"Phil," he asked, "was I the only one in New York who didn't know what the fuck was going on here? Even she was in on it?"

"No, Adam. Calm yourself. Liz knew from the very beginning. Jack told her at the time of the fire, so she knew that when Belloc came to sell the paintings, it would be down to Jack. I'm sorry. I just didn't want you knowingly involved in this sort of business."

"So, let's see then." Mitchell began to count on his fingers. "There is Hastings's wife, both of you, and the Bellocs. Anyone else know about this?"

"Only you and anyone you've told—so far as I know," answered the bishop.

"No one associated with me knows anything," Mitchell said. "That's why I'm here in person talking to you. And that's the way I want it to stay. As far as anyone else is concerned, the paintings are beyond reproach—just so long as Belloc accepts the terms."

"Which are?" Adam asked.

"The offer is in two parts. First, to ensure the lasting cooperation and discretion of Hastings's wife and yourselves in the negotiations and afterward, I'll pay you two point five million U.S. dollars each."

"That's one hell of a drop from thirty million," the bishop said. "I can't see Liz Hastings being too enthusiastic about that!"

"Don't let your own propaganda confuse the realities again, Phil," Mitchell said. "We're not talking about the real thing here. We're talking about acknowledged fakes. Anyway, I was going to continue by offering you the opportunity to handle any subsequent sale of them on my behalf on a ten percent commission basis. Furthermore, I'll cover all your incurred expenses."

Bit by bit, the pattern was becoming clearer to Adam. Having the paintings in his possession, and knowing what he knew, Mitchell was in control. Old Belloc's pride wouldn't allow the paintings to be exposed as fakes—he'd burn them first. Except that he couldn't, as he didn't have them in his possession anymore. Their title would be transferred to Mitchell and he would be free to dispose of them as he wished. He wouldn't want to keep them.

They aren't the ones his father once owned, just replicas. So he'd sell them, and no one would have any interest in undermining them. Belloc wouldn't, since he would want to preserve his reputation and avoid any possibility of an FBI investigation; nor themselves, since they would be paid to remain discreet and also to avoid any similar problems.

The bishop looked thoughtful as he asked, "And the second part of your offer?"

"That deals with old Belloc. He gets back the deeds to the mine that was the main part of the original deal with my dad."

The bishop raised an eyebrow. "I can't see them being too enthusiastic about that. If my memory serves me correctly, the original deal was the cause of some rancor, quite apart from the business with your mother . . . if you'll forgive me bringing that up again. Surely the mine is virtually worthless?"

"Yep, in a sense you're right. It's worth no more than it was worth seventeen years ago, adjusted for inflation, but it allows them to save face." He smiled and said, "Don't forget, my friends. I'm not stealing these pictures."

Shaking his head, Adam said, "You know what the Bellocs are like. You know how far they've gone already. I can't see them taking this lying down."

"Let's give it a burl, shall we?" Mitchell replied. "With a bit of luck, old Belloc's ticker will blow up and he'll shoot through when he hears the news. Jesus, I'd pay extra to see that!" He stood up. The meeting was at an end. "Okay, mates, time to relax and have a bite." Standing between Adam and the bishop, he placed an arm over each of their shoulders, steering them in the direction of the dining room. "Tomorrow," he continued, "the three of us will be jetting off to the New World. And don't worry, she'll be right!"

❦ 24 ❦

A s Liz turned the key in her apartment door, she checked her watch again—nearly nine o'clock—making it about three in the morning in Paris. Sure enough, as she opened the door she could see the light on her answering machine blinking, signaling that calls had been received. That will have been Phil, she thought. She was hanging her top coat on the hall tree when the phone began to peal loudly. She dashed to it to beat the machine pick-up.

The bishop sounded subdued as he spoke, "Tried to catch you earlier. Left a couple of messages on your machine . . ."

"Yes, I've just arrived home, haven't had time to check the calls yet."

"Just wanted to let you know that we'll be catching the Air France Concorde to New York at eleven in the morning; that'll see us arriving into JFK at about 8:45 a.m. local time. But there have been some new developments over here that you need to know about, so we'll come directly to your apartment before flying on down to Florida."

"Why? Are you okay? Is there some kind of problem?" She could hear the despondency in his voice.

"Yes. It's just that there's been a bit of a hiccup, but we're working at salvaging it. Don't worry."

"Don't worry!" she almost shouted. "There's a lot at stake here. How can I not worry? What's the problem? Tell me what it is."

"I'd rather not say on the phone, but it's not as bad as it could be. We'll still do all right out of it. Just get a good night's rest. I'll explain everything when I see you in person. It's early morning here and I need to get some sleep. I'd better go now. Bye." And he hung up.

Liz slammed the phone onto the wall cradle and stood motionless, staring at it with an overwhelming feeling of impotence. Her frustration grew as she realized she didn't even have his number to call him back. She checked her machine and listened. He had called twice earlier, but had delivered no more information and no contact number, just a couple of cryptic messages hinting at something being wrong.

He had sounded strange, too curt, as if someone might be eavesdropping. But she knew all the bases had been covered. What could possibly be the problem—apart from the obvious one?

CNN exploded into one of its interminable cyclical news reports as she hit the TV remote. She poured herself a large whisky, and after swirling it around for some moments, she held it up to her nose and savored the aroma. She knew she had a difficult night ahead, too many worries to allow her to sleep easily. Not only was there this unknown difficulty in France, but there was also Sarah's most recent maddening behavior to keep her awake.

Liz sat down on one of the big couches and killed the sound on the TV, leaving it to flicker as she stared sightlessly at it. She took a sip of the whisky, but the raw alcohol shock barely registered. She was thinking of what Sarah had told her earlier. She was going out to dinner this evening with another entirely unsuitable character for a girl of her age—Joe Rooney.

§

Rooney had been surprised to hear that Sarah was no longer staying at her mother's apartment, and his cab drew up at her new lodgings just before eight.

"Irreconcilable differences!" she had said with a smile to him when he asked her about it. They traveled downtown to a little family-run Italian place on the East Side that Rooney used to frequent in the old days with Anna. It hadn't changed. The food was still as tasty and authentic as his mother's and the vino still exuded the aromas of the dry south Italian earth and sun. It was a slow, relaxing, unpretentious meal—and, he congratulated himself, he hadn't even thought about having a smoke all evening.

Lingering at the table over their wine, they talked for hours. They talked about everything, but mostly about themselves and each other. They swapped common memories and anecdotes. Sarah had laughed when he told her that he even remembered her as a baby. She asked him a million personal questions; he told her very few lies. Time and again, he noted, Sarah steered the conversation around to Adam, and despite some initial unease, he found himself talking freely about him and the bishop and the intertwined lengthy relationship the three of them had. Adam, by far the youngest, was like family, he admitted, and they'd been friends a long time. Nevertheless, as the evening grew on, Sarah's continued references to Adam were beginning to make him uncomfortable. No, even worse, he couldn't deny it—he was jealous.

This realization made him feel a bit ridiculous. In fact, from time to time during the evening, he had caught the occasional curious glance from fellow diners—and he could read their thoughts. What's that old guy doing with a beautiful young girl like that? It was his body language, of course. He wanted to be close to her, to touch her, however innocently. It was too obvious. Even the waiters had noticed, though Sarah herself certainly didn't seem to. Or if she had, it didn't seem to bother her.

In the end there was a small wrangle. Rooney had forgotten, but Sarah hadn't. They didn't actually come to blows, but Sarah reached across the table and grabbed Rooney's nose between her forefinger and thumb, turned it very slightly, and threatened to twist it off if he didn't pass the check over to her so she could pay as agreed. Rooney surrendered as they both nearly fell off their chairs laughing.

Playing the perfect gentleman, he delivered her back to her grandmother's house shortly after midnight. He walked her to the door and kissed her chastely on the cheek before jumping back into the cab to be taken home.

§

The Air France Concorde arrived on schedule, but with customs, immigration checks and the traffic, it was after eleven by the time the bishop and Adam reached Liz's apartment. The lack of sleep and the strain of the past two days showed on them. They sat side by side on one of the big sofas. Adam laid his head back on the cushions and allowed his eyes to close. He knew he had no role to play here. Dealing with Liz was the bishop's responsibility.

Liz, seated opposite them, indicated Adam with a nod of her head and said, "I presume, as he's sitting beside you at the moment, that he's now aware of my involvement?"

"Yes," the bishop said, "Mitchell needed to know how many people knew the paintings weren't right—"

"Mitchell?" Liz interrupted sharply. "Who the hell is Mitchell?"

"I was coming to that. He's the Australian who is the principal behind Tanaka's company and the whole deal. Somehow, he knew the paintings were fakes even before he got his hands on them. Not only that, it turns out they used to belong to his father before Paul Belloc got them. There's a lot of antagonism between them. That's no doubt why Mitchell went to such pains to hide his identity before he could physically take charge of them. I imagine he felt that if Paul Belloc had discovered his involvement, he'd never have dealt with him, and Mitchell would never have managed to lay his hands on them in the first place."

"Are you telling me that this guy, Mitchell, is about to expose the paintings as fakes?"

"No, Liz, calm down; it's not as bad as it seems. Mitchell intends to use his knowledge that the paintings are copies as leverage in a deal with the Bellocs. Admittedly, the deal he proposes is anything but advantageous for them, but at the same time he is prepared to make it worth our while to play along."

The bishop outlined Mitchell's plan to her, summing up: "As long as the Bellocs agree to his terms, there is no great disadvantage to us. After all, he has to keep us happy. Apart from the Bellocs, we're the only ones who know the truth."

Liz sat for a moment, digesting what she'd just heard. Her face tightened and she raised an accusatory finger as she said, "Well, I don't know about you, but from where I sit, settling for two and a half million dollars less than I expected does seem like a bit of a disadvantage. On top of that, once he's done the deal with the Bellocs, we are dispensable. And now that you've told him of my existence, he knows exactly the parties he needs to get rid of, and he has seven and a half million good reasons to do so."

"First of all, Liz, the two and a half million is only part of the deal," the bishop retorted. "Mitchell says he doesn't intend to hold on to the paintings. As far as he's concerned they're only fakes, and they'll have served the purpose of getting his revenge on Paul Belloc. Once the deal is done, he intends to resell them and has promised us, because of what we know and our background, that we can handle the sale," the bishop said.

Liz looked unimpressed. "What does that mean to me?" she asked.

"As all three of us have an equal interest in maintaining the integrity of such a sale, I am happy to share the resulting commission into three equal parts," he answered, then, turning to Adam, he added, "Assuming you're amenable to such a deal, Adam?"

Adam opened his eyes for the first time during the entire conversation. Both of their faces were stern. The little nagging suspicion that had been lurking in the back of his mind ever since

they were confronted with Mitchell's alternative began to surface.
Liz had just spoken it out loud and she was right. Phil and he were
both flattering and fooling themselves with wishful thinking.
Mitchell didn't need them. He and the bishop were surplus to his
requirements. More than that, they would always be a continuing
threat as they knew the truth. Most of all, taking into account the
millions that Mitchell would save, they were worth more dead
than alive. Maybe he had been doing the Bellocs a disservice.
Maybe it had been Mitchell behind Jack and Zannah's deaths all
along, and he had sent the keys to find out who knew what, to tie
up all the loose ends.

"I'll go along with whatever you decide, Phil; that's up to you,"
Adam answered. "But discussing commission sharing at this stage
strikes me as being a little premature. Liz might be right. Once
Mitchell has the paintings legally transferred, the three of us are
the only ones who are superfluous. The Bellocs aren't going to
blow any whistles since they were responsible for the faking, and
God knows what else, but you, me, and Liz—we are a different
matter. It's going to cost him a lot of money to ensure our collabo-
ration. We've got to be a lot cheaper dead. And the problem is that
I don't see how we can do a damn thing about it."

§

As he poured his breakfast coffee, Joe Rooney pondered over
Jack's demise and its associated problems, as he had been doing
quite a bit since the previous evening's dinner with Sarah. Initially,
the circumstances of his death had disturbed him, but as the days
had passed he had considered it less and less. A misadventure,
unusual circumstances certainly, but not homicide. But then there
was Zannah. He had grown up with Jack and had known him well.
Zannah he hardly knew at all. And while Jack's death could have
been simply a bizarre accident—easy to believe for anyone who
had known him—Zannah's was not.

Zannah had definitely been murdered, and by someone who

had either enjoyed doing it from pure sadism or who had tortured her for some reason. What? It wasn't money or jewelry; nothing like that had been taken as far as they could tell. Drugs? There was nothing to speak of—they had discovered evidence of the usual, a bit of weed, cocaine smears on a small mirror, that's all. Just recreational stuff, nothing to indicate that she was a heavy user or dealer. No murder weapon had been recovered, and there were no substantive forensic traces. There were no eyewitnesses, and no one saw or heard anything unusual in the building that evening, just the moderately loud music that had been playing on the radio. The total was nothing, and no suspects—and the further it got away in time, the less the likelihood of anything further being turned up. She would just become another Jane Doe in the statistics, another notch in the well-notched post.

Maybe it had something to do with Jack. But what? Apart from the obvious outrageous visual appearance of both corpses and the fact that they had been lovers, nothing jumped out. Hopefully that was nothing but coincidence, and it was all over. But what about the guy found in the New Jersey parking lot? That made three suspicious deaths that all had a link to the bishop. He spread some honey over his toasted muffin and mused as to whether he was turning into a health freak.

Crunching into the sweetened sourdough, he thought again of Sarah and the evening they had just spent together. He thanked God it had been Zannah and not her. He thought of their age difference; there must be nearly thirty years in it. Thirty years. His heart sank at the thought, and then the Anna guilt swept over him. No, he told himself, it wasn't a matter of one supplanting the other. He still loved Anna, but she was dead. Sarah was alive, and meeting her had rekindled all those emotions and drives that he had thought were gone forever. He may be thirty years older, but he felt a young man again.

By the time he had finished his breakfast, Rooney had made up his mind; he could no longer keep this pressurized inside him. Sarah had to be informed. She had a right to know. But he would have to proceed slowly, have to phrase things very carefully. He didn't want to frighten or alienate her before getting to the point. It was a problem that would be best approached obliquely. Yes, that was the answer. He would have to talk to Liz. Though he dreaded the prospect, he knew she had a right to know as well. He would approach her first of all and have a heart to heart discussion about the relationship between himself and her daughter, Sarah.

❦ 2 5 ❧

I
t was late evening before Adam and the bishop arrived down
in Florida, and they were both wrung out. So many flights
and airports in such a short time mixed badly with the news
they were about to deliver; neither of them was firing on all cylinders. There had been no further detours; the Belloc mansion was
their first stop in their hired sedan.

Paul Belloc Senior sat behind his desk, elbows resting on the
arms of his high-backed wing chair, fingers steepled in front of his
face, eyes closed. Opposite him, in mahogany framed, leather
upholstered chairs, sat the bishop and Adam. Paul Belloc Junior
paced erratically around the three of them before coming to a halt
behind his father.

"How did he find out?" he asked again, staring over his father's
head directly at the two in front. "How did he know all those
details about the paintings? The fire? Jack Hastings?"

The bishop shrugged, at a loss.

"Don't torture yourself with that at the moment, Paul," his
father said, opening his eyes and turning in his chair. "We can look
into that at a later date. As I see it, the situation is a fait accompli,
and it's a mere waste of energy to allow yourself to be sidetracked

by it. Let's concentrate on the problem and decide if there is anything at all we can salvage from it."

"He must be crazy if he thinks we'll agree to this!" Paul Junior spat.

The bishop and Adam said nothing. Old Paul Belloc, in a calm, controlled voice, addressed them all. "He's been very clever. Just like his father. Indeed, it's possible that he may have been even cleverer than we think. Who knows what surprises he may yet have in store?

"Certainly, at the moment, he has possession of the paintings, complete with their provenance. We, on the other hand, would appear to be in an impossible position: if either camp reveals that the paintings are fake, a can of worms of unforeseen proportions may burst open, with both personal and criminal implications too catastrophic to even contemplate risking."

Exasperated by his father's measured tones, Belloc Junior asked, "But if he knows they're fakes, what the hell does he want them for?"

"Revenge maybe," his father explained. "He would have them the way we had them in recent years. You may as well ask why we want them, or indeed why we don't want him to have them. After all, we too know they're fakes."

"That's easy," his son replied. "We want them because the world doesn't know that, and consequently they are worth over a hundred million dollars!"

"I'm afraid that was last week's situation, Paul," the old man said, "and it no longer prevails. This week, a non-sympathetic and powerful player in that world has altered the status quo and has reversed the roles. Now he has them, and we know they're fakes. And that knowledge would appear to be our only strength."

"Hmm, it's a strange sort of victory he's aiming for," the son said. "Although he'd have them, we'd know all he had were worthless fakes. He'd never be able to sell them."

"Unfortunately, I'm sure he thinks he would," old Belloc continued. "He'd have an iron-clad provenance. We could never challenge their authenticity, either in person or through a third party, without taking serious risks. Our complicity in their creation serves as his guarantee of our silence."

"Damn him!" Paul Junior said, arms waving with agitation. "I couldn't just stand by and watch him get away with that. I'd have to blow the whistle and deal with whatever shit happened."

"Maybe that's what he expects you to do—in which case you might be walking straight into his trap," his father said. "It's certainly an interesting situation, with him holding all the aces. He can either sell them when he feels like it, or at any time undermine our reputation and us, and cast doubt on the rest of our collecting integrity by submitting them to a rigorous authentication analysis in France."

"But he could do that now. He doesn't need to go any further with this farce to achieve that."

"You're not looking at this from Mitchell's position, Paul. He isn't on some anti-faking mission to clean up the art world. He's only interested in making me suffer, savoring his revenge. I imagine it doesn't matter one damn to him whether or not the paintings are exposed. He just wants to hurt us."

Paul Junior turned away.

Old Belloc continued, addressing the bishop. "Phil, you say he's here in Florida at the moment?" The bishop nodded and Belloc went on, "I don't want to rush into making irrevocable decisions without thinking this through a little more. So I'll leave it to you to arrange a meeting with Mitchell for tomorrow morning at about ten thirty. That'll give you two a chance to recover from your trip."

"Fine," the bishop said. "I'll speak to him and organize that. I'm sure whatever time suits you will suit him. After all, he has no other reason to be here."

§

Belloc Senior remained seated behind his desk as Adam and the bishop left, escorted out by Paul Junior. He sat back, trying to relax, to clear his mind, to try to anticipate Mitchell's next move. He told himself that he must not allow the Australian to provoke him; he must strive to remain calm and detached. He found himself experiencing a little anticipatory excitement. Yes, he was actually looking forward to tomorrow's confrontation. One hell of a lot.

Sipping at his glass of cold mineral water, he wondered where Paul was. He had expected him to storm right back in after the others had driven away. He didn't have to wait much longer. Paul Junior entered the room, not in the rage he had expected, but somewhat subdued. He approached his father's desk and sat down opposite him in the chair recently vacated by the bishop.

"Dad," he said. His father looked at him and raised his eyebrows as the son continued. "I think I know what's happened—how Mitchell found out about the paintings."

"You do?" his father responded. "How?"

Paul Junior now had his eyes screwed shut, and Belloc Senior could see that he was having difficulty going any further without becoming too emotional. Eventually, eyes still clenched, he uttered, "It was my fault."

"You?" Belloc Senior said. "What do you mean your fault?" His son's eyes opened, fear evident in them.

"Dad, I didn't want to have to tell you this," he stammered, "but I've been having a relationship with Rosa for a while."

His father rolled his eyes and replied, "Do you think I'm blind or stupid? Of course I know that!" He made a dismissive gesture with his hand. "I'm not saying I was entirely happy about it when I first found out." His voice began to calm. "But she's not a blood relation, and I suppose I've grown used to the idea now." He watched with interest as his son's translucent complexion flushed with embarrassment. "I was wondering when you'd ever get around to telling me."

"I'm sorry," the son said. "However, she knows about the paintings and the problems we were having." His voice grew urgent now.

"I think she's the one who's been providing the information to Mitchell."

"What makes you think this?" his father asked.

"You know she left last night to spend the weekend in Washington with friends?"

"Yes."

"Well, I've just called the hotel she was booked into. She's not there. They told me her booking was cancelled. Then I phoned her friends, and none of them knew where she might have gone. It's hard to admit it, but it's now obvious. She was the one best placed to inform on us to her brother. She's double-crossed us . . . double-crossed me!"

Belloc Senior eased himself to his feet and came around the desk to stand beside his son. He put an arm around his shoulders as Paul Junior choked his emotions into his father's chest, but as he looked down on his son's head he felt no pity at all.

§

The legal teams representing both sides remained in an anteroom while the Bellocs, Mitchell, the bishop, and Adam sat spread out around the large, circular conference table on the top floor of TC-SPEED's Miami office building. The vista stretched out over the city toward the ocean, but today no one was looking at the view. Despite being only mid-morning, it was already in the nineties and forecasting higher. The room maintained a comfortable seventy-two. Old Belloc's appearance gave no hint of his terminal condition; dressed in a light grey tropical-weight suit, he looked trim, tanned, calm, and controlled. Belloc Junior sat to his father's right, his face a taut tracery of fine blue veins overlaid by a veneer of strain and tension as he glared at Mitchell, who disregarded him.

The bishop at first attempted to introduce a businesslike normality to the meeting by addressing the reasons they were there, but he was interrupted by Belloc Senior.

"Excuse me, Phil, but let's not drag this out any more than necessary. We all know why we're here, and what for." He paused and addressed Mitchell. "Ray, I've had a few regrets in my life, and I must admit to you that the major one involves your family. We're all driven by different motives at different stages in our lives, and before we go any further in these negotiations, I want to get this out of the way."

Mitchell looked at him with an expression of gentle good humor on his face, as if he were listening to an old friend relate an entertaining yarn.

"I did your father an unforgivable injustice," Belloc went on. "An injustice made many times worse, since he'd been my friend. I could barely justify it to myself then, and I cannot at all now. Call it greed, jealousy, lust—maybe all three—it's irrelevant now. He was a better man than me in so many ways. I would have killed him had the positions been reversed." He paused and took a sip from the water glass on the table. "So, I want to apologize to him through you. Here, on the edge of my life, I can say that I'd change it all if I could. But of course I can't, no one can. I realize you probably see this as no more than a moment of pure self-indulgence on my part, a maudlin reviewing of the completed jigsaw that hindsight is. But for all that, I assure you that I mean it. I'm sorry—and don't worry, I don't expect you to shake my hand."

Mitchell straightened up in his seat and shrugged before replying, "I'm not in the least bit interested in helping you feel any better about yourself, Belloc. If you seriously feel that you fucked up in an earlier part of your life, then good. I'm as delighted as a dog with two dicks. And believe me, I'm really enjoying fucking up this final bit of it, you old bastard!"

Young Belloc's eyes flared, and as he attempted to stand, his father's grip restrained him.

"Now, if that's all you have to say," Mitchell continued, "let's get on with business. I understand our friends here have explained just how much of a barrel I have you over, so I assume you're here to do the deal?"

Though old Belloc maintained his reserve, his son sat wide-eyed and hissing with rage beside him. "You can't let him talk to us like that!" he managed to choke out. "Don't do it! Call it off!" His father sat quietly, saying nothing, just setting one brown, sun-wrinkled hand on his son's sleeve.

Casually, as though addressing a particularly dull child, Mitchell said, "Well, that's entirely up to you, stupid, but rest assured, by the end of today the authentication analysis in Paris will have revealed the three paintings as fakes." He smiled with relish and leaned forward, elbows on the table. "It's your call."

"Relax, Paul," said old Belloc, patting his son's arm and going on to address Mitchell. "You have the paintings, and as you anticipated, you may continue to keep them without further interference from us." All the earlier warmth had gone from his voice. "I probably don't have too much time left and, as you suspect, I've neither the stomach nor the inclination to confront the fallout of such an exposure.

"But before you grow too comfortably complacent, let me warn you. My son, sitting beside me here, doesn't have the emotional baggage that I have, and he assures me that if you attempt to sell these paintings after I'm gone, he will have no hesitation in exposing them as fakes to the world, just as you have threatened to do to us. So keep them, admire them, hang them on your walls, enjoy them in the knowledge that Jack Hastings was a genius; for that is what you have, fakes perpetrated by Jack Hastings—not Picassos. And Paul will never let you forget it."

Belloc Junior continued to glare at Mitchell. His father turned to the bishop and ordered, "Call in the lawyers with the documents, and let's get this farce over with!"

§

Paul Belloc and his son sat opposite each other in the back of the long, blacked-out limousine on the way back up the highway to their Palm Beach home. The divider was up between themselves and the driver, and the intercom was turned off. Paul Junior was nibbling on a hangnail, avoiding his father's gaze.

His father leaned forward and touched his knee with his hand.

"Don't get too screwed-up by all this," he said.

Paul Junior looked up. Determination had replaced the look of rage on his face. "I don't care what it takes, or how long it takes, but I will find her," he vowed, "and when that happens, the bitch will pay for it—I swear to you."

Paul Senior sat back in the deep leather seat. "I don't think that'll be necessary, Paul," he said. "The situation is not quite as black as it's painted." He smiled to himself at the unconscious pun.

His son looked at him uncomprehendingly.

"Don't beat yourself up too much about Rosa. Sure, you're right, she was in the perfect position to betray our secrets to her brother. Indeed, she may even have been in regular correspondence with him, but she has been sharing our lives for a long while —quite apart from sharing your bed—and I'm sure there must be some other explanation for her disappearance."

"Dad, one way or the other—whether Rosa was behind this or not—I just don't see what we can do," Paul Junior said. "He has the paintings and he has the signed documents that transfer the provenance to him. I don't see what else there is."

"Forgive me for not taking you fully into my confidence sooner, but I felt that having you confront Mitchell in a genuine rage was the safest option. Let him see that we are defeated and seething about it. Let him think that he's won the war," the old man said. He winked and touched his nose with the tip of his forefinger. "Don't worry. I may be old, but I still know a few tricks. I'll explain it all to you later, in assured privacy, when we reach home."

❧ 26 ❧

Liz was not happy with the news from Florida. Certainly, two and a half million dollars wasn't to be sneezed at, but she deserved more, wanted more, and had been promised more. Twice that amount. The bishop and Adam had returned and once again were seated side by side on the same sofa in her apartment, each nursing a mug of coffee. As she stood looking at them opposite her, she felt a confusion of emotions. Phil had never before let her down. On countless occasions, he had dealt with problems on her behalf and had always been her dependable stalwart. Now, at this critical moment, which they had spent years anticipating and working toward, he had lost control. He was in retreat. He was failing her.

The presence of Adam Kennedy grated on her more than anything—in the room, in the deal, and in her life. Just a mere matter of weeks ago, his existence barely impinged at a conscious level. He was like the spare wheel in the trunk. You knew it was there, but you hoped you'd never need to have anything to do with it. She made sure their paths rarely crossed, and when they did, she felt nothing more than a vague irritation. That had all changed. Now, since Sarah's return, his presence in her life had grown like a malignant tumor and was proving just as difficult to inhibit. Sure, they had been friends once . . . more than friends. They'd had a fling when she was young and he was younger, but that was a mistake long forgotten by both of them. Now he was just a parasite existing on scraps from the bishop's table. She didn't want him in her home at all. He was a nothing. Without Jack's and her influence on him, and the bishop's impeccable bona fides, which had allowed the entire fraudulent industry to blossom unhindered and unsuspected, he would have nothing. Until last week, he hadn't even known the truth about the paintings, the bishop protecting his sensibilities as if he were a child. He didn't deserve a fraction of what he had received in the past, never mind what was promised from this sale, and most of all, he certainly didn't deserve any of the attention he was getting from Sarah.

They had arrived back from Florida, as Phil had promised, to acquaint her with the development of the deal—a deal which should have been theirs, under their control, with their own substantial profits. Now, as she regarded the two wrung out sights before her, she saw two mere messengers, two lackeys eager to pander to any promise of a pathetic percentage. Manipulated rather than manipulators.

And then there was the irritating problem with Rooney. He had already phoned this afternoon and in his inimitable cop, brow-beating style, had insisted on visiting her this evening. Something important, he claimed. Until Jack's death, he was another she hadn't seen in years, but since the funeral, he too had become a regular intruder in the affairs of Sarah and herself. He had been a handsome young man all those years ago, with dark Italian looks inherited from his mother, but he hadn't aged well. Too much booze, too many cigarettes, and not enough exercise. He had reeked of tobacco smoke the last time he and his young partner called to the apartment after Jack's girlfriend's death, and now the thought of having to entertain him in her home again made her nose wrinkle with distaste. He had been very insistent, no doubt still trying to ingratiate himself with Sarah. In fact, he seemed to have developed an almighty crush on her. Imagine, taking her out to dinner. How ridiculous these pathetic old guys can be.

She had to speak out, to make her concerns known. "So, that's it then, Phil? We simply sit around waiting for someone else to make the next move?"

The bishop spread his palms up in a gesture of spiritual revelation. "Look at this positively, Liz. By Monday afternoon, my Geneva account will have the amount Mitchell agreed upon deposited into it. I will then transfer your share and Adam's to wherever each of you nominate. After that, we'll just have to be patient."

Liz paced about the room, gesticulating. "Yeah—so you say, but I'm not happy about this. I just don't trust this Mitchell person, and even if he keeps his word about the two and a half million, it's very unlikely we're ever going to see any more. Young Belloc is sure to blow the whistle if Mitchell tries to sell them again. You've just told me yourself that he warned Mitchell he would."

Adam shifted his empty coffee mug from hand to hand.

The bishop shrugged. "I don't know, Liz. Yes, I know they've threatened to do that, but it sounded like saber-rattling to me— just an effort to save face. I'm sure, no matter what that brat threatens, he can never be in a position to undermine their authenticity without bringing one hell of a lot of strife down on his own head."

"Well, if you are right and Mitchell calls the Belloc's bluff successfully, he's certainly going to be making a most substantial profit," Liz said. "For an outlay of just seven and a half million dollars, he has acquired assets worth maybe a hundred and twenty or so million more. Even should he live up to his promises, we still won't be grossing as much as was anticipated in the original deal, and this way there's a lot more work, a lot more stress, and a lot more risk. I'm not happy about any of it."

"Sure, I understand your point of view," responded the bishop, "but remember, Liz, we're not talking about the real thing here . . . we're talking about fakes."

"That's not the point!" Liz yelled, slamming her coffee mug down on the breakfast bar section of the kitchen worktop that separated the two areas, her coffee fountaining everywhere.

"What's not the point?" asked Sarah, closing the apartment door behind her. "Am I interrupting something?"

"What are you doing here?" Liz snapped, grabbing a chunk of paper toweling to mop up the mess.

"Joe Rooney asked me to meet him here, so here I am," she answered. Taking her topcoat off, she slung it over a chair and sat on the arm of the sofa beside Adam. "But I didn't know there was going to be a party."

Before Liz had time to respond, the intercom buzzer sounded. It was Rooney. She glanced at the time on her wrist: eight o'clock. Never a weak person, she swept the surge of despair she felt to one side and girded herself to deal with a difficult evening.

As he entered, Rooney's eyebrows rose in surprise. "I sure didn't expect to see you guys here. Thought you'd still be in Paris," he said to the bishop and Adam, then added with a smile, "Hi, Sarah."

Both the bishop and Adam nodded their subdued acknowledgements toward him without bothering to offer any explanation for their presence. Sarah's greeting, on the other hand, was more enthusiastic.

"Hi, Joe! Good to see you again."

Rooney beamed back at her.

As Liz took his overcoat, she noticed the lack of cigarette odor, and glancing at him, it struck her that he looked altogether a good deal tidier than he had only a few days previously. She guided him to a single easy chair and offered him refreshment, which he refused.

An awkward silence followed, during which Rooney became aware that, apart from Sarah, the others were staring at him.

"What's the matter?" he said, dropping his eyes to his clothing, "Is my zipper open? Is there something wrong? Have I come at a bad time?" His eyes darted around the room looking for an answer, eventually resting on the bishop.

"Sorry, Joe," the bishop said, sounding weary. "Please excuse us. It's just that Adam and I have had one hell of an exhausting seventy-two hours. We're zonked. Back and forth to Paris, and then Florida, where we've just come from. On top of which, the French deal hasn't quite worked out the way we'd hoped."

Adam just nodded.

"Huh, sorry about that," Rooney said, as if infected by their depression.

Liz broke the mood. "So, what was it that you wanted to speak to me—and obviously, Sarah—about?"

Rooney looked around, and when he spoke, his voice quavered. "It's sort of—well, confidential. Sort of... personal."

Sarah's arm was resting on the back of the sofa behind Adam's head, her fingers surreptitiously brushing the nape of his neck. The bishop nudged Adam with his elbow.

"I think it's time we were leaving anyway," he said, preparing to rise. "I'll talk to you tomorrow, Liz."

Liz spoke over the bishop's final words, "Just stay where you are, please. If this is what I think it's about, I'd be grateful if you'd stay." Then, turning to Rooney, she said, "Okay, we all know each other here—spit it out!"

"No, no . . . I don't think it would be right, Liz. It's about Sarah and about me. It's not fair to expect me to do it like this," he protested.

"How sweet!" Liz's voice dripped with sarcasm, but she remained firm. "Come on! Do you think I don't have a good idea of what's going on in your deluded *love's young dream* head? I'd already worked that bit out so, for Christ's sake, will you stop pussyfooting around and get on with your protestations of undying love!" she shouted.

Rooney looked dejected as he turned toward the three on the sofa and addressed them. Both the bishop and Adam, uneasy with this unexpected turn of events, looked everywhere but into Rooney's face.

"This isn't how I wanted this to come out," he said, "but I suppose you two would've heard tomorrow anyway . . ." He shrugged. "I suppose."

Liz stood drumming the fingers of her right hand against her thigh.

Rooney swallowed, took a deep breath and cleared his throat. Then he spoke directly to Sarah, "Okay, look, I hate to bring this up again—Jack's terrible death. And I know it was an awful time for you." Sarah sat quietly on the sofa arm, now covertly kneading Adam's neck.

"A couple of things were established at the time through the forensic tests. First, Jack wasn't under the influence of alcohol or any drugs when he died. He was in perfect health; no sign of cancer, tumors or any other terminal condition that may have influenced him to take his own life. As you know, hanging was the cause of his death." Rooney dropped his head and paused before taking another deep breath before continuing. "But what you may not know is that hanging invariably causes involuntary ejaculation in males, and Jack was no exception."

Sarah squeezed down onto the main body of the sofa beside Adam and reached for his hand. Liz glared at her.

"The ejaculate was discovered during the preliminary examination and, routinely, it was tested. The result was a surprise."

The three on the sofa were now looking at him. Liz remained standing, sphinxlike.

"Jack was sterile," he said.

"Sterile!" Sarah was the first to speak. "How could that have happened?"

"It didn't *happen*, Sarah," Rooney replied. "I'm afraid Jack was congenitally sterile; it wasn't a condition that had only recently occurred."

"Congenitally sterile!" Sarah said. "Are you telling me that he was always sterile?"

"I'm sorry, Sarah, but that's correct," he said, nodding.

Consternation widened Sarah's eyes as the implication slowly dawned. She looked over toward her mother, whose face, though still impassive, had grown paler. "Is this right? Did you know this?" she demanded.

All eyes were now staring at Liz, whose gaze was fixed on Rooney. She made no reply.

"Mom!" she shouted, "If Jack was sterile, who was my father?"

Liz reached for her purse, rummaged for a Kleenex, and glared at Rooney again. "Why are you doing this?" she asked, her voice strong but vibrating with anger. "What's the good of bringing all this stuff up now with Jack dead?"

"Mom, answer me! Who the hell is my real father?" Sarah yelled.

Liz stood, breasts heaving, turning to stare directly into her daughter's eyes as if deciding whether to tell her or not. "He's sitting there beside you," she said.

Sarah, Adam and Rooney all looked toward the bishop, whose mouth had suddenly fallen open. He, in turn, snatched staccato glances around, as if to see who else could possibly be sitting on the couch.

"Oh my God, the bishop! He's my father?" Tears were now welling in her eyes.

"No, not Phil! Beside you! The person I've been trying to keep you from jumping into bed with ever since you've come back from Europe!"

Sarah leapt from the settee and bolted into the kitchen area. She grabbed a bunched handful of paper towels from the roll holder and muffled her cries into them, leaning into the bowl of one of the double sinks. Adam, now also on his feet, was yelling as well. "Me! Sarah's father? You must be crazy! I was only a kid! We hardly knew each other! It only lasted a short time!"

She retorted, "It only takes once if you're unlucky."

Liz walked over and cradled her sobbing daughter in her arms and murmured, "Sorry, Sarah, I didn't think that's what he was going to bring up. I thought it was something else—I was wrong."

Rooney had already stood up and had joined Liz and Sarah. He stroked Sarah's hair, trying to comfort her, to calm her down.

"Liz," he said during a break in Sarah's sobbing, "you're wrong; it's not Adam."

His quiet words reverberated around the room like thunder. Once again, he was the focus of attention. Adam took a step backward and collapsed onto the sofa again, the bishop placing a hand on his jacketed arm. Liz became still, and Sarah's sobbing eased a little, her head still buried in her mother's supporting shoulder.

"It's not Adam, and it's not Phil. I've had all the tests done, and there is no room for doubt. I'm sorry, Liz." Rooney put his hand on the shoulder with which she was supporting Sarah. "Sarah's my daughter!" he said.

It was one of those snapshot moments when the world stops and everything is frozen; one of those moments when there is enough time to count the hairs on the back of your hand, the pores on the face opposite. You have forever; time no longer exists. No sound, no movement; even Sarah's mewling ceased. But it didn't last. Liz erupted into recovery.

"Yours?" she screamed, shrugging Rooney's hand off. "That can't be right!"

"As you've just said yourself, it only takes once if you're unlucky, but believe me, it's true. I can show you the report."

"Fuck the report . . . and fuck you! I can't believe it. It can't have been more than once or twice!"

"Look, Liz, it was as big a shock to me as well. I had no idea either. But from the moment I saw her at the funeral, I knew she looked familiar, knew I'd seen that look before. Even when I saw in the report that Jack was sterile, I still didn't make the connection. It was only when I came across an old photograph of my mother when she was a girl that it clicked. After that, well . . ."

Sarah spun from out of her mother's grasp. Her tears had ceased, but her face was red and swollen and her voice when she spoke sounded strong. She was back in control and turned to her mother. "Thank God there are only three men here tonight, or this may have taken even longer! I can't believe that for all these years you thought Adam Kennedy was my father! That's why you were giving me such a hard time—to stop us from committing incest! Well, I'm pleased to tell you, you failed!" She threw her hands up and ran them back through her hair. "And now this—I'm nothing but a fucking cuckoo!"

"Calm down, Sarah, that's not true. The most important thing is that you're *my* daughter. I bore you, and raised you, and loved you—nothing else matters!" She put her hand out and moved toward Sarah, who instantly recoiled.

"No! I can't look at any of you," she said, turning and tearing off more paper towels before swerving past her mother in the direction of the bedrooms.

Liz turned to Rooney. "Thanks one hell of a lot for that! But don't think that we're ever gonna be playing Happy Families!" and without another word, she turned and strode out of the room after her daughter.

§

The bishop broke the lengthy silence. "You've given us all quite a shock there, Joe. One thing's sure—you'll never get a transfer to the diplomatic corps." He stood up and went over to the fridge, taking out a beer. "Anyone else want one?"

"Thanks," said Adam, moving over to take the proffered can. "My tongue feels like it's part of the roof of my mouth."

Rooney nodded and the bishop handed him another. They all returned to their seats.

"Phil, I'm sorry. You know I didn't want it to come out like that. She forced me."

"Perhaps," the bishop said, "but it's out in the open now, and who knows? Maybe deep down, you just needed an excuse to get it out—any excuse."

DANN FARRELL

As Adam and the bishop opened their cans and guzzled long draughts, Rooney said, "Who knows? Maybe you're right." They sat in silence drinking, then Rooney said, "By the way, where's André at the moment . . . still in Africa?"

The bishop answered, "Yes, he's still there, though I haven't heard from him in a couple of days since we've been away. Why do you ask?"

"Just something that came up made me think of him," he answered. "Have you thought anymore about the guy calling himself Snow—you know, the one who phoned you from his cell-phone?" he added.

"No. I must admit I haven't thought of him since. We've been so busy. You got a photo of him yet?"

"Yeah, but not on me—down at the office."

Adam interrupted, "Who's Snow, and what's he got to do with anything?"

"Maybe nothing, Adam, but the New Jersey cops found a body in a car a few days ago," Rooney answered. "Driver's license identi-fied him as John Snow—but it was a counterfeit."

"What would that have to do with Phil?"

"The guy didn't have much with him: driver's license, untrace-able credit card in the same name, a few hundred bucks in cash, a knife, a loaded pistol and an armful of groceries lying on the rear seat. But, as I've already explained to Phil, he also had a burner phone on which he'd made only one call. This call, I'm afraid, was to Phil's unlisted number, and a conversation took place lasting forty-seven seconds exactly. Too long for a wrong number, don't you think?"

"And there were no other calls on this phone?"

"No, none outgoing, though he did receive one from a public phone later on the same evening, the evening he was killed. The second call was a bit longer, nearly three minutes."

Rooney moved closer, pulling up his chair until his knees were nearly touching the bishop's. "Phil, I don't know what's been going on, but I do have certain suspicions. Is there anything you'd like to share with me . . . not as a cop, but as a friend?"

The bishop answered him, "I appreciate your concern, Joe, but you've lost me. Anyway, why would you be interested in a John Doe homicide in another state? Do you think it's linked to Zannah's killing somehow? In any case, I don't know how you can imagine that this man, Snow, had anything to do with me. I can't be held responsible for other people calling my number—unlisted or not."

"This wasn't just a regular homicide, Phil. There were a couple of unusual things." Rooney looked around and lowered his voice a little. Adam leaned forward to catch his words as he continued. "To start with, it was all very tidy and efficient. Two rounds right into the cranial cavity, obviously a reduced charge as they didn't exit, just scrambled his brains. No ejected brass left in the vehicle. And, from traces of latex rubber melted into the skin and on the victim's jacket, it looks like the killer had a condom stretched completely over the weapon. Serves as a makeshift silencer, and stops the brass flying everywhere. Sounded professional to me, more like a hit than anything else. Then when your phone number entered the equation, the mist cleared."

The bishop wore a horrified look on his face, "Joe, I don't know what you're implying . . ."

"It's more of an observation than an accusation, Phil. And really, I don't give two fucks about that guy. He's proving to be so invisible that he probably deserved it. Most likely a hired killer, maybe Russian Mafia, who knows? Certainly, his dental work is reckoned to be of Eastern European origin." He leaned closer to the bishop, and gesturing with his beer can, said, "But anyway, Phil, we know: you, me, and probably Adam. We all know that André, with his background, would fit the bill one hundred percent. Come on, level with me. Did that guy slice Zannah up? Did André even the score?"

The bishop sat back on the sofa as though he had been pushed, "You can't be serious, Joe! André's not a killer!"

"Yeah, I know he's retired, Phil, but maybe he made an exception for old time's sake," Rooney responded. Then he shrugged. "You know, there's a lot been going on here that I'm in the dark about; but I suspect both of you could shed some light on it if you cared to. However, I did get a line on some things during this investigation—in particular, something about Zannah's death, or more accurately, *life,* that, because of our friendship, I've kept quiet."

"What's that?" Adam asked, his face grim at the memory of Zannah.

"Well, we all know she was pregnant, and yes, we know it wasn't yours," he added to Adam. "So, who was the father? Her phone records showed calls to both of you, among others. But quite a lot to you, Phil."

"Of course they did. Jack would have called me from her place often, and she herself called me several times after Jack's death," the bishop answered.

"Sorry, Phil—but I know," Rooney said. "It was a long shot, but when I learned about Snow and the phone call, I took some samples from your bathroom when I was round at your place the other day. Of course, because of the way I took them it couldn't ever be admissible in court, but I just needed to check it out for myself. The fact is that, through the DNA analysis, I know you're the father of her embryo."

Adam sat back, astonishment on his face. The bishop was in the process of drawing breath to protest when Rooney continued, "I know you were down in Florida that night, Phil, so, off the record—tell me who killed Zannah and why. Was it Snow? Was it André?"

The bishop sat still and unresponsive for a moment, then he calmly stated, "May Jesus Christ be my judge, neither myself nor André had anything to do with her terrible murder. I swear to you, Joe. In fact—as I've already told you—that was the weekend I sent him to Boston, and from there to Africa on a couple of charity-related problems that had cropped up. As for this person, Snow, I just couldn't say."

"I want to believe you, Phil," Rooney said. "But I know not to put too much reliance on your oath. I know better than most who you are, who the person is under the cassock. I hate to say it, since I like you and we go back a long way, but essentially your life has been one long lie that has provided you with power and a very comfortable lifestyle. You're not a real priest, a believing priest. You're a fake."

The bishop's tone was earnest now. "Joe, I can't deny that some of what you say is true, but many of us find ourselves living lives that are like badly fitting garments that we're uncomfortable in, and unfortunately, many of us die in them. The truth is that we're all prisoners of the decisions made for us either by our family, our circumstances, or our youth. Some of us have been more fortunate than others, and sure, I won't deny I've made the best of my opportunities. And though I may have found myself representing beliefs that I no longer hold, I've never publicly undermined them, out of respect for the congregation and gratitude to the hand that's fed me for all these years. You may sit there and accuse me of hypocrisy, but you can't accuse me of ingratitude or lack of fellow feeling for others. And I'm damn sure you can't accuse me of murder!"

In the silence that followed, Adam watched Rooney and the bishop sit motionless. He addressed Rooney, "It's unbelievable . . . first you and Sarah and then him and Zannah!" He turned to the bishop. "You've not only been deceiving me for years, but you've been fucking Zannah as well!"

"Adam—sure, I know you have a right to complain about some of the things I've kept from you. However, I can't apologize for things that weren't really any of your concern—and strange as it may sound coming from me, my sexual life fits into that category."

"Phil, you can screw around as much as you want, but Zannah! She's dead—pregnant and dead—and you were the father!"

"I didn't know—honestly—she never told me." He turned to Rooney. "Even when I heard, I never thought it might be me."

"Why? Did you stick to the Church's line on contraception and just rely on Divine intervention?"

"She was a modern woman, Joe. I simply assumed—"

"Hold on, both of you," Adam interjected. "Neither of you is in any position to be casting stones, and this certainly isn't the place to be having this argument, with Sarah, and what she's gone through, just next door."

Rooney remained silent for a moment before saying, "Yeah, maybe you're right. Maybe I got a bit carried away. Sorry, Phil."

The bishop raised his hand in acknowledgement.

"Let's grab a cab and go elsewhere," Adam said.

"It's not necessary. I have a car downstairs," Rooney said. Standing up and walking toward the bishop, he grabbed his outstretched hand and heaved him out of his seat. "Come on, let's go and sort out all this shit over a drink." He draped his arm around the bishop's shoulders and steered him toward the door as Adam walked ahead of both of them.

As they pulled the door closed, Liz emerged from the hallway, looking after them.

❦ 27 ❦

I t was shortly before dawn when Liz left the apartment, leaving Sarah alone, deep in a sedated sleep. She drove fast through the sparse early Sunday morning traffic, feeling adrenaline-sharp despite having had a sleepless night, brooding about the implications of the previous evening. She had overheard everything Rooney and the others had said. It wasn't the fact that the bishop had screwed Zannah that was upsetting—that wasn't important to her—but he'd been doing it on a regular basis. He'd been having an affair with the bitch. This signaled another strong possibility—that he'd been planning to use Zannah to sideline her, to try to cut her out of her share. It's been part of his plan all along. Ungrateful, lying, hypocritical bastard—Rooney was right.

As she swung into the private Church-property parking lot, the grey morning light was beginning its inexorable creep in from the East, improving nothing in the grim material world nor in her disposition. The streets and buildings looked dismal, damp, and abandoned, mirroring her mood. She seethed as she thought of all she had done for him. It was her influence that had loomed over everything, that had encouraged Jack to accommodate Phil with repairs and restoration of old paintings in the beginning, and then encouraged him to accommodate him further with the occasional fake. An impulse that had grown into an industry. Now, it was obvious, no use trying to fool herself. All the signs pointed to the fact that his loyalties had shifted. She had been used, merely strung along. No wonder he was so upset when he heard of Zannah's death, she thought, his plan was obviously to fuck her and fuck me over. She slammed the car door closed behind her.

The bishop's bleary eyes widened in surprise as he opened the door. He looked tired and disheveled, dressed only in a white bathrobe, his feet bare. He stood to one side, and as she brushed past him in the hallway, she could see ahead of her the evidence of a long night's drinking spread over the big central coffee table: empty bottles of beer, whiskey and vodka. Lingering above it all hung the stink of stale booze.

"Been having a few with the boys?" Her voice was scathing.

"Something like that," he murmured. "Would you like a coffee?"

"I'm not here on a social visit," she replied as she walked ahead of him into the lounge. Quickly scanning the room, she satisfied herself that they were alone and turned to face him. "I overheard everything that meddler, Rooney, told you last night, and I can't let it go. You were screwing that bitch, Zannah, behind my back. That's bad enough, but she was carrying your child. I just can't believe it!"

"Calm down, Liz, it's not what it seems." He touched her on the elbow, urging her to take a seat.

She pulled her arm away, remaining on her feet. "No, you're exactly right. It's not what it seemed, but it's all pretty clear to me now. You and she were going to double-cross me and maybe even Jack, then you, your new mistress, her child and probably your protégé, Kennedy, could just sail off into the retirement sunset. For a celibate, you've got one hell of a big family!"

"Don't be crazy, Liz, I was just keeping her sweet. You know how erratic Jack was becoming. This way I had a spy in the camp and could gain an insight into his intentions. At the same time, it meant that I could try to control her greed and ambition. Believe me, the last thing I expected was for her to become pregnant."

"I don't believe you, you ungrateful bastard." Her voice was rising. "Have you forgotten all that I've done for you? That it was me who encouraged Jack to paint the pictures you wanted in the beginning? All those years—all that we've meant to each other—and you do this to me!"

"Calm down! I've done nothing to you. Jack always got a fair percentage for any work that he did, and you can't claim to have been neglected either."

"Yes, but of course you, your charity, and your acolyte benefited with the lion's share. For all I know, the famous charity is also a fiction." The bishop shook his head in exasperation. "And then this whole Mitchell story. It sounded fishy from the beginning. But I stupidly trusted you. It's just your way of fobbing me off with scrapings!"

"Liz, I've said it before, but two and a half million dollars isn't scrapings in anyone's money," he explained in a patient tone, "but whether you believe me or not, it's the truth. Adam was there with me; he'll confirm it."

"Sure! You expect me to believe him?"

"Look, this is a bad time for this sort of argument. I've had a very late night and very little sleep. Let's relax and have a coffee."

He moved to put his arm around her.

She shrugged him away. "I won't be condescended to. I won't be treated like the little woman. If it weren't for me, you wouldn't be where you are today."

The bishop's patience with her was beginning to wear. "Don't overstate it, Liz. I know you've done a lot. Jack could be a loose cannon and you often kept him in check, but don't for one moment think you were indispensable. I could've handled him on my own."

"Like hell you could! Ever since Jack and I split, you've been losing influence with him. That's why he was becoming awkward, more demanding, not jumping to your every request, and holding you to ransom!"

"Give it a rest, Liz," he said with a dismissive wave.

"Give it a rest! I haven't started yet. You're a fool if you think that without my perseverance with Jack, you'd ever have had the paintings."

"Nonsense!"

"No, it was me Jack couldn't do without. He only moved out and into his studio because I insisted, because it was what I wanted."

She pointed a finger at him. "And why do you think I wanted it?" She paused, waiting for the bishop to answer.

"Why ask me? How the hell should I know?" he barked in return. "You're well practiced at being an enigma. I stopped trying to rationalize your behavior a long time ago."

"It was you, you blind fool. With Sarah away, I was making room for our relationship to fulfil its promise after all those years —especially with the upcoming windfall of the paintings' sale and you always dreaming of your retirement. It was to prepare for a future for both of us together.

"Jack had always hoped it was a temporary arrangement, that I would take him back. Zannah and the others were nothing to him —just candies. I saw him when necessary, pushed all the right buttons, kept him in line. It was *me* who ensured he didn't go too much off message. Toward the end, of course, the prospect of the money was going to his head, and he became more difficult to handle. Like you, he didn't realize how important I was."

"Are you telling me that all the time you and he have been apart, you've been seeing him? That you've been . . .?"

"Fucking him? Yes, whenever necessary," she said. "Keeping him sweet, controlling his greed and ambition. Sound familiar?"

The bishop's chin dropped to his chest as he shook his head, stunned.

"That was nothing," Liz continued, "just the beginning. What sickens me is that I've invested the most important things I have in you—my emotions and my future—I've taken countless risks for you. And you've just been using me. I'm nothing to you! I've often wondered why you were so concerned with keeping your apprentice squeaky-clean. He mustn't know this; he mustn't know that! He's your alter ego, your conscience; that's why you wanted to keep him pure!"

"That's not true, Liz." He sounded as though he was pleading. "You know how important you are to me. I've just been doing what I thought was for the best for everyone. But I never dreamed of you and Jack—"

"Sauce for the goose, Phil, but at base it would mean nothing. Except, unlike you, I wasn't planning to start another family!"

"I swear, Liz, I didn't know. I thought it was harmless. She meant nothing to me."

"You're pathetic! Playing around with that greedy, stupid bitch, while I had to do the real work."

"What d'you mean?"

"That cunt had no influence at all with Jack. If I'd taken him back, he would've done anything—painted a hundred Picassos— but I didn't want him. I wanted what you and I had, and so I had to do it the other way."

"You've lost me, I'm sorry."

"Must be your lack of sleep that's making you so dense this morning. So let me spell it out. I knew he had the paintings finished. He told me, and he offered to hand them over if he could move back in. I pretended to consider it, let him think that there was a chance I would change my mind. In the meantime, I tried to bargain with him, accommodate him in his little games, get him to release them to you. Eventually, though, it became obvious that he felt that as long as he held them, he had the upper hand—that he could control me. Of course, he didn't admit that out loud. He just tried to string me along.

"The cross-dressing fetish that killed him was his favorite game. He'd been at it for a while before I found out. But having scared himself once, doing it on his own, he introduced me as a safety device. Of course, when he found that having me as a spectator was an even bigger turn on, it became regular—either as an end in itself, or as extreme foreplay.

"So the last time, on his birthday, when he was being particularly difficult about the paintings and virtually blackmailing me into assisting him with his transvestite games, I got fed up with it. I had to teach him a lesson, so I kicked the stool away and strung him along for a change!"

Liz didn't see it coming: the flat of the bishop's hand cracked across the left side of her face with such force that it sent her spinning onto the floor.

"God forgive you!" he shouted, stepping forward as though he was about to follow up.

Adam's voice interrupted, "I thought I heard . . . Christ, what's going on?" He entered from the hallway leading to the bedrooms, buttoning up his shirt. "Phil? What's happened? Is that Liz?"

The bishop held his hand out toward him and cried, "It's okay, it's okay! I can handle this. Go back inside. Please leave us alone!"

Liz had started to pick herself up, lifting her purse from the floor beside her and producing a small, black automatic pistol. Flipping the safety off with her right thumb, she straightened up and pointed it at the bishop.

"Pretty typical of you, still trying to protect him. Last night, my daughter lost her father for the second time when she discovered that she is the child of a complete stranger. How do you think that makes me feel? That was something she never needed to find out. So let's face your surrogate son with a few home truths!"

"Liz, please," the bishop pleaded, "put the gun down."

She ignored his plea; the muzzle of the automatic maintained its steady aim.

"Yes, you kept him in the dark for all those years, but you made sure he benefited handsomely when it came to sharing the profits. All the rewards and none of the risks. I never liked it. Well, I can tell him a few things that can implicate him, sully his conscience!"

"What's she talking about, Phil?"

Phil closed his eyes and almost whispered, "She killed Jack for the Belloc paintings."

Liz motioned with the gun barrel, beckoning Adam to move closer to the bishop.

"I did it for your friend and mine," she said, indicating the bishop. "My ungrateful, holier than thou, two-timing lover of fifteen years!"

The bishop clutched his temples. "God forgive you," he said again.

"Are you trying to tell me that you had no idea?" Liz spat back. "That you didn't suspect?"

The bishop shook his head from side to side in silent reply.

"I suppose you didn't know that I disposed of Belloc's goon either, after you phoned me about him?"

Adam stared at her open-mouthed as the bishop lifted his head again to look at her. He didn't need to speak. Liz knew what he was thinking. He had been fooling himself.

"How did you think he so conveniently disappeared?" she asked. "A guardian angel? And then, of course there was your mistress and the matter of the keys to the New Jersey studio. Now that I know what was going on between you, I'm really glad that she held out so long."

"No!" Adam found himself yelling, "You killed Zannah! You cut her up like that!"

Liz shook her head, the left side of her face beginning to discolor and swell from the bishop's blow. "No, I didn't. But to ensure we got the keys and all the information, I arranged for someone more skilled than myself to deal with her."

"Who did it? What animal did that to her?" Adam shouted.

"Unlike your mentor here, I'm not one to betray friends and helpers," Liz said.

She calmly watched the tensing and angling of Adam's physique, signaling an attack, and, with the slightest movement of her wrist, retrained her weapon on him. As he started to move, she began to squeeze the trigger.

The bishop lunged sideways at Adam as the hammer fell, the report a subdued crack like an axe on dry kindling. Blood was already blackening the shoulder area of his white bathrobe as he landed in a jumble on top of Adam on the floor.

It was so easy. Liz marveled at just how easy she found it. As if pre-programmed, she watched herself perform: detached, emotionless, but nonetheless admiring. Stepping forward to administer the coup de grâce, she stood over the tangle of bodies. She gripped the bishop's hair tightly with her left hand, yanking his head to one side. She had a clear shot to the back of Adam's skull.

She only just heard the sound of the subsonic .38 slug before it took a chunk off the back of her own head.

❧ 28 ❧

Joe Rooney had not been into the office in the days following Liz's death. Now that the police interviews were over, he simply wished to be left alone. No need to leave the house; just make a phone order, charge it, and have it delivered. Booze, cigarettes and fast food, and not even that much of the latter passed his lips. He was avoiding everyone, or almost everyone; let the machine do the talking. He wasn't even going to attend the funeral, though the turmoil surrounding that decision only depressed him more. He felt even more of a coward for not doing so.

It was just after noon and the room was dark except for a thin triangle of dust-particled light slicing through a gap in the still-drawn drapes. He sat slumped in the La-Z-Boy where he had passed the night amid overflowing ashtrays, empty beer cans and liquor bottles. Unshaven and disheveled, wearing the same clothes he had slept in since the shooting, his eyelids barely flickered as his phone began to ring beside him. The machine picked up after four rings.

"Joe, if you're there, pick up. It's me, Carl."

He remained motionless, eyes still closed. There was only one person he wanted to receive a call from.

"I went to the memorial service at the funeral home this morning. I spoke to Sarah," Carl continued into the machine.

Rooney shifted in his seat, leaned over to the side table, lifted the handset and punched a button to stop the recording.

"I'm here. You spoke to Sarah?"

"Yeah. Are you okay, Joe?"

"I'm okay," he replied in a subdued voice. "You were saying . . . the memorial service?"

"Yeah, there was quite a big turnout, just a few familiar faces missing."

Rooney only grunted in response.

"Neither the bishop nor Adam Kennedy were there—not surprising, I suppose. The medical examiner will be releasing the body to the funeral director later today—it's to be directly cremated by the funeral home."

"You were talking to Sarah? Did she . . ."

"I paid my respects, and though I'm sure she remembered me, I'm afraid your name was never mentioned."

Rooney remained silent.

"I did hear from some others I was talking to that she's planning on leaving New York, though. Moving back to Europe, they said."

"When?"

"Don't know exactly, but I got the impression it's sometime soon." Carl's voice took on a concerned edge. "Look, Joe, can I get you anything?"

"No thanks, I've got everything I need."

"Yeah, but with the holiday tomorrow . . ."

Rooney concentrated, what was Carl talking about? Then he remembered. Today was Wednesday; tomorrow would be Thursday . . . Thanksgiving!

"I was thinking that maybe you'd like it if we spent it together."

Thanksgiving! This was the last thing Rooney needed. "Carl," he said, "I appreciate your concern, but I'm okay. I just need some time to myself. Remember, I've been through worse."

"Okay, Joe. But one thing's just come up that you might like to know."

"Mm . . ." Joe grunted.

"The ballistic report on Liz's pistol's come through. It's the one that was used in New Jersey—unregistered and so far untraceable. All the remaining rounds in the magazine are the same as those used on Snow, all hand-prepared with a reduced propellant charge. Lucky for the bishop, I suppose, but I wonder where she got her hands on that?"

"I don't know, Carl." Rooney sounded weary. "I just don't know."

"Well, think about it, and if you need anything at all, at any time, don't hesitate, just call me," Carl said. "Even if you just need someone to yell at, I'm only a phone call away."

"Yeah, thanks." And he hung up.

§

Rooney had tried several times, but he had never managed to get through to her. There was never any answer at her grandmother's home, so he tried her mother's apartment. That was worse; each time he called, the machine picked up and the voice of the woman he'd killed invited him to leave a message. After the third time, he couldn't face her again. He had shot dead the mother of his only child, and now that child was going to leave New York, the continent and his life. He lit up another Marlboro and poured himself a whiskey. A lead-colored Smith & Wesson .38 lay amongst the debris on the table beside him. Many times in the past few days, he had looked at it and been tempted to solve everything, to stop the pain. Maybe, if even a small percentage of the myths that the world's religions propagate were true, he might even see Anna again. Only the thought of Sarah, alive and out there in the world, alone, and an orphan, made him hesitate.

He had been crazy. No, worse than that—he'd been impulsive and stupid. He should have waited, should have told them privately, discreetly. If he'd been more careful, none of this would've happened.

Now, Liz was dead by his hand, and Sarah was alone, distraught, and probably seething with hatred for him. Phil, too, had been shot, and it was all down to him. If only he'd kept his mouth shut until they'd arrived back at Phil's place, then Liz wouldn't have known anything about his relationship with Zannah. Rooney lifted the revolver in his hand as he had done countless times in the last three days. He didn't need to check the cylinder; he knew it was ready. It had all been his fault. Sucking the last from the cigarette, he stubbed it out, causing more ash to cascade from the overfilled ashtray onto the coffee table. He belched, trying to relieve his nauseous stomach, wincing at the burning acid indigestion that followed. Leaning back, he closed his eyes, the weapon heavy in his lap.

The door chimes woke him. He checked his watch; it was nearly three. He had dozed off again. The gun had slipped between his thighs butt first, and he looked down to see the black eye of the muzzle staring up at him. He lifted it by the thick barrel and tossed it onto the coffee table. The doorbell chimed again. Stumbling to his feet, the effort left him breathless. He peered out through the chink in the drapes. There was someone on the porch. It looked like a woman. Then another chime sounded. As he moved to the door, he brushed down his shirt and trousers with his hands, scattering crumbs and cigarette ash onto the floor. He glanced in a wall mirror, and, horrified at the decrepit wreck that faced him, he swept a hand through his thinning hair in an attempt to tidy his appearance. No doubt thinking that the house was deserted, she had turned and was walking away by the time he opened the door.

She was dressed for the cold, and in black, wearing a long, dark woolen overcoat over slacks and shoes. A heavy black scarf filled the space between the coat collar and the brim of the soft black hat pulled firmly down on her head. No flesh showed. Even her hands were sheathed in fine black leather gloves.

Even from the back, he knew it was her, and the sight made his heart race. "Sarah," he called, flinching at the pain he knew his voice would cause her.

Sarah turned at the sound and walked back toward him. The little of her face that was exposed to the weather told him nothing.

"Come in," he said, moving aside to allow her to enter. He reached to take her gloved hand, but she pulled it back. He indicated the couch opposite his seat, offering to take her coat and hat.

She pulled her scarf down so that it fell in a draped loop across her chest, revealing her unmade-up features. The sight of her made him want to cry.

"I won't be staying that long," she said, wrinkling her nose at the stale tobacco and booze odors as she sat down in the semi-darkness.

"Can I get you something? Coffee, tea, a soda?"

She shook her head, and he eased himself back down into the security of the ash-dusted nest of his last few days.

"You're leaving," he said. It wasn't a question.

She just nodded in response, her eyes expressing no interest in how he knew.

"When are you going? Where are you going to?"

"I'm going back to Europe." She shrugged. "I don't know when yet . . . soon."

He saw her eyes drawn to the gun, lying on the coffee table.

"Is that what you killed my mother with?"

"Sarah, don't . . ."

"It seems a reasonable enough question to me," she insisted. "Is that it?"

"No," he said, "they took it away for ballistic tests . . . that's my personal weapon, a spare. But I'm sure that's not what you came here for."

"Oh, I'd forgotten how good you are at reading people," she said. "How you have that special insight into people's souls. What do you think I came over here for? Coffee and cookies, or to say goodbye?"

Her usually sallow complexion was pale, her skin almost translucent. He was reminded of his mother in her casket.

"Sarah, you don't know how sorry I am, but I had no choice," he said, looking directly at her. "The raised voices woke me. I heard the shouting, and I knew it was Liz. Even so, I was almost too late. Phil had already been hit. Another second and Adam would've been dead."

She said nothing, merely stared at him.

"I'm sorry, I had no choice," he repeated. "She was going to kill him."

Sarah's gaze dropped. "No," she said, "I suppose you didn't." Her voice had lost a bit of its edge.

"But I know the whole thing was my fault—barging in, upsetting everyone, screwing up everyone's life, thinking only of myself."

She looked up at him again. "Yeah, well, you're a cop. It's hard to break the habit of a lifetime."

He watched as she removed her scarf, placing it beside her on the couch. He ached to touch her, for her to touch him.

"What can I do?" he asked her, as if it was a question that only she had the answer to.

"I don't know," she replied. "I came here hating you. Hating you for what you did to her, to me, and to all our lives. But I see now that you've done it to yourself as well."

"I deserve it. My stupidity started a chain reaction that put us all in a hell of a predicament that morning. No matter what I'd done—if I'd just stood by while Adam was killed, you'd have ended up hating me anyway. There was no easy answer, and I had no time."

"Sometimes, all you can do is the right thing," she murmured, impassive as an oracle. Her gaze drifted to the table between them.

Following her look, he reached over to the mess on the coffee table, lifted the revolver, and hunching forward, cradled it in his interlocked palms on his lap. Staring down at the weapon, his body began an almost imperceptible swaying, to and fro. He made no sound.

§

Standing up, Sarah reached into her coat pocket for a Kleenex and walked over into the thin beam of daylight piercing the slightly open drapes. She stared outside while blotting her silent weeping with the tissue. She turned at the sound of sobbing. Rooney sat swaying, kneading the hard metal in his hands as if it were dough. Tears brimmed and rolled in plump globules down his stubbled face. His rocking became more pronounced as she watched. She moved back over to the couch and stared at the man who had dealt such an ugly death to her mother as he broke down in front of her.

In the short time she had known him, she had grown to really like him. In merely a matter of days, he had become a father figure to her. But, damn it, he had shot her mother dead. Her only mother—the one she had loved and had known all her life. The woman who had made her and shaped her into what she was. What was he but an interloper, intruding on their lives, trespassing on her history? He had no right—or had he? He was her biological father.

§

He saw the tension in her face quiet as she looked down at him, and he felt the knot in his own throat relax. Sitting down on the edge of the cushioned seat opposite, she leaned forward toward him, stretching out her hands. A few stray black strands curled from under her soft cloche hat. His mother's southern brown-eyed gaze suffused him with aching sorrow. Her two small, gloved hands reached out, encasing his fists and the revolver, lessening his rocking motion and stressing a trembling in his limbs he had been unaware of. Yielding, his fingers relaxed their grip at her touch, freeing the weapon into her grasp. She hefted the weapon in her right hand as they stared into each other's faces. It was pointing straight at him. Everything would be fine now, he knew. Her left forefinger caressed the back of his hand, calming and reassuring. The sweat felt cold on his brow. Looking at Sarah, his tears created a penumbral halo around her face. He saw her lips move but could hear no sound. But he got the message: one way or the other, he knew everything was all right now. He would suffer his penance, and he would be forgiven.

Even in the gloom, he saw her brown irises enlarge. His mother's eyes. She lifted the pistol to chest level. His mother's face leaned toward him, and he felt his daughter's lips against his tear-soaked face. She cast the gun beside her onto the couch.

He felt her arms encircle him and he bent forward, holding her tightly in turn. They wept against each other, saying nothing. As they embraced, he became aware of the awkwardness of his posture, the bending causing a rising discomfort in his abdomen. He tried to ignore it, to relish the warmth of her arms around him, but it grew more intense. His head began to pound as the discomfort turned to pain. Slowly it radiated up through his chest toward his shoulders and neck, even into his jaw. Suddenly, the pain shot down his left arm. In horror, he pulled back from her, trying to breathe, clutching at the now binding ache in his chest. The dampness on his face felt like ice, and he knew what it was.

As he pulled backward into his seat, the look of surprise on Sarah's face turned to realization. Without hesitation, she grabbed the telephone beside her and dialed 911.

29

ndré's African location had made him difficult to contact, but when he heard the news of the shootings, he had insisted on returning to New York at once despite Adam's assurances that the bishop's condition was comfortable.

The day before Thanksgiving was one of the busiest for airports nationwide, and the JFK arrivals terminal was thronged. As André emerged into the hall from immigration trailing only a compact hard-shell carry-on, Adam could see he looked drained. Not surprising, he thought, since, with his changeover at Paris, he had been traveling for over twenty-four hours. Still, Adam knew André was no stranger to hardship.

André grasped Adam's outstretched hand firmly. "Good to see you, Adam. How is he now?"

"He's recovering," Adam replied. "He's still in a bit of pain . . . mostly it's just soft tissue damage and severe bruising. He's still suffering from the shock of it though."

As they walked to the exit, Adam filled André in on the major details of the evening of the shootings, but omitting Liz's homicide confessions or anything to do with the paintings.

"Certainly, she was a formidable woman," André said in a

respectful tone. "I liked her and always admired her strength and single-mindedness."

Adam looked sideways at him. "Hold on, André. Let's not forget that she shot the bishop, and it's only luck that she didn't kill me."

"Sorry, Adam, I'm just being objective. That's the sort of woman she was: she knew what she wanted, and she knew what she had to do—and did it. You were very fortunate that Rooney was there as well, though I don't think she would've killed the bishop."

As Adam opened his vehicle, André tossed his case into the rear before getting into the front passenger seat.

"You weren't there, I was," Adam said. "If Rooney hadn't come out of the bedroom at that moment, it would've been Phil and me instead of her. I have absolutely no doubt about it." He started the engine and drove toward the parking lot exit.

"Maybe you're right." André shrugged, more placating than agreeing. "But I think the bishop meant too much to her, and I don't mean to insult you, but you didn't."

Adam grunted and increased his speed.

"Where is the bishop now?" André asked, breaking the silence as they joined the Expressway.

"He's at my place. I picked him up from the hospital earlier. He'll be staying with me for a week or two. He doesn't want to return to his own apartment at the moment—too many unpleasant memories, not to mention the mess. The police have finished with it now."

"Don't worry," André said, "I'll deal with whatever tidying up needs done."

"Good, but he's depressed about not attending the memorial service later this morning."

André shrugged. "They had been friends for a long time, even though she did shoot him. And you? Are you going?"

Adam's eyes widened as he turned toward his passenger. "Are you joking? She tried to kill me."

André settled back in his seat and closed his eyes. "Yes, I understand, but you have to acknowledge it," he said. "She was a formidable woman." Adam ignored him and drove.

The bishop was napping in what looked like an uncomfortable fashion on the couch as they entered Adam's apartment. Half-reclining, he had his torso twisted in order to avoid any undue pressure on his wound. His shoeless feet rested on the cushions. His breathing was shallow but regular. He woke at the noise of their entry and pushed himself into an upright seated position with his good left arm before struggling to his feet.

He welcomed André with a wry smile. "I must've dropped off there. Probably something they gave me at the hospital." André squeezed the bishop's left hand in greeting and helped him ease back down onto the sofa.

"It's probably just the shock of the physical trauma; it can take quite a bit of time to recover fully," André said.

"I know, but it's not just the physical. Every time I allow myself to think of that moment, I begin to feel so sick I could almost throw up. Sometimes it feels worse than when I was shot!"

"Don't worry," André said, "that's normal; it's always worse afterward, especially when you have such an added emotional aspect to it." He pointed to the bandaged, sling-covered shoulder. "Just be careful and try to prevent the wound from becoming infected".

Adam prepared coffee as André produced sheaves of docu-ments from his briefcase and began to acquaint the bishop with the developments in the African projects he had been visiting.

As André was preparing to leave for the episcopal apartment, the bishop drained his coffee mug and informed Adam, "There was a call when you were away at the airport. Your machine answered and I wasn't going to interrupt, but when Mitchell started to leave a message, I lifted the handset and spoke to him."

Adam looked surprised, feeling some slight amazement at how the drama of the past few days had distracted him. "What did he say?"

"Naturally, he'd heard about the problems we've had," he said, taking a Kleenex and blowing his nose. "About Liz and me." Adam could see his struggle to compose himself against the raw emotion of the memory.

"Did he mention the money transaction?" Adam asked in an attempt to distract him.

"Yes. He said everything had been carried out. The funds have been transferred as promised. But he'd like us to pay him a visit if I'm fit enough—preferably tomorrow, if possible."

"Tomorrow! What's he planning, a Thanksgiving reunion? You're just out of the hospital. You're not ready to start flying around the country again. What can he want in that much of a hurry?"

"Who knows? But he did say it was important, it could be that he wants to discuss the further sale. After his call, I checked with Switzerland to make sure the money had been transferred, and sure enough, he's been as good as his word. So far, it appears your fears about him have been groundless. Then I called him back and agreed to see him tomorrow."

"Where?" André interrupted.

"He has a place in Connecticut, no more than a couple of hours' drive, he says." He nodded in the direction of Adam's desk. "He faxed through directions and a rough location sketch."

André lifted the fax from the tray and studied it briefly before handing it over to Adam. "I'll drive you both up there, in that case," he offered.

"No," the bishop said, "I'd rather you sorted out the mess back at the apartment, though I can't imagine ever staying there again. Anyway, you'll need a rest after your long journey. Adam can drive me; it's not too far."

In the face of a direct instruction, André prepared to leave, the reluctance evident on his face. "I'll pick up a cab outside, but I'll speak to you in the morning in case you should change your mind or have any other instructions." He lifted his small case and left.

Once alone, Adam felt freer to talk. "I don't know, Phil. You should be taking it easier. A long drive might be a bit much for you. Anyway, I still don't trust Mitchell, and I certainly feel that young Belloc could turn kamikaze if he tries to sell the paintings. To tell you the truth, I'd be happier if I never heard from Mitchell again."

"Look, there were no bones broken. Sure, I lost a little blood, and I admit it gave me quite a scare, but physically I'll be fine." He raised his damaged arm out from his side to illustrate his words.

He continued, "As far as the paintings are concerned, we have to be involved whether we like it or not. If we opt out, we'll be sending the wrong signals to Mitchell. Certainly, he'd be able to sell them without us, and, on the face of it, that would be the more profitable route for him. But it leaves the possibility of a permanent threat that we might, at any stage, undermine their authenticity, and we have already seen what extremes people will go to when such vast amounts of money are involved. Much better to play along until the game is well and truly over."

"And you're not concerned about the Bellocs?" Adam asked.

"Think about it, Adam. No matter what they said, there's really nothing they can do. Those were just empty threats. They're too deeply involved to risk exposing them as fakes now."

Adam pulled a face that showed he was less than convinced.

"Let's drive up and see Mitchell tomorrow, find out what he wants, tie up any loose ends, and then get on with the rest of our lives," the bishop urged.

Like André, Adam found himself overruled. They were going to Mitchell's in the morning, but he still felt uncomfortable with the prospect. Even now, knowing that Mitchell had been in no way responsible for the deaths of Jack and Zannah, he felt threatened by the prospect of him. Crazy, he told himself, particularly since the man had already enriched him by two and a half million dollars this week.

The intercom buzzer interrupted his thoughts. "That'll be André back, probably pretending to have forgotten something. He just won't take no for an answer." Adam opened the intercom channel and pressed the entrance release as he said, "There you are, it's open, come on up," before turning back to the bishop. "Stick to your guns, Phil. I know he's an asset, and is the essence of discretion, but you've made your decision, so don't let him railroad you into coming along."

"Don't worry," the bishop replied. "He'll do as he's told."

From habit, Adam knew how long it took to reach his apartment from the lobby, and he was almost at the door to open it when he heard a gentle rap. She was dressed in a dark blue topcoat and matching pants that perfectly complemented the shining gold of her shoulder-length hair. For a moment, he thought there was a mistake. This was a stranger—a beautiful stranger, but a stranger nonetheless.

She just stood there, head tilted to one side, and asked, "Adam, isn't it? I'm Rosa—Rosa Mitchell. We've met several times in the past down in Florida." She hesitated for a moment before asking, "Can I come in?"

Adam was flustered. "Rosa, of course, yes. I'm sorry, you gave me a shock. I was expecting someone else. Please, come in." Taking her coat, he guided her into the lounge.

No wonder he didn't recognize her, Adam thought, never having seen her dressed for winter weather before.

She saw the bishop sitting on the couch. "Bishop, how are you? I heard that you had been hospitalized. Are you feeling a bit better?"

Adam could feel the tension building in the pit of his stomach. Rosa, Ray Mitchell's estranged sister, and the step-daughter of old Paul Belloc, was the last person he ever expected to see walking into his apartment. He couldn't remember the last time he'd spoken to her, and he certainly hadn't seen her since the sale of the Picassos had been mooted. So what the hell was she doing here?

The bishop looked at her, confusion in his eyes, "Rosa? What are you doing here? Did the Bellocs send you?"

"No, not the Bellocs. My brother, Ray, reckoned that it might be better if I dropped out of sight while the negotiations were going on, just in case. So I decided to drive up to New York, take my time, sort of combine seeing the sights with keeping out of sight." She smiled.

"And your brother told you to come visit us here?" the bishop asked.

Adam butted in. "So you've been involved with your brother all along?"

"Yes, to both questions," she answered, "Ray says that you are going up to his place in Connecticut tomorrow, and suggested I tag along. I hope that's okay."

The bishop and Adam looked at each other.

"That explains a lot of things," the bishop said, then added to Rosa, "You're certainly an unusual chaperone, but if that's what he wants, you're welcome to join us."

Adam wasn't quite so enamored with the idea, but Phil was the boss.

§

The morning was crisp and bright as they drove northeast into the glare of the low winter sun with Rosa sitting in the rear. Earlier, André had called again, and the bishop had difficulty persuading him that he wasn't needed on this trip. He was behaving as though he was responsible for the debacle that had occurred while he was away, and he was determined to compensate for it.

Today, though, Phil felt much better. The pain in his shoulder had subsided to not much more than an uncomfortable throbbing stiffness, allowing him to feel less like an invalid and more like his old self. He sat comfortably, with only one arm in the sleeve of his dark jacket, the right arm still in a sling with the coat draped over it. To complement his physical improvement, he tried to stop obsessing on the past, which couldn't alter anything. Even though Liz's death was tough to come to terms with, he knew he had to get past it. Yes, she'd done some terrible things, some unbelievable things, and he knew that, if not for Rooney's interception, Adam, and possibly even himself, would have joined her list of victims.

But now she was dead. The impact of the slug had slammed her clean over his head, crashing her face down onto the floor. He saw her beautiful, shapely, dead legs twisted in impossible angles, her left arm wedged beneath her torso with the fingers trapped, crunched back into a wristlock position by her own bodyweight.

He saw her facial features damaged beyond casual recognition, her hair slick with gore behind her ear, diamond stud still in place, right eye open. But it hadn't mattered. She had suffered no pain. He felt the shame and regret for her and a strange sorrow for the inelegance of this final scene. He feared that this would be the image he would forever hold with him: this last view of her before the ambulance arrived, which, sirens screaming and whooping, whisked him from the scene to the emergency room.

Now he planned for change. Retire from the Church, the charity and his dealings. He had more than enough accumulated over the years to accommodate him for the rest of his life, even before the two point five million from Mitchell. For Adam as well, things would be different. They could both afford to abandon this place, which was stained by so many ugly memories. Move somewhere else, abroad even. Start new lives unsullied by deceit. Suddenly he wanted to do it now, immediately, without having to undertake this particular detour.

§

Adam interrupted the bishop's reverie. "Can't be too far now to the turnoff." He glanced down at the fax sheet, which now sat balanced on the steering wheel. "Yeah, we take the next exit, and from there it looks like it's not more than a couple of miles."

Mitchell's instructions were impeccable. The immense wrought iron gates that sealed the driveway to his estate were unmistakable. Adam lowered his window and pressed the call button. A camera mounted high above the gate pillar moved imperceptibly, and the gates began to open. Mitchell's metallic voice welcomed them from a concealed speaker and instructed Adam to drive up to the front of the house. As the Mercedes station wagon drove through the gates, they glided closed behind it. At the first turn, they passed a two-storied, red brick gatehouse with a tall, pitched roof and fretwork bargeboards. "Who lives there?" Adam wondered out loud.

"Ray has a couple who maintain this place for him. That's where they live, though I believe they're away visiting family for Thanksgiving this week," Rosa informed him.

The Mercedes hissed along the asphalt driveway, lined by dense evergreen bushes and tall, leafless winter trees. The two-storied, turn of the century, herringboned brick and half-timbered home dominated a cluster of adjoining red brick buildings to the rear that suggested stables and carriage houses. From somewhere beyond, a plume of oily smoke rose above the outbuilding roofline. No doubt burning garden waste, Adam thought as he pulled up in front of the big stone-stepped front porch. Before he could make it around the Mercedes to open the bishop's door, Mitchell appeared, well wrapped up against the cold, and began to help the bishop out of his seat.

"How's the crook wing?" he asked, indicating the bishop's sling-covered arm.

"It's on the mend, thanks."

He glanced over in the direction of his sister. "I see Rosa made it as well, thanks for bringing her along," he said, though they all were aware that her presence hadn't really involved a choice. "Let's go inside."

Over coffee, Mitchell sat beside his sister on one of a pair of walnut-framed, bergere-caned settees facing each other either side of a guarded log fire, which crackled in the big, stone-framed hearth. The bishop and Adam sat on its twin opposite while Mitchell commiserated with them over the tragic events of the past couple of weeks.

"You guys have had the rough end of the pineapple, and no

mistake," he said, adding, "and I must admit I do feel a bit responsible for at least some of your problems."

Adam looked at him. "I lean a bit in that direction myself," he said without a trace of humor.

"Of course, I can't undo what has already been done, but let's just explore the world of clouds and silver linings for a moment and maybe I can come up with something to compensate you both."

"I don't know whether or not you're responsible for anything that's happened," the bishop interrupted, his eyes hard. "What I do know is that we had a deal that, for better or worse, has been completed. We did our bit, and you yours. That's all. I'm not a little boy who's just fallen and skinned his knee, and who can be given a lollipop to take his mind off it. Someone I've known and been close to for half a lifetime has been killed, literally on top of me, after shooting me and trying to kill Adam. A lot of people's lives have been utterly changed. We've suffered physical as well as psychological trauma. We can't—I certainly can't—simply forget it all, dump it like yesterday's newspaper. Part of my life has been amputated, so don't talk to me about clouds and silver linings."

"Yep, fair enough, I'm sorry," Mitchell apologized. "That was a bit glib, and I understand how you must be feeling." he leaned forward and touched the elbow of the bishop's injured arm. "Forgive me. I was just trying in my awkward fashion to say that the despair will pass. You, as a priest, know this is the case. Focus on the future. You, and others you care for, are still alive."

Adam leaned forward, and said in a businesslike tone, "Fine. Let's do that. Let's focus on the future. We've driven up here at short notice, as you requested. What is it? Why are we here?"

Mitchell nodded. "Okay. First of all, we just need to take a bit of a walk outside. Are you up to it, Phil? Just to the stables, at the back?"

The bishop nodded.

With Mitchell leading the way and his sister behind him, Adam and the bishop followed through the big high-ceilinged kitchen, via a dimly lit, paneled corridor to a back door with a large stained glass panel in its top half. The door was flanked on one side by a glazed gun cabinet containing two shotguns and a sporting rifle, while on the other stood a large, early twentieth-century American, tiger-oak, mirrored hallstand draped with a selection of heavy quilted jackets. Mitchell snatched one of them and slipped it over the several layers he was already wearing. Outside they were facing the open end of the old U-shaped brick built stable block. In the middle of the cobbled courtyard, the fire Adam had noticed signs of as they drove up still flickered and smoldered, giving off a damp, smoky, winter garden smell. Mitchell led them over to one of the storeroom doors. He unlocked the bulky grey metal padlock and pulled back a heavy steel bolt. With a different key, he turned another lock mortised into the body of the door, switched on the overhead light, and stood to one side so they could all enter.

The traditional appearance of the outside of the storeroom belied the interior. This had been refurbished with security in mind. The entire interior, including the door, had been sheeted in steel. Movement detectors flickered red-eyed from the top corners. The room was almost empty, except, stacked against the wall leaned the three paintings.

"Recognize those?" Mitchell asked.

No one else spoke. Adam was the first to move. He went straight over to the paintings, lifted the largest one of the three and began examining it minutely. Setting it down, he repeated the procedure with the second one, eventually placing it alongside the first. As he got to the bottom corner of the third one, he turned to the bishop and said, "These last two are definitely Jack's. The corners are bruised where I dropped them the evening we took them from his studio." Turning to Mitchell, he said, "So I suppose the other one's Jack's too?"

Mitchell nodded.

"What are they doing here? I thought they were in France," Adam asked.

"I reckoned there wasn't much point transporting them all the way across the Atlantic for nothing," he answered with a shrug. "Let's face it, what are they? They're only fakes."

"So all the threats of having them tested and exposed as fraudulent was just a bluff?" Adam said, as Mitchell came forward past them, lifted the two smaller paintings, one in each hand, and easing past the others, carried them out into the courtyard and over toward the bonfire.

They moved out after him, and Adam felt the bishop's restraining hand on his arm as Mitchell tossed the paintings onto the flames. Smothered, the fire paused for a moment, then licked tentatively as if tasting the new additions. Within moments, as if approving of the flammable accelerants on the canvases, the fire blazed, crackled, and then devoured them.

"What the hell are you doing? You said you were going to sell them again!" Adam shouted.

"Relax, Adam, just a moment. One more to go," Mitchell replied, as he fetched the final painting from the storeroom and threw it straight onto what was now a raging conflagration.

Adam looked at the bishop in concern, and though he still gripped his arm, the bishop's face was expressionless.

"Jesus, Phil! After all we've been through, they're gone!" he hissed at him.

Mitchell walked back over to the group.

The bishop spoke first. "Reading between the lines, I assume the Bellocs don't have any idea, otherwise they wouldn't have allowed you to succeed this far?"

"No," Mitchell replied, "they had no idea at all."

"What are you talking about?" Adam asked, looking from one to the other.

The bishop answered, "It would appear that Mr. Mitchell here has been much cleverer and more devious than anyone, including us, has given him credit for."

"What do you mean? Those are Jack's paintings. At least, two of them definitely are. The bruises on the corners from where I dropped them are so insignificant that no one would've faked them. They are the same ones!"

"Let's go back inside where it's more comfortable," Mitchell urged them. Turning to Adam, he said, "I have something else to show you that should make things a lot clearer."

Back inside the centrally heated cocoon of the house, in front of the blazing log fire, Mitchell warmed his hands before peeling off the jacket and tossing it onto a chair. He checked his wristwatch, produced a long chromed key from a trouser pocket, and approached the paneled oak door to the right hand side of the fireplace.

"This vault is on a time delay switch set at thirty minutes. I initiated it as you drove through the gates. Come and have a look," he said.

Behind the oak door lay a small vestibule, again paneled in oak but with a polished steel electronic keypad at the far end of it. Facing them, straight ahead, was a stainless metal door, which matched the keypad. Mitchell inserted the key in the lock and turned it, then pressed down on the long, shiny steel handle and pulled the vault door open. The vault was well lit and the size of a suburban bathroom. Metal lined, there were racks along the right hand wall with a few document boxes stacked on them. But the blaze of color that drew everyone's eyes came from the three framed paintings lined alongside each other, leaning against the walls.

Adam and the bishop just stared; even Rosa, who had watched the earlier burnings dispassionately, stood wide-eyed.

Adam was the first to speak, "I don't know about the paintings themselves, but those sure look like the original frames, the ones that were destroyed when the Bellocs' collection was burned."

"Let's go and grab a seat in front of the fire, and I'll explain everything. Rosa, maybe you'd grab a few tinnies from the fridge for our guests?"

Mitchell closed the heavy vault door without locking it, and they returned to the big room and arranged themselves on the couches on either side of the large coffee table in front of the fire. Mitchell took a beer while Adam and the bishop both accepted sodas from his sister.

Sitting back, Mitchell began to explain.

"When my dad died in eighty-nine I was still youngish, embittered, and determined to get my own back on that old bastard, Belloc. I decided that the most poetic punishment I could inflict on him was to break into the gallery at his corporate headquarters, where the Picassos and the rest of his collection were on display, and destroy my dad's paintings.

"I knew that would inflame him, which was all I wanted. But before I could do anything, I heard that his insurance company had decided that as Picassos were now making such an obscene amount of money on the world art market, they wouldn't cover them if they remained hanging on open display. So he was going to be forced to remove them to somewhere more secure, and specially commissioned copies would be hung in their places. By the time I heard this, it was too late. I wasn't going to be able to organize a raid at such short notice, so I abandoned the idea.

"Then shortly afterward, my mum, who, as you know, was living with Belloc, was taken ill and hospitalized. She was suffering from an inoperable cancerous tumor, and the lookout was bad. They only gave her weeks to live."

While he was speaking, Adam had noticed Rosa's eyes grow watery with emotion. Mitchell must have noticed as well, for, as she stood up and moved away from the others to stare out the window, he said, "Rosa, why don't you go up and unpack? You know this bit of the story." Without replying or looking over at them, she hurried out of the room.

He continued, "At this stage, I hadn't seen, heard from, or spoken to my mum since she left my dad in eighty-five. Over five years without a word, and then out of the blue she phones me. She's sobbing down the line, telling me she's sorry, and that she doesn't have long to live. I don't mind admitting to you that, despite everything, it got to me. So, I took the next plane to Miami."

despite everything, it got to me. So, I took the next plane to Miami."

Adam could see that the memory was disturbing Mitchell as well.

"Of course, at the hospital she took care to keep me and Belloc apart. In fact, I didn't see the old bugger until the funeral. The personal details of our reconciliation, if you can call it that, are irrelevant here, but in our long talks before she became incoherent, she told me very interesting stuff. The guilt of what she had done to my dad had consumed her, and the embodiment of this guilt was the paintings. They confronted and accused her, and as the core of Belloc's collection, she could never escape from them.

"*More trouble than they were worth*, was what she called them. Particularly when the insurance underwriters decided that they couldn't be both exhibited and covered for risk at the display facilities. Belloc was furious, she told me. Then she confided that even though he commissioned copies, his ego wouldn't stand being dictated to by a mob of insurance people. And so, while pretending that only the copies were on display, Belloc enjoyed the knowledge that everything he viewed every day as he walked to and from his office was the real McCoy."

"So you were responsible for the break-in and the fire which destroyed them, after all?" Adam interjected.

"Yes and no. After my mother died, I certainly organized a break-in, and I did set a small fire which caused a bit of damage to other stuff, but not to the Picassos. They remained safe and well, only now, I had them."

With disbelief in his voice, Adam asked, "You mean they weren't destroyed after all? You took them from the Belloc headquarters at the time of the fire, and you've had them sitting here in that vault all this time?"

Mitchell nodded, a slight smile on his lips.

"And the Bellocs didn't know?" Adam shook his head in amazement, adding, "Was Rosa involved?"

"No, not at first. We didn't really know each other very well at that time. But, unknown to Belloc, we kept in contact via letters, emails, and the occasional phone call. Then, as she grew older, I arranged for her to come to visit me here secretly from time to time. However, she proved her worth in the end. She overheard Belloc and his son discussing Hastings being commissioned to create perfect replicas with the intention of eventually putting them on the market. Well, it was too good an opportunity to resist."

"An opportunity to legitimize the real ones! Once you had the fakes, you had the second most important thing—provenance!" Adam exclaimed.

Mitchell held up a forefinger in emphasis. "The most important thing to me was to even the score with Belloc. I knew what a proud, arrogant bastard he was. This art he had spent a lifetime collecting had become what defined him, essential to his self-image. After the fire, everyone thought it was the copies that had been destroyed while the real ones were safe in the security of the Belloc's home. I knew his ego wouldn't allow him to admit to the world that the core paintings of the famous Belloc collection were fakes."

Shifting on the settee in order to make his injured shoulder more comfortable, the bishop spoke up, "And now, I assume, they are back on the market?"

"Correct," Mitchell replied. "The paintings aren't, and never were, up my street. Their value to me lies in their value as irritants to Belloc, and, as I promised you in France, I'm giving you and Adam the opportunity to handle the sale on my behalf, though I have to admit not for an entirely selfless reason."

"Rubbing salt in the wounds," the bishop said.

"Too right! It'll really annoy the old bugger to have his own former agents handling the sale. And, once they've squirmed and squealed enough—even if they set their pride aside to denounce the pictures, or suggest to certain ears that tests for authenticity should be made—then you can assure them that I'm not selling

Jack's copies. You can admit that you saw me incinerate the fakes in front of you.

"And to back it up, you can tell them that I'll make them available to the Getty Institute or anywhere of equivalent standing for authentication and testing. Above all, I want to be sure the old bastard knows beyond any doubt that the paintings I have are the bee's knees. I don't even care if he tries to buy them back, so long as he pays top market value."

"What had you in mind? One hundred and fifty again?" asked Adam.

"Special price to the Bellocs." He laughed. "One hundred and sixty million!" He turned to the bishop, "But whatever we sell them for, with your whack of the ten percent commission, as agreed, you can put your feet up, just nurse your wound and take it easy."

"And you will have netted a very handsome hundred million plus profit," the bishop retorted.

Mitchell nodded in agreement. "The money's a bonus, but don't forget, they were my dad's originally, and he was cheated out of them by Belloc."

They were interrupted by a loud rasping buzzer noise emanating from a handset on the coffee table. Mitchell frowned, lifted it, pointed it in the direction of a small monitor screen set close to the main entrance door of the room, and pressed a button. Powering on, the screen showed a camera shot of a long, pewter-colored Chevrolet Suburban at the front gates. Even through the tinted front windshield they could see the two front seat occupants. They all recognized them immediately. The driver's window was down, the driver waiting for a reply from inside the house.

"Mitchell here," he said into the handset.

The driver was looking directly up at the camera lens, "Glad we caught you at home. Aren't you going to invite us in?" The voice made no attempt to disguise its sneering arrogance.

Without speaking, Mitchell pressed the handset button that activated the gate opening mechanism and looked over toward the bishop and Adam. They had all seen the face looking at them from the screen. It was Paul Belloc Junior.

Mitchell stood up and went over to a side table, opened a drawer, and produced a small, stubby revolver, swung the cylinder out to check it, and satisfied, weighed it in his palm, the muzzle pointing at Phil and Adam on the sofa.

"How'd you suppose Belloc found his way here?" Mitchell asked

The bishop was the first to reply. "Believe me, this is as big a surprise to us as it is to you. He certainly didn't learn from us."

Mitchell nodded. "Yeah? Well, maybe he's had your phones under surveillance," he said, his voice steely, "but if I find out that either of you have had a hand in this, believe me, you'll pay for it."

He tucked the revolver into his waistband underneath his sweater.

"If you've had nothing to do with this, I apologize. I know you've both had tough times with firearms recently, but I've seen the craziness in that bloke's eyes the couple of times I've met him. So, I'm just going to be careful."

He pressed another button on the handset, and the driveway in front of the house filled the screen. As they watched the Suburban drive up and pull to a stop, he ordered, "Don't either of you move from here. I'll meet them on my own."

✺ 30 ✺

Leaning back on the bishop's desk chair, André set the phone handset down and stared out the window in quiet reflection. No, irrespective of how it happens, whether in the course of duty, misadventure, or natural causes, you never get used to the sudden death of those you have bonded with. First Jack Hastings, then, only the other day, Liz Hastings, and now, this morning, it was the turn of the one who killed her. Joe Rooney was dead.

Carl Lummus had sounded very upset on the phone, but at least he had the consideration to try to contact the bishop to inform him. Joe's heart had finally given up shortly before seven, having struggled through the night—a massive attack, Carl told him. Sarah Hastings had been at his side throughout, having even called the emergency medical services from Rooney's home in the first place.

However, all André's attempts to contact the bishop or Adam after Carl's call had been fruitless. He knew they were leaving town early to avoid the unpredictable holiday traffic, and a voicemail response was the most he could get to the bishop's cellphone. Not wanting to record such a distressing message, he realized that this was the excuse he needed. He had been uneasy about the bishop and Adam traveling to Connecticut alone; this business concerning Mitchell was proving risky. Sure, the bishop wouldn't be happy about his wishes being disregarded like this, but another one of his oldest friends had just died, and André was certain he would want to be informed. And there was only one way for him to find out.

As he tossed his overcoat onto the back seat of the bishop's Mercedes in the parking lot, a piercing whistle attracted his attention. A girl standing on the pavement waved toward him as she thrust a banknote through the front window of the cab she had just alighted from. Hat on her head, scarf wrapped around the lower part of her face and long coat flying, she approached him at a run. She was close to him before he recognized her. It was Sarah Hastings.

"André, do you know where Adam is? I've just been to his apartment, and he's not there. They told me he, the bishop and some girl left a couple of hours ago."

André paused when he saw her. She must know that her mother had been killed while trying to kill Adam, or the bishop, or both; he had to make reference to her loss.

"Sarah, I'm so sorry about your mother. I was in Africa. I only heard the details when I returned yesterday."

She stopped, and gave a nod of accepted sympathy. "Thanks," she said.

"And you were with Rooney when he died this morning."

"How'd you know that?" she asked.

"His partner, Carl Lummus, phoned a short time ago hoping to speak to the bishop, to pass on the news. He told me."

She nodded. "I've decided I've had enough. I'm getting away from here for a while, maybe even for good, going back to Europe. Too many bad memories. I just wanted to see Adam before I leave." Her fingers fidgeted with her accessories, her scarf, her gloves, checking from button to button her already buttoned-up coat. "Have you any idea where I can find him?"

What a predicament this child has found herself in, he thought, as he looked at her standing vulnerable and desperate before him. First Jack and then her mother dying violently in quick succession, then being uniquely orphaned again after learning, on top of it all, that she was the biological child of the man who killed her mother. Poor girl.

"Adam and the bishop were driving upstate early this morning," he admitted to her.

"Do you know where they're going—and who was the girl with them?"

"Girl? Sorry, I have no idea who any girl might be. They were on their own when I left Adam's apartment yesterday, and there was no mention of anyone else going with them."

"Where were they heading?"

André was not in the habit of giving out confidential information, but this was different. Circumstances had changed. She was Rooney's natural daughter, and her presence would enhance the justification for following them to Mitchell's. Furthermore, the existence of an anonymous third party, a girl, whose presence notably wasn't mentioned when he'd spoken to the bishop on the phone before they set off earlier this morning, raised even further concerns.

"Connecticut," he said. "I'm driving up there now. You're welcome to accompany me, if you wish."

She jumped at his offer, running to the passenger side and sliding onto the soft leather front seat.

"But first, we have to go to Adam's apartment," he said.

"Why?"

"Directions and a sketch map were faxed through to him yesterday. I need to have another look at them."

"Won't they have them with them?"

"Yes, but Adam has a plain paper fax which uses imaging film. It's like a more sophisticated version of the old black carbon paper that everyone used to use for making copies on manual typewriters in the past, except that the image is thermally transferred. I just need to take it out of the machine and hold the film up to the light, and if we're lucky, I'll be able to read off all the details."

André powered up the Mercedes and drove toward Adam's apartment. Being Thanksgiving, all the usual business and commuter traffic was missing, and he was able to make good time through the nearly empty streets. The concierge at Adam's building knew André well and was aware that the bishop was staying with Adam in the meantime, so he admitted him into the apartment when André said he had to collect some documents that had been forgotten.

He quickly clicked open the fax machine, removed the half-used roll of film, and keeping it tightly secured in its frame, raised it against the morning light. Carefully turning the green plastic cogs on the bottom reel, he rewound the thermal paper past a couple of junk faxes and a note from the gallery. There it was—the sketch and the directions. He recognized it as the copy he had glanced at yesterday. Grabbing a notepad from among the clutter on Adam's desk, he made a rough copy of the map and jotted down the details.

As they headed up to intersect with Interstate 95, Sarah removed her hat and scarf, unbuttoned her coat and relaxed back in the passenger seat while André explained to her exactly where they were going, mentioning Mitchell's name for the first time.

"Mitchell!" she said, sounding surprised. "I've never met him, but I have heard the name before. In fact, they were talking about him when I arrived in my mother's apartment the evening before she was killed. I don't know any of the details, but my mom's comments about him were less than complimentary."

André looked over at her, encouraging her to continue.

"I think she was unhappy about his involvement in whatever deal they were doing, and I think Adam had reservations about him as well."

Her words did nothing to reassure André. If there turned out to be any basis to Sarah's comments about Mitchell, then the bishop and Adam may be walking into more trouble. He didn't know exactly what the deal was with Mitchell, though he did know it had something to do with the Bellocs and the Picassos and that it involved a considerable amount of money. Of course, he could be wrong, but so what? André believed that it was always better to try to anticipate events rather than just react to them.

He was now barreling north on the freeway at an indicated seventy-five, ten miles per hour over the posted speed limit. The day was fine, though cold, and they moved with ease through the light interstate traffic. However, it was ten o'clock, and he knew they were well behind the bishop and Adam. Despite his misgivings about the plague of traffic cops on the highways, he pressed the throttle further to the floor.

§

Trooper Mike Reisner of the Connecticut State Police was feeling relaxed. The sky was clear and the traffic light as he cruised south in the outside lane at seventy in his brown Ford Crown Victoria. It had been a stress-free morning so far, a real and welcome holiday in every sense of the word. Today he wasn't even in danger of becoming bored, for this weekend marked the start of his retirement and today was his next-to-last day on the job. Between his years in the Marine Corps and his years on the force he would be reaping a substantial pension, and he had plans. So, today and tomorrow he was taking no chances. Yes, he was going to avoid trouble if at all possible. Today and tomorrow, he was going to be extra careful not to get killed.

As he crested the hill, his heart sank. The big black Mercedes sedan coming toward him on the other side of the median had just overtaken another vehicle and was sitting in the outside lane, well exceeding both the posted limit and Reisner's own tolerance threshold. His radar and laser system on the console was on hold in order to avoid giving constant warning to all those out there with radar detectors, and he hit the "instant-on" button. Even before the console display confirmed what he believed, the high-pitched tone told him that this violator was really moving. The display came up: ninety-three. He couldn't ignore it. He pressed his foot down on the accelerator and turned on his light bar. He knew a highway turning point was no more than a quarter of a mile further on. He set off in pursuit.

§

As André saw the police cruiser crest the hill toward him, he cursed his impatience. They were everywhere; he should have known better. Now, only a miracle could save him if that cop had caught him on his radar. He had eased off the throttle immediately upon seeing the police silhouette and had dabbed at the brake. He glanced at his dash display and grimaced in dismay. He was still traveling at nearly ninety. He slowed to just above the limit, anticipating the inevitable.

Sarah had been lying back with the passenger seat partially reclined, resting with her eyes closed. André wasn't sure if she had been sleeping or not, but the sudden change of momentum caused her to open her eyes. "What's wrong? Why are we slowing down?" she asked.

"Looks like we've just been caught by police radar coming toward us," André replied, glancing in the rearview mirror. "Either that or he's received an emergency call, since his roof lights went on after he passed us, and he sped up." André checked the mirror again, adding, "Don't turn around. I was right, there he is now. He's crossed over and is coming after us. Let me do all the talking."

He indicated turning right, slowed down, pulled well over onto the shoulder, and turned the engine off. Light bar still flashing, the patrol car pulled in a little distance behind him.

Sarah maneuvered herself so she could see what was happening through the door-mounted mirrors. "He's just sitting there. Why isn't he getting out? We're running late enough as it is," she said.

"He's radioing in our details to check us out, just in case we have outstanding tickets or have been reported for any other reason. Just be patient, and remember: he is in control." André removed his sunglasses, lowered his side window, and placed both his hands on the steering wheel in full view, as he saw, in the mirror, the cop open his door and carefully approach him with his right hand resting on his holstered weapon.

"License, insurance, and registration, please," Trooper Reisner said.

"The registration and insurance details are in the glove box, Trooper," André said, indicating the closed receptacle in front of Sarah, "my license is here, in my pocket." André was playing the game, showing his throat, demonstrating to the officer that he was not a threat.

Reisner nodded, "Go ahead," and took a small step back, avoiding being in a direct line with André's hand and allowing a better view of the contents of the glove box.

"This is not my vehicle; it is registered to Bishop Philip Connor. I'm his personal assistant, and we're traveling at the moment to bring him some extremely sad personal news," André said as he handed over the documents.

Reisner perused them. "Do you know why I pulled you over?" he asked, ignoring André's statement.

"I suspect I was speeding, officer."

"What speed do you think you were traveling at?"

"I know I was exceeding sixty-five," he admitted.

"I've clocked you at ninety-three," the officer said.

Reisner bent down low enough for a quick scan of the interior. "Remain in the vehicle, sir," he ordered, before moving back to his patrol car.

§

As Mike Reisner prepared to run checks on the driver's license and car registration paperwork he held in his hand, something niggled at the back of his mind. It was the signet ring he'd noticed on the driver's left hand: a plain gold band with an engraved emblem—not ostentatious, but rather understated—just a small circle with what looked like flames coming out of the top of it. He had seen it somewhere before, and he knew it held some significance for him. Damn it, he thought, wouldn't that be a bitch—to retire after all these years only to start slipping into Alzheimer's?

Still irked, he began to dictate the document details into the microphone for checking. He tapped the steering wheel with his fingertips as he waited for a reply, all the time racking his brains. The dispatch understaffing at Thanksgiving was slowing the check-up process down, but eventually the reply came through—nothing flagged against either the vehicle registration or the license of André Leroux.

That was it! How could he have missed it after having seen such an obviously French name? That emblem had flown above his head every day for a month on a joint military training exercise on the Horn of Africa. It was the Flaming Grenade of the French Foreign Legion.

The realization sent a surge of adrenaline through him. What the hell was a legionnaire doing as the supposed personal assistant to a Catholic bishop? As he asked himself the question, he saw the driver's door of the Mercedes open and the driver begin to get out. Mike Reisner scrabbled for his pistol as he thrust open his door.

§

Sarah turned up her collar and pulled her coat around her more tightly as she said, "André, do you think we could have the window up? It's getting cold in here."

Without taking his eyes from the rearview mirror, André replied, "I don't think that would be a good idea. These guys don't like any deviation from the status quo. Button up well and just think ourselves lucky that he didn't ask us to open *all* the windows. Remember, in this situation, he is in control and has all the power, and we mustn't make the mistake of giving him an excuse to use it."

Her hat on her head, gloves on her hands, and her scarf wrapped around the lower part of her face, little of Sarah was still visible. "Jesus, André, this is ridiculous! It must be over five minutes since he went back to his cruiser," she complained.

"Relax, Sarah. It shouldn't take much longer."

"Couldn't you tell him that we're rushing to pass on the news that Joe Rooney, a fellow officer, has just died this morning?" she hesitated for a moment before continuing, "You could even tell him that he was my father."

André thought for a moment. He was more aware than Sarah that it might be important to catch up with the bishop sooner rather than later, and she was correct, this was taking much too long. Furtively, to avoid attracting attention from behind, he slipped his fingers into the side door pocket. No, there was nothing there. Then he checked the central storage and found them. Business cards. He knew they were there somewhere. Yes, as he remembered, among others, there were cards of Rooney's and even ones belonging to Carl Lummus.

He showed them to Sarah "It's against my better judgement, but you may be right. As it is Thanksgiving today, the police traffic control is bound to be on a skeleton staff. We could be sitting here for ages. So, I'll get out—but, above all, I don't want you to move, turn around, or leave the car. Let me do all the explaining. Remember, this will make him very jumpy."

Holding the business cards between the thumb and forefinger of his raised right hand, André placed his other hand on the outside door handle, pulled on it, and as the door opened, slowly proceeded to get out.

§

Before the driver had fully emerged from the Mercedes front compartment, Mike Reisner was standing upright behind his partially opened door, pointing his semi-automatic pistol in a two-handed grip. "Step away from the car!" he yelled. "Keep your hands high!"

He watched as the driver followed his instructions. "Now, face toward the front of the vehicle!" The driver did as commanded. "Now, with your hands high, slowly walk backward toward the sound of my voice!" Reisner came from behind his opened door and, still training his pistol on the driver, approached him with care. "Keep walking! I'll tell you when to stop!" By now, they were within yards of each other, and Reisner could see that the driver was holding what looked like business cards in his raised right hand. "Now kneel! Both knees on the ground!" Once the driver was in the kneeling position, Reisner ordered, "Cross your feet at the ankles!" Reisner was now within feet of him. He moved to his right and grew closer, weapon trained at the driver's torso. Adjusting his pistol grip, he snatched the cards, shouting, "Don't move!" as he did so.

Taking a few steps backward, he scanned the cards: two NYPD officers' cards. "What are these?" he demanded.

"Trooper, I'm sorry for causing you trouble, but I'm afraid I'm on an extremely tragic errand. One of those cards belonged to Detective Joe Rooney, who died suddenly just a matter of hours ago. That's his daughter sitting in the passenger seat. He was a good friend of my employer, the bishop. But as the bishop left town early this morning, and all I can reach on his cellphone is his voicemail, we are on our way to tell him the terrible news. And, as I'm sure you can appreciate, that's not the sort of news I'm happy to leave on a recording."

Reisner glanced at the other card. "And Lummus—who's that?"

"Carl Lummus is Joe's colleague. He was the first one to call me this morning with the news. All his details are on the card, so you can check it out easily."

"The girl's his daughter, you say?"

"Yes, he had a heart attack when she was with him yesterday. She's been by his bedside all night."

Reisner stared at the kneeling figure for a long moment and then glanced over at the girl in the passenger seat.

"And that ring you're wearing on your left hand—what's that signify?"

There was a moment's hesitation before he answered, "Oh, it's *La grenade à sept flammes*; it's the emblem of my old military unit."

"And how did a legionnaire come to be a bishop's aide?" Reisner asked, his tone sounding casual. The driver partially turned his head, a look of surprise on his face.

"I assisted him from time to time when he was developing charity projects in Djibouti, in East Africa," he answered, adding, "And how would a Connecticut State Trooper recognize a symbol that not one in a million Americans would know?"

Reisner said, "Okay, André Leroux, you can stand up and turn around."

As André rose to his feet, Mike Reisner holstered his pistol and approached him, hand held out. "Sorry about that, André, but you can never be too careful—as you know." They shook hands as he went on to explain, "I was involved in a bilateral training exercise down with your crew on the Horn when I was in the Marines a long time ago—and I remember the legion emblem on the barracks wall and fluttering on the flag. I was there for a month. What a hellhole!"

"That is Africa, Trooper," André said, as they walked back to the front of the Mercedes.

Opening the driver's door, Reisner addressed Sarah, "My apologies, Miss. I wasn't aware . . . please accept my sincere sympathies."

Sarah gave a weak smile and nodded. "Thank you."

Reisner turned to André, "Can I help you? How far are you going?" André explained that he had never been to their destination and only had the address and a sketch map with directions. Reisner studied it for a moment. "I know it," he said. "I was brought up not too far from there. It's no more than a thirty-minute drive—less if you continue at the speed you were driving at. You can't see the house from the road, but you can't miss the big black gates on your left." He gave André rapid but detailed navigation instructions.

"Now, just go!" Reisner said. "I'll make a couple of calls, and you shouldn't get pulled in again. Just don't kill anybody!" They shook hands.

"Thank you," André said as he jumped back into the driver's seat, buckled his seat belt, and powered away.

Reisner ambled back to his cruiser. Resuming his patrol in the same direction as the Mercedes, he marveled to himself at what a small world it was. As he began making the promised calls, he didn't notice André's driver's license and documents slip from where he'd discarded them earlier and fall behind his right heel in the footwell.

$$\S$$

André drove fast. Only once did they see another cruiser, and again it was in the oncoming carriageway. He eased off the accelerator, then resumed his speed as the police vehicle flashed its headlights and the trooper acknowledged him with a wave.

Now, nearly two hours after leaving New York, they left the freeway, and, according to the sketch and Reisner's advice, they didn't have much further to go. At the beginning of the journey, André hadn't wanted to alarm Sarah by sharing his concerns with her, but as they drove and discussed the potential problems ahead, she impressed him as being her mother's daughter. Without melodrama André outlined what he felt they should do once they arrived at Mitchell's. If his fears proved groundless, there would be no harm done. She listened with interest and approval to the various suggestions he made. She was an attentive student, and as they rehearsed the plan, he felt confident that she could pull her own weight.

Less than ten minutes later, the bishop's big black Mercedes swooshed along the damp secondary road lined with bare-fingered trees which led toward Mitchell's New England hideaway with Sarah at the wheel.

🎋 31 🎋

Mitchell was standing at the driver's door of the big Suburban before Belloc Junior opened it. As the door opened and young Belloc swung a leg out, Mitchell grabbed his left arm, swiveled it up his back, and spun him around hard against the side of the vehicle.

He pressed the short muzzle of the revolver into Belloc's kidney area. "When I let go of your arm, place your hands on the roof and don't move. Is there anyone else in the rear?"

"No, there are just the two of us here," young Belloc answered, his voice cracking.

With his free left hand, Mitchell began to frisk him. Immediately, he hit a crisp nylon shoulder holster under his left arm. He pulled a black automatic pistol from it and stuck it in his waistband before skimming the rest of Belloc's body profile. Then he stood back, his gun still trained on him.

"Not a very friendly way to come visiting," Mitchell said to him. "You're no longer in the Deep South here, you know. The cops up here don't take kindly to civilians carrying concealed firearms across state lines." Mitchell nodded toward old Belloc, who still remained seated. "Is he armed too? If so, throw it out here."

From the front of the Suburban, Belloc Senior answered, "Don't be absurd, of course I'm not armed. Now, if you've finished your ridiculous game of cowboys, are you going to invite us in?"

Mitchell stood back as the elder Belloc climbed out of his front seat and walked around to the driver's side.

"After you," Mitchell said to him, lowering his pistol and indicating the front entrance. Belloc Junior dropped his hands as Mitchell ordered him to follow his father.

There were no exclamations of surprise or greetings from either group as the Bellocs walked in front of Mitchell into the big room. No one looked comfortable. After placing Belloc Junior's weapon on a table by the doorway, Mitchell stuck his own revolver back into his waistband and faced the newcomers, making absolutely no pretense at hospitality.

"What d'you want? I don't suppose you just happened to be in the neighborhood?" he said.

Belloc Senior settled himself into a mahogany-framed elbow chair before saying, "We've come to try to sort things out, amicably or otherwise, once and for all. And from your welcoming behavior, I fear it may have to be otherwise."

"Our business is already settled," Mitchell said. "You agreed to the terms. It's all been sealed, signed and even delivered. There were no loose ends, nothing left to sort out."

"And the paintings," Belloc asked, "what do you intend to do with them?"

"Not that it's any of your bloody business, but I'm going to sell them, of course." Mitchell indicated the bishop and Adam with an inclination of his head. "In fact, the three of us were just discussing it before you arrived."

Paul Junior looked around and pulled a chair up beside his father. Old Belloc's eyebrows lifted. "Despite the threat of us undermining their authenticity?" he said.

"For a start, I don't think you could risk that," Mitchell replied. "There are too many things at stake way beyond ruining your *valued* reputation." As he glanced at Paul Junior he noticed his eyes narrow. "Anyway," he continued, "I think you'd find that not only would you be demolishing your precious status, but you would be in danger of becoming the prize laughing stock of the entire art world."

Belloc Senior raised his eyebrows again in silent question.

Mitchell indicated the closed paneled door that led to the strong room. "I think you should take a look in there."

Together, both father and son half-turned and followed Mitchell's gaze. Belloc Junior grabbed the arms of his chair as if to rise, but hesitated. His father, however, moved quickly to his feet, waited for his son to join him, then led the way across the dark oak flooring and pulled open the paneled door to see the vault gleaming in front of them at the end of the lighted corridor.

"Go ahead. Push down on the bar and pull it open. It's not locked," Mitchell said from close behind them. Adam and the bishop had also risen and, following them to the vestibule, viewed the scene from the rear.

§

Adam could feel the knot of tension in his stomach. This was the second time in less than a week that he found himself in the presence of a loaded firearm that was being waved about in an intimidating manner. He knew he should have more forcefully opposed the bishop's inclination to visit here. He would've been happier never to have seen any of these three again. And how did the Bellocs know to come up here? They certainly weren't just passing by.

He watched Belloc Junior as he moved forward, levered the bar down and pulled the heavy door open. The vault was still lit. Old Belloc entered first and regarded the paintings. His son joined him by his side. No one spoke as the Bellocs examined them.

Belloc Senior said, "Interesting frames. They look original. I used to own some very similar." He turned away and, solemn faced, shouldered his way out through the bottleneck of the others.

Mitchell closed the wall door behind him and leaned against it. "Yep, something tells me you're right," he said to Belloc. "You used to have a few identical in your possession."

Belloc spun around on his chair to face him. "You'll have to do better than that. The frame alone doesn't make the painting."

"But they are the real McCoy, I'm sure you'll be pleased to hear," Mitchell said with a smile. "All of them."

Belloc looked over to where the bishop was supporting himself half-seated on the arm of the sofa, seeking his input.

"He's telling the truth, Paul," the bishop said. "We watched him burn Jack's copies outside in the stable yard not long before you arrived. Those are the originals."

"Are you sure? How can you know the paintings you saw burned were the ones Hastings painted?"

Adam resented having to become part of this dispute. It was over. What the hell business of the Bellocs was it anyway? Nevertheless, he had to support the bishop. He had to share the pressure with him. "Phil is right," he said, "the ones we saw being burned were Jack's copies."

Belloc looked at him as if he were little more than a nuisance. "And how can *you* be so confident about that?"

"When we were moving them from Jack's studio, two of them were accidentally dropped and their corners were slightly bruised," Adam answered. "Just a couple of barely noticeable scuffs and dents on the edges, but I checked and there was no doubt about it —they were the same ones."

"Anyway," Mitchell added, "I'll make it clear to any prospective purchaser that I welcome any non-destructive authentication being carried out."

Old Belloc nodded, half to himself. "In recent years I've wondered, and I've had my suspicions. I realized the fire could merely have been a diversion to cover up the disappearance of the paintings, and since the Picassos were the only major works that were supposedly destroyed, I had an inkling you might've been involved." His tone was unemotional. "But suspecting you had them wasn't enough. I needed to know for sure, and I needed to know where they were. Now I want them back." He spoke with the confidence of a man in command, with the air of a professional who had been forced to play a game with a mere amateur. And now it was time to show who the boss really was.

"You can have them. The price is one hundred and sixty million dollars," Mitchell replied. "And just to show there are no hard feelings, I'll let you keep the mine into the bargain."

Adam watched as Belloc's stern visage began to relax. He could see that the old man was fighting against too much of a smile.

Belloc began to chuckle. "One hundred and sixty million! You really have it in for me, don't you? And you think you've been so clever." Belloc's eyes moved past Mitchell over to the hallway entrance. "But you just haven't been clever enough."

Adam and the others swiveled their heads in the direction of his gaze. Rosa, her blonde hair tied back from her face, stood framed in the doorway. A cocked, dark charcoal-colored automatic pistol in her grip contrasted starkly against her white blouse, her aim directed at the torso of her brother. For a brief moment, Adam was confused. Rosa, with yet another pistol? But she didn't have to speak. Her actions were unambiguous. Belloc Senior nudged his son, who stepped over and removed Mitchell's gun from his waistband and then recovered his own weapon from the table.

"Rosa, what are you doing? I'm your brother, for Christ's sake!"

She made no reply, simply continuing to train the gun on him.

"Maybe I can help you there," Belloc Senior said. "My suspicions about you were confirmed when I was shown some of your early correspondence to Rosa sometime after the fire. Too many casual questions about the paintings puzzled her, as did your undisguised hatred for us. You overlooked the fact that I raised her, treated her and loved her as my own. Emotionally, she is much more my daughter than she is your sister, so I encouraged her to lead you on, let you play out your hand."

"I can't believe it!" Mitchell said. "Rosa, why are you doing this?"

"You wouldn't understand, just as you didn't understand my mom." Her voice faltered with emotion as she spoke. "All she wanted was a reconciliation before she died—some sign of forgiveness from you—but she never got it. She told me that, even as she lay there dying, she could still see the reproach in your eyes, even after all those years. 'A hard, heartless, self-obsessed bastard, just like his father,' is what she said."

Adam could see the anger glowing in Mitchell's eyes as he turned back toward Belloc. "So what d'you think that coming here like this is going to achieve? Now you know where they are, d'you think you can just walk in here and take them?"

"Actually, that's exactly right. They are mine, after all; they have never belonged to you. You stole them from me." Belloc smiled. "You might say I occupy the moral high ground."

The bishop interjected, "So the whole scenario of Jack and the replacement copies was merely a ploy to flush the stolen ones, the originals, out into the open?"

"No, not a ploy, Phil. Your idea of representing Jack's original copies as the real ones and having him prepare virtually unassailable copies for eventual sale was both timely and ingenious.

"It meant that whatever the truth of the situation was, they would have a role to play. If the originals did exist and weren't destroyed in the fire, then whoever had possession of them was most likely going to want to purchase the copies with their provenance. If, on the other hand, they had indeed perished in the flames, well, I had nothing extra to lose, and in an ideal world, maybe a hundred million dollars or so to gain. However, as you see, my suspicions were correct, and now I'm about to repossess them."

His son, glaring at Mitchell, beckoned him with his gun to move away from the front of the vestibule door where the vault lay. Opening both doors, he entered the vault and carried the paintings out one at a time. He stacked them against the oak paneling while Rosa kept her weapon trained on Mitchell.

This is total madness, Adam thought. They were going to steal the paintings—just physically take them away! How the hell did they imagine they could get away with that? Images of Jack and Zannah flashed through his head, and he knew they would have only one option. He felt the goosebumps prickle on his skin and the adrenaline begin to fizz through his system, just as Belloc Senior addressed him.

"Adam, would you please assist Paul with the paintings? We'd like them carefully packed in the rear of our vehicle outside."

Adam looked from Mitchell to the bishop, and then at Rosa. He had no choice. Without replying, he stood up from the couch and approached the paintings.

Young Belloc handed Mitchell's revolver to Rosa, who stuck it into her waistband. As Adam lifted the first of the paintings, Belloc Junior stood back to allow him to carry it past. "I'm going outside with him," he told her, following Adam at a distance of several paces while keeping his weapon trained on his back.

As Adam, still in front of young Belloc, was returning for the next painting, he heard Mitchell protesting.

"You know that this is absurd! You can't simply steal these and expect to get away with it. First of all, the paintings are now legally mine in the eyes of the world, and secondly, the bishop and Adam are witnesses to this ridiculous armed robbery." He paused, before adding, "Unless, of course, they've been in on it all along too?"

"No, they weren't," Belloc replied. "They didn't need to know —though I must say they have been the biggest disappointments to me." He looked over at the bishop. "Phil, after all these years we've been doing business, what did you do? You let me down. Sold me out. I thought we were friends, and at the first hiccup in the most important deal we've ever done together, you changed sides!"

"It wasn't a matter of sides, Paul," the bishop said. "Throughout, I've just been trying to salvage what I could from the deal. I realize it may not appear like that to you, but at the time I didn't know all that you've just told us."

As Belloc dismissed the bishop's words with a wave of the hand, Adam lifted the next canvas, urged on by the gun at his back.

Once the final painting, the largest one, had been placed in the back of the Suburban, Belloc Junior thrust a plastic bag into Adam's hands and ordered him back into the house.

Back with the others, Belloc Junior addressed Mitchell. "Hold your hands out in front of you, wrists together," he ordered, indicating with his pistol for Adam to secure Mitchell's wrists with long plastic cable ties from inside the bag. "Now cuff the ankles, and make sure they're tight!"

"Next the bishop," he instructed, once Mitchell was tightly bound.

The bishop winced in pain as Adam helped him remove his jacket and sling and straightened out his wounded arm for binding. Then, in turn, Adam tied the bishop's ankles, hobbling him. Finally, under the gun, Adam was bound by Belloc Junior.

"Paul," the bishop appealed to Belloc Senior, "come on, don't make this situation any worse than it already is. Tell him to free us. We can sort this out."

"I'm afraid it's already sorted out, Phil. We have been manipulated into a corner, and it leaves us with no alternative. You, Adam, and your Australian friend here are going to have to die together . . ."

"Have you gone flaming mad?" Mitchell yelled at him. "Once the paintings turn up in your possession, the alarm bells will go off. They'll suspect you at once."

Belloc Senior smiled. "Not at all. It will appear as if you all had a disagreement. Your two friends will be killed with your gun. The untraceable pistol Rosa has in her hand will be the one that they used to shoot you. A fall out, that's all. And the fire—I know how fond you are of fires—which will accidentally burn most of the house down will consume your plastic restraints along with everything else. Fortunately, I'm informed that, with commendable foresight, you have already established in your will that your little sister, Rosa, is your only living relative and heir."

Rosa still stood expressionless in the doorway, weapon in her hand.

"Sweet Jesus," moaned the bishop. "You mean to tell me that she inherits everything!"

"I'm glad to see you're returning to your Lord in your last moments, Phil." Belloc smiled.

"Damn you, Paul. Hell won't be full till you're in it!" the bishop yelled back at him.

Mitchell turned to his sister, his eyes beseeching her. "Come on, Rosa, you can't really be part of this. No matter what you say, you're my sister, my own blood."

The younger Belloc walked over beside Rosa, put one arm around her shoulder, and sneered. "Blood may be thicker than water, but there are other bodily fluids thicker than even that."

Mitchell lifted his bound hands up to his face and wiped away the build-up of tears that were affecting his vision. "My God, I can't fucking believe it," he spat at her. "You're lower than a snake's armpit—just like your mum!"

Rosa eyes narrowed at the remark as she raised her two hands into the firing position, shrugged Belloc Junior's encircling arm off, and took quick aim at her brother's chest. Her right forefinger moved to the inside of the trigger guard. She did not say goodbye.

❧ 3 2 ❧

Adam ceased straining at the tight plastic bindings around his wrists. Along with everyone else in the room, he stared at Rosa, mesmerized with horror, anticipating the shot. A sudden rasping noise made everyone start in shock. Rosa spun her head in the direction of the gate controller handset and lowered her gun.

"It's the buzzer at the front gates," she said, moving across to the coffee table to pick the handset up. She turned back to her brother and said, "Are you expecting someone else?"

"Yeah, the cavalry," he said with a sneer.

She activated it in the direction of the monitor and the front entrance glowed into wide-angled view. Adam saw a familiar big black Mercedes sedan ticking over in front of the gates. Rosa zoomed the camera in to the face of the driver who, window fully down, was looking up at it.

"Who the hell is that?" she asked her brother.

"I have no idea," he replied.

The Bellocs gazed at the stranger's face on the screen. "Don't know, never saw her before," said the son.

"It's Sarah, Liz Hastings's daughter!" Adam cried. "What the hell is she doing here?" Though he thought it, he didn't add . . . *and driving the bishop's Mercedes?*

"Let's find out," said Rosa, lifting the handset to her face. "Hi, this is Rosa Mitchell speaking. Can I help you?" she said in a cheerful, friendly voice.

Sarah's voice replied out of the monitor, "Yeah, hi, my name's Sarah Hastings. I've come to see Adam Kennedy and Bishop Connor. I believe they're visiting with Mister Mitchell today."

Rosa looked over at old Belloc, who was sitting looking at the monitor with concern. "Better admit her. We can't just send her away now that she knows there's someone else here," he said.

Rosa manipulated the camera remotely, scanning the vehicle to check for other occupants. Sarah was alone in the car. Rosa spoke cheerily into the handset again. "Yes, that's right, they're both here. When I open the gates, just drive up to the front of the house. I'll meet you there," she said, and pressed the button to open them. They all watched as Sarah drove through, whereupon Rosa closed the gates behind her before switching cameras with the handset to the one that covered the driveway in front of the house.

As he waited for the Mercedes to appear in the monitor, Adam's head was spinning with questions. How did Sarah know we were here, or where it was? How did she come to be driving the bishop's car? Is she going to walk in here and become another victim?

As they all watched the car emerge from the shadows of the driveway, Rosa headed for the front door, her gun hand concealed behind her as she walked. Adam's heart sunk when, on the little screen, he saw Rosa approach Sarah as she got out of the vehicle. He could see Sarah anticipating it as a handshake gesture; her own right hand was halfway to meet Rosa's when she saw the weapon. She recoiled as if it were a snake. Moments later, she was entering the room, walking in front of Rosa at gunpoint.

On seeing Adam seated on the couch, bound hand and foot,

Sarah ran straight over to him, oblivious to the gun pointed at her back and Rosa's shouted command not to move.

"Adam," she cried, "what's happening here? Why are you and the bishop tied up? Who are all these people?" She glanced around at the others. Tears were now beginning to flow down her face. She scrabbled in her purse and withdrew a bunched handful of Kleenex before falling sobbing onto her knees directly in front of Adam, her hands grasping his. Adam felt her transferring something solid from the Kleenex into his clasped palms. From the feel of the metal spirals of the screw, he knew what it was. It was 'the Waiter's Friend'.

Rosa walked across and tugged on Sarah's hair. "Get onto the seat," she ordered, holding the pistol only inches from Sarah's temple. "How did you find this place? Who told you they were here?"

Sarah squeezed down onto the couch beside Adam, placing a hand on his. "They knew at his apartment building. He'd left a copy of directions in case anyone was looking for them."

Adam felt Rosa's gaze burn into him. "Why is she lying?" Rosa demanded of him. "I was there all the time, and I'd have noticed if you'd left any instructions or directions." He saw the surprise register in Sarah's face at her words and she saved him from having to make a reply.

"So you were the girl who left with them?" Sarah almost shouted, ignoring the muzzle pointing at her, "What were you doing at his apartment?" To Adam's ears, she sounded a lot like her late mother, but he could feel from her touch that the anger he heard was contrived. Under the cover of Sarah's hand, he now had the small serrated blade open.

Rosa ignored her question and turned to Belloc Senior, who was seated on a single elbow chair between the couches, facing the fire. His son stood glowering behind him. "What d'you think, does she change anything?" she asked.

Old Paul Belloc, who had watched in silence until now, spoke. "Sarah, let me first of all commiserate with you for the loss of your parents so recently. I knew them both and held them in high regard. However, as you see, we find ourselves in a bit of an awkward situation now. A situation that calls for some serious life or death decisions to be made, and to make these decisions we need to be sure of certain facts. Now the primary thing we need to establish is how you came to find out that the bishop and Adam were both here, and how you found your way to the house."

"I've just told you!" she replied.

"This time I want the truth. Let me assure you, if you lie you will be killed," he said.

Sarah sighed and looked around at Adam and the bishop. "Rooney is dead—"

The bishop leaned forward, interrupting her. "Joe is dead? How, what happened?"

"He had a heart attack—late yesterday afternoon. I was with him. He died early this morning," she replied.

Adam sat speechless.

"Who's that, and what's it got to do with the question?" Rosa asked.

"The policeman who shot her mother," explained Belloc Senior. "Go on," he instructed Sarah.

"Rooney's partner, Carl Lummus, wanted to locate these two to inform them, and it turns out the bishop's aide had seen the directions and remembered them. Lummus is probably close to here now."

"And where did you get the directions?" Belloc asked.

"From the same place," came the reply in an unmistakably French accent.

André stood framed in the doorway of the entrance hall, armed with the essential close-quarters weapon, a semi-automatic shotgun he had taken from the gun cupboard, pointed at the Bellocs. Paul Junior, still holding his pistol, raised his hands. Rosa, standing at the end of the couch with her back toward the door, was beginning to turn when André barked at her, "Don't move, or I'll fire!" She froze.

DANN FARRELL

Belloc Senior responded first. "André. What a surprise."

"Now, both of you," André said, ignoring Belloc, "slowly lower your weapons to the ground, then kick them away from you. Now!"

Belloc Junior obeyed with the deliberation of a mime artist. Rosa didn't budge.

"Rosa, put it down!" André insisted.

Rosa's shoulders had relaxed, regaining her earlier composure. "Surely you wouldn't harm a girl, André? Not an old friend like me?" she said.

"You wouldn't be the first," he answered. "I do whatever is necessary. Now, put it down!"

The ice in André's voice caused Adam to glance at the bishop in horror as Rosa started to obey. He twisted around further toward André.

"Jesus, André! Don't tell me Rooney's suspicions were right. Did you kill Zannah?"

André's eyes never left Rosa's back as she slowly placed her weapon onto the floor. "Now, kick it away from you!" he ordered.

"André! Is he right?" the bishop insisted.

André shifted his gaze to the couch where Adam and the bishop were half-turned, waiting for him to answer.

"It had to be done. Liz Hastings told me you needed certain items. The girl was very stubborn."

"But what you did to her . . ."

"She lied at first, tried to make a fool of me. Time was short. I had to get to Boston, and I knew you had to have them."

The bishop closed his eyes and began to shake his head from side to side, "God forgive you . . . God forgive you . . ." he repeated.

They were interrupted by a scream from Sarah. "She has another one! Look out!"

Rosa dipped as she spun, pulling Mitchell's revolver from her waistband, raised it one-handed, and fired. André caught the movement, altered his aim, and pulled the trigger.

The combined noise in the room was deafening. Adam felt the blast on his face and saw Rosa pirouette crazily into one of the piers between the tall latticed windows, her blouse reddening as her body crashed against the woodwork before sliding down the wall onto the floor. He saw her blood dripping onto the polished parquet floor around the fallen revolver lying in the angle between her arm and her torso.

André, too, had fallen and lost his weapon, having been hit on the right deltoid by Rosa's shot. He scrabbled with his good arm to regain control of the shotgun on the floor at his side. Young Belloc, a look of shock still on his face, dragged his eyes away from Rosa's body and lurched toward where his pistol lay. As he reached it, Mitchell slammed into his side, sending them both sprawling onto the floor, Belloc's pistol spinning toward the fireplace. Before any of the others could move, the elder Belloc lifted an eighteen-inch high bronze statuette of a dancing faun and bounded toward André, brandishing it above his head. André, right arm dysfunctional, struggled with the ungainly length of the weapon, trying to wedge the stock under his good left arm to take aim. Belloc, almost on top of him, hand held high to bludgeon, took the full force of the shotgun blast in the chest, catapulting him backward, his torso a mess of red and black, to land almost across the carcass of his stepdaughter, Rosa.

The bronze, fallen from his father's dead hand, clattered close to where young Belloc was trying to escape the limited pummeling he was receiving from the bound Mitchell. Managing to drag himself to one knee, he snatched it up from the floor and swung the bronze at Mitchell's head. Despite his own head being jerked back by Sarah yanking on his two ears, the bronze still found its target. Mitchell fell onto the floor, bleeding heavily from above the flap of scalp and hair now fringing his left eye, and lay still. Adam, still sawing at his wrist bindings, saw Belloc drive his elbow back and up into Sarah's stomach. The blow dislodged her grip on him and bent her over in agony. Staggering to his feet, Belloc turned and kneed her hard again in the solar plexus. She collapsed onto the ground retching. With craziness in his eyes, he swung his foot back and kicked her torso while she lay writhing and moaning. He snatched his gun from the hearth and turned again to André.

His wrists bleeding from his efforts, Adam watched the rapidly evolving spectacle with horror. Belloc Senior lay sprawled motionless, bloody and dead, almost sideways across Rosa's jeaned legs. His features were a hash of blood, meat and staring scared eyeballs from the stray fringe of shot pattern, and blood was now beginning to pool around the bodies. Across from them, Mitchell lay bleeding onto the deep red hues of the finely knotted central rug.

André with the shotgun, though injured, was still armed and moving. The slight projection of the chimney breast and the bulk of the furniture shielded Paul Belloc from the doorway where the bishop's aide, still on the floor, was struggling to control the wavering of the twenty-inch barrel and hefty wooden stock. Adam knew taking a hit from the shotgun at this short range would mean slaughter, but Belloc was being cautious despite the shooter being on the floor and effectively one-armed.

From his concealed position, Belloc dived flat onto the floor, keeping Mitchell's motionless form between him and the doorway where his opponent had propped himself up. André, shotgun stock wedged beneath his left arm, pivoted to follow Belloc's movement, the barrel describing an erratic arc toward the floor. Belloc's first two shots impacted into André's torso. The shotgun clattered to the floor as his close cropped head smacked back with a dull thud against the doorpost. A third shot put a hole in his temple, tipping him over into the hallway.

Belloc raced toward Sarah, who was still doubled up from the beating. He approached her from behind and aimed his pistol at the back of her still jerking head as she gasped for breath.

Abandoning all attempts to free himself, Adam shuffled to his feet and, hands held high above his head, gripping 'the waiter's friend' tightly, he launched himself at Belloc's back. The advantage of surprise allowed him one clean blow, and he drove the little one-and-a-half-inch blade solidly into the left side of Belloc's shoulder, just missing his neck and spine. Belloc screamed and erupted into rage. He swung around before Adam could withdraw the knife and swiped him across the forehead with the pistol. Adam crumpled unconscious onto the floor.

§

Still holding his weapon, Belloc lifted his good arm over his shoulder and pulled the little blade from his damaged trapezius. He dropped it to the floor and took aim again.

This time he ignored Sarah and focused on Adam's skull, the muzzle inches from his bleeding temple. He squeezed the trigger —but nothing happened. Misfire. He tried again, but still the same result. He slammed his palm up against the magazine base at the bottom of the pistol grip before pulling the slide back; the jammed round ejected and another chambered. As he bent and picked the problem round up from the floor and placed it in his pocket, he complimented himself on his presence of mind. Again, he squeezed on the trigger, and again nothing happened. Aware that if what the girl said was true and others were on their way, he was working against a deadline, so he couldn't waste any more time on this. The jamming could be due to a weak magazine spring, or a fault with the ammunition, but he knew he had a spare magazine in the front of the Suburban. He groped for the bag with the cable ties, turned back to Sarah, and secured her wrists and ankles instead.

Belloc felt detached and calm; his hands no longer shook. He felt no pain from his abrasions, bruises, or shoulder wound. Glancing over at his father and Rosa, he knew they were no longer there. He knew mourning would have to be left until later. He looked over at the bishop, who had managed to shuffle over to the doorway where the body of his aide lay, and he allowed himself another flush of pleasure at the thought of the slow, painful, roasting death they all had ahead of them. This is one revenge dish that will be eaten hot, he thought.

It was time to go. But first he tossed the brass mesh fireguard to one side, grabbed the big metal fireside tongs from the hearth and lifted one of the flaming logs from the fire. Dashing around the big room from window to window, he set each set of drapes alight. By the time he reached where his father and Rosa lay, thick grey smoke was rushing to the ceiling behind him and the old varnish on the wood paneling was beginning to blister and bubble from the heat. He tossed the still flaming brand onto one of the now empty couches before grabbing another from the fire and tossing it onto its twin. The cane-work panels on the sides and backs of the settees ignited immediately and began to flame, crackle and spit as sparks shot onto the rug. Still gripping the long tongs, he dashed over to where the bishop was leaning over his dead aide, pointlessly striving to revive him, and swung the long implement at the bishop's head. The impact of the blow smashed the cleric down on top of the corpse while the momentum of the swing embedded the tips of the tongs in the wooden wainscot. The bishop lay motionless, blood flooding from his scalp.

Belloc rushed to the remote controller, aimed it at the monitor and hit one button, then another, and another. The view on the monitor screen began to shuttle: out front, the view of the three parked vehicles; the mid-drive camera showed blacktop and foliage; the inside view of the closed front gates; the view from the high gateway camera; then back to the front as the sequence began again. He pressed another button and he saw the gates start to move. Pistol in hand, he ran into the hallway and out through the front door. A quick visual check assured him that the paintings were still in the back of the Suburban. He started up the big five-liter V-8 and, gas pedal to the floor, roared off down the drive.

❧ 33 ❧

Adam gradually became aware of a pain that seemed to be everywhere. It was exploding outward from his head to his extremities, especially his wrists, which felt on fire. Opening his eyes, he saw the bishop bent over him, his face dripping with blood, with the little knife gripped between his bound hands slicing at Adam's bindings. He held them steady, trying to ignore the pain from the bishop's sawing, until at last they parted. Above him, he saw clouds of smoke rolling out across the ceiling, threatening to fill the room. Snatching the blade from the bishop, he sliced at his ankle ties.

He could see the small blue darting tongues of fire grow into yellow sheets as the wall paneling, cracking and spitting, flamed upward into the dense smoke. He guessed the beams supporting the floor above would be next. At last free, and starting to cough from the smoke now wisping around him, he turned to cut the bishop's bonds.

"What's happened, Phil?" Adam asked as he started to cut.

"Belloc knocked you unconscious with his pistol after you stabbed him. Then he started the fire and has driven off with the paintings."

"What happened to your head?"

"I'd made it over to André and was checking in case he was still alive, when Belloc hit me with the fire irons. I glimpsed him coming and tried to crouch a bit lower just when he swung at me, but they still caught me quite a whack. It's damn painful, but it could've been worse. The ends of the tongs embedded into the wall and must've absorbed some of the force of the blow. I just fell on top of André and lay there until he went."

"How long ago was that?"

"He's only just left. I wasted no time before I started to cut you free."

Adam could see the pressure from each slice of the little knife blade was causing pain to the bishop's wounded shoulder, but there was no time to be gentle. The couches were now fully ablaze, and he could feel the hair on his head begin to singe from their heat. Greasy black streams of smoke spewed from the cushions. They had to get out.

"Almost through, Phil," he said as he made the final cut. "We've got to get the others out of here now! I'll get Sarah. Do you think you can deal with Mitchell?"

Without waiting for an answer, Adam jumped up, ran to Sarah, and, keeping low to try to stay below the smoke, he grabbed her under the arms and dragged her outside, across the tarmac, to the grass verge opposite.

Belloc's Suburban was gone. Adam ran back into the house, where the bishop was trying to manhandle the still unconscious Mitchell to safety.

Once back inside the half-blazing room, Adam scanned about for the remote gate controller. There it was, lying on the floor close to the flaming couches. Lifting the remote, he could feel the plastic growing tacky from the heat. The monitor view was still in shuttle mode, and he could see that the Suburban had not yet passed the mid-drive camera. Coughing now from the fumes, he pressed what he guessed was the gate control button and watched in desperate anticipation as the big metal railings started to move together with the all the urgency of a childhood summer. The front parking area appeared once more on screen, then the mid-drive view again, showing the rear of the speeding Suburban.

Steeling himself, Adam stooped under the lowering smoke ceiling and made his way toward Rosa's body. His face almost level with her legs, he could see the smoky outline of old Belloc half on top of her. He reached out and hooked his fingers into the waistband of her jeans and tugged at the corpse, her belly skin still warm against his knuckles. Twisting around, he pushed old Belloc's body free from on top of hers with one foot. He could see the revolver now—a metal island in the small lake of blood which had formed on the parquet flooring between her body and the bound edge of the big rug. With his free hand he snatched it, and just as he was about to release his hold on her waistband, her left hand gripped his wrist with the savage strength of desperation. The shock of realizing she was still alive electrified him. Peering through the descending smoke, he could see her face, swollen and splattered in blood.

She was mouthing something at him. He didn't need to be a lip reader to know what it was: "Help me!" she was pleading. "Help me!"

This was no time for internal discussions or making moral judgements; she was alive, that was enough. Gripping her hand, he hauled her body backward toward the doorway. As he pulled, he glimpsed the monitor as the new view showed the big vehicle slewing in a four-wheel slide almost off the driveway and into the undergrowth as Belloc attempted to avoid smashing into the gates —and then the screen went blank. The electricity was gone.

Once outside the building, Adam hoisted Rosa over his shoulder and deposited her, still bleeding, close to where Sarah lay on the grass opposite. He glanced up to see the dark grey smoke as it gushed from the windows, now cracked and broken from the heat. What was keeping Phil?

Taking a deep breath, he rushed back inside, keeping as low as he could yet remain on his feet. In the thickening fog of smoke, he almost fell over the bishop still struggling with Mitchell's limp body.

The bishop yelled, "It's no good, I can't move him any further. He's too heavy. I need help."

Without words or waste of breath, Adam shouldered the bishop out of the way, grabbed Mitchell under the armpits and heaved him backward toward the door. No wonder Phil had been having trouble. Mitchell's dead weight felt glued to the floor. Pull harder! The smoke stung his eyes, starting the tears. Even this low to the ground, he knew he mustn't breathe, or that could be it. With each heave, the choking pain in his chest and throat grew worse. He needed to breathe. How much further? He knew he couldn't keep going. His head, where he had been struck by Belloc, felt as if it was about to explode. His eyes were streaming. He would have to abandon Mitchell and save himself.

Eyes now closed against the acrid burning smoke, he felt someone brush against, then past him. Abruptly his burden lightened; he had help. Marshalling one last enormous effort, his left shoulder whacked against the hallway doorframe. He knew where he was. Not far to go now, if he could make it. His helper, beside him now, hauled Mitchell with an energy he no longer had. Aiming his back toward where he anticipated the front doorway to be, he stumbled the last few feet and felt the lip of the doorsill at his heel. One final pull, and the blast of cold air told him they were out.

At last, sucking in the crisp clean air, Adam was able to breathe again, but still unable to see for the streaming tears. He called out to whomever was still dragging Mitchell with him, "Phil, is that you?"

"Yeah! I'm sorry I had to leave you, but I needed to get some air! Are you okay?"

"I can't see. I need to wipe my eyes!"

"Keep pulling him, we're almost at the lawn!" the bishop yelled.

Adam felt his shoes sticking on the hot asphalt and renewed his effort until he caught his heel on the granite edging and tumbled backward onto the grass. He wiped his eyes on his shirt-sleeves and blinked repeatedly, the stinging of the smoke still causing tears to stream—but at least he could see. With the bishop's help, he manhandled Mitchell onto the grass. "Phil, you'll need to see if he's still breathing!" he yelled against the increasing crackle and roar of the flames. He put his hand into his pocket and produced the little knife. "Take this, and cut Sarah free!" he shouted. "I managed to close the front gates before Belloc made it through. I'm going to see what I can do." Producing the bloody revolver from his waistband, he wiped his eyes again and set off at a run down the half-mile driveway.

He ran unsteadily at first, still feeling the phantom bindings of his ankle restraints each time a foot pounded on the hard surface. Running faster, each impact jarred searing pain up into his injured head, but, as he struck a rhythm, the urgency masked it to little more than discomfort. Reassured by the weight of the weapon in his hand as he ran, he anticipated the probabilities. Adam knew that Belloc's only option would be to force an entry into the gatehouse, as there was bound to be some means of opening the front gates from inside. With luck, he should be in time.

The moment he spotted the edge of the bargeboard and the weathered red brick corner of the gatehouse, he slowed to a trot, then to little more than a walk. He tried to control his breathing, to slow his hammering pulse, to proceed with caution. Too many were already lying dead this morning and he, himself, had walked blindly into trouble once too often today. He kept to the edge of the asphalt, crouching in order to take advantage of whatever cover was offered by the evergreen shrubbery.

A shot made him start. He felt the goosebumps flare on his flesh and the hair stand on the back of his neck. But nothing happened around him. Another shot followed, and he realized that the empty gatehouse wasn't proving that easy to force open. Belloc was trying to shoot his way in.

Rather than risk passing Belloc and the house on the exposed driveway, Adam crossed over and, still crouching low, scraped his way downhill through the thick undergrowth. Within a minute he could see the dark smoked glass and the light cluster of the rear quarter of the Suburban, the iron lacework of the closed front gates rising beyond it.

Glancing around to make sure he wasn't being watched, he opened the tailgate; the Picassos were still there. Two-handed, though still holding the revolver, he lifted the large one, partially wrapped in a blue padded packing blanket. Ignoring the pain in his head, he edged some yards into the vegetation before maneuvering it beneath the dense greenery of a large rhododendron bush. Returning to the open Suburban, he grabbed the second one, which was similarly wrapped, and carried it too into the undergrowth. His heart was hammering as he went back for the final painting. There was still no sign of Belloc, or of the gates opening. If Belloc has managed to get into the house, he thought, he's obviously not finding it easy to open the gates.

Now the last one. He picked it up, revolver still in his hand. Bending low, trying not to hurry or make too much noise, he pushed through the vegetation. Just need to stash this one, he thought, then get back and close the tailgate of the Suburban, and with a bit of luck Belloc will drive off without noticing his loss. Suddenly, his left toe caught under a partially exposed root and he crashed forward. Desperate to avoid smashing on top of the painting, he dropped the revolver, while grabbing at the flimsy branches around him for support. Missing the painting, he sprawled, face scratched and bleeding from the bushes, beside it.

In the second after landing, he heard Belloc's mocking tones above him. "Well done, you gave me a bit of a scare there. I was afraid you were going to wreck it. Now, I want you to rise to your knees very slowly and don't turn around—or I'll shoot."

Sick from his failure, he did as Belloc ordered.

"Now, place a hand on each side of the frame and don't even dream about trying to grab that gun." Adam leaned forward and gripped the padded blue cover. Belloc bent and picked up the fallen revolver. "Now, stand up and walk slowly backward until you can put it back where you've taken it from."

He could feel Belloc shadowing his every unsteady backward movement. Something was affecting the vision in his right eye; it felt like rain on his face. Reaching the back of the vehicle, he turned and set the painting down on the carpeted flat bed. As he was bent over and sliding it further into the back, he saw a drip of blood land on top of the cover, and then another. Lifting his hand, he wiped the blood from his eye and received a glancing, though painful, blow from the pistol barrel to the back of his skull.

"Keep your hands down!" Belloc growled. "Just get back there and get the others."

At gunpoint, Adam recovered another of the paintings from under the bush and stacked it on top of the one already in the Suburban, before returning for the final one. Shadowed by Belloc at every step, he fetched it, and as slowly as he dared, replaced it with the others. He closed the tailgate and for the first time saw his reflection darkly in the rear window. He barely recognized himself. Black rivulets of blood and dirt streaked his face, torn from his fall. For a fleeting instant that felt like an hour, he found the image rivetingly interesting—right up until the black shadow behind it rammed a pistol muzzle hard into the base of his skull. Belloc's reflection grew bigger in the tailgate glass as he drew close to speak.

"This isn't just because you let us down. I've never liked you, you parasite!" he hissed.

The muzzle pressure in his neck increased as Belloc straightened his arm, forcing Adam's head closer to the rear windshield. Powerless, Adam knew what was coming next.

As the force smashed his face into the tailgate glass, Adam heard the shot as if from far off. His eyes opened wide as he slid down the back of the Suburban. Both his arms flailed as he tried to scrabble for the rear wiper blade, but his hands slipped on the blood and brain matter, allowing him no purchase, and he sank onto his knees and then face down onto the ground. The earthy smell of moldy organic matter filled his nostrils. Nutrition arising from decay, he realized, is the simple fate of us all. He felt heavier than tons. He wanted to shrug the weight off. Memories from his childhood, the teaching of the clergy flooded back; this is the way it is supposed to be. At this point the corpus is redundant; we must slough it like a snake's skin. He felt a smug pleasure at having remembered this. There was no pain, just numbness.

Distantly, as in a dream, he heard the undergrowth crunch and swish. The weight that constricted him, crushed him, suddenly eased. He felt himself being lifted into a sitting position.

A curt command ordered, "Police officer! Stay just where you are!"

Adam felt hands quickly frisking him. He could feel, he could move! He wiped the debris from around his eyes and blinked at the uniformed figure hunkered down beside him.

"Are you all right?" the officer asked.

"I don't know," Adam answered, feeling confused.

Tentatively at first, he felt around his shoulders, head and face, raking gore and tissue from his hair before examining it in his hands. Feeling no emotions, he examined it, and eased himself back against the chromed rear fender of the Suburban.

"No. I don't think any of it belongs to me . . . it's all his," he said, indicating the still twitching bloody remains of Belloc lying to one side of him. "I heard a gunshot. I thought I was dying."

"What's your name? Who are you?" the officer asked, pistol still in his hand, scanning around him.

"Adam Kennedy. I'm here with Bishop Phil Connor."

"Are there any other shooters?" he asked, quickly adding, "Where's the bishop's aide, André Leroux?"

"No," Adam answered, indicating Belloc. "He was the last." Puzzled at how this stranger knew so much, he continued, "André is dead. That man lying there killed him."

Adam was struggling to his feet with the police officer's help when they heard the crashing noise of someone approaching at a run through the shrubbery. Despite Adam's reassurances, the officer readied his weapon. Moments later, the bishop burst from cover, closely followed by Sarah.

Phil stopped dead at the sight of the firearm pointed at him and raised his hands.

Sarah drew up by his side. "Thank God!" she cried, "This is the trooper who helped André and me on the way here. Where did you come from?"

The trooper holstered his weapon. "After you and André drove off, I found his documents on the floor, where I'd mislaid them. So, as it wasn't too far out of my way, and I knew where you were headed, I decided I'd deliver them back to him.

"But on the approach, the first thing I noticed was the smoke and reckoned the house was on fire, so I called it in. And when I stopped I heard gunshots. So, after I called for backup, I made my way into the grounds—just in time to save Mr. Kennedy here from having his head blown off."

Peering at his savior's identity badge on his chest, Adam grasped the trooper's hand and said, "Trooper Reisner, Thank you!"

Adam looked up through the trees toward the house where the black billowing smoke was forming a cloud above the treetops. "Come on," he said, "We'd better get back up there and check out the others."

As they hurried back up to the house they could hear the distant whooping and wailing of the approaching emergency services' sirens.

❦ 34 ❧

As the house came into view, Adam could see that the main part of the building was now totally engulfed. Black and grey smoke billowed from every fissure while yellow and orange-streaked flames shot high above the roof and flared from the damaged windows.

"Trooper, the fire trucks!" he shouted over the combustion roar. "How're they going to get through the gates? They're still closed."

Reisner didn't falter in his stride as they raced toward the two shapes lying near the bushes opposite the house. "Don't worry!" he yelled. "The crews will manually override them. They'll open them in seconds!"

Both Mitchell and his sister lay in the recovery position in the grass where Adam had left them. Ray, his head wound bound with Sarah's scarf, was semi-conscious. Rosa, the left side of her torso a seeping, bloody mess, lay immobile but still alive.

"Give me a hand here!" Reisner called, "We've got to move these folks further away—they could be asphyxiated, or even burned to a cinder!"

Adam rushed to help him. Between them, they heaved Ray further from the inferno, while the bishop and Sarah struggled with the slack form of Rosa. Just as they reached a safe distance with their burdens, two gigantic red and white Fire and Rescue trucks arrived, blasting up the driveway in a cacophony of screaming sirens and flashing lights, and accompanied by the full spectrum of first responder emergency services. The various vehicles disgorged a host of protective-suited personnel even as they slowed.

Immediately upon seeing Rosa's condition, the triage crew ordered a medical helicopter deployment, then they stretchered her and her brother, Ray, to the nearest suitable landing zone—the paddock at the rear of the stable block. The firefighters, using grappling hooks, hauled both already badly scorched vehicles away from the front of the building while the fire hoses were put into position.

Very soon it was evident that the battle was in vain: the heart of Mitchell's house was a furnace blazing beyond control and with such ferocity that the fire-fighters shifted their emphasis to dousing the surrounding trees and vegetation to contain the inferno as much as possible and prevent it spreading. By the late afternoon, as the light faded, all that was left of the home was a smoking, stinking, blackened ruin.

One by one, the emergency services wound down their operation, drifting off with none of the deliberation or urgency of their arrival. An emergency generator chugged noisily, powering the arc lights that illuminated the still steaming mess, while the presence of a police cruiser, parked well away from the smoke and the smell, ensured the integrity of the crime scene until it could be safely investigated.

In the closing darkness, Adam, bruised and bandaged, leaned against a tree, his arm around Sarah in an exhausted but comforting embrace, and gazed in silence at the illuminated scene of destruction while a blanket of ash and debris drifted down around them. Yards away, the bishop, resting on a small stone garden seat, talked quietly with Carl Lummus—who had lately arrived, after being informed of the incident by Trooper Reisner earlier in the day. But now there was little more to say, and, having ensured the safekeeping of the paintings from Belloc's vehicle, nothing else for them to do. After thanking Reisner again, Sarah, Adam and the bishop prepared to return to New York.

As both Mercedes—the bishop's and Adam's—were burned beyond repair, the three were happy to accept the offer of a ride back to the city with Carl. However, they didn't afford much in the way of company for the return journey. Phil, seated in the front, began snoring even before they reached the end of the driveway, while Adam and Sarah, in the rear, slumped together into a deep sleep within minutes of hitting the highway.

35

Sarah's grandmother, Maria Halliday, had returned to her New York residence immediately upon hearing the news of her daughter's death. Despite her normally resilient nature, Liz's demise was taking its toll on her. Sure, they had fought incessantly when they were together, but, Maria reflected, once they parted and each had some time to themselves, the bad feelings ebbed away like water through sand. Liz was her own flesh and blood; she had always loved her and admired her for her strength of character, despite occasionally feeling like strangling her. Liz had always been her own woman, if a bit of a spitfire.

Now, with Liz gone, Maria reflected, the only family left is Sarah—and she was talking about leaving, going back to Europe. Why? All because of the madness that has erupted since Jack's funeral? Not only the horrible killing of that girlfriend, Zannah, but also the crazy revelation that Sarah wasn't Jack's natural child, but the daughter of Rooney, the cop. The man who killed her mother. And now, to find she is visiting at his home as he goes into cardiac arrest, then spends the night by his bedside until he dies! My God, no wonder the child is bewildered.

But Europe? It's just an escapist reflex action. There is nothing or nobody for her there. Here, she would at least have the benefit of the love and support of what little family was left. She mustn't go away.

Maria looked out at the fading light and wondered where Sarah was. It was getting late, and she hadn't heard anything from her since the news this morning that Rooney had died. No doubt she's involved with the bishop or some other of Rooney's friends. Loath to be a meddler, she nevertheless resolved to try to locate her if there was no word within the hour. She settled down in front of the roaring fire.

Maria was dozing when the call woke her. It was Sarah, and she was on her way from Connecticut and would be arriving home in about an hour. Don't worry, Sarah told her, she would explain everything shortly. Connecticut? What in God's name was she doing there? But she sounded okay, that was the important thing.

Indeed, within the hour, Maria heard the front door chimes, followed by the noise of the lock turning and the door scraping open on the sill. She also heard voices. She stood up, took a cursory glance at herself in the large gilt overmantle mirror, then, satisfied, she walked out to greet her guests.

She clasped her hands to her bosom at the sight before her. "Oh, Jesus, what's happened to you?" she screamed, running toward the visitors walking toward her. "Have you been in a pile-up?"

"It's okay, Grandma. We've been in a house fire, that's why we're so filthy, but we're all right. I'm just a bit bruised with a few scratches, there's nothing broken."

Maria guided them into the kitchen area where she made coffee for them all as Sarah introduced Carl and provided her grandmother with an outline of the day's events.

As the three of them sat at the breakfast bar drinking their coffees, Maria began shaking her head from side to side. "Unbelievable! The two of you could've been killed. When is this madness going to stop? Sarah, you are the only person I have left." Tears started to roll down her cheeks; she ripped a paper towel from a roll. "I don't know what I'd do without you." Sarah moved over to her grandmother, put her arms around her, and whispered consolations as Adam and Carl quietly said their goodnights and left.

The pair hugged and kissed, each of them dripping with tears, until Maria—with a final, intense hug, stood back from her granddaughter and said, "You frightened the life out of me there, Sarah, but I know it wasn't your fault. You're back safe, that's all that matters. Now, look at you, you're like a chimney sweep. Go up and get undressed, and I'll run a big, hot bath for you." She looked down at herself, noticing the grime and soot that had transferred onto her clothing and skin during their embraces. "Once you're tucked in, I can see I'm going to have to take one, too." They began to giggle as they made their way upstairs.

§

Sarah didn't wake up until after ten when Maria pulled the drapes open, having carried in coffee and a light breakfast on a tray. She clenched her teeth from the ache in her abdominal region as she rolled over onto her side before levering herself up into a sitting position.

"There are some painkillers beside the orange juice, if you need them," Maria said.

Lifting the tablets, Sarah smiled a thank-you. She ate the fruit and the warm croissant while her grandmother tidied around the bedroom.

"Thanks again, Grandma. I needed that."

Maria Halliday sat beside her on the bed and put an arm around her. "Darlin', you've had one hell of a time these past couple of weeks. I just want you to take it easy for a while. You need comfort, security and love, not more stress. So, please, forget about going away. Stay here with me, I'll look after you. It's time to relax and recuperate."

Snuggling her face against her grandmother, Sarah laughed. "You've been spending too much time south of the Mason-Dixon

Line . . . you're losing your New York edginess. I'm okay. I'm just surprised you didn't bring me biscuits, gravy and grits for breakfast instead."

Maria smiled back. "Touché. But maybe there's something in what you say, and your mom's death has brought it home to me. Ever since then, I've been feeling more emotional and weepy than I ever have before. Remember, you're all I've got left in the world, and the last thing I want is to see you gallivanting around Europe on your own, aimlessly." They hugged each other.

"You're a hell of a girl," her grandmother added. "You have a lot of my dad in you. He would've bounced back just like you, and though you wouldn't have wanted him for an enemy, he was also kind and considerate."

"I would've thought I was more like my mom?" Sarah said. "And you know as well as I do, not too many would've called her kind and considerate. To tell you the truth, it worries me a bit. I feel the anger rising in me from time to time, and I hate it."

Maria kissed her cheek. "You may have inherited her hot temper, but with you it's defused easily and fades quickly."

Sarah said nothing for a few moments, just closed her eyes and relaxed against her grandmother's shoulder. "You know, Grandma, I was almost killed yesterday," she said in a whisper. "Almost shot in the head, just like Mom. Adam saved my life."

Maria squeezed her hand. "The way both Adam and young Lummus told it last night was that it was you who saved Adam and Phil Connor . . . and the other man . . . Mitchell, isn't it? And by the way, Adam's already been on the phone for you this morning. I told him you were still sleeping. He said he'd call back this afternoon."

Sarah replied, "I'll call him once I'm dressed."

"Before you start making too many arrangements for today, young lady, I must remind you that we need to go to your mom's apartment and have a search through her files—if you're up to it, that is? The lawyers will need to make a start on her estate, which shouldn't be too difficult as you inherit everything, but we'll have to try to collate what she has and what she inherited from Jack. This might be more of a problem as she probably hadn't even started that, and we'll have to do it."

"No, it won't be difficult," Sarah said. "I know where she kept all her files. As for Jack's estate, that should be simple enough too, as it's mainly his paintings, and I know Adam was meeting Mom last week, at the studio, to compile an inventory of them. I'm sure she'll have all the details somewhere in her office. So, we can zip down there after I shower, if that suits you?"

Maria smiled. "As long as you feel up to it, it'll be a relief to get it over with."

Dressed and ready to leave, Sarah called Adam's apartment number. It was answered immediately.

"You were just sitting and waiting for my call, I suppose?" Sarah said with a chuckle.

"Yes and no," Adam replied. "I've been hoping you'd call, but Trooper Reisner just beat you to it. It turns out that, despite officially retiring this weekend, he still has to tidy up all the paperwork generated by the mess yesterday."

"Poor guy."

"Yeah, well, he says he has no regrets—says he was just glad he was able to help. But, if you guys hadn't arrived when you did, I reckon we wouldn't even be talking now."

"And if Reisner hadn't arrived when he did . . . well, I just don't want to contemplate that," she said.

"Yeah, you're right, me neither. Anyway, Reisner was with Mitchell early this morning taking his witness statement. He says he's recovering well and is being released today."

"What about that bitch I helped the bishop with yesterday?"

"I'm afraid she didn't make it. She was dead on arrival at the hospital; she'd lost too much blood."

Their conversation was interrupted by the sound of Sarah's grandmother calling for her.

"Sorry, Adam. I'll have to go," she said. "We're going down to my mom's to go through her files and records to allow the lawyers to start winding up her estate. We'll be back in the afternoon, so I'll call you then."

"Good," Adam said. "I look forward to it."

SARAH AND HER GRANDMOTHER WERE IN LIZ'S APARTMENT before lunchtime.

Sarah peeled off her gloves and topcoat. "I haven't been back since Sunday, you know. But it all feels so normal—it's even warm. If there were cut flowers about the place, I'd almost expect Mom to come swinging in at any moment."

Maria agreed. "Yes, the heating's been kept on, but you'll have to decide what you're going to do with the property. Sell it, or lease it out."

A tremor in her grandmother's voice made Sarah glance at her. For the first time, she looked like a little lost waif and her eyes were brimming. Sarah embraced her and held her as she began to sob onto her shoulder.

As her sobbing waned, Maria shuddered an enormous sigh, gave Sarah a wet-faced smile and shook herself like a dog just in from the rain. She produced a little floral handkerchief from her pocket and dabbed her eyes and nose. "Let's get on with it," she said, setting her large purse down and searching in it. "Here are all the keys I've been able to find," she said, clattering several large bunches and a couple of single chromed keys onto the surface.

Sarah grabbed one of the bundles. "This has the file cabinet and mom's desk drawer keys on it. Those chrome keys are for the little safe under the desk—but she never kept much in there, maybe a little bit of spare cash. Why don't you have a look around the desk and safe while I'm checking the files?"

As Sarah was busy in the filing cabinet, Maria opened the little metal safe and pulled the contents out onto the desk top. "Yes, you were right, Sarah. There's not a lot in here—just a billfold with about six hundred dollars in it, and a video camera with its associated bits and pieces, all in a plastic bag."

"I'm having a lot more luck here," Sarah said, adding another folder to the pile she already had on the workspace along the wall. "I've got insurance policies, property deeds, the inventory for all the paintings, and all sorts of other interesting stuff."

Her grandmother examined the camera and accessories through the thick plastic. "Liz never struck me as the sort for home movies," she murmured, half to herself.

Sarah bunched all the folders together and scanned around the study till she spotted a large laptop case that she knew would hold them all. "Me neither, maybe she was using it for inventory purposes or something," she said. "Anyway, just stick it in your purse and we can check it out later. I think we have everything we need here." She slotted all the assembled documents into the expanding case; they were ready to leave.

The house phone was ringing as they arrived in through Maria's front door. Sarah lifted the handset. It was Adam.

"Adam, sorry, it all took a bit longer than I expected. We were just coming in through the door when I heard the phone."

"No need to apologize, Sarah. In fact, make a note never to apologize for anything again. Everyone—me, Mitchell and Phil, we all owe our lives to you and your quick thinking yesterday."

"Well . . . thanks, but don't forget, if it weren't for you, that creep would've blown my head off—just like mom's . . ." Her voice dropped in volume. "You saved *my* life, Adam." She wiped at her eyes with a tissue.

Adam's tone brightened, "Now Sarah, don't let's get into an argument about who saved whose life here. Do you feel up to going out for something to eat this evening?"

Sarah beamed. "Yes, I'd love to. In fact, if it's okay with you, I'd love to go to the little Italian restaurant Joe took me to last week —one that he and his wife used to frequent—do you know it?"

"I sure do. I'll make the arrangements for about seven thirty, if that suits?"

"Perfect! Already, I can't wait!"

She was still smiling when she hung up, then she made her way through to her grandmother's study with the case of folders and began to unpack them onto the desk.

Sarah helped her grandmother light the one remaining open fire in the house that was still authentic—all the rest having been converted to gas. Maria still favored the look, sound and smell of real wood combustion—said it reminded her of her childhood—and Sarah tended to agree. Once the kindling was well alight and the big logs started to burn, Sarah closed the chimney flue down to control the draught and placed the brass mesh fireguard in front of it. They both sat down in the long Chesterfield sofa and, enjoying the flickering in front of her, Sarah relaxed, snuggling into her grandmother's arms. Within minutes, she was fast asleep.

By seven, when Adam arrived, Sarah was ready. Opening the door, she saw him standing smiling, arms wide, gripping a big bunch of flowers in his right fist. She ran into his open arms.

"Oh, Adam! It's so lovely to see you!"

Adam squeezed her tightly to him, multi-colored petals crushing into her hair.

"Not too tight!" She laughed. "Don't forget, I had quite a kicking yesterday."

Adam apologized with a look of concern on his face, which she waved away, taking the flowers from him. She led him inside, where her grandmother stood up to greet him.

"Good to see you again, Mrs. Halliday," he said

"It's Maria, Adam." She smiled at him. "Can I get you something?"

"No, thank you, Maria. We have a cab waiting outside."

"Well, maybe later, when you both come back?"

Adam nodded. "Thank you, I look forward to it."

Sarah had her top coat on now and grabbed Adam by the hand.

"See y'all later," Maria said with a smile as they walked out.

§

Maria had been sitting and staring into the fire for some time, her daughter Liz foremost in her thoughts. The little girl who'd once been everybody's darling—particularly her grandfather's, the man who'd spoiled her rotten. She'd been so bright, so loving; a tomboy, yet so feminine. What had happened to her? What on earth had made her become so ornery?

Standing up, she fetched her purse and removed the thick semi-opaque plastic bag from it. Spilling the contents onto the sofa beside her, she picked through them. Locating the mini video tape, she read the handwritten details on the label: "AK & ME @ JACK'S NOV 17th 99". As Sarah had said, probably some inventory filming. A few moments browsing the instruction booklet allowed her to grasp the operating fundamentals. She popped the tape in, unfolded the screen, pressed the power button, and then the "Play" button.

A full color scene of one of Jack's rooms filled the display. There was no action, just the same shot showing a number of unframed paintings leaning against the wall with several larger ones lined along out of the picture. The only movement was the digital counter on the screen ticking by. She pressed another button and the digital readout speeded up . . . but there's something! She stopped it with two figures frozen in front of the pile of paintings. It was Liz and a man. A short burst of rewinding brought her back to the vacant room scene. Again, she pressed 'Play'.

There was no sound on the playback as Maria watched her daughter enter the room leading a man by the hand and walking over to the paintings. Indicating the canvases with her free hand, Liz hunkered down alongside them, pulling the man with her. As he crouched down, his profile turned into view. As she expected, it was Adam Kennedy, the "AK" on the tape.

Liz, taking control as usual, Maria thought, feeling a gushing of pride, love and loss for her stunning daughter in front of her. She couldn't take her eyes off her; so beautiful in that blue dress—maybe a little revealing for a business meeting—but then Liz was never a slave to convention. As Liz began to riffle through the paintings with her free hand, Maria felt her throat tighten with emotion. Tears began to pool in her eyes. She fumbled for the small handkerchief in her cuff.

In that split second she had taken her eyes from the screen to locate her handkerchief, something had happened, for now there was a fury of passion raging in front of her. It was like powerlessly watching a shocking crime being committed—or a murder. Hand trembling, Maria pressed the rewind to search for the point of transition; the segue from control and discussion to rampant, tempestuous lust. She hit 'Play' again.

§

Sitting opposite Sarah in a quieter corner of the restaurant, Adam reached across the tabletop and caressed her hand. Despite the aches, bruises and scratches around his head and face, Adam couldn't keep from smiling. He felt free: free from any restraints, free from any of the nagging guilt that had haunted him, free to turn a new page, an immaculate clean sheet for him to compose this new, most promising, chapter of his life. Watching her smile back at him in return, he basked in the euphoric glow of love and certainty. Nothing can ever go wrong between them now.

"So, have you arranged that vacation you promised we'd being going on yet?" Sarah said.

Adam took her other hand and squeezed it. "Until now, I felt that might've been a bit presumptuous of me given all the recent trauma, but you just say the word and I'll get straight to it."

"Consider it said, then." She smiled, squeezing his hand.

Adam looked around to ensure they weren't being overheard. "I have a bit of news for you though. Something pretty momentous . . ."

Her eyes opened wider.

"Now, I know nothing can compensate for the bereavements and everything that you've suffered since you've come home, but you might say it's a movement in a new direction, a more positive direction . . ."

Sarah tightened her grip on his hands and leaned forward across the table toward him and whispered, "Adam, I'm so happy simply to be here with you, just sitting holding hands. This is the positive direction I want to travel, and I hope you feel the same. If you do, I can't believe anything could help me feel better than this."

Adam eased her forward, then leaned over and brushed his lips against hers. "I do, Sarah. You have become the most important thing to me. You have changed my life."

Still holding hands, she straightened up, leaned back in her chair, and smiling said, "That's all I really needed to hear. But about this other new positive direction . . . go on, try me."

Adam laughed. "Ray Mitchell phoned my apartment this afternoon and spoke to Phil. According to Mitchell, you're a cross between Mother Teresa and an avenging angel."

"I'm flattered—as long as he's not referring to my dress sense."

"He reckons he owes his life to you, and he's determined to recompense you in any and every way he can."

"Very nice of him, but really, it was all down to you."

"Yeah, well, he was quite complimentary about me as well," Adam said, affecting a faux-modest expression, "but, and I have to agree, if you hadn't turned up the way you did, we'd all have had it.

"Anyway, I don't know how much you know about what was going on with Mitchell and me, the bishop, and Liz, but, in a nutshell, he had agreed to pay the three of us two and a half million dollars each—which, by the way, he's already done. The payment was made into an overseas account of Phil's, and he has Liz's share for you."

Sarah widened her eyes, looked around and whispered, "Two and a half million?"

"But that's not all," Adam added. "When the paintings are resold—which will be in the spring—he'd agreed to pay us a commission of ten percent of the hammer price!"

"And what'll they fetch?"

"Probably between one hundred and one forty million, maybe even more."

"So you're talking about another ten plus million—that's crazy! Why would he do that?"

"It's a long story, which I'll explain later. But crucially, Liz was due to receive an equal share of this ten percent as well. However, this morning when Mitchell called Phil, he insisted on renegotiating the terms of the commission. He insisted on increasing it up to ten percent each—in total, thirty percent!"

Adam noticed tears welling and beginning to trickle down Sarah's cheeks.

"Sorry," she whispered, blotting her tears. "I know I should be delighted, and I appreciate the intention, but sitting here talking of mom, and thinking of Joe Rooney, and Jack, and André, and those other people who died yesterday . . . money, reward—they don't seem to mean a whole lot. I know that we're all born to die, but I'm sure three or four weeks ago none of those people would've had an inkling that they'd be away already."

Adam spoke softly, and looked directly into her eyes. "You're right, Sarah. And we all know you've had a horrendous time since you've come home. Now, I can't bring any of them back, or even replace any of those you loved and were close to, but I want to try my best."

She squeezed his hand as her tears cascaded. He fumbled in his jacket pocket and produced a crumpled Kleenex for her.

"I know," she said, "and I want you to. It's just maybe I haven't cried enough. Maybe I knew that it wasn't over and . . ." She sat up straight, breathed deeply and patted her face dry. "Come on!" she rebuked herself. She inhaled deeply, then added to Adam, "Not that I'm planning to adopt her as a role model, but Mom would never have reacted like this."

§

Maria was sitting on the couch reading in front of the blazing log fire when she heard Sarah and Adam arrive back. It was just after eleven.

"Cold night outside?" Maria asked.

"Freezing," Sarah said, "but it's like a furnace in here. Are you planning to sit up all night, Grandma?"

"Oh, sorry! I never thought . . ." Maria said, closing her book and preparing to stand up. "Of course, you two will want some privacy."

"No, no, don't leave. I didn't mean that. I just meant that it was a big fire for this time of the night," Sarah protested. "Please, stay where you are. I'll get us all a nightcap."

As Sarah removed her coat and took Adam's, Maria patted the cushion beside her.

"Sit here, Adam. It's very cozy and there's plenty of room for three."

Adam joined her.

"So like her mother, don't you think?" she said as Sarah left the room.

"Well . . ." Adam hesitated. "There are resemblances, obviously, but there are big differences as well."

Lowering her voice, Maria said, "Of course, from whispers I heard after the funeral, you knew Liz pretty well, didn't you?"

Adam cleared his throat. "I used to know her better, a long time ago—if that's what you're referring to."

"Oh! So are you saying that you and she weren't . . . you know, secretly an item or anything like that? You weren't the reason for the split from Jack?"

"No, absolutely not!" Adam struggled to keep his voice low. "Look, Maria. It's not my place to talk about Liz's . . . personal arrangements. I may know some of the answers, but I assure you, I wasn't in the picture at all as far as Liz was concerned—unless she wanted to manipulate or discredit me, of course." He hesitated, and added in a more sympathetic tone, "No offence meant, of course . . ."

"Hmm. . . That's interesting," she said, half to herself

"I'm sorry, Maria, if that sounds callous, especially as she's no longer with us. I don't know who you've been talking to, but I assure you, you've got the wrong idea."

"It's just that she and I had a hell of a row after Jack's cremation," Maria said. "She went overboard, criticizing me for making the suggestion that you accompany Sarah home, rather than her coming along to the funeral lunch. So, when I heard these rumors they made sense. I assumed she'd just been jealous."

Adam said, "No, it wasn't jealousy. It was something else. I suppose you're entitled to know at this stage, but please don't mention it to Sarah."

Maria said nothing, made no promises.

He continued, "I knew nothing of Liz's suspicions until the evening before she died. But, it turned out that she had believed for years that I was Sarah's biological father as a result of a brief fling we had all that time ago, back when I was little more than a kid. So, she went on a crusade to keep us apart once she discovered Sarah and I had a mutual attraction. Joe Rooney, of course, put her straight on that—as you no doubt know?"

Maria nodded her head. "So that's why she was so hostile! I imagine she would've threatened to tell Sarah, if you persisted against her wishes."

Despite the heat of the fire, Adam felt a shiver as a wave of goosebumps prickled his body hair. "How did you know that?"

"It's the easy answer. She had you by the balls—end of story. Simple blackmail, that's all."

At the sound of a door opening and the clink of glasses on a tray, Adam touched Maria's hand. "Please don't say anything about all this. It's very important to both of us."

Maria smiled at him and squeezed his hand in return, adding, "It's very important to the three of us—don't forget that."

"What's important to the three of us, then?" Sarah said, smiling, as she entered with the drinks.

Maria kept a hold of Adam's hand. "I've just been giving your boyfriend here a little pep-talk. After all, you're the only grand-daughter I have, and I have a duty to look out for you." She smiled as she added, "Don't think your mother was the only ruthless one in this family."

Sarah reddened as she passed out the drinks. "Grandma, what a thing to say!"

Sarah squeezed up alongside Adam as all three toasted each other's health and chatted about the evening at the restaurant. Maria, lifting her book and purse, bent over and kissed her grand-daughter on the cheek and stood up. As if part of her nightly ritual, she moved the fireguard aside and, hefting the big brass poker in her free hand, stirred it around the blaze in the hearth, agitating something that fell into the flames, briefly flared and hissed, unnoticed.

"You'll hardly need any further logs on tonight," Maria said.

Sarah murmured in agreement.

Satisfied there was no residue from the flimsy plastic case or the magnetic tape still evident in the ashes, Maria leaned the poker against the fireplace, realigned the fireguard, bade them both goodnight, and went off to bed.

THE END

I hope you enjoyed THE PICASSO PROVENANCE . . . If so, I'd love you to do me a big favor and spend a moment leaving a short (or long, it's up to you) review on the book's Amazon page. This can be a big help in attracting attention to my books and growing my audience.
To go directly to the review page just click on the appropriate button below:
Amazon.com
Amazon.co.uk

Thank you.

Don't forget to visit my website: dannfarrell.com where you can
pick up the following exclusive FREE offering.

Antiques and Art lovers should enjoy the ebook DIRTY
DEALINGS, which contains tales, insights and tips from my
worldwide dealings in everything from the conventional to the
eccentric during my twenty-five-plus years in the business.

Printed in Great Britain
by Amazon

18540355R00181